LINDA HOWARD

AUTHOR OF *PREY*

SHADOW

A NOVEL

WOMAN

Don't miss these

c suspense
l:

AN

T

BURN
DEATH ANGEL
UP CLOSE AND DANGEROUS
DROP DEAD GORGEOUS
COVER OF NIGHT
KILLING TIME
KISS ME WHILE I SLEEP
CRY NO MORE
TO DIE FOR
DYING TO PLEASE

Or these novels,
co-authored
with Linda Jones:

RUNNING WILD
BLOOD BORN

ISBN 978-0-345-50694-8
U.S.A. $7.99 CANADA $9.99

9 780345 506948

50799

S EAN

"Lizzy," he said, his deep voice calm and dark, a little cautious, as if he didn't want to spook her. She realized he didn't know what, if anything, she'd remembered. "I won't hurt you. Do you remember me?"

Yes. There were still big gaps in her memory, but she remembered *him*.

She had loved him. Whether or not he'd loved her had been up in the air, still was, because she didn't know what had happened. But one thing definitely hadn't changed: She still did love him, she realized, otherwise her heart wouldn't be feeling as if it were about to burst. He was here. The long time apart felt as if she hadn't been living at all, as if her world had been gray and empty. Pain and joy and all kinds of anger unfurled in her, and she briefly closed her eyes. This was too much; she couldn't get a grip on any of her emotions, couldn't put any of her tumultuous thoughts into any kind of order.

"Yes," she finally managed, all but whispering the word. She drove the knife point into the post, left it sticking there. She looked back at him, her lips trembling. "*Preciousssssss.*"

No sooner had the word left her lips than he lunged, was on her, the impact of his body knocking the hoe to the ground. It would have knocked her to the ground as well except for the grip he had on her, both arms around her, and he lifted her off her feet and kissed her.

Books published by The Random House Publishing Group are available at quantity discounts on bulk purchases for premium, educational, fund-raising, and special sales use. For details, please call 1-800-733-3000.

SHADOW WOMAN

A NOVEL

LINDA HOWARD

BALLANTINE BOOKS • NEW YORK

Shadow Woman is a work of fiction. Names, characters, places, and incidents are the products of the author's imagination or are used fictitiously. Any resemblance to actual events, locales, or persons, living or dead, is entirely coincidental.

2013 Ballantine Books Mass Market Edition

Published in the United States by Ballantine Books, an imprint of The Random House Publishing Group, a division of Random House, Inc., New York.

BALLANTINE and the HOUSE colophon are registered trademarks of Random House, Inc.

Originally published in hardcover in the United States by Ballantine Books, an imprint of The Random House Publishing Group, a division of Random House, Inc., in 2013.

ISBN 978-0-345-50694-8
eBook ISBN 978-0-345-53592-4

Cover design and illustration: Jae Song, incorporating photograph © Steve Prezant/age fotostock

Printed in the United States of America

www.ballantinebooks.com

9 8 7 6 5 4 3 2 1

Ballantine mass market edition: December 2013

To my sister, Joyce.
I love you. I miss you. Rest in peace.

SHADOW
WOMAN

Prologue

San Francisco, Four years earlier

Eleven p.m. The President and First Lady, Eli and Natalie Thorndike, had retired to their hotel suite for the evening. It had been a long day, beginning with the President's cross-country flight, then going straight into a flurry of campaign speeches—supposedly *not* campaign speeches, but all of them really were—then culminating in a huge fund-raising dinner where each plate was ten thousand dollars. The First Lady had been by his side the entire time, so she had not only logged the same number of hours, she'd done it wearing three-inch heels.

Laurel Rose, an eleven-year veteran currently assigned to the First Lady's detail, was so tired she could barely see straight, but at last her shift was over. She hadn't been wearing heels, but her feet were killing her anyway. She tried her best not to limp as she made her way to her assigned room, down the hall but on the same floor as the President's suite, so she would be swiftly available if needed. The on-duty agents were in two rooms, one directly across the hall, another with a connecting door to the suite, though that door was locked from the suite side. She didn't envy them the graveyard shift, but at least now, with POTUS and FLOTUS in for the night, they could relax somewhat.

Three entire floors of the hotel had been taken over, with the President and First Lady on the middle floor. Guests who lived in the hotel had been relocated to other rooms, the stairways and elevators were secured, the hotel staff had been investigated and cleared, and the buildings across the street had been secured; all known risks in the area had been contacted to let them know the Secret Service was watching them, though most had been judged incapable of carrying through on their threats. The First Couple was as safe as the Service could make them.

That didn't mean nothing could go wrong; it just meant they had made it as difficult as possible for anything to happen. There was always an uneasy feeling deep inside Laurel's gut that reminded her anything *could* happen, keeping some small part of her perpetually on edge.

"You're limping," observed her fellow agent, Tyrone Ebert, as he fell in beside her on his way to his own room. So much for hiding how much her feet hurt, she thought wryly. She didn't bother denying it, because he'd just look down at her with one of those see-through-you-like-glass looks of his. There was something a bit spooky about him, his dark eyes seeing everything while he himself revealed nothing, but Laurel trusted his razor-sharp instincts. So far he wasn't showing any signs of burnout, something she deeply appreciated, because she herself was hanging on by a thread.

"Yeah, it's been a long day."

Nothing new about that. The days were all long. Since the Service had been moved from Treasury to Homeland Security, in her opinion things had pretty much gone to shit. Not that they'd ever been great— Secret Service management was an oxymoron; *mis*-management was more like it. But now the long hours were longer, morale was in the crapper, their equipment was shit, and on another subject entirely, her mother, who lived in Indianapolis, was getting old and less able to do things for herself. Laurel had put in for a transfer to the Indianapolis area, but she had little hope of getting transferred even though there was a position open. That wasn't the way things worked; unless you had some juice and knew someone who could pull strings, you weren't likely to get what you requested.

Laurel didn't have the needed juice. She hated office politics, so she'd never played the games, and now she was seeing far too clearly that her career with the Secret Service was nearing an end. That was another big problem with the Service: they couldn't keep good people because of their asinine policies. And, damn it, Laurel knew she was a good agent, despite the underfunding, understaffing, outdated weaponry, and increasingly long hours. She just couldn't take it any longer. Well, for not much longer, anyway. She hadn't quite brought herself to the quitting point.

It was such a cool job, in some ways. Not great pay, but cool. She loved what they did, and was able to compartmentalize her emotions so it didn't matter who sat in the Oval Office: the job was what mattered. She didn't have to like the First Lady; she just had to protect her. The job would have been easier if the Thorndikes had been more personable, but at least they weren't as horrendous as some of the previous First Families, if you believed some of the tales she'd heard. Natalie Thorndike wasn't rude, or a lush, or hateful. It was more as if she didn't see the agents protecting her as people; she was proud and cool and remote. Sometimes Laurel wished Mrs. Thorndike *was* a lush, which would at least have made for more interesting detail work.

The President was pretty much the same way, cool and remote, disconnected from everything except politics. On camera, or in campaign mode, he exuded warmth and likability, but he was a superb actor. In private, he was calculating and manipulative—not that Mrs. Thorndike seemed to care. Occasionally they were on the outs with each other; the agents could always tell because the typical coolness would become downright glacial, but other than that there was no outward sign of discord, no loud arguments, no verbal sniping, no slamming doors. For the most part, though, the political power couple marched in lockstep. Their unity had already gotten them to the White House, where they planned on spending another term. With the President's ruthless instincts and the First Lady's powerful family behind them, they would be part of the nation's inner political circle for years to come, amassing wealth and power, even after he was no longer in office.

"See you in the morning," Tyrone said as they reached his room.

"Good night," she said automatically, a little surprised he'd said as much as he had. He wasn't much on small talk, or on socializing. She actually knew very little about him, other than that he performed his duties impeccably. She'd worked beside him for two years now, since he'd come on the First Lady's detail, and—come to think of it—she still didn't even know if he was married or not. He didn't wear a ring, but that wasn't necessarily indicative of anything. If he *was* married, or involved with anyone, he'd never mentioned it. On the other hand, he never hit on her either, or on any of the other female agents. Tyrone was . . . solitary.

As Laurel continued to her room, two down from his and on the opposite side of the hall, she realized for the first time that something about him gave her a little thrill in her stomach. She'd blocked it out because of the job, but now that she'd admitted to herself she probably wouldn't be here much longer, it was as if she'd given her subconscious permission to bring the attraction to her attention.

She liked him. He wasn't a pretty boy, but he was damn striking, in a take-no-prisoners, dangerous kind of way. Tyrone would never blend into a crowd. He was tall and muscled, and moved with the kind of graceful power one saw in professional athletes, or trained special forces soldiers. Physically, he did it for her. She liked being around him, even though he wasn't much of a talker. And she trusted him, which was big.

She slid her key card into the slot and turned the handle when the green light came on, stepping into the cool of her room. The bedside lamp was on, and the bathroom light, just the way she'd left them. She still took a moment to check her room, because double-checking was what she did. Everything was normal.

Wincing, she toed off her shoes, then groaned with relief as she rotated each ankle in turn, arching her feet, stretching the ligaments. The soles of her feet still burned, though, and nothing would help that other than getting off them for the next few hours, which she planned to do as fast as possible.

She stripped off her jacket and dropped it on the bed, and was starting to shrug out of her shoulder holster when she heard a faint *pop-pop-pop*. She didn't have to stop and listen, didn't have to think; she *knew* what the sound was. Adrenaline seared her veins in a huge rush. She wasn't aware of leaping for the door, only of surging into the hall and seeing Tyrone right ahead of her, doing the same thing, his weapon in his hand as he charged full speed down the hall toward the President's suite. They weren't the only ones. The night shift had erupted from the room they occupied and the head of the President's detail, Charlie Dankins, was kicking in the double door.

Oh my God. The shots had come from *inside* the suite.

The doors and locks were sturdy; Charlie had made several attempts by the time Laurel and Tyrone and a swarm of other agents had reached them. Tyrone positioned himself beside Charlie and said, "Now," and they kicked together, the combined force finally crashing the doors inward. The agents went in high and low, weapons ready, rapidly sweeping the parlor for the threat.

The room was empty. She couldn't hear anything, which was even more horrifying, but her heartbeat was thundering in her ears so maybe it was drowning out any sounds. To the right, the door to the First Lady's bedroom stood open, but Laurel controlled her instinct to rush toward it. Right now, their priority was the President, which meant Charlie was in charge.

The door to the President's bedroom, on the left, was closed. Charlie rapidly assessed the situation; until they knew where the President was, they could assume nothing. He pointed at Laurel and Tyrone and the rest of the First Lady's detail, indicating they should check her half of the suite, while he and the others swept the President's quarters.

His tactics were sound. The detail moved toward the First Lady's bedroom in an endlessly rehearsed procedure.

The lamps had been turned off in the bedroom, but light from the open bathroom door streamed across the polished marble floor and plush Oriental rug. They rushed the room in precision, halting when they spotted Natalie Thorndike standing motionless on the other side of the sofa, her left side turned toward them.

Laurel had taken the left-hand position as they moved into the room, with Adam Heycs, the detail leader, to her right, and Tyrone to Adam's right. Adam said sharply, "Ma'am, are you—"

Then they saw that someone was lying on the floor in front of the First Lady, someone with thick dark hair that had gone mostly gray: the President.

The next couple of seconds came in lightning-fast slices, as if time had become a strobe light.

Flash.

Mrs. Thorndike swung around, and that's when they saw the weapon in her hand.

Flash.

Laurel had a split second, a frozen instant, to register the horrible blankness of the First Lady's expression; then light flashed from the muzzle of the weapon and what had been only a "pop" from a distance was an endless blast of noise in the confines of the hotel room as the First Lady fired and kept firing, her finger jerking on the trigger.

Flash.

A huge force slammed into Laurel, knocking her backward to the floor. On some distant level she knew she'd been shot, even recognized that she was dying.

Flash.

She had another of those split seconds of sharp awareness: Adam was down, too, sprawled beside her. Her dimming vision caught Tyrone's expression, set and grim, as he fired his own weapon.

Doing what he had to do.

Dear God, Laurel thought.

Maybe it was a prayer, maybe an expression of the horror she couldn't fully realize. There were no more flashes. She gave a small exhalation, and quietly died.

The assassination of the President of the United States by his own wife, and her subsequent death at the hands of the Secret Service when she opened fire on them, killing one of the agents in her own protective detail and wounding another, was almost too massive a blow for the national psyche to take in. The country as a whole was in shock, but the mechanism of government automatically kept moving. On the other side of the country, the Vice President, William Berry, was sworn into office almost before the news of the President's death hit the wire services. The military went on high alert, in case this was the beginning of a bigger attack, but gradually the pieces were put together to form a sordid picture.

The picture was literally a photograph, found in the First Lady's luggage, of the President engaged in intimate relations with her own sister. Whitney Porter Leightman, four years younger than the First Lady and a power in Washington in her own right, immediately went into seclusion. Her husband, Senator David Leightman, had no comment other than, "The President's death is a tragedy for the nation." He didn't file for divorce, but then no one in the know in the Capitol expected him to; regardless of the situation, his wife was still a member of the power Porter family, and he wasn't about to cut his political throat because the President had been banging his wife.

A few people wondered what had made the First Lady snap, because the liaison wasn't exactly a secret and she had to have known about it for some time, but in the end it was decided that no one would ever know for certain.

Secret Service agent Laurel Rose was buried with honor, and her name immortalized among those others who had given their lives in the performance of their duties. Adam Heyes was severely wounded, his recovery taking months, and had to retire from the Service. After several months, the agent who had shot and killed the First Lady, Tyrone Ebert, quietly resigned.

And the government ticked on, the wheels turning, the papers shuffled, the computers humming.

Chapter One

It was a normal morning. Lizette Henry—once upon a time Zette-the-Jet to her family and childhood friends—rolled out of bed at her usual time of 5:59 a.m., one minute before her alarm was set to go off. In the kitchen, the automatic timer on the coffeemaker would have just started the brewing process. Yawning, Lizette went into her bathroom, turned on the water in the shower, then while the water was heating took a desperately needed pee. By the time she was finished, the water in the shower was just right.

She liked starting her mornings off with a nice, relaxing shower. She didn't sing, she didn't plan her day, she didn't worry about politics or the economy or anything else. While she was in the shower, she simply chilled—or more aptly, warmed.

On this particular July morning, her routine so honed and finely tuned she didn't need to look at a clock to know what time it was at any point, she showered for almost precisely how long it would take the coffeemaker to finish its brewing process, then wrapped a towel around her wet hair and dried herself with a second towel.

Through the open door of the bathroom, the wonderful aroma of the coffee called to her. The bathroom mirror was fogged over with steam, but that would be clear by the time she'd fetched her first cup of the morning. Wrapping herself in her knee-length terry-cloth robe, she padded barefoot into the kitchen and grabbed one of the mugs from the cabinet. She liked her coffee sweet and light, so she added sugar and milk first, then poured the hot coffee into the mixture. It was like having dessert first thing in the morning, which in her book was a nice way to start off any day.

She took the coffee with her into the bathroom, to sip while she blow-dried her hair and put on the small amount of makeup she wore to work.

Setting the cup on the vanity, she unwound the towel from her head and bent forward from the waist, vigorously rubbing her shoulder-length dark brown hair. Then she straightened, tossing her hair back, and turned to the mirror—

—and stared into the face of a stranger.

The damp towel slid from her suddenly nerveless fingers, puddling on the floor at her feet.

Who is that woman?

It wasn't her. Lizette knew what she looked like, and this wasn't her reflection. She whirled wildly around, looking for the woman reflected in the mirror, ready to duck, ready to run, ready to fight for her life, but no one was there. She was alone in the bathroom, alone in the house, alone—

Alone.

The word whispered through her mind, a ghost of a sound, barely registering. Turning back to the mirror, she fought through confusion and terror, studying this new person as though she were an adversary rather than . . . rather than what? Or, *who*?

This didn't make sense. Her breathing came in swift, shallow gulps, the sound distant and panicked. What the hell was going on? She didn't have amnesia. She knew who she was, where she was, remembered her childhood, her friend Diana and her other coworkers, what clothes were in her closet and what she'd planned to wear today. She remembered what she'd had for dinner the night before. She remembered everything, it seemed—except that face.

It wasn't hers.

Her own features, what she saw in her mind, were softer, rounder, maybe even prettier, though the face she was looking at was attractive, if more angular. The eyes were the same: blue, the same distance apart, maybe a little deeper-set. How was that possible? How could her eyes have gotten more deep-set?

What else was the same? She leaned closer to the mirror, looking for the faint freckle on the left side of her chin. Yes, there it was, where it had always been; darker when she'd been younger, almost invisible now, but still there.

Everything else was . . . wrong. This nose was thinner, and more aquiline; her cheekbones more prominent, higher than they should have been; her jawline was more square, her chin more defined.

She was so completely befuddled and frightened that she stood there, paralyzed, incapable of any action even if one had occurred to her. She kept staring into the mirror, her thoughts darting around in search of any reasonable explanation.

There wasn't one. What could account for this? If

she'd been in an accident and required massive facial reconstruction, while she might not remember the accident itself, surely she'd remember afterward, know if she'd been in a hospital and undergone multiple surgeries, remember the rehab; someone would have *told* her about everything, even if she'd been in a coma during her recovery. But she hadn't been in a coma. Ever.

She *remembered* her life. There hadn't been any accident, except for the one when she was eighteen that had killed her parents and turned her world completely upside down, but she hadn't been in the car; she'd dealt with the aftermath, with the crushing grief, the sense of floating untethered in the black space of her life with all of her former security gone in the space of a heartbeat.

She had that same feeling now, of such unfathomable *wrongness* that she didn't know what to do, couldn't take in all the meanings at once, couldn't grasp how fully this affected everything she knew.

Maybe she was crazy. Maybe she'd had a stroke during the night. Yes. A stroke; that would make sense, because it could screw with her memory. To test herself, she smiled, and in the mirror watched both sides of her mouth turn up evenly. In turn, she winked each eye. Then she held both arms up. They both worked, though after showering and washing her hair she thought she'd have already noticed if either of them hadn't.

"Ten, twelve, one, forty-two, eighteen," she whispered. Then she waited thirty seconds, and said them again. "Ten, twelve, one, forty-two, eighteen." She was certain she'd said the same numbers, in the same sequence, though if she'd had a stroke would she be in any shape to judge?

Brain and body both appeared to be in working order, so that likely ruled out a stroke.

Now what?

Call someone. Who?

Diana. Of course. Her best friend would know, though Lizette wasn't certain how she could possibly phrase the question. *Hey, Di; when I get to work this morning, look at me and let me know if I have the same face today that I had yesterday, okay?*

The idea was ludicrous, but the need was compelling. Lizette was already on her way to the phone when sudden panic froze her in mid-step.

No.

She couldn't call anyone.

If she did, *they* would know.

They? Who were *"they"*?

On the heels of that thought she was suddenly drenched in sweat, and nausea convulsed her stomach. She lurched back to the bathroom, barely making it to the toilet in time before she couldn't hold back any longer. After throwing up the small amount of coffee she'd drunk, she clutched her stomach as dry heaves seized her body and wouldn't let go. Sharp pain stabbed behind her eyes, so intense that tears blurred her vision, ran down her cheeks.

When the convulsive vomiting stopped, she weakly sat down on the cool bathroom floor and reached for the toilet tissue to mop her eyes, blow her nose. The terrible pain behind her eyes eased, as if an internal vise were being loosened. Panting, she closed her eyes and let her head drop back until it rested against the wall. She was so tired it reminded her of how she'd felt after just finishing a 30K run.

30K? How would she know what running thirty kilometers felt like? She wasn't a runner, never had been. She walked on occasion, and when she was a kid she'd done some riding, but she wasn't a fitness nut by any means.

The stabbing pain behind her eyes was back, and her stomach rolled. She sucked in air through her mouth, willing herself not to start heaving again. Putting her fingers on the inside corners of her eyes she pushed hard, as if she could force the pain out. Maybe the pressure worked; the stabbing eased, just as it had before.

The nausea and headache were kind of comforting, though. Maybe she was just sick. Maybe she had a weird virus that was making her hallucinate, and what she thought she was seeing in the mirror was just that: a hallucination.

Except she didn't feel sick. And that was strange, because she'd just thrown up so violently her stomach muscles ached, and she'd had that piercing headache, but she didn't feel *sick*. Now that it was over with, she felt perfectly well.

She also felt annoyed. Her schedule was completely shot; by now her hair should be dry, and her makeup on. She *hated* when anything disrupted the timeline she'd laid out for herself; she was so regimented, she made a Swiss watch look harum-scarum—

Wait a minute. Regimented? *Her?* When had *that* happened? It felt wrong, as if she were thinking of someone else entirely.

Abruptly she was retching again; she surged to her

knees and bent over the toilet, choking, her stomach rolling, saliva dripping from her open mouth. This time the stiletto of pain behind her eyes was blinding. She gripped the edge of the sink beside her, holding on to prevent herself from collapsing on the floor—or headfirst into the toilet. Even as awful as the nausea and pain were, somewhere deep inside she felt an incongruous tickle of humor at the idea.

The spasms gradually faded and now she did collapse, but at least it was on her ass on the floor. Leaning back against the vanity, she tilted her head back and closed her eyes, mentally watching the pain pull back like a visible tide.

Obviously, she had to have some kind of bug. Just as obviously, no way could she go to work. Not only did she not want to make a spectacle of herself dry-heaving all over the place—or worse, wet-heaving—she didn't want to give this to anyone else. After they recovered, they'd probably be after her with torches and pitchforks.

This was crazy. She didn't think this way, about toilet-diving being funny, or about mobs with pitchforks. She thought about work, and her friends, and keeping the house clean and her laundry done. She thought about normal stuff.

Pain twinged again, not as sharp, not blinding, but there behind her eyes. She froze, waiting for the beast to grab her. Her stomach rolled, then calmed; the pain faded.

She needed to call in sick, the first time she'd done so since she began working at Becker Investments. Her department head, Maryjo Winchell, had a company-issued cell phone for this type of thing, and, being the careful type she was, Lizette had programmed Maryjo's number into her own cell phone.

They would know.

The eerie words echoed through her brain again and Lizette tensed, but this time they weren't followed by debilitating pain and nausea. Why hadn't it happened now?

Because she'd had that thought before.

Yes. The answer felt right. She didn't know why, because on the surface it was both stupid and paranoid, but—yes.

Okay. The best thing to do, then, was to not let people know she'd flipped out, and just act normal—sick, but normal.

She got her cell phone from the table where she'd left it, and turned it on. She always turned it off at night, because . . . She didn't know why. No answer came to mind; she just did.

When the phone had booted up, she scrolled through her contacts until she found "Maryjo," selected the number, and hit the green call icon. She heard ringing almost right away, but she'd read that the first couple of rings were placebo rings, put in place so the caller would think something was happening, when in reality the connection took a few seconds longer to happen. She tried to think where she'd read that, and when, but came up blank. Maybe it no longer held true; cell-phone technology changed so fast—

A click, and "This is Maryjo" sounded in her ear. Lizette was so caught up in thinking about cell-phone technology that for a second she was blank, trying to remember why she'd called. *Sick. Right.*

"Maryjo, this is Lizette." Until she spoke, she hadn't

realized how ragged she sounded, her voice thick from throwing up, her breath still too fast. "I'm sorry, I won't be able to make it to work today. I think I have a bug. Trust me, you don't want me spreading it around."

"Throwing up?" Maryjo asked sympathetically.

"Yes. And a splitting headache."

"A stomach virus is going around. My kids had it last week. It lasts about twenty-four hours, so you should feel better tomorrow."

"I hate that it's such short notice." Though how she could have anticipated getting sick, she didn't know.

"Not your fault. This is the first sick day you've had in three years, so don't sweat it."

"Thanks," Lizette managed to say. Something rang an alarm bell deep in her mind, something that felt as if there was something else— Her stomach lurched. "I'm sorry, I have to run—" And she did, stumbling, gagging. She hung over the toilet and awful choking noises tore out of her throat, but there was nothing else to come up.

By the time she could catch her breath, every muscle was trembling. Straightening, she held on to the vanity for a moment, then turned on the cold water in the sink. Bending over, she splashed water over her hot face, over and over again until she felt calmer and could breathe without a hard ragged edge tearing at her throat.

Better. This was better. But she didn't let herself look at the stranger in the mirror; instead she closed her eyes and just stood there for a moment. Finally she grabbed the towel and blotted the water from her eyes, swiped it across her face and neck.

Her heart was still pounding. What on earth had set off this last bout? Was it something Maryjo had said? Nothing jumped out at her, yet she distinctly remembered that sense of alarm, as if Maryjo had ventured into dangerous territory. She mentally replayed the conversation, trying to find anything out of whack, even something trivial. Maryjo's kids had had a stomach virus, it had lasted about twenty-four hours, blah blah blah. There literally was nothing else, except for the comment about how long it had been since she'd taken a sick day.

Pain streaked through her head like a warning shot. She gripped the edge of the sink and waited it out, trying to keep her mind clear of thoughts, and the pain faded.

Okay.

Something nagged at her, something she felt she should remember but that stayed maddeningly at the edge of—

No. There it was. And so trivial. Exactly when *had* she last taken a sick day?

She hadn't, not that she could remember. Not in the entire five years she'd worked at Becker Investments. So why had Maryjo said she hadn't taken a sick day in *three* years? When had she been sick? Surely she'd remember, because she was almost never sick. The few times she had been really stuck in her memory, such as when she was twelve and picked up a gross, nasty bug at summer camp that totally knocked her on her keister. She didn't even catch the normal assortment of head colds that circulated around the office every winter.

So when, other than now, had she ever been absent from work?

She thought back to when she started work at Becker.

This time the pain simply exploded in her head and nausea twisted her stomach. She hung over the toilet, heaving and gasping—and while she did so, she dropped her cell phone on the floor and stomped on it, breaking it apart.

That was insane. And yet—the impulse to destroy her cell phone was so strong that she'd simply acted on it, without hesitation, without question.

When she got control again, she first blew her nose, then splashed more cold water on her face, as she fought for a logical explanation.

There was none. She couldn't remember ever being sick enough to be out of work, but that wasn't what had made her insides curdle with fear. She felt as if a stranger were fighting her for control of her body, and sometimes the stranger won.

Whatever was going on, whether she was having a complete mental breakdown or there really was something colossally *off,* she'd find out, and she'd deal with it.

Until then, she could only go with her instincts, such as stomping the cell phone to smithereens. She felt almost painfully foolish, but—

Maybe not.

She looked down at the cell phone. Just in case it was still working, she said, "Oh, crap," in her ragged voice, and picked up the little plastic carcass. "Now I have to buy a new phone." Then she popped out the battery to be certain it was dead, and dropped both the phone and the battery in the trash. After a second she fished the pieces out, put them in the sink, and ran water over them before once again dumping everything.

She was so scared she didn't know what to do next, but what frightened her most of all was the realization that *she didn't remember starting work at Becker Investments*.

Chapter Two

Xavier got up before dawn and ran his usual five miles. He liked running in the relative cool of darkness; not only was it more comfortable, occasionally it offered some chance entertainment: once some shit-head had made the serious mistake of trying to mug him, and had finally managed to crawl away with nothing more serious than a few cracked ribs, some crushed fingers, and Xavier's size eleven-and-a-half track shoe planted halfway up his ass. He'd considered breaking the shit-head's neck, just to make the citizens of D.C. a little safer, but bodies could lead to complications so he'd refrained. There had been a few other interesting moments, but in general, once the shit-heads got a good look at him, the smart ones would back away and let him run in peace.

He was a big man, pushing six-four, and muscled in a way that had little to do with a gym and a lot to do with staying alive in all sorts of going-to-shit situations. He could swim ten, fifteen miles, and run twice that many, while carrying up to a hundred pounds of equipment. He could fly a helicopter, pilot a boat, and he'd had so many hours of weapons training that almost any weapon fit his hand as naturally as his own skin. It wasn't his size, though, that made would-be muggers think twice; it was the way he moved, the hyper-alert vigilance of a predator—not that any muggers would ever think in those terms. Their survival instincts would more than likely whisper, "bad dude," and they'd decide to wait for a more likely victim. Xavier was a lot of things; victim wasn't one of them.

He was back home by five thirty, and twenty minutes later he was already showered and dressed, which today meant jeans and boots, and a black tee shirt. The color of the tee shirt changed from day to day, but the rest of it was pretty much standard. "Dressed" meant he'd also checked his weapon, then situated his holster so it rode his right kidney. The big Glock wasn't the only weapon he carried, but it was the only one that was readily visible. Even in his own home—perhaps most particularly there—he was always armed with two or more weapons, and never more than a step away from others in his private arsenal.

He didn't feel paranoid; most of the other black ops people he knew did the same. Home was a point of vulnerability, for him and for everyone in the business, because it was a fixed point. People who stayed on the move were much harder to target. The good news was that, as far as he knew, no one was gunning for him . . . yet. The "yet" was always there, acknowledged but unspoken.

Because of that, he'd taken the precaution of buying two condo units, side by side. One was in his name; the other was in the name of J. P. Halston. If anyone checked deeper, they'd find that the "J. P." stood for Joan Paulette. A lot of single women went by their initials. Joan had a Social Security number and a bank account, paid her maintenance and utility bills on time, and had no love life at all. He knew because he was Joan and she didn't really exist, except on paper. Currently, his and Joan's love lives had a lot in common, which was a real pisser, but that was reality and he could deal.

He slept in one condo and kept the other as a safety valve; he'd installed a hidden door, which could be opened only with the fingerprint of his left little finger, in the back-to-back closets linking the two. He'd put other safety measures in place as well, because someone in his line of work couldn't be too careful. He hoped to God most of them were a waste of time, because if he ever really needed them, then it meant he was chin-deep in a world of shit. His particular skill set was valuable because he was both bold and careful, an attitude he applied to his private life as well as his work.

The powers that be were stupid as hell if they didn't expect that, so he operated under the premise that they *did*. He felt more comfortable when everyone—within a limited circle—knew what everyone else was doing. Probably that was why he was still alive; they figured he'd set a trigger to expose them if they ever made a move against him. In that case, they were one hundred percent correct. That didn't mean they wouldn't someday try to find a way around, over, or under the situation; when that happened the political shit-bomb would be about to explode and everyone would be scrambling to survive, which was the exact situation he watched for. He'd known the price going in and had judged the end result worth the cost. Unfortunately, the cost had turned out to be higher than he'd expected.

Like he did every morning, he sat in the small, shielded room in the safety-valve condo, which served as the nerve center for all of his various alerts, electronic trip wires, and information-gathering programs, drinking coffee while he listened and read, and monitored the monitorers. He'd piggybacked onto their systems, so when her house was swept they picked up only their own bugs, but, again, he figured they knew anyway. If they hadn't been smart, he wouldn't have been working with them in the first place. Not that he didn't trust his own people; he did, up to a point. Beyond that point, he trusted only himself. He was surprised they'd kept him in the loop this long, but then, he was intimately involved, and he wasn't someone they wanted to piss off. He had friends with power, and even more dangerous friends with skills; he didn't know which one of the two had more influenced the decision to keep him informed, but as long as it worked, he didn't give a fuck why.

Still. They watched her; he watched them, and made certain what they reported was what he already knew. And because he already knew, they were careful to keep the status quo going. They couldn't withhold information, or give him the wrong intel. What he couldn't control was if they initiated an action without there being a trigger, if someday someone in power simply decided the risk was too great to let the situation continue.

That was where he trusted his gut instinct, honed to a lethal edge by all the action he'd seen. The day that instinct whispered to him was the day he acted.

Mutual assured destruction, a fancy way of saying "Mexican standoff," was a fine concept when it came to keeping the peace.

At the moment, he was reading about the state of the euro—not that he was any kind of financial guru, but then, he wasn't reading for investment information. Money drove everything in politics, in national security—hell, it drove everything, period. Desperate nations did desperate things, and a ripple in the monetary market could have him on a jet within the hour, traveling to God only knew where, to do whatever had to be done. Because he wasn't available to oversee her all the time, he had a backup in place, to act if necessary. He tried to anticipate those times, predict when his services might be needed. While he was reading, he was also listening for anything the least out of the ordinary. So far, her routine had seemed to go as usual. Anything *un*usual would trigger a tidal wave of reaction.

"Ten, twelve, one, forty-two, eighteen."

The whispered numbers grabbed his attention as abruptly and completely as if a shot had been fired. He set down his cup and swiveled his chair around, his head cocked, his entire body alert. Automatically he reached for a pen, jotted down the numbers. *What the hell—?*

Seconds later, she repeated the sequence of numbers, though this time in a slightly stronger voice.

There was a pause. Then came sounds of movement, at first normal, then hurrying, followed by the unmistakable noises of prolonged and violent vomiting.

Fuck! He wished he had eyes on her, but the surveillance network had allowed her that privacy. Nothing she said, either on her house phone or cell phone or even her work phone, not to mention what she watched on TV or did on her computer, was private. Her car was constantly tracked by a GPS device. But video had been nixed; not out of any concern for her constitutional rights, which had pretty much been shredded and trampled in the mud, but because it had been deemed unnecessary. They didn't need to see her go to the toilet, or take a shower, so long as they knew that was what she was doing.

Surveilling her had been easy. She never deviated from her routine. She was calm, predictable—and now, it seemed, sick. But what the fuck were those numbers?

He listened to a couple more episodes of vomiting. Definitely sick. Then came the signal that she'd turned on her cell phone. The name of her department supervisor at work, Maryjo Winchell, popped up on his screen.

He'd cloned her cell, so he listened in real time to the call. What he heard reassured him. She thought she had a bug, she was throwing up—he already knew that—and had a splitting headache. Maryjo confirmed there was a stomach virus making the rounds, her kids had had it, blah blah blah.

His tension had just begun to fade when Maryjo threw a grenade in his face. *"This is the first sick day you've had in three years, so don't sweat it."*

Fuck! Fuck fuck fuck! He'd long ago learned to control his temper—most of the time—but now he really wanted to throw his coffee cup through the computer screen. Why the *hell* would Maryjo Winchell keep up with how long someone had gone without taking a sick day?

Thank God, Lizette didn't seem to notice. Maybe she was too sick. She mumbled a thanks, then said, *"I'm sorry, I have to run."* He listened to her do just that, listened to a bout of vomiting, running water, a long pause, another bout—then there was a clatter, and the cell-phone connection went dead.

Simultaneously, from the other bugs, he heard a clatter and heavy thud. After a few minutes, she blew her nose. There was the sound of heavy breathing, more running water. Then, in the thick voice of someone who had been vomiting and whose nose was stopped up, she muttered, *"Oh, crap, now I have to buy a new phone."*

More noises, as if she was fiddling with the phone. Water running again. Then came the sound of the hair dryer. That made sense; she washed her hair in the shower every morning. Even though she was sick, she was drying her hair. That was her routine, one she hadn't deviated from in the three years he'd been surveilling her. Not going in to work, even though she was sick, was the equivalent of an earthquake in her well-ordered life.

After she turned off the hair dryer, he followed the sounds as she went back into her bedroom; from what he could tell, she was going back to bed.

Everything should be all right. The other listeners would have noticed Maryjo's verbal bomb, but the important thing was whether or not Lizette had noticed, and she hadn't seemed to. She was sick, she'd been on the verge of heaving again, so she might not have been listening all that closely.

Could they take that chance?

He knew her. Her biggest talent had been her ability to think on her feet, to take a fluid situation and flow with it, letting her instinct lead her. She was undoubtedly puking her guts up, but given the Winchell woman's slip, it was too much of a coincidence, at least to him, for Lizette to "accidentally" drop and destroy her cell phone almost immediately on the heels of that revelation.

On the one hand, something like this was never supposed to happen. She was shut down, and the process was permanent.

Maybe. It had never before been tried to the extent that they'd used it on Lizette. She was supposed to have been forever altered, the way an amputee is altered; she would function, she would have a life, but would never again be the way she had been before. But because the process hadn't been pushed to that extreme, how could anyone know for certain exactly how she'd respond?

That was where his own gut instinct kicked in. He had to factor in the fluidity of her thinking, which maybe made her more resilient. Add that to the damaged cell phone, and his gut said, *"She's back."*

So the question wasn't whether or not they could take the chance of ignoring the alarm sounded by Winchell's slip, but could *he*?

Chapter Three

Information was everything. The gathering of it went on ceaselessly, every second of every day. Eyes and ears were everywhere, in one form or another. There were cameras, wiretaps—some warranted and some not—and keystroke loggers; cell phones were cloned or their calls simply captured; there was thermal imaging; there were GPS units that logged the position of both vehicles and cell phones, and even the old-fashioned method of human surveillance. Sifting through that monumental collection of information, separating the meaningful from the mundane, was a chore that never ended. With the completion of the NSA's data center in Utah, there would be even more details about every call, every text, every e-mail for the computers to sort through, based on certain keywords that would trigger a closer look.

But even with all the high-tech stuff, there were still real-time, human eyes and ears that watched and listened, especially to sensitive cases that couldn't be trusted to any computer program, no matter how advanced and top secret. If it was never in the data banks, then it couldn't be mined, couldn't be hacked.

Dereon Ashe had one of those sensitive-case jobs. He didn't know everything about it, but what he did know was enough to make him wish he didn't know *anything,* because he was damn certain this was the kind of shit that got people killed. Nevertheless, he and at least five other people endlessly monitored the woman known as Subject C—which always made him wonder exactly what had happened to subjects A and B—and examined every move she made, every call she placed or received, every detail of her life. It didn't matter that her life was, as far as he could tell, pretty damn boring; it was minutely examined.

Damn boring, that is, until now.

First there were those weird numbers, which made him tense and quickly scribble them down, in case they meant something, then— *"Oh, shit!"* It was definitely an "oh shit" moment. Dereon rubbed his eyes, not because he was tired, but to give himself time to think. He was incredulous that something so simple— calling in sick—could blow up in their faces like this.

Quickly he punched the numbers to connect him with the agent in charge of this operation.

"Forge."

The brusque identification by Al Forge made Dereon grimace with a combination of worry and alarm; he didn't want this decision to be on him so he had to notify Forge, but at the same time, he didn't like being in the crosshairs of Al's attention. It gave him a goosey feeling, like ice cubes dripping down his back.

Swiftly and without any embroidering, he related what had just happened with Subject C. Though of course they knew her name, in conversation she was never identified. Subject C existed only to a very select group of people, of which he was one—damn his luck. He didn't know what had happened with Subject C, and he never wanted to know. He watched her, he reported his findings, and he kept his nose out of business that wasn't his. It seemed safer that way, because whatever had gone down had to have been seriously big shit.

"I'll be right there," said Forge, and dead air filled Dereon's headset as the call was terminated.

He keyed back in to the surveillance audio and continued listening to Subject C, picking up where he'd left off. By the time Al Forge arrived, Dereon was able to bring him up to date on what had happened in that short interval.

Al scratched his jaw, his sharp gaze turned inward as he weighed events against possibilities. He was pushing sixty, his short hair gone mostly gray, his pale eyes a little less icy as age began to cloud them, but he was still as lean and hard as he had been when he was in the field. His face was lined by the weight of decisions he'd made, actions he'd taken. Dereon didn't ever want to be in Al Forge's position; nevertheless, he'd be hard put to think of anyone he respected more.

The silence wore on as Al stood there in thought, the seconds ticking past.

"C might not have noticed." Dereon finally felt compelled to point out the obvious, just to break the silence.

The flicker of Al's gaze sliced at him for the waste of time. Abruptly he said, "Put me through to Xavier."

That was one of the most puzzling aspects about this job. Everything that happened with Subject C was reported to this Xavier, who, as far as Dereon could find out, was nothing more than someone who worked black ops; he wasn't a supervisor, wasn't in any position of power. There were, in fact, very few details readily available about the man, which in its way signaled that there was more to him than those few details revealed. Al was always the one who talked to him; even more remarkably, none of those conversations were ever recorded. But then, nothing about this situation was on the record. After every shift, all of the data on Subject C was erased.

A few strokes of the computer keys accomplished that. Al slipped on a headset. After a moment Xavier answered, his deep voice familiar and remote, as if he had never been touched by any emotion. "Yeah." There was something in that remoteness that made Dereon glad he'd never have to meet Xavier in person, that Xavier didn't know he even existed. His world and that of the black ops people were eons apart, and carefully kept that way.

Al said, "Subject C has possibly been alerted to a discrepancy in the timeline." He paused. "Given that you've piggybacked your own surveillance system to ours, you already know this. I trust you haven't done anything precipitous."

Dereon swiveled around in his chair and stared at his superior in open astonishment. Of course they'd known that Xavier was in their system, but they never gave away information. Never. The smallest detail could give them an invaluable advantage—or, conversely, give one to the enemy. Exactly who the enemy was in this situation wasn't clear, but he did know strategy, and knowledge was power. Al had just given away some power by letting Xavier know that they were aware of his activities. Now he knew that they knew that he knew—God, this sounded like some old vaudeville routine.

"You'd have been an amateur if you thought for a second that I wouldn't." The cool, disembodied voice registered a faint amusement.

Okay, that was another wrinkle, Dereon thought. Xavier had already known that they knew about his surveillance. Vaudeville? No, this was a chess game, played by two masters who evidently knew each other well. Dereon hated chess. It made his head hurt. For someone who was in his line of work, he really preferred that things be straightforward, uncomplicated, and exactly what they seemed.

He should have gone into accounting.

Al made an impatient gesture, then swiftly brought himself back to stillness, as if impatience was a luxury he couldn't allow himself. "The point is, I'm not going to pretend to give you update reports that I know you already have. You want to know if I've been straight with you. I have, all the way. You also need to know that I'm not working with a hair trigger here. There's no indication that the situation with Subject C has changed, and every reason to think it won't."

"So you called me because, what, you want reassurance that I won't make a preemptive move? You know better than that. If I said so I'd be lying, and you wouldn't believe me anyway because if you were in my position you'd be lying your ass off."

That went without saying, so Al didn't bother trying to deny it. In his job, in their jobs, they did whatever was necessary. Sometimes the necessary was ugly; that didn't make it any less necessary.

"I don't want to do anything that will cause harm

to Subject C," Al said, choosing his words carefully. "The situation is balanced."

Xavier gave a short, humorless bark of laughter. "I've known from day one—hell, before that—that the situation is only as balanced as I make it. Your dilemma is that you don't know what safeguards I put in place, or how many trip wires. Otherwise I'd have been dead years ago. You know it and I know it."

"My job isn't to kill patriots," Al said, a quiet note entering his voice. He was a man who'd fought for his country on multiple levels for most of his adult life, and his creed was the same as Truman's: the buck stopped with him. He wouldn't throw any of the black ops people under the bus; if it became necessary, he'd sacrifice his own career and freedom first. The people who worked under him knew it; Dereon knew it. That inspired a very deep level of loyalty—except, it seemed, in Xavier.

"No, your job is to protect the country, whatever that means on any given day." Cynicism laced Xavier's words. "And I'm with you on that, normally."

"Except in this situation."

"Let's just say I trust you as much as you trust me."

"If I didn't trust you, you wouldn't still be on the job."

"Unless your motive was to keep me busy and maybe out of the country."

"I'd assume your trip wires would cover that contingency."

"You'd assume right."

"So we're at a stalemate."

"Remember the Cold War term? Mutual assured destruction? That works for me."

"You're making enemies," Al said. "Powerful enemies, people who wonder why they should trust you when you obviously don't trust them. You're forcing them to see you as a threat."

"I *am* a threat, unless they behave themselves. Yeah, I know, we can all hang together or we can hang separately, but I know these people. At some point, some son of a bitch is going to figure he can outsmart me and put this thing away forever. He'll be wrong, but the shit will have hit the fan before he figures that out. So, yeah, regardless of what reassurances you give me, I'll make my own decisions."

Al was silent for a moment, deep in his stillness mode. Then he said, "Don't assume that I'm the enemy. Just remember that. If I can help you, I will."

Dereon worked that over in his head. With Al Forge, you never knew; he could either be on the level or he could be playing Xavier. Only time would tell.

That same curt laugh sounded in their headsets. "There's another Cold War saying: Trust, but verify. Talk to you later, Forge." There was a brief pause. "You too, Ashe. It *is* Dereon's shift today, isn't it? Or have I lost track?" The connection ended.

Dereon's blood ran cold. He jerked his headset off and stared at Al, his expression frozen with horror. "H-how did he know that?" he stammered. "How the fuck did he know my name?" Or what shift he worked, or anything at all about him? This was like attracting the attention of a velociraptor: nothing good could come of it.

Al closed his eyes and pinched the bridge of his nose. "Because he's Xavier, that's how. Shit. This means he has a mole in here, or somehow he's got eyes and ears on us that our sweepers didn't pick up, or he got this location and followed us all to our homes. He's a patient bastard; he'd spend weeks figuring everything out."

Followed him home? Panicked nausea rose in Dereon's throat. "He knows where I *live*? Where my wife and kids are?"

"Don't worry. He won't kill you unless he needs to."

"That's reassuring!" Dereon said sarcastically, too alarmed to care how he was talking to his superior.

"It is, actually." Al heaved a weary sigh. "If he wanted you dead, you already would be. You have to understand how Xavier thinks. He didn't let us in on that little secret to scare you shitless—though evidently he succeeded in doing that anyway."

Being Forge, he couldn't let Dereon's panic pass by unremarked. He expected his people to be in control—of their jobs, of the situation, and most of all, of themselves. "He let us know that he's on top of us, and he also knows that we now have to spend a lot of time and effort trying to find out exactly *how* he found out. We have to run security checks, we have to put fresh eyeballs on everyone who works here, and we have to turn our vehicles and homes inside out, looking for bugs."

Dereon took a deep breath, forcing himself to look at this strategically, the way Forge was doing. "Will we have to move locations?"

"Possibly, but there's no guarantee that he doesn't have physical eyes on us and will simply have us followed to the new location, in which case we've gained nothing and wasted resources. There's also the possibility that by reacting the way we now have to react, he'll be able to learn even more about us by watching what we do."

In other words, Xavier had them by the short hairs, and had his own reasons for letting them in on the secret.

Chapter Four

Lizette lay quietly in bed, her mind racing. It was weird, but she felt okay, as if the awful sickness had never happened. She was a little shaky from throwing up so much, but overall . . . okay. No headache, no nausea, just an almost overwhelming sense of urgency. But, an urgency to do *what*? She had no idea, unless it was to act as normal as possible.

Something was seriously wrong when she felt as if acting normal were crucial. She felt well enough to get up, but lying in bed seemed the safest thing she could do right now. Wouldn't someone who was really sick be lying down? *Act normal.*

So many alarming things had happened in such a short space of time that she could barely catch a thought to examine it before another one booted it out, demanding attention. She'd worked at Becker Investments for five years . . . maybe. She didn't know. Maryjo had said she hadn't had a sick day in three years, so did that mean she'd worked there only three years, or had Maryjo simply pulled "three years" out of her hat without any reason? People did that; Maryjo had probably been rushing around, getting ready for work, her mind half on the day ahead of her, so she'd already mentally disconnected from the conversation and "three years" had popped out. It didn't mean anything.

Rather, it might not mean anything; taken in context with the fact that she didn't actually remember going to work for Becker Investments, it could mean a lot.

Going to work somewhere wasn't something that would be forgotten. You might forget the last date you went to the dentist; you didn't forget the first day at a new job—or getting the job in the first place. That was the biggest gap. She had no memory of putting in an application, of talking to anyone. All she could remember was simply living in this house and working at Becker, her routine set and unremarkable, going about every day as if it were exactly like the day before.

Living . . . in this house. Dear God, she didn't remember moving here, either, didn't remember choosing to live in this suburb of D.C. She just *did*. She'd simply accepted it, without curiosity, the way she accepted that grass was green, but now that she truly thought about it the gap was terrifying.

Item: The face in the mirror didn't match the one in her memory. That was somehow the most important one, yet she quickly shied away from examining it more closely right now.

Item: She thought she'd worked at Becker Investments for five years, but if it was really three, what had happened to those other two years?

Item: She didn't remember starting work at Becker Investments, period.

Item: She didn't even remember moving to this little house.

Item: She was suddenly, inexplicably certain that

she was being watched, that her calls were being monitored, that there might even be cameras in the house watching her.

The most likely explanation for all of those things was that she had either become seriously mentally ill—and overnight, too—or she'd developed a degenerative brain disease, a tumor, something logical even though the possibility was terrifying. A tumor would also explain the nausea, the headache, even the paranoia. The idea was weirdly comforting, because that meant she was sick instead of crazy—

The phone rang, interrupting that line of thought, and she rolled over to grab the cordless unit from the charger on her bedside table. Diana's name and cell number showed in the caller ID window. Quickly she thumbed the talk button. "Hi," she said. Her voice still sounded thick and nasally.

"How are you feeling? Maryjo said you have that stomach virus."

Startled, Lizette glanced at the clock and saw that it was after eight. She'd been lying in bed worrying over what had happened—what was happening—for a lot longer than it seemed. Diana was already at work, and of course would have talked to Maryjo when Lizette didn't show up on time.

"The vomiting has eased off, at least for right now," she replied. "But I think the headache was the worst. It was so bad I thought I might be having a stroke, so I did the stroke test on myself—you know, checked that I could smile, then that I could raise both arms, recited numbers to see if I could remember them."

Diana laughed. "I'm sorry, I know you must feel terrible, but I can just see you doing that. Smile—

check. Raise arms—check. Remember numbers—check. Even when you're sick, you make all of your ducks get in a row."

"Ducks are unpredictable; you have to crack the whip over them or they go renegade and cause all sorts of trouble."

"Your ducks are the most well-behaved ducks I've ever seen," Diana assured her, still laughing a little. "Now, have you called your doctor?"

"No, I went back to bed and must have dozed off. I don't have a regular doctor, anyway. If I don't start feeling better, I'll go to a pharmacy and pick up something for nausea. Or see a doc-in-a-box."

"You need a regular doctor."

"Doctors are for sick people. I don't need one when I'm healthy." And yet . . . she'd had a regular doctor, Dr. Kazinski, when she was younger. She'd had regular checkups and flu vaccinations, Pap smears and mammograms, the whole be-responsible-for-your-health deal. But then she'd moved, and for some reason she hadn't gotten a new primary care physician. Why hadn't—pain speared her temples, and she leaped off that train of thought like a hobo. Sure enough, the pain ebbed, and she could concentrate on what Diana was saying.

"But you aren't healthy now, and here you are, without a regular doctor."

"It's just a virus. It'll wear off on its own. The only danger is if I get dehydrated, and I'll be on the watch for that."

Diana sighed. "Well, I can't make you go. But I'll check on you again when I get off work, okay?"

"Okay. And—thanks." *Thanks for caring. Thanks*

for taking the time to check on me. It struck Lizette as she disconnected the call that, other than Diana, there was literally no one else in her life who would do these things.

How had that happened? *When* had it happened? Growing up, and in college, she'd had a multitude of friends around her. Family, not so much, not since her parents died. She had an uncle in Washington State . . . maybe. She hadn't had any contact with him in years, so he might have moved—hell, might have *died*. There were also some cousins she hadn't seen since she started grade school; she wasn't certain she could remember their names, had no idea who her female cousins might have married or where they lived. She wished she'd made more of an effort to stay in touch, wished they had done the same. But when you weren't close to begin with, becoming close was sometimes not in the cards.

She'd been eighteen when her parents died, so even though Uncle Ted and Aunt Millie had come to the funeral, they evidently considered her a full adult because they hadn't offered any aid other than a "call us if you need anything" platitude before they were on the plane going home. She'd been on her own. The mortgage on the house had been paid for by her parents' life insurance policies, plus she'd had a chunk of change left over in addition to her college fund, so she hadn't been in any financial difficulty.

Emotional difficulty, yeah. To be suddenly severed from her family ties had been an unbearable shock. For a year, she'd mostly stayed in the house, talking to her friends sometimes, but gradually that contact had dwindled down to almost nothing. She hadn't wanted to leave the last place on earth where she'd felt safe, hadn't wanted to socialize, hadn't laughed even though she'd spent hours in front of the TV watching sitcoms that had presented an unrealistic and sometimes twisted version of what her life had been before her parents died in a mass of twisted steel and plastic.

Eventually her friends had stopped calling. Slowly but surely, though, she'd begun to pull herself out of the abyss. Her mom and dad wouldn't have wanted her to drown in grief, to stop living her own life because theirs had ended. They'd been investigating colleges with her, talking about where she might like to go, what she was most interested in doing as a career. So, at nineteen, she'd started sending out feelers to the real world, in the form of college applications. Before the accident, she'd really wanted to go to Southern Cal, to stay near home, and because the house was now paid for that still seemed like the most practical option. Forcing herself out of her cocoon wasn't easy, but she'd done it. Her friends from high school might have faded away, but once she began living a real life again, she made new ones at college. Funny how they'd dropped away, too, except for a very occasional—as in maybe once a year—e-mail or Christmas card.

From Uncle Ted and Aunt Millie, there had been nothing, and for a while that had really hurt. Now, though, they seldom even crossed her mind. When they did, she'd feel nothing except distaste. She didn't *want* to have anything to do with them; what kind of asshole jerks would leave an eighteen-year-old on her own like that, without even a weekly phone call to check how she was doing? To hell with them and their kids, the cousins whose names she couldn't remember.

When she'd left college and sold the house, moved to the other side of the country, she hadn't bothered to send them her new address.

Which, in a way, brought her back full circle. She remembered her life, remembered the details, the emotions, all of the big things and some of the little ones, like snapshots in her head. So why didn't she remember going to work at Becker? And why didn't she remember buying this house? It was her house. She made payments to the bank every month. But—no. Nothing.

She stared up at the ceiling. Just how big was this gap in her memory?

Very methodically she started back at the beginning. Okay, so there was nothing for the first two years. How many people remembered anything from their babyhood, anyway? Very damn few. She'd met only one, as a matter of fact, a—

The pain that exploded in her head was blinding, leaving her clutching her head and moaning. Right behind it came a rush of nausea. She shot out of bed, stumbled and lurched to the john, hung over the toilet for what felt like an endless amount of time. This was the worst episode yet. It left her wrung out and weak, sitting on the cool bathroom floor with weak tears running down her cheeks.

She hated feeling like a wuss.

But—damn, hadn't this episode been triggered by some elusive memory that seemed to be knocking on the door of her consciousness, trying to get in? Like the reason why she hadn't set herself up with a new primary care physician. She didn't try to pull the memories up, didn't try to isolate them, because that would just set off another episode. Instead she tried to think *around* them, to isolate the problem, just as she'd been doing when she'd gotten sidetracked by that baby-memory thing.

She leaned her head against the wall. If she was going to do this, she probably should stay near the toilet.

So, what was her first memory?

Maybe when she was three, she thought. She remembered a gorgeous pink and white dress with a big flirty skirt that she'd worn for Easter; she even remembered a picture of her with her mom when she was wearing the dress, her arm stretched up as her mother held her hand. Besides remembering the photo, she also remembered being in the dress, admiring how the skirt kicked up with every bouncing step she took. She'd bounced and jumped a lot.

Okay, that year was taken care of. How about four?

She remembered starting kindergarten. Or maybe it was pre-kindergarten. Whatever. She'd sat in a teeny chair at a small round table with a girl who had fat red ringlets, and a boy named Chad whom she'd *hated* because he kept picking boogers out of his nose and wiping them on her, at least until she punched him in the nose. There had been other kids, of course, but all she remembered was the girl with red hair and booger-wiping Chad, the little shit.

When she was five, she'd learned how to read. She'd sat at the kitchen table and proudly traced her finger from word to word, sounding them out, while her mom cooked supper.

Six—first grade, and a fight with a bigger girl who called her a name and pushed her down, making her skin her knees. She'd jumped up and tackled the girl and pulled her hair.

Seven—some first grader had thrown up in the school lunchroom and set off a massive chain-reaction of vomiting that had even involved some of the teachers.

Year by year she went, sometimes remembering what her schoolmates had done, sometimes what she'd done, and sometimes the memory had been rooted in her parents. The year she was nine, her parents had taken her to her grandparents' house in Colorado for Christmas, and the snow had been amazing.

There was something for every year, until five years ago.

She skirted around a wall in her memory, sensing that it was there but afraid to try tearing it down because whatever was behind those walls caused the headaches and nausea. Five years ago, there was nothing.

Four years ago, there was nothing.

Three years ago, suddenly she was living here, and working at Becker, going about her placid routine as if the two-year gap in her life didn't exist.

Could a tumor cause such a clearly defined memory loss? Wouldn't it be more spotty, and include more recent memories? Short-term memories were the hardest to retain—hence the "short term." But moving to a new location and getting a new job were important things that would jump the short-term and go straight into the long-term memory bank. Some things just did.

Where had she moved from?

She remembered that. She'd been living in Chicago

at the time, having moved there when she was twenty-three.

Except . . . maybe she hadn't moved directly here from Chicago. She didn't remember. What had happened during those two years that had wiped out her memory of them? And what the hell had happened to her face?

Suddenly she thought of a way she could verify that her face wasn't hers, which was an incredibly weird concept. Grabbing the edge of the bathroom vanity, she hauled herself to her feet and stared at the face that wasn't her. On the off-chance she might have had some horrific accident herself and had to have reconstructive surgery, she pulled her hair back from her face and leaned close to the mirror, looking for scars.

There. Oh my God, there.

In her hairline, faint but definitely there. She pulled her ears forward, trying to see behind them, which was kind of an exercise in futility. Frustrated, she grabbed a hand mirror and held it so it reflected behind her ears, and—yes. More scars.

Stunned, she put the hand mirror down. Then she picked it up again and rechecked behind her ears. Yep, the scars were still there. Very fine, and very faint. Whoever the cosmetic surgeon was, he or she had been very good.

So this face *was* hers, or at least what hers had been made to be. The real question now was, how in hell had this happened, and how could she find out?

Chapter Five

I thought I might be having a stroke.

The knotted tension in Xavier's shoulders eased when he heard that, because it was the perfect explanation for that string of numbers she'd twice recited. Even better, she hadn't asked her best friend how long she'd actually been working at Becker, hadn't mentioned the conversation with Maryjo Winchell at all. Good. With luck, they'd skate by this without a shit storm blowing up in their faces.

It helped that she really was sick. Yet another episode of nausea came in loud and clear over the speakers.

But—luck? He'd never trusted that bitch.

He'd rather go with his own instincts, his own knowledge of *her*, that said the cell-phone bit was too coincidental to be a coincidence.

He wanted eyes on her, but as long as she stayed in the house he had to stay put so he could monitor the situation. Instead he sent a secure message to a friend who would make sure nothing unusual was going on in her vicinity: "Heads up. If she leaves the house, or if you see any unusual activity—repairmen, poll takers, insurance salesmen, anything—let me know asap."

An IM popped up on his screen within seconds: "Will do."

If she did anything the least bit suspicious, he'd have to move fast, and having someone already there would give him an enormous advantage. Al Forge had a formidable network, but Xavier wasn't without his own resources; he'd spent years cultivating a spider's web of allies and assets, knowing that he was walking a tightrope between being too dangerous to kill and too dangerous *not* to kill. He still took assignments knowing that putting himself in harm's way made it easier for him to be eliminated without it appearing to be anything more than part of the job, but he needed the extremely good money he made from those assignments. What he did wasn't cheap, and neither were the safeguards he'd put in place. Moreover, his services were needed, and that meant something. He could probably make more money by selling his skills on the black market, but he hadn't crossed over to the dark side yet.

The "yet" was always there, looming like a storm cloud that never quite reached him, but kept him checking its position. If push came to shove, would he go there?

Probably.

Six years ago, he'd have said "no."

Five years ago, he'd faced a hard reality that sometimes doing the right thing was the wrong thing to do, and vice versa.

Four years ago, he'd been enraged at the trap they were caught in.

Three years ago, he'd become the trapper.

He had no idea how in hell this situation was going

to play out, but none of them could quit the game. He was in it to the end, whatever that end happened to be. But, *damn,* he was so tired of the status quo he was almost ready to push some buttons just to make things *change.*

He needed to see her. There had been pictures, clips, audio, but he hadn't seen her in person in four years. As dangerous as it was, he needed to actually put eyes on her, hear her voice, make contact, and see for himself if she had any reaction to him or if the block was still holding. The next time she left the house would be the perfect opportunity, a small gap in surveillance now that her cell phone was no longer operational. She'd get a new one, it would be duly cloned and bugged, but until then there wouldn't be any ears listening unless she was in the house or in her car.

She'd probably be watched, of course, but if so he'd be able to spot that ahead of time. There was also the possibility that he himself would be followed, but the day he couldn't lose a tail would be the day he quit the business. Actually, the day he couldn't lose a tail would be the day he died, which equaled "quitting the business."

There was nothing he could do now except wait.

Lizette dozed off again, and woke feeling as if she'd been beaten up and tossed into a ditch on the side of the road. The headache and nausea were gone, but they'd taken a lot out of her. Did she know what it felt like to be beaten up and tossed into a ditch? She could almost laugh, if she didn't have an uneasy feeling that sometime during those missing two years she might actually have found that out.

Instead of actively searching her mind for memories, because she was afraid of what the result would be if she did, she took a deep breath, rolled from bed, and tried to think of something to do. This was Friday, so she was supposed to be at work, and doing something other than that wasn't in her routine. She'd stayed home sick, so it felt vaguely like cheating to do anything other than *be* sick.

Now that she felt better—aside from the beaten-and-tossed-into-a-ditch thing—she could go to a doctor, but that seemed stupid. What could she say? "I was sick this morning but I'm feeling better now, and, by the way, I appear to have had facial surgery during two years that I don't remember at all. Am I crazy, or brain-damaged?" She didn't want to be admitted to a hospital for observation, and that alarm buried deep inside recoiled at the idea that someone might make some inquiries into her medical history.

But her stomach was calm, and her head wasn't hurting, so she felt as if she should be doing something. It made the most sense to do what she did on the weekends, just to get a jump on things. She liked everything around her to be very organized. She was good at that, keeping things orderly—her ducks marching in a row—and following a routine.

She eased upright in the bed, took stock. So far, so good. Gingerly she stood, feeling as if her system might go haywire if she moved too fast, and shuffled out of the bedroom. In the kitchen, she put her hand to the coffeepot; it had long ago turned off, and the coffee was stone cold, but she could reheat it in the microwave. A big cup of coffee would go a long way toward making her feel better.

Uh—maybe not yet. She didn't want anything in her stomach until she was certain it would stay there. She'd thrown up so much the muscles in her abdomen were sore from strain.

Instead she went into the small spare bedroom down the hall that she'd turned into a home office, not that she worked at home very often. Here was where she paid bills, balanced her checkbook, and occasionally played computer card games to pass the time. Now and then she browsed the Internet, and every year she filled out her taxes online.

Taxes.

That was it. Though she didn't have to keep more than three years of past taxes on file, she didn't remember deleting any of the older ones. They were ducks, like the others; just old ducks.

Moving with purpose now, she sat down in front of the computer, hesitated, then got up and disconnected her DSL modem. Could anything she did while she was disconnected from the Internet be detected? She had no idea, but at least she'd made the effort. She opened her files and clicked on "taxes." In an effort to ward off a headache she silently told herself, *I'm cleaning out my files. That's all. This is an ordinary activity, not an attempt to access an old memory.*

When she saw three years of tax returns in the folder, the beginnings of a headache teased her. She closed her eyes and thought about the show she'd watched on television last night, then about the next-door neighbor's dog, the furry yapper. She liked dogs, but that one was a PITA, a pain in the ass. She deliberately thought about a song she'd heard on the radio yesterday, one that had turned into an earworm she'd been able to dislodge only by deliberately listening to something else just as repetitive; evidently the two had cancelled each other out. To her relief, the headache that teased her faded away.

She took a deep breath and resumed her research. All right, just three years of files in the "taxes" folder. Whether or not she remembered deleting the files, evidently she had. She couldn't say that would be a noteworthy action, anyway, so not remembering doing so didn't mean a thing.

Next she opened the right-hand drawer of her desk and pulled out her checkbook. She still paid bills the old-fashioned way, with a check in the mail rather than an electronic transfer, because it struck her as more orderly and safer, speed be damned. There was a neat, short stack of check registers, one for each of the past two years. Year three was with the checks in a neat, black cover. Lizette reached to the bottom of the stack and pulled out the oldest check register.

Was that her handwriting? Yes, definitely. Were there any payments that might indicate unusual activity? *No*, just as definitely. As she flipped all the way through that register, and then the next one, alarm began to grow. She paid her bills, but apparently that was it. She didn't appear to have any outside interests, hadn't gone on any trips, or done much of anything. Had she always been this way? She felt a definite reluctance to think about the subject at all, but, no, she didn't think so. This didn't feel right.

Hell, she knew this wasn't *her,* any more than this face was hers!

Another idea struck: credit cards. She pulled out the file folder containing her paid credit card bills. She had two cards, an American Express and a Visa. Flipping through the statements, looking at what her charges had been, she could only shake her head. Her charges were few, seldom more than one or two a month, and for the most mundane things: gas, groceries, stuff like that. The oldest statement was from three years ago.

She got up and fetched her wallet, pulled out her American Express card. She'd been a "member" for three years.

Oh, shit.

The realization that she didn't remember applying for and receiving the American Express card was another piece of the monstrous puzzle.

She returned to the credit card statements, looking through them, noting what she'd purchased. As with her checkbook, none of the charges said anything about her as a person. Nothing here helped her reconcile what she saw, what she remembered, with the woman she knew herself to be.

She hadn't bought a concert ticket, or any jewelry, or a special pair of shoes. That was kind of good, because she didn't remember going to a concert and if she'd bought a ticket and not gone she'd have been pissed. Nothing stood out; her financial records were as blah as what she remembered. Why, there wasn't even a single charge to a gun store—

The attack blindsided her, hitting brutally fast, and was so severe she was literally blinded by the pain.

Her body lurched in response and she gripped the armrests of her chair to keep from falling to the floor. Her stomach rolled, but before the nausea could hit she wrenched her thoughts to the song she'd heard on the radio yesterday, the one that had stuck in her mind for a while. She even sang a few bars—badly, because she couldn't sing worth crap. But yes, that was her voice, the voice she'd always had: a little too deep, a little rough, and entirely off key. It was nice to know some things hadn't changed.

As soon as she felt in control once again, and the headache faded to a manageable pang, she sat for a moment thinking over other avenues she could explore. Finally she plugged the computer back into the modem, let them connect, and clicked on the "history" tab. She didn't expect to see anything that she didn't remember from yesterday or the day before; she was simply looking back over a few days, that was all. She wasn't looking for anything in the missing years; she was looking for herself.

Why did she never check out any of the news outlets? She didn't care one bit about politics now, but once she had—

Lizette stopped that thought before her body attacked itself.

Let's see. Swiftly she glanced down the list of sites, all so familiar. She played solitaire. She didn't have an account at a single social media site. Occasionally she'd listen to a song on YouTube. That was about it.

Asking why would bring on another attack, so she hummed that song again, took a deep breath, and in one portion of her mind she asked . . . *when did I become a zombie?*

She almost laughed. Now and then her coworkers would make a joke about "the coming zombie apocalypse." If there ever was one, she was better equipped than most people to— This time there was no stopping the pain that exploded in her skull. It happened too fast, slamming into her like a sledgehammer. *Not a headache,* she thought as she fell out of her chair and curled into the fetal position. It wasn't a headache; it was an attack . . . maybe even a warning. She lay on the floor whimpering until she could see well enough to focus on a spot on the rug beneath the plain desk and chair. Concentrating on that helped, and as the pain eased off she began singing softly to herself.

Chapter Six

Two hours later, her stomach now settled enough that she could tolerate putting something in it, Lizette sat on the floor with a cup of coffee—lightened, sweetened, and warmed in the microwave—sitting on the coffee table within reach and the only photo album she could find open in her lap. There were baby pictures, photos of her with her parents, school pictures—not from every grade, but from most. Toward the end of the book there were some snapshots from college, always with friends with whom she had since lost contact. After that, nothing.

When had she stopped taking photographs? Not that she was a particularly good photographer, but still, who didn't take pictures of . . .

Of what? She went to work, she read, she watched television. She didn't participate in sports or join clubs or even date—at least not in a long while, which was weird, because she could remember a time when she'd had an active social life. But that was then, and this was . . . this was pitiful. What would she take pictures of now? Lunch at her desk?

Over the past two hours she'd been experimenting, exploring the boundaries of this weird crap that was happening to her. Now she could recognize the signs that the headache and nausea were coming, and she no longer doubted that it was any thought of the missing two years that brought on the pain. She had no explanation for that, not even a plausible theory, but she did have the good sense to believe what she saw—or rather, what she felt.

Thinking about—or trying to think about—why she'd stopped taking pictures brought on the first, very recognizable signs of distress, so she stopped trying to figure it out and turned back in the album to photos of her childhood. Halloween, Christmas, a summer vacation at the beach. *Damn,* she'd been skinny. *Look at those beanpole legs!* Concentrating on things she definitely remembered did the trick, and once again she was in control of her own body.

The doorbell rang, and she almost jumped out of her skin. Her shoulder bumped against the coffee table, her mug shook, and caramel-colored liquid splashed close to the rim. She steadied the cup, set the photo album aside, and stood.

The hair on the back of her neck was standing up. She could feel alarm like a cold chill all over her body, shouting a warning.

Who would come to her door in the morning, when anyone who knew her would know she was normally at work at this hour? It was too early for the mail, not that she expected a package or anything that would need to be signed for, which would be the only reason the mailman would knock. Door-to-door salesmen were kind of rare these days, and the only friend she had who would check on her—Diana—already had.

Lizette approached the door cautiously, her hands opening and closing as if seeking a weapon that wasn't there. She eased around to the side, so if anyone shot through the door—*shit!* Quickly she hummed a song under her breath, concentrating on the tune, warding off the hammer of pain that had drawn back in preparation to knock her block off.

The sickening sensation ebbed, but she still eyed the door uneasily. Her heart was suddenly pounding, as if she expected a snake to be on the other side, waiting to strike when she opened the door. Her reaction was . . . new, and definitely disturbing. On any other day she'd have answered the door like a normal person, with curiosity but also confidence. Now she was very wary of who might be on the other side, and she couldn't bring herself to relax. What should she do now? Maybe if she was quiet, whoever was on the other side would go away. On the other hand, maybe it was a burglar checking to see if anyone was at home before circling around to the back and breaking in, in which case she could yell *Who is it?* or even look through the peephole, if she could steel her nerves to take that chance.

But before she could do either, a familiar voice called out, "Yoo-hoo. Lizette, are you home?"

Her heart returned to a normal rhythm; her muscles uncoiled. Not a snake, just a busybody—a busybody who actually said "yoo-hoo," for God's sake. Who did that, outside of old sitcoms?

With a different kind of dread, Lizette blew out a breath, resigned herself, and opened the door. Her next-door neighbor stood on the porch. Maggie Rogers lived in the house on the left, and she'd been there as long as Lizette could remember—which, evidently, was only about three years. Maggie was a widow, too young for retirement but living well enough on her late husband's insurance money. She had silvery gray hair cut in a short, slightly edgy, and definitely fashionable style, a pretty face that looked younger than her hair said she was, a trim and athletic figure, and a small yapping dog that was, oddly enough, almost exactly the same color as her hair.

The dog was in her arms, peering at Lizette with beady dark eyes. Lizette normally liked dogs. She just didn't like dogs that looked as if they had rodent DNA. To keep from being hypnotized by that beady gaze, she forced herself to look only at Maggie.

"Are you all right?" Maggie asked. "I saw your car in the driveway and I was so worried." Maggie stepped forward and Lizette automatically stepped back and, bingo, just like that, Maggie was inside without having been invited. Lizette was annoyed with herself for not standing her ground, though she had to admit her normal modus operandi was to avoid confrontation, to not speak up, to be . . . passive.

Maggie held the dog close in her arms, to keep the little varmint from jumping down and playing "can't catch me" throughout Lizette's house. Her gaze scanned the room, but that was nothing unusual. Every time Lizette had encountered Maggie, the other woman had checked out everything, as if looking for some little clue that Lizette had a secret bondage fetish, or drug addiction, or anything else salacious. She was doomed in that, because Lizette couldn't think of even a tiny salacious detail in her life—damn it. "You never miss work," Maggie said almost accusingly, as if Lizette had disrupted *her* life by being sick.

Okay, it was kind of creepy that Maggie knew so

much about her schedule, but not surprising. Maggie was the type of woman who sat where she could see out her windows and keep tabs on all her neighbors, a champion curtain-twitcher. Lizette managed to keep her expression neutral. Even if she did have enough money that she never needed to work, this woman needed a job in the worst way. Her day revolved around watching her neighbors and monitoring their every move; she gave real meaning to the phrase "get a life," because the only one she seemed to have belonged to everyone around her.

Still . . . "I don't feel well," Lizette found herself explaining. The sweatpants and tee shirt she wore, along with no makeup and a face that had been, at last glance, much too pale, should have given that away. Give Maggie an F in observation skills.

"I was afraid of that. What can I do to help?" Maggie finally looked directly at Lizette, her pale blue eyes probing, alight with curiosity. "God, you do look awful," she added, sounding sincere.

Gee, thanks, Lizette thought sarcastically, then felt guilty because, even if her main motivation was curiosity, Maggie *had* come over to check on her and offer to help. "Nothing major, just a bug. I'm feeling somewhat better now. I still haven't tried any solid food, but I'm keeping liquids down. As a matter of fact, I was about to change clothes and go to a pharmacy or Walmart to pick up a few things."

"I'll be happy to do that for you. Just give me a list."

Aspirin, Pepto-Bismol, an ice bag, a throwaway cell phone . . . The items ticked off in her head. She shut that inner voice off before it triggered another attack.

"Thanks, but I think the fresh air will make me feel better." That was a polite enough way of saying *"Thanks but no thanks, and bye-bye."*

But Maggie didn't take the hint. She went to the sofa and sat down; the dog squirmed to get down, but she held him tighter. Glancing down, she saw the photo album that was open on the floor near the coffee table. "Oh, you've been looking at old pictures."

"Yes." Lizette stood at the end of the couch and looked down at her neighbor, who had made herself comfortable and showed no sign of taking the hint and going home. An idea niggled at her; maybe she could ask Maggie if she remembered exactly when Lizette had moved in—was it three years ago, or five?—but that was a strange question to ask anyone. Not only that, what if the house was bugged?

Maggie gave her a strange look. "Are you all right?"

"Hmm? As well as I've been all day, so far. Why?"

Maggie made an odd sound in her throat, one of either concern or curiosity; sometimes it was hard to tell the difference between the two. "You were humming. Not that humming is strange," she added hastily, "just that you had the weirdest expression on your face."

"Sorry," Lizette said, though she wondered why she was apologizing for humming. When one of those thunderbolt headaches threatened, switching her thoughts to the song she'd heard yesterday had become so automatic, she'd barely been aware that she'd started to hum. "You know how annoying it is when you hear a song and then can't get it out of your head?

Like that old Oscar Mayer wiener song? That kind of thing."

Suddenly she found herself wondering exactly why Maggie was here. Why had she come over, instead of just calling? Before, she'd simply accepted the woman as the stereotypical nosy neighbor, but what if she wasn't? Lizette covertly studied her visitor. Exactly how old was she? Fifty, maybe? She could be younger than that; the silvery gray hair made her look older, but she wasn't what anyone would call elderly. Her skin was smooth, a lot smoother than her hair color should indicate. She didn't wear a lot of makeup, and what she did wear was tasteful and almost undetectable, which took skill. And beneath the baggy, nondescript outfit she wore, she was trim. Was she also muscular? In good physical shape? Maybe. She didn't move as if she had any problems with arthritis or worn-out joints.

Maggie's hands were all but hidden in the thick, long hair of the yapper. Lizette studied what she could see, because hands could say a lot about someone's age. What little she could see seemed to be smooth and spotless.

And the dog. The ornate collar could be hiding anything—a camera, a voice recorder—

Lizette grabbed her coffee cup and stepped back. This time she didn't sing or hum aloud, but she let the song play in her mind, concentrating on the words until they drowned out everything else. *Normal,* her mind shouted behind the lyrics, *be normal.*

"I'm sorry," she said swiftly. "My manners are terrible. I'll blame it on the bug; I haven't been sick in so long I can't remember the last time. Thank goodness these things don't last very long." She headed for the kitchen. "Would you like some coffee? I'm going to make a fresh pot."

"That sounds great," Maggie chirped, killing Lizette's hopes that instead of accepting she would say she'd just wanted to check that everything was all right, and now she'd get back home.

Lizette breathed deeply as she stepped into the kitchen. *Normal.*

Almost an hour had passed before Maggie finally took herself and the yapper—whose name happened to be Roosevelt, which came close to taking first place for the most incongruous name for a tiny dog she'd ever heard—back to her own house. What kind of woman would have such a lengthy visit with someone who'd had such a recent bout with a nasty bug? A hypochondriac who wanted to *really* be sick for a change? Someone who was so hungry for companionship she'd run the risk of catching the bug herself? Just a nosy neighbor? Or was she snooping around trying to find out . . . what?

Every time Lizette reached that point in her thought loop, a headache would threaten and she'd have to mentally back away.

While she was getting ready to go out, Diana called to check on her. Lizette dutifully reported that she was feeling better, hadn't thrown up in several hours, and was about to go pick up some OTC stuff in case things got worse. It was weird, but she felt as if she had to carefully choose every word, that everything she said was being analyzed and weighed—

Quickly she began humming, and the pain faded. *Dang,* she was getting good at this. Paranoid, but good.

What was the saying? Just because you're paranoid, that doesn't mean people aren't out to get you. But if you were paranoid, how did you know which enemies were real and which were imaginary? Look how suspicious she'd been of Maggie; would she have been as suspicious if Maggie didn't insist on taking that rodent-dog with her everywhere she went? Was dislike of the yapper coloring her thoughts about Maggie?

Well, sure. But that didn't mean she was wrong.

Being paranoid was a lot of work; she had no idea what to think.

But she knew what she knew, and she knew what she didn't know. She didn't know when she moved into this house. She didn't know when she went to work for Becker Investments. She didn't know *anything* that had happened during that two-year gap in her life.

The most alarming fact of all was that she'd spent three years *not noticing* any of this stuff, not even that she had a different face.

Until she knew exactly what was going on, wouldn't the safest thing be to assume that all of her paranoid thoughts were *true?* If they weren't, no harm, no foul. But if they were, then she should do her best to protect herself . . . from whatever.

She locked up and went to her car, which was parked in the driveway between her house and Maggie's, very deliberately not looking up at Maggie's windows in case the other woman was standing there watching. Her car was a silver Camry, with all the bells and whistles available, reliable, unremarkable. A chill went down her back when she realized she didn't know how long she'd had it, that she had no memory at all of buying it. She didn't even know what model year it was.

The insurance card and registration were in the glove compartment. She started to open it up and take the paperwork out, but remembered that Maggie would have a very good view of what she was doing if she did it there, so instead she started the engine and smoothly reversed to the end of her driveway, where she stopped completely and checked in both directions, as she did every time she left, before continuing to back out.

It was as if caution, routine, and a complete lack of curiosity were as much a part of her as her blue eyes. And it felt wrong—not the blue eyes, those were definitely unchanged, but everything else about this life she was living. She didn't let herself actively think about it because she didn't want to bring on one of those killer headaches while she was driving, but deep inside she accepted that everything about her life now was just *wrong*. The car was wrong, the house was wrong, her job was wrong—*she* was wrong.

She didn't know what she could do about it, but there had to be something, damn it. Maybe she should stop trying to reason everything out, which gave her nothing except a headache—with vomiting thrown in as a bonus—and just go with her instincts.

* * *

She was on the move.

Thanks to the extra electronics installed in her car, he'd be able to tell exactly where she went. So would Forge's people, but with luck, they wouldn't bother putting extra eyes on her. They knew where she was, what she was doing, and why. Besides, right about now Forge had his hands full trying to figure out how Xavier had gotten so much information on Forge's people and plugging the hole in his security. That should keep them busy for a while.

In the meantime, he had things to do.

When she stopped at the first red traffic light, Lizette leaned over and opened the glove compartment to pull out the registration papers and the original sale papers. She'd known they were there, but she'd never read them before—again, there was that lack of curiosity that now seemed so foreign to her. The traffic light turned green almost right away; before, Lizette would have either laid the papers on the seat beside her and waited until she stopped the next time or pulled into a parking lot to read them, but now she swiftly unfolded the papers and held them against the steering wheel, flipping through them, checking the date.

Three years. Everything went back three years, as if the person she'd been had ceased to exist five years ago, then after a gap of two years she'd come back to life as this new cautious, unexciting, routine-bound woman who hadn't even had a real date that she could remember during those three years.

Maybe the reason was nothing more sinister than some sort of accident, which would explain the cosmetic surgery on her face and the gap in her memories. What it *wouldn't* explain was the fact that she'd evidently been functional enough to buy a house and a car and get a job, which didn't jibe with the whole not-remembering thing. People with brain injuries severe enough to cause that kind of amnesia didn't just go forth again as a fully functional person; there would be all kinds of intense therapies that she'd remember, because as far as she knew amnesia happened from the time of injury backward, not the time of injury *forward*. Operating on sheer logic, the reason for all this couldn't be a physical injury.

Mental illness, paranoia—that was more likely than an accident, which was a bummer because she didn't want to be paranoid. But did mentally ill people ever consider that possibility, or did they simply assume the opposite?

She was doubting herself again, after deciding to go with her instincts.

The navigation screen in the dashboard caught her eye. The car had a GPS. That meant it was possible to monitor the position of her car, wherever she went. This was a car she didn't remember buying, and it didn't feel as if it were a car she *would* buy. Maybe it had been picked out for her, and came to her with all sorts of bugs and tracking devices installed. She didn't know how to check for anything like that, but she knew it was possible.

Act normal. She just had to act normal.

She pulled into the parking lot of the Walgreens pharmacy closest to her house. There was an open parking slot right beside the door, the premium spot, the one everyone wanted. She started to wheel into it, then abruptly changed direction and circled around the interior parking spaces until she found two end-to-end empty ones. She pulled in and through, so she was facing out of the parking slot and could simply pull out and drive away. If she had to leave suddenly, not having to back out of the parking space would save precious seconds, and maybe her life.

A chill went down her back, prickled over her skull. Her instincts were suddenly shouting at her, and she didn't like what they were saying.

They're watching.
They're listening.
They know where you are.

Chapter Seven

Xavier eyed the screen of the laptop that was sitting beside him in his truck. Her car was indicated by a blinking chevron, and the chevron had stopped moving. The map overlay told him she was in a Walgreens parking lot, which was good, because she'd said she was going to a pharmacy and that was the closest one to her house. She'd gone directly there, hadn't made any unscheduled stops—in other words, she was acting exactly the way she should.

The big question was: would she do anything differently whether she'd remembered or not? If she'd remembered anything at all, wouldn't she logically try to carry on as normal while she figured things out and made arrangements? From a distance, there was no way to tell.

Despite taking quick looks at the laptop to make certain she wasn't on the move again, he drove hard and fast; he cut through parking lots, raced through yellow lights, and in general made it impossible for anyone to follow him without being spotted. His six stayed clear, though. In another few hours he might have eyes on him, depending on what Lizzy did, but not yet. He knew he didn't have a tracer on the truck because he made damn sure it was clean, and it was an older model that didn't have navigation or any of the other Big Brother shit that made it possible for anyone to know where he was, how long he'd been there, or how fast he'd been driving. His gas mileage sucked, but his doors were reinforced to stop anything short of armor-piercing rounds, he had enough power in the big eight-cylinder to outrun most street cars, a large-capacity gas tank, and with the big push bars on front he could bull his way through most attempts to block him. So far he hadn't needed the truck's extra capabilities, but he always planned for the possibility.

He was sweating the time factor. If she went into the store, got what she wanted, and checked out without taking the time to browse, he'd miss her. She might go straight back home, in which case this chance was blown. He wanted to see her for himself; he'd stayed away from her for years, not even driving past her house, but that was when the status quo was holding. If things were changing, he needed to know. He was taking a big risk, but because it was such a risk it wasn't a move Forge would anticipate that he'd make.

Sometimes the smartest thing to do was the one that made the least amount of sense—especially when others expected him to hold the line.

Getting around the D.C. area was an exercise in patience at the best of times, but thank God it wasn't rush hour; he wheeled into the Walgreens parking lot in record time. If he hadn't had the tracer, allowing him to move at almost the same time she had, he wouldn't have made it.

Rapidly he scanned the parked cars; he knew her

make and model, the color, even the license plate number. There were several empty parking slots right against the building, close to the door, but none of the cars were hers. Then he spotted the unremarkable silver car, which she'd parked toward the back of the lot and pulled forward through a double space so she was facing out.

His heart gave one hard thump. He himself always parked that way. Everyone he knew in the trade parked that way, because a split second could save their lives. Park so you're ready to go, without having to back out, turn, change directions—all little things that caused delays and could make the difference between getting out alive, or not.

And now Lizzy had parked like that, even though there were empty parking slots closer to the building. Maybe those slots had been full when she'd arrived, but that didn't explain the way she'd parked now. Maybe he was reading too much into it; people did park that way, sometimes on a whim, or because they sucked at reversing. Maybe she was pulling into the parking slot and the person parked in front of her had just been leaving, so she'd simply pulled forward. He shouldn't read too much into it. Neither should he ignore it.

He circled around, backed into an empty slot in the very last row, and got out of the truck. Before leaving the condo he'd thrown a denim work shirt on over his tee shirt, leaving it unbuttoned so he had easy access to his weapons. A discerning eye might catch that he was armed, but if anyone noticed he could always flip out his fake badge. Yeah, the badge was against the law; a lot of what he did was, so he didn't sweat it.

Even if he did get busted, he'd be released as soon as they ran his ID.

A rush of adrenaline burned in his veins, then his heart, his whole body; then he settled into the cool calm, every sense heightened, that always came over him when he closed in on his prey.

The automatic doors swooshed open and the particular scent of a pharmacy hit him, part plastic, part medicinal, barely detectable under the sweet scents of cosmetics and lotions. Cool air washed over his face as he stepped inside, already scanning left and right as he went in, something he'd have done even if he hadn't been looking for her. She'd be in the pharmacy section, probably, so he bypassed the makeup and toys and candy, his long legs covering the territory fast.

There. *There,* ambling down an aisle of shampoo and other crap. Her back was to him, and she carried a wire shopping basket with plastic-covered handles. No doubt it was her, though; he knew that mane of dark hair, the erect set of her shoulders, the way she carried her head and, holy shit, the inverted-heart curve of her ass. *Lizzy*—in person, after years of only hearing her voice or seeing photos.

Even so, he took the time to pause and make a deliberate survey of the area. No one was watching her. No one was watching him. The aisle was empty except for her; the next closest person was a plump, gray-haired staffer, two aisles over and busy shelving items.

One of the wire shopping baskets sat beside a center display of leftover Fourth of July stuff. He grabbed it up, seized a spray can of deodorant and a bag of candy as camouflage, tossed them both into the basket, then closed in, his rubber-soled boots silent on the tiled floor. Deliberately he turned so his shoulder was to her and bumped into her, hard enough to almost throw her off balance.

Someone pushed her, hard, making her take a half-step back to keep from falling on her keister. Without thinking, Lizette transferred her weight to her back foot and whirled, alarm skittering through her, her grip tightening on the basket handles as she instinctively prepared to swing it at her attacker as hard as she could.

"Sorry!" a man said in a deep, slightly rough voice as he turned toward her. "I wasn't paying attention to what I was doing."

On some level she noted that he'd been turned away from her, and the spurt of panic eased. He was carrying a shopping basket, and a quick flick of her gaze told her that the most dangerous thing in it was a can of deodorant—well, maybe the chocolate candy, depending on whether or not she was on a diet or looking for a weapon.

Then she looked up at his face, and her heartbeat stuttered. Her skin registered what felt like a physical impact, as if every nerve in her body was reacting to . . . something: chemistry, body heat, testosterone—whatever it was, it was too much, too strong and direct. The hair on the back of her neck lifted, chills ran up and down her arms, and her nipples shrank to tight nubs.

The harsh fluorescent lights of the pharmacy faded, sound receded, and for a few disconcerting seconds her vision narrowed to him, just him, as if they were alone in the middle of the store. The volatile mixture of reactions was so confusing she reached behind herself to grip a shelf for support as she backed up a step, needing some distance between them. *He* was too much.

Her eyes big, her lips going numb, she all but gawked at him as she tried to come to grips with herself. She didn't react to men this way, not even nice, sweet, stable, gainfully employed men any normal woman would love to meet, and certainly not this—this *predator*. "Nice" and "sweet" were two words she was certain had never been applied to him. She should run. She should obey her gut instinct and get as far away from him as fast as she could.

She knew that. She agreed with her gut instinct. But she couldn't get her feet to move.

She shivered, her body still battling with the overwhelming, conflicting signals her brain was sending. Maybe she was going to faint, she thought, alarmed by the possibility but unable to look away from him.

He was a head taller than she, broad-shouldered, tough and lean in boots, jeans, and a denim shirt unbuttoned over a black tee shirt. More than his size, though, was the aura of coiled power about him, even though he was just standing there. His stance, the way he was perfectly balanced so he could go in any direction without hesitation, the powerfully muscled legs so plainly revealed by his tight jeans, all spoke to a man in top physical condition.

The bone structure of his face was lean and angular, with chiseled high cheekbones and a thin, high-bridged nose that made her think he must have some

Native American in his heritage, though it could be Middle Eastern. But it was his eyes that marked him for what he was. He was dark-haired, olive-skinned, and his heavy-lidded eyes such a dark shade of brown that the irises almost blended with the blackness of his pupils. His gaze was direct, coldly intense, and as it focused on her she felt as if she'd suddenly been put in the crosshairs—

She felt a sharp, warning stab of pain, and that finally broke the spell she'd been under. Swiftly she looked away, concentrating on the label of a shampoo bottle, because she'd look like an idiot if she started humming mindlessly. The pain ebbed and she said, "That's okay," not looking at him again because something about his eyes made her feel as if she were standing on the edge of a cliff, about to fall into the unknown.

His big hand appeared in her field of vision as he reached for a bottle of shampoo. "This stuff makes me feel like an idiot," he muttered, startling her into glancing at him.

"Shampoo?" She knit her brows together in a slight frown. "What's hard about shampoo? Wet, lather, rinse. Don't tell me you failed Shampoo 101." The words popped out, and it felt as if someone else was saying them. She knew better; don't engage with strangers—especially strangers who looked as if they could snap her neck with one hand—don't be provocative, don't . . . She knew there were more "don'ts," more directives she should be following, but they were fraying, falling apart even as she tried to bring them to mind. She wasn't a smart-ass; she tried to be polite to everyone, tried not to be intrusive, yet here she was busting this guy's chops and the weird thing was . . . it felt almost natural.

"Passed with flying colors; I was the teacher's pet," he returned, his mouth quirking up on one side in a lopsided half-smile that showed he wasn't at all offended. "But look at this." He turned the bottle so she could see it. " 'Volumizing and clarifying.' What is it, and do I need it? Will it make my hair stand straight out, and I'll understand the universe better?"

She looked up at his dark hair, thick, straight, and slightly unruly, as if he'd combed it by dragging his fingers through it. "I don't think you need any volumizing." Pointing down the aisle, she said, "Besides, this is a woman's shampoo. You need that manly man stuff down there."

He looked where she was pointing. "What's the difference?"

"Packaging."

His gaze returned to her and his lips quirked again. "So I'll still understand the universe better?"

Her heart started beating a little harder, a little faster. "No, but you'll feel more manly while you're not understanding it."

The expression in his eyes changed, lit, and he laughed, kind of, a rough little chuckle as if he didn't make the sound very often and didn't know how to let it go. Her heart gave a funny little bump, followed by another skin-prickling chill as she abruptly realized she'd let her guard down. She had to get away from him, had to be safe, because whatever he was, was more than she could handle.

"Excuse me," she said, turning on her heel before he could say anything else. She reached the end of the aisle as fast as she could without actually running, darted to the left, set her basket down, and headed for the door. She needed the antinausea stuff in the basket, as well as the aspirin, but taking the time to check out was more time than she had. She'd go somewhere else to get what she needed. She'd go to Walmart. She had to get away from him and she didn't care if she made a fool of herself doing it.

Her heart was pounding as she all but sprinted across the parking lot to her car. She used the remote to unlock it just before she reached for the door, threw herself inside, and relocked the doors. Fumbling a little, she pushed the key into the ignition and started the engine.

No one followed her out of the store.

Knucklehead.

She sat for a few seconds, breathing hard, exasperated with herself. She'd panicked for no good reason, just because some big guy had made some casual conversation with her.

Maybe. Maybe that was all he'd been doing. But maybe there was more, something she didn't understand and couldn't remember. How could she tell the difference?

Answer: she couldn't.

She blew out a breath. Oh, well, she needed to go to Walmart anyway, to buy a replacement for her cell phone. She'd still have to pay for her plan with her current cell server, but until she figured out what was going on, she wanted a phone that was more anonymous. Make that two phones, because she needed a burner phone—

Shit!

She didn't have time to hum or read labels. The agony in her head made her whimper as she tried to curl into a ball, but the steering wheel was in the way and she banged her knee, hard. That helped, in a strange way, as if she could process only so much pain at one time, and this new source jerked her focus away from her head. The headache promptly began ebbing.

Her eyes were watering from the pain, but at least she hadn't started vomiting again. She wiped her eyes and sank back in the seat, breathing hard and gathering her energy. *Okay.* She'd just learned another coping strategy. The next time an attack sneaked past her guard, all she needed to do was punch herself in the mouth.

She didn't remember him. That was good. That was bad. When she suddenly bolted, running from him as if snakes had sprouted from his head, Xavier forced himself to remain where he was. He didn't want to panic her into doing something that would trigger a response from Forge's people. Simply approaching her himself was risky enough, but now he had the answer he wanted.

She was coming back. He knew it, even though she hadn't recognized him. She'd still reacted to him, to the almost electric connection they'd always had. The shampoo conversation had been so similar to one they'd once had about deodorant that he hadn't been able to mask his reaction. *You'll still smell better, but you'll feel more manly about not stinking.* He could still hear her saying that, see her smirk before he grabbed her and kissed it off. She'd had a smart mouth on her that had required a lot of kissing to keep her under control; listening to her these past few years, hearing how dulled down they'd made her, had driven him nuts even though he'd been forced to accept it.

She was alive, though she hadn't really been living. He'd had to be content with that. But now things were changing; he'd heard it in her voice, seen it in the sparkle that had lit her eyes. The situation might hold together for another week, another month, maybe not progress any further than it had already, but he wasn't betting on that.

Instead he'd bet that she was going to come roaring back, because that was who she was, and all hell was going to break loose.

Chapter Eight

Lizette surveyed the array of cell phones at Walmart. Something was niggling at her, something she needed to think through if she could just figure out whatever the niggling thing was.

"Need help with a phone?" the barely-twenty-something clerk asked. He was lanky and earnest, and wore glasses that sat crookedly on his nose.

"I don't know," she replied. She'd come in here fully intending to pick up a basic phone, but now that she was here in front of the display she wasn't certain she'd be accomplishing anything.

"Are you thinking smart phone, or a more basic model?"

"I'm really just browsing. Thanks."

Did she really need a burner cell phone? The idea was one of those weird thoughts that had popped out of the blackness of those missing two years, but if she applied it to now, what use was it? She had no one to call who she couldn't call with her normal phone—which she'd destroyed in a sudden panicked certainty that it was bugged. *Bugs.* That was the point, not secrecy. What she knew about prepaid cell phones wasn't a lot, but she did know the phone had to be activated online, which meant it was registered in her name. What would she be accomplishing?

Nothing.

Okay, that question was answered. What she needed was a phone she knew wasn't bugged, which she might as well get from her regular service provider, given that she was already paying for a contract. If she kept the battery out of it, then she couldn't be tracked by the phone's GPS. Likewise, if the phone was dead, it couldn't be cloned. A separate bug installed in the phone might be able to pick up her conversations if she was in the room, but first someone would have to have access to her phone, and she could definitely control that.

She felt as if she'd been lost in a wilderness of ignorance and was slowly beginning to find her way out. Nothing made sense, but order was beginning to assert itself; she wasn't as panicked now and she could think logically.

She had walked in the doors hell-bent on getting a prepaid cell phone that she didn't need, but getting one would send an alert to the mysterious "They," which was what she wanted to avoid. A true burner was one a third party had picked up and passed on, so it wasn't linked to her. She didn't know how she knew this little detail, but she did, and it wasn't giving her a headache, either. Yay for her.

She left the store without buying anything, not even OTC meds for headaches and nausea. She obviously didn't have any kind of virus, because what bug could be stopped by concentrating on songs or other trivial stuff? No, both symptoms were obviously triggered by surfacing memories from the missing two years.

Something had happened to her, something cata-strophic and maybe even sinister, though she had no evidence of the latter. Instead she seemed to have been set adrift in a new life, and left to her own devices.

Maybe she'd had some kind of weird reaction to anesthesia whenever she'd had the facial surgery. Maybe it was nothing more than that, and all these suspicions about bugged cell phones and being watched were by-products of movies she'd watched in the past.

She'd be careful because she didn't know for cer-tain what was going on, she thought as she drove to her cell service provider to get a new phone, but she wouldn't let this drive her crazy.

That was the smart thing to do—right?

For the rest of the day and evening, things were nor-mal enough, at least on the surface. Lizette did what she routinely did, ate soup for dinner, fielded another call from Diana, and reported that she was feeling a little shaky but overall much better. She watched TV. She read—or tried to read. The whole time, she was thinking about the creepy-crawly feeling that her house had been bugged—not just the phone, not just her car, but the house, too. If someone really was going to all that trouble, *not* bugging the house would leave a big hole in the electronic fence, and she simply couldn't see that.

But how in hell could she check her house for bugs? She could look at all the lighting fixtures, all the lamps, but wouldn't that be a dead giveaway if there really were bugs there? Besides that, she'd changed all the bulbs in all the fixtures several times while she'd been living here, and she'd never noticed anything unusual. A really good bugging job would be in the electrical outlets, and she wouldn't be able to find out for sure unless she had a meter to measure amperage—

Whoa. Headache. She hummed a little, made it go away. She was getting damned tired of these stupid headaches. What if she had one at a critical time, say, when she was driving? She could plow right into a semi, or a van full of kids, or any number of awful things.

Okay, nothing she could do about bugs. She'd be better off going to bed and trying to get some sleep, so she could recover from the roller-coaster ride of pain, nausea, and jangly nerves she'd been on for most of the day. The problem with that was, those jangly nerves were still with her. Her face still wasn't the face she remembered, at least two years were completely missing from her life, and she couldn't shake the bone-deep sensation that some unknown, malevolent *they*—whoever *they* were—were behind the whole thing, not only in stealing part of her life but keeping her in the dark and standing guard to make certain she stayed there.

That really pissed her off. Why her? What had she done? Was it nothing more than chance, or had she agreed to be a part of a medical study that had gone awry—big understatement there—and this was the result? No, that didn't explain the new face. Nothing did.

Until she found out exactly what was going on, she figured jangly nerves would become her new norm, and she'd have to learn how to deal with them. Take that guy in Walgreens today; she'd panicked over nothing, which was embarrassing, but at least he was a stranger and she hadn't done something stupid like start screaming because he asked her a question about shampoo.

Thinking about him was a welcome distraction. For a few minutes she allowed herself to wallow in pure female pleasure as she remembered the impact he'd had on her senses. Was he a walking testament to the truth about pheromones, or what? She'd been both turned on and scared at the same time, which was an exhilarating kind of rush all on its own.

If she hadn't been such a wienie, maybe he'd have asked for her number. The next big question was, would she have been brave enough to give it to him?

He wasn't safe. She knew it instinctively. Even though there hadn't been anything outwardly threatening about him, she knew he didn't fit into the mold of a safe, normal, everyday type of man.

Strange that she could remember his face so clearly. It was those dark, dangerous, intense eyes that stood out the most. A man like him—

No, she was letting her hormone-driven imagination run away with her, which fit right in with the rest of the day she'd had. She had to laugh at herself. At least thinking about a hot guy was better than worrying about the house being bugged.

Eventually she wound down enough that she thought she might sleep, and dragged herself off to bed. She was restless, though, and her subconscious went over and over the day's events, trying to make sense of them, trying to solve the puzzle. Then—finally—she slept.

And she dreamed. She knew it was a dream, the way she sometimes did when she had almost surfaced enough to wake up, but not quite. Her surroundings looked real enough, and she was herself in this dream, which was a relief, because after the day she'd had she didn't want to dream about being someone else.

She'd dreamed about houses before: houses with hidden rooms and steep staircases, other houses she could almost remember as being from the real world, such as the house she'd grown up in; her fifth-grade best friend's house; even this very house, though with hidden doors and underground rooms that she actually kind of enjoyed, because there was something magical about it. But this . . . this was a new house, sprawling and meandering, with room after room after room, all white, all airy and strangely peaceful even though as she looked around, she knew she was lost. How the hell was she supposed to get out of here? Every time she thought she'd found the way to the front door, she'd find herself in some other part of the house. She'd look out a window and see the front door off to the left, or the right, but she could never find it.

Then she realized that *he* was here—somewhere, lost in the big house the same way she was. He was looking for her and she was looking for him, but walls and doors got in the way. She didn't feel worried about it, though, just annoyed at the delay. She'd find him, or he'd find her. He always did.

She should have asked what his name was, when he'd bumped into her at Walgreens. She didn't normally strike up conversations with strange men, especially men like him, but he'd started it, so she could have kept it going. How hard would it have been? While they'd been talking about shampoo—or had it been deodorant?—she could have said, "I'm Lizette. Who are you?"

Instead, he didn't have a name. She supposed she could always call her mystery man Mr. X, which was better than nothing. She even kind of liked it.

She kept circling through the house, trying to find him. For some reason her path kept going through the largest room of all, a huge room with white walls, white couches and chairs, white billowing curtains. The fourth time she found herself in that big room she got really pissed, and in a fit of temper pushed through a door she hadn't noticed before—and there he was, in the one room of the house that *wasn't* all white. There was color here, reds and blues and greens and browns, like nature itself. There was texture, and smell, as if it were real. *He* was real enough, just as he'd been in the pharmacy, big and hard and unexpectedly appealing. What a dope she'd been, to have been afraid of him for even a minute. She should have looked into his dark eyes and allowed herself to fall in; she should have trusted him.

No—wait. She didn't trust anyone, not anymore.

Lizette wanted to tell X that she'd missed him, but her voice wouldn't work. *Crap.* It was her dream, she should be able to say whatever she wanted, but for some reason she was mute. All she could do was look at him and wonder how he'd look naked.

She hadn't had a sex life in the past three years. Maybe longer. Okay, that was real life. Beyond that . . .

she knew she wasn't a virgin, but she couldn't remember ever wanting anyone the way she wanted X.
There was an aching emptiness between her legs, a
clawing, almost desperate need to have him inside
her.

It wasn't love, wasn't a niggling need for a little
sexual release. She needed him the way she needed
air, inside her, over her, under her . . .

He laughed a little, the way he had in Walgreens,
and walked toward her. He didn't speak either, but
she knew that he wanted her as much as she wanted
him. He reached out and touched her cheek, and she
closed her eyes, nestled her face in his big, rough
hand. That touch felt right, and warm, and . . . not
enough.

Because this was a dream, one second they were
face-to-face and fully clothed, then the scene changed
and they were naked, lying in a bed in the room of
color. The bed hadn't been there before, but whatever; it was there now, deep and wide, just what they
needed. *Good dream,* she cooed approvingly in her
thoughts.

She wanted him right now. They were naked, they
both wanted it, she was wet and he was hard—there
was no reason she shouldn't be able to have him. Instead he laughed as he pinned her wrists to the bed
and lowered his head to kiss her neck . . . simply
kissed. She couldn't believe it. He was hard, so how
could he kiss her so softly and with such aggravating
and unnecessary *patience?* She squirmed impatiently
and he moved on top of her, his heavy weight pressing her down as he held her still.

Skin to skin, his scent filling her, his mouth on her,

everything stopped. Time stopped. There was just his body and hers, this big bed that stretched forever, this room of color. This felt so real she forgot it was a dream, lost herself in the sensation.

She found her voice, just enough for one word. "Now."

Finally he spoke, too, in that deep, rough voice of his, a voice that matched the dark eyes and hardness of him. It was a voice she *almost* knew. "Relax, Lizzy. We have all night."

That sounded all well and good, but what if they didn't have all night? Oh, right—she remembered again that this was just a dream. Not real, no matter how real it felt. But dreams didn't last forever; what if she woke up before they were finished? That had happened before, dreaming that she was falling off a cliff and waking up just before she hit the ground, or coming face-to-face with a tiger and waking with a gasp just as it lunged. In this case she wanted to hit the ground; she wanted to be eaten alive. She wanted the dream to last.

She knew how to make X hurry, how to make sure he didn't drag this out too long. She reached down, their bodies so tightly pressed together she had difficulty working her arm between them, but she managed to get her fingers around the thickness of his erection and began stroking. He growled in her ear and caught her earlobe between his white teeth, biting down just enough for her to feel the sharp pinch, but he didn't roll on top of her and push between her legs where she ached. Frustrated, annoyed even in sleep, she stroked harder, longer, and after another low growl in his throat he whispered, "Keep it up and I'll come in your hand."

Crap! That would definitely defeat the purpose. She snatched her hand away, scowling at him, and he laughed.

He kept on kissing her, his mouth moving from her ear to her throat, throat to chest, chest to nipple. His tongue circled the tight point, then suddenly he clamped his mouth on her and sucked hard, strong, pulling at her until he wrung a sharp cry from her. Her back arched and she wrapped her legs around him, straining, trying to lift herself to his engorged penis so she could take him in.

Diabolically, he moved back just enough that she couldn't get into position, and she made a feral sound deep in her throat that earned her another of those wicked, gloating laughs.

Thinking furiously, calculating grip and balance and momentum, she worked out how she might toss X onto his back and straddle him, taking him in before he could stop her and ending this painful wanting. *Damn him,* he was always like this, pushing her out of her comfort zone of control. He was big, but not so big that she couldn't handle him, if she took him by surprise. *Fuck* foreplay.

Even in her dream, that sentence startled her into laughing.

Somehow, he knew. This was *her* dream but he was in control, and instantly he whipped out a pair of handcuffs and shackled her to the headboard, both wrists. The handcuffs must have come out of the ether, because being naked, he didn't have a pocket to hide them in. Dreams were such a hoot.

X grinned at her. It was a predator's smile, all teeth, very much like the lunging tiger.

She tugged on the handcuffs, torn between excitement and fury. "That's not very nice." She'd have pouted if things like that ever worked on him, but they never did. Still, she wasn't afraid, not of him. Never of him.

"You want nice?" His eyes narrowed. "Since when?" He ran big, rough hands over her body, from neck to waist, from waist to thighs and downward, as if he were tracing her outline so slowly the complete study would take hours . . . days. She shook with wanting him. She trembled, when he lowered his head and kissed her on the neck again while his hands . . . played. His skin was burning hot, but his touch was so gentle and hard and demanding and patient, all at the same time, despite the steely hardness of his erection that betrayed how turned on he was. He'd be the perfect lover . . . if she could just get him in the right position. Didn't he want her as much as she wanted him? Wasn't he as hungry?

Hungry like a tiger whose dinner had been handcuffed to the dinner table.

She wanted to touch him, but with her hands above her head she couldn't. She was restrained, he was in complete control, but if he thought she was helpless he was about to learn otherwise. She closed her eyes and turned her head away, concentrating on his position, calculating the distance. She'd already tried this, but he might not be expecting the same move twice. The thick, bulbous head of his penis brushed between her legs, teasing, and like lightning she scissored her strong legs around him and pulled him in to the very point of entry.

Time froze. Everything in her waited, caught on the cusp of orgasm. He was right there, touching her, almost inside her. Almost, almost.

Then she heard something, a faint noise intruding on the intimate battle between them. She was suddenly aware that they weren't alone in the big, rambling house. Someone was searching through all the white rooms for her. Maybe they didn't know she'd found this room of color. Maybe they didn't know that she'd found him. X. Her lover.

He was right *there,* and she needed him more than ever, but they were running out of time. She wanted to hold him, but she couldn't. She wanted to scream, but if she did they would hear. The searchers would find them any minute and she didn't want to be caught naked, didn't want to be *caught,* period, yet she couldn't make herself let him go. So she lifted her head up and whispered in his ear.

Desperately she pressed her mouth against his ear, whispered, demanded, "Fuck me!"

He gave another of those growling laughs that she could feel as well as hear, and pushed inside, filling her deep and hard.

Lizette woke with a lurch of her body, a moan tearing from her throat as the dream orgasm faded away. Her covers had been tossed aside; her pillows were on the floor. In spite of the overhead fan and the air conditioning, she was sweating.

Oh, God, that had been good.

How long had it been since she'd had a really hot dream? She couldn't remember, and she didn't miss the irony that the dream had been about a stranger who'd frightened the crap out of her in a pharmacy aisle.

One thing for certain: dreaming about sex was way better than dreaming that unknown strangers were watching her.

She glanced at the clock as she grabbed the pillows from the floor. Three sixteen in the morning, which was way too early to get up, especially considering what a tough time she'd had going to sleep last night. She was thoroughly relaxed now, so maybe the hot dream had been her mind's way of dealing with the stress of the day.

Good deal.

She thought of the name she'd given him in the dream. Mr. X. It fit him. It felt right. She drifted back to sleep thinking of how he'd tasted in her dream.

Chapter Nine

Lizette warily approached Saturday; Friday had been such a day of upheaval that she was almost afraid of what the new day would bring. The wrong face still stared at her from the mirror, she still had at least two years missing from her memory, but at least she wasn't spending the morning either curled up in pain or hanging over the toilet puking her guts out. She'd take any improvement she could get.

But the day felt odd, as if she were just waiting for something else to happen. Briefly—very briefly—she entertained the idea of going back to Walgreens to see if by chance Mr. X would be there, but she had to roll her eyes at herself on that one. *Not going to happen.* He'd bought his shampoo yesterday; he wouldn't be back for more.

Saturday was her day for errands, one of which was grocery shopping. Normally she shopped at Walmart for the majority of her groceries, and at the small neighborhood store closer to the house when she needed only a few things. Today she went to neither, and she couldn't have said why, other than breaking out of her routine seemed like a good idea.

Instead she stopped at a store she passed on the way to and from work every day but had never entered. It was a nice store, large, clean, just a bit fancy, so she took her time. The prices were a bit higher than at Walmart, but she was actually having fun finding different foods.

Leisurely shopping was a decent enough way to spend a Saturday afternoon when it seemed as if her body and mind were turning against her and nothing about her life made sense anymore. It was nice to get away from her worries for a while, to deal with nothing more dramatic than what this store had or didn't have, to study labels, plan a meal or two, and think about . . . nothing.

Except—suddenly, the damnedest things were perplexing. She stopped, staring into the case of frozen foods. Blueberry pomegranate frozen yogurt. Something about it resonated, though she couldn't remember ever trying it before. Did she like it? Would she like it? She tended to stick with vanilla, and she was damn tired of vanilla. So . . . maybe. Opening the door, she took out a carton of blueberry pomegranate and placed it in her grocery cart, next to the cinnamon raisin bagels and the oatmeal raisin cookies. *Carbs, much?* She usually made certain her diet was more healthy than not, but today she was having problems with her selections. What if all this time she'd been eating foods she really didn't like? After everything she'd gone through the day before, that didn't feel as ridiculous as it sounded.

She couldn't live on carbs alone, so she made herself go back through the produce aisle, adding fruits and vegetables to the cart. Normally she ate turkey: turkey breast, ground turkey, turkey bacon, turkey sausage . . . she was so sick of turkey, she never wanted to see it again. She bought some real bacon, though a package of chicken breasts probably balanced that out. Before she totally flipped out and added something like sardines to the growing pile, she wheeled the cart to one of the checkout lanes.

As the cashier efficiently scanned the items, Lizette looked out the wide front windows, studying the parking lot. Her car was parked to the right and several spaces down, facing out—again—so she could drive straight out of the space and into the lane that led to the side exit of the parking lot. She didn't even remember purposely choosing that space, but looking at it now, from this distance, it was plain to see. She was poised for a quick getaway.

And, *huh*, no headache or nausea, just a clear observation of her surroundings.

She paid with a swipe of her credit card and plucked the keys from her purse so they were in her hand and ready. She grabbed her bags—plastic, not paper—and placed them so they hung over her forearms but didn't restrict her hands. The plastic straps of the heaviest bag bit into her flesh and pinched a bit, but she wanted both of her hands free. She couldn't remember ever worrying about that before, but she had a new reality now.

She stepped off the curb and headed toward her car, her gaze automatically scanning the area. She was alert, in a way she hadn't ever been. No, that wasn't quite right: she hadn't been this aware in a *long time*. So what if she couldn't remember exactly when she had been this aware? What was fascinating was how oblivious most people were.

The woman who had checked out beside and just

before Lizette was loading her groceries into the back of her Highlander, while two children—one boy, one girl—argued about who was going to sit where. Most of the other cars were empty, though a man sat in the driver's seat of a gray sedan, probably waiting for his wife or girlfriend. He was looking down, as if texting or playing a game on his phone, but she couldn't see what was in his hands. A store employee, a young and bored guy probably working a summer job, was collecting grocery carts. One young couple was headed into the store; she held a piece of paper, most likely a list, in her right hand. Lizette could tell they'd probably been arguing. Neither spoke or looked directly at one another at any time, and there was a good three feet between them, a distance neither felt compelled to narrow. His shoulders were tight; her mouth was pursed.

Lizette used the remote to pop the trunk open. After storing her groceries there she closed the trunk, and once again looked around. A car was just pulling into the parking lot—a female driver, alone. The woman circled the parking lot, looking for a slot as close to the store as she could get.

Lizette unlocked her door, got inside, and immediately relocked the door.

She sat there for a long moment before starting the engine. A long chill ran down her spine. Someone was watching her. Damn it, she *felt* eyes on her, though she hadn't seen anything out of the ordinary.

But maybe not. Maybe being hyper-alert was just putting herself in the mindset that she *could* be watched, and her imagination was taking over from there. Half convinced she was being watched, half certain she wasn't, Lizette pulled out of the parking slot and turned toward the traffic light.

The gray sedan, the one with the man who'd been texting, or whatever, in the driver's seat, was just leaving the parking lot as well and he fell in behind her. Frowning, she glanced into the rearview mirror. He was still alone.

What were the possibilities? Rapidly she ran through a few scenarios. Maybe he'd run into the store, picked up a few things, checked out ahead of her, and then sat in his car for a few minutes to send a text. She hadn't seen him in the store, but that didn't mean anything. Maybe he had planned to shop, but something or someone had called him away before he could take care of that chore. That was plausible. Unlikely, but still plausible.

Then again, maybe he was following her. Had he picked her out of all the women who'd walked in that parking lot and chosen her as his victim? She had been careful, she'd been alert, so what had marked her as an easy target? Or had he been behind her on the drive from her house to the store where she had never shopped before? Would she have noticed?

No, an inner voice said, *you wouldn't have. You were thinking about Mr. X, and doing normal things, like getting on with your life as if nothing had changed in the past day and a half.* Her big thing today had been shopping at a grocery store she hadn't been in before.

Her heart jumped up in her throat. What should she do?

A left turn would take her toward home. She didn't dare lead this guy to her house, though if he'd followed her from there he already knew where she lived. She tried to think through the ramifications of that, but things were happening too fast for her right now and she needed to concentrate on what she was doing. When the traffic light changed to green, Lizette turned right.

So did the car behind her.

She drove down the main street that would, eventually, take her past the office building where she worked. This was a part of town she knew well. She'd driven these streets enough. For the past three years—maybe three—she'd driven this route to work five days a week. She had rarely deviated from the route, though every day she'd gone out for lunch and gotten to know the area that way. Once, for a five-week period, a detour had taken her by another route while this one was being repaired and repaved.

Now, as she kept her speed at precisely the speed limit, she realized that while she'd never consciously paid much attention, she really did know a lot about this area. It was as if a part of her subconscious had been operating on a different level all along.

The road coming up led to an apartment complex: dead end. The next three streets to the left would take her into a middle-class neighborhood. She wasn't sure what was back there besides houses: cross streets, maybe a park. Farther down this street there were a number of restaurants, an office building much larger than her own, and a couple of nice strip malls.

The gray car was still behind her, but it wasn't right on her tail. A Highlander—maybe the one with the woman and two kids and their groceries—had passed the gray car and then pulled between them. Lizette flipped her turn signal and moved into the left lane. So did the Highlander. Her heart pounded; her palms began to sweat. Surely she wasn't being followed by *two* vehicles, especially since the one behind her had kids in it. On the other hand, what great camouflage! And multiple cars doing a tail were always better than one—

Not now, not now! she thought frantically as pain stabbed through her head. She couldn't afford to be blinded by a headache. The only song she could think of at the moment was "Oscar Mayer Wiener," so she hummed it and concentrated on the words until the pain dimmed and she could see clearly again.

Then the Highlander turned into the middle-class neighborhood, and Lizette breathed a sigh of relief.

The relief didn't last long. The gray sedan was still a short distance behind her, not riding her bumper but staying fairly close.

Without using her turn indicator, she took the next left, sharply and cleanly. *Huh.* The Camry, which she didn't think she'd have chosen for herself, handled pretty well. On the side road, she slowed her speed. She checked the rearview mirror and saw the gray car turn onto the road behind her.

Her pulse rate jumped. She took a deep breath, and something deep inside her seemed to settle down. Coincidence, like the Highlander? Hell, no. One coincidence was more than enough for one day. She wouldn't take the risk that this was another. She checked for oncoming traffic, then slammed on her brakes and spun the steering wheel, making a one-eighty turn in the middle of the street and heading back toward the main road. As she zipped past the gray car she didn't look at the driver, not directly. She could see well enough with her peripheral vision to identify him as the man from the grocery store parking lot, though.

He didn't look directly at her, either.

Stalker, robber, rapist . . . innocent bystander? She wasn't going to take a chance, regardless.

She pulled back onto the main drag and hit the gas. Traffic was light, so she didn't have any problems swerving in and out between cars, changing lanes, putting some asphalt between her and the man in the gray car. She was so intent on the traffic, on the cars she passed with no more than a hair's breadth between them, that she didn't dare check her rearview mirror to see if the gray car was behind her.

But when she hit a fairly clear stretch of road, she checked the mirror. Was that him, a quarter of a mile or so back? His car was so ordinary, it was impossible to tell, and she couldn't make out the details of his grill and headlights.

Several blocks past her office building she took a fast right, slowing just enough that she could maintain control. She took the next right, too, then a left. She passed a slower-moving black pickup, made another turn, then pulled into the parking lot of a small apartment complex, turned a corner, and slid her vehicle into a small space between a white van and a gray pickup, two high-profile vehicles that hid her smaller car from view, if anyone had been able to follow her to this point.

Just in case, she popped her seat belt and slid down low in the seat so that anyone who did drive by wouldn't see that she was in the car. Automatically she reached for her purse, as if there should be something there she needed, but her fingers stopped well short of the leather strap. What was she reaching for? Her breath mints? Fingernail clippers?

Yeah, she could be flip about it, but in the back of her mind she knew exactly what she'd been reaching for. *I need my weapon.*

Her heart was beating hard but not terribly fast; her legs trembled in reaction, to either fear or adrenaline. Right now, she couldn't tell which.

Maybe she should call the police, but what the hell would she say? She hadn't gotten a license plate number, and even if she had, the man in the gray car hadn't done anything illegal. Scaring a paranoid woman wasn't a crime, last she'd heard. *No, no police.* Besides, putting the battery in her cell phone and turning it on would let whoever was following her triangulate her position.

Oh, shit. The car had a GPS. It might have a separate tracker hidden on it somewhere, for all she knew. If her pursuer was tracking her movements, the gray car would show up any minute now, and there was no way she could evade him for good, at least as long as she stayed with the car. A part of her mind screamed that she should get out of the car now, that sitting here she was in a position of weakness, but out there . . . out there in an unfamiliar neighborhood with no gun, no backup, no one to call, was she any better off than she was right here?

No gray sedan showed up, and after a while she had to conclude that it wasn't going to. If the guy had been following her, she'd lost him. Which brought up two possibilities: either her car *didn't* have a tracker on it, or he was some random pervert who didn't belong with *Them*. He might have seen where she'd turned off the main road, but there were too many possible routes after that, including more than one that would have taken her back to the main road. In her mind she replayed the drive, the twists and turns, the close calls, the speed.

The freakin' *rush*.

Where in hell had she learned how to do that?

Well, maybe she was getting a little too proud of herself. She hadn't exactly driven a Le Mans race. There was also the more-than-fifty-fifty chance that the guy hadn't been following her at all, and she'd risked life and limb escaping from nothing.

She waited another five minutes, then finally sat up in the seat. Then she waited some more, wanting to see what was going on around her. Her position here was a good one, she decided. No one passing by on the street would see her vehicle. They'd have to be in the parking lot and right up on her to have a clue. And if that happened she was pretty much screwed, unless she put the car into a low gear and rammed them. She'd have to keep that in mind.

But no one drove past. The only activity she saw was apartment residents coming and going from the Dumpster twenty yards away. She made herself sit there a while longer. How long did she need to wait before she could safely leave? She couldn't stay here, but she didn't see how she could leave before dark. Hours from now. Finally she grabbed her purse and pulled the strap over her shoulder, then left the car, easing around the van on the driver's side to sneak a peek toward the road. There was no traffic, nothing but a few kids playing ball. There wasn't much beyond this complex, so the road didn't serve as a throughway to anywhere. Anyone who drove back this way was either coming here or lost.

No one would expect her to hide here.

She popped the trunk, shaking off that weird thought, and ruefully lifted the grocery bag with the softening frozen yogurt in it out. No way would it survive much longer; and she wasn't leaving this parking lot anytime soon. The chicken would have to go, too. The temperature in the trunk was plain damn hot, and she didn't want the yogurt melting and the chicken spoiling there. She might as well get rid of them both while she could.

She walked toward the Dumpster, purse strap cross body, one bag of groceries—a.k.a. garbage—in hand. What a waste! Now she'd have to wait until next week to find out if she liked blueberry pomegranate frozen yogurt, because she was damned if she was going back to the grocery store until then. She almost laughed; she was losing her mind—or not—and she was worried about the yogurt.

She was aware of the girl's presence long before the kid opened her mouth.

"If you don't live here you can't use our Dumpster, and you don't live here. I know everybody here, so don't lie to me."

Stifling an inner sigh, Lizette turned to face the girl. Twelve years old or so, she guessed. Skinny, stringy blond hair under a faded blue baseball cap, blue eyes, good bones. She'd be very pretty, one day, if no one messed with her face. She kept a cautious distance between them.

"I didn't know." She lifted the bag slightly. "Do

you like blueberry pomegranate frozen yogurt? Slightly melted, of course."

The girl narrowed her eyes. She was so young, but her gaze was already suspicious. "I don't know. Never tried it."

"Neither have I, but it looked good. Wanna trade? Frozen yogurt and chicken for that hat."

A hat would hide her hair, disguise her profile when she finally did leave here. Such caution was probably an exercise in uselessness, but she couldn't stop herself from making the effort.

"I'm not an idiot," the girl snapped. She scowled. "Is it poisoned? Drugged?"

"Of course not," Lizette said indignantly. "I'm just not going home as soon as I thought I would, and I'd hate for it to go to waste."

"You were headed for the Dumpster with it. Why should I give up my hat for your garbage?"

Good point. At least she was no longer being accused of trying to poison random children. "Fine. Twenty bucks for the hat."

The girl's eyes widened. "Deal," she said promptly.

Lizette set the bag down, reached into her purse for a twenty, and approached the girl. "I'm Lizzy. What's your name?"

"I'm not supposed to tell strangers my name."

"I'm not a stranger, I'm the woman who's about to seriously overpay for a used hat."

That got a smile out of the girl. "I'm Madison."

"Anyone ever call you Maddy?"

Madison shook her head briefly and scowled, letting Lizette know she didn't care for the nickname.

"No." Then she removed the cap and they made the exchange.

Picking up the bag, Lizette turned and heaved it into the Dumpster.

"Hey!" Madison said, shocked. "You threw the ice cream away!"

"You didn't trade for the ice cream. You want it, you'll have to do something else for me."

"I'm not Dumpster-diving for ice cream."

"Fine. You want to earn another twenty?"

"Doing what? You're not a perv, are you? I ain't taking off my clothes."

"Thank God. I just need some help with my car."

"I don't know how to fix a car."

"It doesn't need to be fixed. It needs to be disguised."

A couple of hours later, after full dark had fallen, Lizette tucked her hair under the ball cap and got behind her steering wheel. There was no doubt she'd gone way beyond caution and rode hard on the edge of downright nuts, but in a way she'd had fun. Once Madison had gotten into the swing of things, she'd even laughed. The hubcaps had been removed, and a good dose of mud covered not only the license plate but the bumper and tires, as well. Her neat-as-a-pin Camry now looked anything but. Her car now sported a bumper sticker proclaiming her daughter an honor roll student at the local middle school, and an honest-to-goodness hula girl swayed on her dash. Madison had even gotten some duct tape and put a patch of it on the left passenger window, as if covering a hole. If by chance the man who had followed her out of the market parking lot that afternoon, or anyone else who knew her car by sight, was still out there, watching and waiting, he'd never recognize her or her car.

It was kind of sad that no one came to check on Madison in all that time—she said her mom wouldn't be off work until after nine—and that she could deface a car that might not be her own with no adult coming to inquire about her activities.

"Hey!" Madison called as Lizette started the engine. Lizette rolled down her window, and the girl leaned in. "I know it's none of my business, and you don't have to tell me if you don't want to, but . . . who are you running from?"

Lizette eyed her from beneath the rim of her ball cap and gave a wry smile. "Honey, I have no idea."

Chapter Ten

"Al."

Al Forge turned as his name was said in a clipped, calm tone that told him the identity of the speaker even before he saw her. It was a fucking fact of life: everyone had someone to answer to, even if, at the end, it was Death, or God, or whatever they thought they were facing. As high up on the food chain as he was, he still had a superior, and her name was Felice McGowan.

"Yes?" he said, making it a polite query as if she were a visitor who was interrupting him—which technically she was, because this was his territory— mainly because he knew that even though she wouldn't show a flicker of reaction, it would annoy her. Annoying Felice was a game he enjoyed playing. Some days an interruption was welcome, but today he had a feeling he knew why she was here, and he wasn't looking forward to the looming conversation.

"Tank," she said calmly, turning on her heel and striding away. Al didn't let himself show any outward signs of concern, but he definitely felt them as he followed her to the tank, an interior soundproof room that was as secure from eavesdropping as they could make it, which was pretty damn secure. No cell phones were allowed in the room, no cameras, no recorders, no weapons, and everyone who entered was scanned to make certain they didn't have any of those devices. What was said in the tank stayed and died in the tank.

On TV he'd seen clear Plexiglas versions of the tank, with all the inhabitants in clear view, but this tank was a regular room that had been shielded and reinforced, with jammers that prevented both reception and transmission. It wasn't as cutting edge as the TV versions, but it worked.

Before he entered, he removed his cell phone from his belt and placed it in a vault. Then he pushed open the heavy reinforced door and went inside.

The tank was an ordinary room on the inside, with a conference table lined with high-backed office chairs, a coffeemaker and all the accoutrements sitting on a credenza at one end, and harsh fluorescent lighting that they'd recently replaced with pink-tinted bulbs because they'd noticed they all got headaches and wanted to kill each other when they were in here. Their jobs were stressful enough without throwing bad lighting into the mix.

"What's up?" he asked casually after he'd closed the door behind him, as if he didn't already know, but this was part of the game.

"Subject C." She propped one hip on the table, a dominant position that he was positive she took on purpose. Because she was nothing if not thorough, Felice would have studied body language, microexpressions, and every other area that could possibly give her an edge in a field that was dominated by men.

He took a few seconds to admire the picture. Felice was an attractive, classy woman: forty-eight years old, divorced, mother of one adult daughter. She had clear gray eyes and her streaked blond hair was cut in a short, almost masculine style that was stylishly feminine on her. Her tailored trouser suit was a muted dark gray, but the blouse under the fitted jacket was a rich blue that deepened the color of her eyes. She trod the narrow line of being both professional and feminine without a single misstep.

She was also the one person he'd worried about most in this situation. Not because she was a screwup, but because she wasn't. She was cold and logical and would take whatever steps she deemed necessary to contain the damage. In this situation, though, logic could actually work against them. Al worked hard to stay on top of things so he could head off any destructive decisions she might make, but he'd always been aware that the status could turn on a dime and he wouldn't be able to stop her.

Xavier had always known it, too.

"Subject C," she said again.

"Everything seems unchanged with Subject C."

"Except for the security breach concerning the time lapse."

He hadn't tried to hide the slip by the Winchell woman from Felice, because straight up was the only way to play this. "It wasn't a security breach. We know about the time lapse, but Subject C doesn't. She didn't react in any way. She was sick, and as far as we can tell from her subsequent actions, she didn't attach any importance to the statement."

"You can't know that. Remember that she was very, very good."

"That was before. Her memory was wiped. Now

she's just an ordinary person who lives in a very small world."

"The process has never been tried to this extent before. I don't put as much trust in it as you appear to."

"I haven't decided to *not* trust it on no evidence to the contrary," he said with some bite to his tone. Felice might outrank him, but Al didn't operate from a position of fear; it simply wasn't part of his makeup.

In a world with a population of over seven billion people, there were six people alive who knew what had really happened four years before. Originally there had been eight, but one had died of natural causes and the other Xavier had taken care of—not that Felice knew that particular detail, but Al did. Six was such a small percentage he couldn't begin to mentally calculate how many decimal points that was. But Felice was one of the six—and so was Subject C. Technically, Subject C *didn't* know, but the possibility that she might one day recover her memory was what kept them watching her. She was the weak link, the one who'd been brought in from the outside and wasn't part of the team. Felice had never really trusted her, but they hadn't had any other option.

"I'm ordering physical surveillance," Felice said, not asking his opinion, simply telling him what she'd decided.

Shit! That could be an unmitigated disaster. He gave her an exasperated look. "You're overreacting, and you may well push Xavier into overreacting, which is the one thing guaranteed to make this blow up in our faces."

Being Felice, she didn't respond to his charges, simply made a counter-charge of her own. She was accustomed to dealing with congressmen and -women, with committees and bureaucrats and generals. He doubted she'd have blinked at being charged by an angry rhino, so she certainly wasn't going to back down from him. "You've always been far too cautious concerning Xavier. He's as mortal as the rest of us."

Al cocked his head. "I could have had him killed at any time," he retorted. "Hell, he could have killed *us* at any time. He knows that, I know that, and you know that. Do you think he hasn't made preparations? He has the goods on all of us, and he's set more trip lines than we could ever find."

"He *says*. Why would he incriminate himself?"

"Because he figures he'll be dead, so it won't matter about him. It's too big, Felice; you can't contain the damage if this blows open, and it will if you don't stay calm."

That got a flash of ire from her, because Felice was nothing if not calm. If emotion had ever figured into any of her decisions, Al hadn't seen it. She actually drummed her fingernails on the table, once, before smoothing out her expression. "I'm not sending a wet team out after her. I just want to make certain she isn't doing anything unusual, something we can't pick up from audio."

"Then I should tell Xavier."

"No. Absolutely not. He'll think it's just a means of getting to her before he can react."

That was entirely possible, knowing how Xavier thought, how he allowed for every contingency. On the other hand— "Do you think he won't *know* you've put a team on her? Not alerting him is the riskiest thing you can do."

"So send him out on a job."

She really hadn't dealt with Xavier enough to know he wasn't "sent" anywhere. He was offered jobs. He took them if he wanted to. Al had worked with him, trained him, and he trusted him in the field more than he'd ever trusted another human being. The one thing he'd never do was underestimate the man.

"He won't go. Not now. He has his own ears on Subject C; he knew about the breach at the same time we did."

"What? *What?*" She almost shouted the last word, which for Felice meant she was about to explode with fury. "You knew that, and you didn't prevent it?"

"He isn't going to trust us if we don't trust him. He knows we know." To ease the tension from the atmosphere, Al went to the coffeemaker and selected a pod, popped it into the machine, and slid a polystyrene cup into place. The machine hissed and popped, and a few seconds later began dribbling hot coffee into the cup. "What's more, he knows where our operational base is, who our analysts are, what shifts they work, and where they live. He knows your routine, he knows your house, he knows your daughter's house. If you don't believe anything else I've said, Felice, believe that. Of all the operators in the world, he's the one I wouldn't want to piss off."

She was silent for a moment, her nostrils flaring as she processed that she was as much of a target as any of them. He'd learned a long time ago that people who felt safe were a lot more willing to risk the lives of others than were people who were in the trenches themselves. It was a completely different viewpoint.

Still, this reaction was because she wanted to contain the threat to herself. He imagined she'd have *him* knocked off without losing a minute's sleep if she thought he would ever be a security risk, but he was part of her team, and she trusted him. He trusted her too, as far as that went, not to turn on him. But Subject C was a different matter, and now she was seeing Xavier, too, as not being part of her team. That was her mindset, and one of Felice's strongest points—and also one of her weak points—was that she didn't doubt her own decisions. She considered options, and she made the call.

He sipped on his coffee, and she mentally poked and prodded at the situation. Finally she straightened from the table. "You'll have to handle Xavier," she said, her eyes cold. "I want reassurance that everything with Subject C is status quo, so the active surveillance will be in place asap. I'll handle it. You may alert him if you think he absolutely has to know, but I advise against it. Be very careful what you do."

Annoyed, Al registered that by handling it herself, Felice meant she didn't want him using his people; she wanted to use people he didn't know. Fine. Reducing his measure of control was a slap at him, but it was also something that could backfire, and with that last comment she had put the responsibility on him no matter what happened. If he told Xavier and things still went south, it was on him—but not telling Xavier was a risk no sane person would take.

"Oh, I'll tell him," he said mildly, reining in his temper. "After all, you wouldn't want your men to get their throats sliced while they were sitting in their cars."

Her lips pressed together. "If that happens, then all bets are off, and I'll move on him. I'll think of a way to handle the fallout. Just make sure he understands that."

She left the tank, her heels clicking smartly against the tile floor. Al took another fortifying gulp of coffee. No way was he telling Xavier what she'd just said, because that would guarantee she didn't wake up tomorrow. How could she not realize that?

Because she felt safe.

But she wasn't. None of them were.

Chapter Eleven

Lizette's Sunday was completely uneventful, mainly because she didn't leave the house. Instead she cleaned, and in cleaning looked as intensely as she dared for hidden microphones and cameras. She rolled back rugs, dusted lamps, even rearranged the furniture a bit. All the wiring that hooked up her TV to boxes and recorders and such had seemed like prime possibilities, but her TV was wall mounted, which meant she couldn't unhook everything under the guise of moving it to another location. Besides, as far as she could tell, everything had looked normal.

On TV, bugs were always planted in the phones, or the lamps; cameras were mounted behind stacks of books, peeping through tiny openings, though of course they were always spotted because of blinking red lights. What kind of idiot would use a covert surveillance camera that had a blinking red light, for crap's sake?

With that thought she braced for a headache, but—nope, not even a twinge. Hallelujah! Not that she had any clue why her *thoughts* would cause such savage headaches, but she was all for anything that stopped them. She couldn't say definitely, but it seemed as if the first time she had these weird thoughts was when the headaches were most hellish. By now, she'd thought about bugs and cameras so often that the subject felt commonplace.

Finally she concluded that if the house was bugged, it was in the wiring, which she couldn't check. She slid the battery cover off her cordless phone and examined the compartment, but couldn't see anything suspicious.

There were three conclusions she could draw from her findings. One, the bugging was a professional job. Two, she didn't know enough about the subject to do a thorough search. Or, three, she was completely nuts. She threw that last one in just to allow for the possibility, but everything in her rejected it. She knew she was missing two years of memories. She knew she'd had surgery on her face, which she also didn't remember. Every time she started to doubt herself, those two irrefutable items pulled her back into full doubt-everything, trust-nothing mode.

Not being able to figure out what was going on was the most frustrating situation she'd ever dealt with in her life. It wasn't just that there was no obvious reason for the no-memory, altered-face deal, but she couldn't think of any off-the-wall, subtle reasons, either. No medical condition that she knew of fit the parameters. Nothing in her life as she knew it fit the parameters.

As she knew it. Those were the key words.

All that was left to her was some sort of conspiracy theory, which, as far-fetched as it seemed when compared to her very ordinary and unexciting life, did fit the details better than anything else she could imagine. How else could she explain the suspicion about her cell phone being bugged—something that had never before occurred to her—or her car having a tracker on it, or suddenly discovered driving skills that were completely out of place with her normal driving habits? And what did she know about burner phones?

It was as if a different person was inside her, fighting to the surface. No—that sounded kind of split-personality, and that wasn't how she felt at all. She felt as if she, the real person, was trying to escape the drab prison *They* had put her in. The life she lived now, the withdrawn, no-fun, dull, and completely predictable day-in-and-day-out, didn't jibe with the person she'd been before. She'd always been up for an adventure, for pushing herself. At her job in Chicago, she'd—

Damn, damn, damn! She dropped to the floor, clutching her head and trying to stifle her moans as she curled into a tight ball and fought to focus on something, anything, that would break the grip this unbearable pain had on her. If anyone was listening, she didn't want them to know anything was wrong, because suddenly this seemed like a weakness that they might be able to exploit. She was helpless enough if one of these attacks caught her, without someone figuring out how they were triggered. What if they could just ask her a question about her past, and trying to think of the answer would do this to her?

Working out that possibility shifted her focus enough to let the pain ebb to a bearable level. Evidently anything that she could concentrate on would do the job, which gave her a strategy for handling the headaches. They weren't coming as often, and most of the time now she could catch herself before the pain really got her. It was only when an entirely different subject would pop into her head that she'd get ambushed now.

But these thoughts were clues to her past. If the headaches were the price she had to pay to find out exactly what had happened to her, she'd deal. Instead of trying to avoid the triggers, maybe she should be exploring them. She knew she'd lived in Chicago; she remembered that. So the problem was with the job she'd done; that part of her life was vague and misty, shrouded in mental fog. For now, it was enough to identify the problem. Trying to clear away the fog would be like probing a sore tooth. Maybe the fog would gradually clear away on its own, maybe not. She didn't know if she had the luxury of waiting to find out, so she had to assume that she didn't. Now that she knew the area to check, she could revisit the subject occasionally, see if things became any clearer.

Chicago had to be the key. That was when she'd lost touch, because she didn't remember getting from Chicago to D.C. Something had happened in Chicago. At least now she had a starting point.

By bedtime, she was tired from all the cleaning and frustrated because she hadn't found anything, but definitely ready for bed. She showered because she was dirty from cleaning—wasn't that just wrong on some level?—and crawled into bed ten minutes earlier than her usual time.

Maybe she'd dream about the hot guy in the pharmacy again. Every time she thought about Friday night's dream her heartbeat would speed up a little. It had been so great, the dream so intense and realistic that she'd actually *felt* him enter her; if she closed her eyes, she could still clearly recall the heat and sensation, and, wow, her climax had been explosive. Yeah, waking up that way in the middle of the night was well worth the lost sleep.

But Mr. X didn't visit her dreams, and she woke Monday morning feeling a little disgruntled about it. She went through her normal routine, not because she found comfort in the familiar but because for now she sensed being normal was critical to her well-being.

She left on schedule and took her normal route to work. Every so often she'd check her rearview mirror, but the rush-hour traffic was so chaotic, with vehicles dodging back and forth in the lanes, jockeying for position, that she could barely keep track of who was directly behind her at any given time. There were a lot of similar cars and SUVs, too; a vehicle would seem familiar and she'd try to watch it, only to notice a moment or two later that, wait, there was another one that was identical in color, but the headlights were a little different. And she couldn't constantly watch the mirror and drive at the same time, unless she wanted to rear-end someone. In the end, she gave up and simply concentrated on getting to work.

At the office, she felt a little more secure. She smiled at the guard as she paused to sign in. Her ID card was clipped to a lanyard that she wore around her neck; the guard knew her, of course, but the procedure was strictly enforced. Entry into the building was controlled, and everyone had to check in at the security desk.

She got into the elevator with several other people and punched in the code that would make the eleva-

tor stop on the floor where Becker Investments was
housed. The car began rising, the motor and cables
whining. The elevator-code thing was more for im-
pressing clients than anything else. After all, the
stairwells were still free access, and had to be because
of fire codes. Still, she had walls and people around
her, and whatever was going on didn't seem to war-
rant an entire assault team roping down from the top
of the building.

Headache.

Willing herself not to make a sound, not to collapse
on the floor, she stared hard at the abstract patterned
blouse the woman in front of her was wearing. The
pattern was wild but the colors were kind of muted,
in grays and creams and blues, which made a nice
mix.

Okay, good. Concentrating on the pattern worked
as well as anything else, and she hadn't had to resort
to humming.

She got off on her floor. The receptionist was just
arriving too, emerging from another elevator car, and
together they walked down the carpeted hallway.
"Good morning, how are you?" the receptionist said.
Her name was Rae; she was pretty and maybe twenty-
three, twenty-four. Lizette got a glimpse of the book
she was carrying: a textbook on marketing. Evidently, Rae was going to school at night, with an eye
on a different field of work. Lizette had done her
share of receptionist work when she'd been straight
out of college, as well as waitressing. Strange, but
she'd take waitressing over being a receptionist any
day. It was much harder work, but at least she'd been

moving, and every day had been different even though most of the customers had been regulars.

If she'd still been in school, it might have been a different story; she might have needed a quieter job, so she could get in some studying.

Then she thought back to the energetic kid she'd been. No, she would still have picked waitressing. She'd even liked the challenge of keeping certain customers under control.

Those memories, she noticed, didn't trigger any kind of reaction. They were normal memories. But now she knew she could add assault teams, and roping down the outside of buildings, to her list of avenues to explore, along with Chicago. Evidently she'd really been into some derring-do kind of stuff.

Deep down, she felt a sense of rightness. Whatever she'd done, wherever she'd been, she hadn't been content to sit in an office building every day.

Almost as soon as she stored her purse in the bottom drawer of her desk, Diana stuck her head around the cubicle wall. "Hi! Still feeling okay? I meant to call you this weekend, but things went nuts with the kids. I'd think about calling you, then Armageddon would break out and it would slip my mind, and I'd remember again after we'd already gone to bed."

Diana's kids were four and five years of age, a boy and a girl, and both of them seemingly hell-bent on breaking their necks before first grade. Having been around them before, Lizette completely understood.

"I'm still getting headaches, but it's more off than on." She said that to give herself some cover in case she had one of the attacks. "No more nausea. That was over with by Friday afternoon."

"Good. You sounded awful when I talked to you. Feel well enough to grab some lunch today?"

"Sure. See you then."

Diana waved and headed for her own cubicle. They had lunch together at least a couple of days a week, whenever Diana didn't have errands to run. Her kids seemed to generate a lot of errands, everything from doctor's visits to picking up stuff for birthday parties for their day-care buddies and replacing broken items. Diana's life was a study in damage control—real, physical damage, not the bad-news kind.

Then it hit her. Diana's kids were four and five, which meant that if Lizette had truly worked at Becker Investments for five years, she'd at least remember *one* of her friend's pregnancies . . . but she didn't. She couldn't remember when Diana didn't have the two kids.

She'd hardly needed more proof that something was very wrong, but somehow the personal nature of this was way more convincing than her car registration, driver's license, and tax returns. She remembered Diana's birthday, the kids' birthdays, things like that, so if she'd been here she definitely would have remembered them being *born*.

Ergo, she hadn't been here. She'd worked here, and lived in her house, for roughly three years. The couple of years before that—anyone's guess.

She'd been a different person, and she needed to find out who that person was, and what she'd done. Everything hinged on that.

Chapter Twelve

She thought about it all day, knowing inside that she was living a life that wasn't hers, that the person she'd been had somehow been stolen. She had been concentrating on appearing as if nothing had changed, but maybe the key to unlocking her past was in breaking free of routine, in acting more as she imagined she'd have acted in that forgotten life.

She didn't have to do the same thing day after day after mind-numbing day. *If* she was being survcilled—and where in hell had that word come from?—as long as she didn't do anything really out of character, such as suddenly signing up for martial arts classes, she shouldn't set off any alarms. Not that she wouldn't like to get in some martial arts training, but she wanted to take this gradually.

With that in mind, when she left work that afternoon, Lizette took a different route away from the office building, heading away from home, losing herself in new twists and turns, losing herself in ordinary, maddening rush-hour traffic. She wasn't going anywhere in particular, so she wasn't in a hurry.

The workday had been uneventful—normal—and should have lulled the sense of urgency that kept her internally on edge, but it hadn't. Normal didn't feel normal, it felt fake, as if she should be more on guard now than she had been before. Every so often during the day she'd felt as if the hairs on the nape of her neck were standing up, warning her, indicating a high level of alarm. The fact that she couldn't detect anything in her immediate surroundings that could possibly be alarming wasn't reassuring. Was her office bugged? Was someone in the office keeping an eye on her? Was every keystroke on her computer being logged?

She *needed* a long, leisurely drive to settle her down. If anyone followed her, that would give her a chance to spot them. If no one followed her, then she'd have scouted out the territory past her usual boundaries, and she'd feel more settled when she did go home. There was nothing like a good, long drive to clear the mind; she could remember taking drives in the past when something was bothering her, not going anywhere in particular, and how her subconscious would take over and the solution to her problem would surface.

She drove a little faster than normal, too, whenever she'd catch a break in the traffic and could. Zipping in and out, moving smoothly and quickly among and around the other cars, gave her a mild shot of adrenaline that almost felt like relief, as if she'd loosened a too-tight belt. She usually stuck to the speed limit and the right lane, puttering along like an old lady. Not today, though.

She'd headed west, into Virginia. The miles unspooled beneath her wheels. For a moment, just a moment, she felt as if she could truly breathe. No one would be looking for her here; no one would care. If she'd been followed, she hadn't spotted the tail.

There was no reason to just drive forever, so she took an exit off I-66, then looped around and headed back toward D.C. She hadn't gone all that far when she noticed a sign for a large chain store. Her heart gave a little thump. Sporting goods.

She took the designated exit and followed her nose, working her way toward the large, red and green sign she could see off to the right. A few minutes later she saw the store, straight ahead, in a large, bustling strip mall.

Cool.

She couldn't drive aimlessly all the time—well, she could, but there were better ways to let her mind drift, ways that wouldn't cost her a fortune in gas. She used to be in better shape; in college she'd run quite a bit, swam, did some yoga. She didn't do any of that now. Oh, she walked around the neighborhood now and then, ate a healthy if unexciting diet, even occasionally dragged out an exercise DVD when it was too hot or too cold to walk, but it had been a while since she'd gotten anything resembling a workout, if one could call walking around the block a time or two a workout.

One couldn't. She seriously needed to work on getting in shape.

There were a lot of things she could do. She could buy some free weights and start lifting, work on her muscle mass. She could jog instead of walk. She thought longingly of a martial arts class, but she'd already discarded that as being too alarming to whoever They were.

Okay, jogging would be a decent start. She'd need a new pair of running shoes, though. The shoes she had weren't worn out, but she needed better support for running than she did for walking.

She couldn't find a decent place to park in front of the sporting goods store, meaning she couldn't find two end-to-end open parking spaces, and it was busy enough that she didn't want to make people wait while she backed the car into a spot. Instead she went a few aisles down, in front of a children's clothing store and a bakery, and found what she wanted. She even parked down at the end, closer to the exit. She had to walk a little farther, but given that she'd decided she needed to get in shape, that wasn't a bad thing.

The strip mall was fairly crowded. People were in and out of the stores, up and down the sidewalks, winding their way through the lines of cars in the parking lot. There were kids and parents, older men, a harried woman in purple scrubs and sensible white shoes, teenagers in packs of varying numbers. One kid was texting as he crossed the street, tempting fate. Thank goodness there was a nurse nearby, in case he took a header or, God forbid, got clipped by a car. Looking around, Lizette didn't see a single person who looked as if he or she didn't belong here. She didn't see anyone just sitting in a car, watching her. If she'd been followed whoever was on her tail was good, because she hadn't spotted a thing.

Briskly she strode toward the store. The doors in front of her whooshed open. Almost instantly, the smell of the store engulfed her, and she took a deep, appreciative breath, pulling in the scents of leather and oil and metal blended. You wouldn't think a sporting goods store would have a specific smell, its own perfume, but this one did. Probably they all did; she'd just . . . forgotten.

A sense of excitement bubbled up. This was her kind of place. Just in case she found more than new running shoes, she snagged one of the big shopping carts and headed down the main aisle.

The store felt strange and new and familiar, all at once. Her head swiveled back and forth as she looked up and down all the side aisles, taking in this and that, wondering what she needed, what might be of interest. At the same time, she checked out the other shoppers. No one paid her any undue attention; no one looked out of place.

But they wouldn't, would they? No, they'd blend right in, and she wouldn't see them coming until it was too late.

Her attention was drawn toward the rear right corner of the store, and she swiftly decided that shoes could wait. She wheeled her cart toward the hunting section as if it were pulling her in like a magnet. The area was marked well, with a big green, black, and brown camo sign hanging high: HUNTING AND FISHING GEAR. Just what she wanted—not that she had any desire to take up fishing.

She felt kind of like a kid in a candy store, almost giddy, and definitely thrilled. This didn't feel like foreign territory.

What captured her attention first was an impressive display of weapons against the rear wall: rifles, mostly; some shotguns, air rifles. An employee stood at the counter, closely watching the aisles, on the lookout for shoplifters. Swiftly, automatically, she assessed him. Brown hair, small eyes. Maybe thirty, skinny, not much in the way of upper body strength. He looked at her, nodded, and immediately dismissed her as not being a likely customer.

Fat lot he knew. She didn't bother nodding back. He'd already looked away.

She scanned the weapons display and remembered wishing for a gun when she'd thought she might be cornered in the parking lot of a slightly seedy apartment complex.

But you want a handgun that can't be traced, and you sure as hell don't want anyone doing a background check and alerting Them.

A big display of hunting knives caught her eye. There were other, more expensive knives in a locked display case, but these were encased in hard plastic and hanging on an end cap. Obviously they weren't top of the line, but she didn't want to blow a couple of hundred dollars on a knife, either. She pulled one from the peg and examined it. It had a six-inch stainless-steel fixed blade with a very slight curve. It wasn't fancy, but it was a decent length, and the grip was small enough to fit her hand better than one of the behemoth hunting knives would. She dropped the clamshell package in her cart, along with a leather sheath that hung nearby. On the next aisle over, she almost crowed with joy. Bear spray! It was really pepper spray, extra strength, which wasn't as good as a handgun but way better than nothing. And if she was going to jog alone, pepper spray would be a good thing to have on hand. What had she been thinking, walking in her neighborhood without it all these years?

She put two canisters into her cart, paused, then got another one. Three wasn't too many. Over by the camping gear she found some wasp and hornet spray and almost automatically dropped two big cans into her cart. One would go by her bed, the other in the bathroom. It was just as good as pepper spray and could shoot a stream a good twenty feet. *Huzzah!*

In the camping section there was a huge selection of backpacks. She took her time selecting one that spoke to her, as in wasn't too big but had plenty of zippers and pockets. Nylon rope. Some carabiners. She paused, looking at the last two items, remembering just this morning when she'd thought about an assault team roping down the outside of a building. The image didn't bring on a headache attack now, but it did give her a tight feeling in her stomach, one almost of . . . anticipation. Good God, had she actually *done* something like that?

Probably not. Some weekend rock climbing was far more likely. Still, the idea was tantalizing.

She got some protein bars, a rain poncho, other items that appealed to her on some level. Her shopping was almost automatic; she barely gave any thought to the things she grabbed and threw into her cart. If she stopped to think she'd make herself sick, and she'd had enough of that. She *needed* these things; she needed them all.

Finally she made it to the middle of the store and the impressive display of running shoes.

Half an hour later, with shoes, thick socks, and a sleek new black jogging outfit—because who started a new exercise regime without all new gear?—she headed for the checkout counter. The days were still long; it wouldn't be dark for a while. Even though she'd be late getting home, she could eat one of the protein bars on the way, dump her shopping bags, change clothes, and hit the pavement before dark. She wouldn't run for long, not on her first day, but she was oddly interested in pushing herself, to see what she could do.

When she reached the counter, she stopped and considered the contents of her cart. Pulling out the knife and pepper spray, the protein bars, the rain poncho, and anything else that could even remotely be considered as preparation for the coming zombie invasion, she pushed them toward the cashier. "I'm paying cash for these," she said. "The rest I'll put on a credit card."

Maybe her caution was useless. Maybe someone was watching her check out, noting everything she'd bought. She had no way of knowing, and it made sense to her to make the extra effort anyway.

She did fleetingly wonder if the cashier thought her request was odd—especially paired with her purchases—but a closer look at the young woman made her realize the cashier wouldn't have blinked if she'd bought a bow and arrow, a red bikini, and a miner's headlamp. She probably saw all sorts of strange combinations every day.

But after she paid for her haul, Lizette blew out a weary sigh. She'd have to make one more stop on her way home: an ATM. She'd just blown almost every cent of cash she'd had with her. She really needed to start carrying more cash anyway, as a precaution. A machine would allow her to withdraw only two hundred dollars at a time, but she'd make a withdrawal tonight and tomorrow she'd go by the bank at lunch for a larger transaction.

They won't like that, either.

Tough shit.

Dealing with invisible people was tiring. Still, even though she didn't know what was going on, she didn't think her problem was mental. If she ever sat down to make a foil hat, then she might concede that she was the problem. Until then she'd carry on.

On the way home, she didn't zigzag in and out of traffic, and she didn't speed . . . much. She'd already had her quota of excitement for the day, and though she'd liked it, she had to ease into this new/old persona. On familiar ground again, she went to her bank and through the drive-through ATM. She felt more secure with that cash in her handbag. She'd feel even better tomorrow after another trip to the bank.

She parked in the driveway, grabbed her bags from the backseat, and nodded to Maggie, who peeked through the side window of her house. Maggie waved her fingers, then let the curtain flutter closed. Keys in hand, Lizette headed for the front door. And again, the hairs on the back of her neck danced.

Don't turn around. Don't let them know you know.

She didn't know whether to laugh or cry. But she didn't turn around.

The man sat back in the driver's seat, a cup of cold coffee in the drink holder to his right, his cell in his left hand. This was a quiet neighborhood, too quiet. It was nearly dark, and only a few kids remained on the street. He couldn't stay here much longer; one of the subject's neighbors had already asked him if he needed help.

This was, bar none, the most boring assignment ever. Who the hell had he pissed off?

"Yes, I lost her for a while," he explained again. "But I found her." He glanced at the laptop on the passenger seat, looked at the beeping red light that indicated the subject's vehicle. "She went shopping. At a strip mall in Virginia."

No, he explained again, he didn't know exactly where she'd gone shopping or why she'd chosen Virginia. Maybe there had been a big sale. She was a woman, after all. He'd driven through the parking lot and found her car in front of a bakery. Where she'd gone from there he had no idea, but there had been a bookstore, a shoe store, and a women's clothing store off to the right.

After about an hour she'd returned to her car carrying several shopping bags. From where he'd parked, he hadn't been able to identify her bags, but she'd been alone and she'd been shopping, so there wasn't any big deal about it. Afterward she went to her bank's ATM. After shopping, that made sense.

The last guy who had lost the subject had already been sent on some shit job in the Middle East. In their line of work, they either produced the goods or someone else was brought in to do the job. The boss didn't reward employees who screwed up by sending them to Paris.

Her history told him the subject was in for the

night. He didn't know what went on inside the house, didn't need to know. In an hour he'd be relieved. If he was lucky, he might make it home in time to see the last couple of innings of the Nationals' game.

Then the subject's front door opened, and his boredom fled. *What the hell?*

She stepped into her driveway and executed a couple of quick stretches. Gone was the staid office worker he'd been watching; he wouldn't have recognized her if he hadn't seen her walk out of that house.

Her hair was pulled back into a thick ponytail. Her face looked sharper this way, more . . . dangerous. She was dressed all in black, with the exception of her shoes, which were a dark gray. No baggy shorts and muscle shirts for this runner, not even in the notorious D.C. heat and humidity. Her shirt was short-sleeved and loose—loose enough to hide a weapon beneath, if necessary—and the pants were long and fitted.

This duty was new, but he *had* been briefed. Once the subject was in, she should have been in for the night. He'd seen pictures of her, walking in the neighborhood, iPod on, earbuds in, zoned out, and dressed in shorts and a tank top that didn't leave room for her to hide so much as a piece of gum. So, leaving the house was unusual but not unheard of. Still . . . this was an entirely different look for her.

She jogged toward the street, and he got ready to throw his jacket over the computer and start the engine if she headed his way. Instead she turned and ran in the opposite direction, and he relaxed again as he kept an eye on her: back straight, form good, she ran slowly past her neighbor's house and then increased her speed. She didn't keep her eyes straight ahead, but instead studied her surroundings, keeping good situational awareness. No iPod. People were stupid to run alone with their ears plugged so they couldn't hear anyone coming up behind them. A lot of people got mugged that way.

The subject hadn't looked straight at him as she'd hit the street, but he was sure she knew he was here.

Quickly he dialed a number on his cell phone. When the call was answered, he said, "I think something's going on."

There was a short silence, then an exasperated, "Like *what*, for fuck's sake?"

"I may be wrong, but it looks as if she's going into some physical training. Not a casual jog; the look's all wrong, like she's about to get into some serious running. No iPod, noticing everything around her. I'm pretty sure she spotted me."

There was another curse, then: "Clear out. You don't need to be there when she comes back home. I'll get someone else on her."

Chapter Thirteen

Three a.m. was prime time for any self-respecting burglar. Houses were dark; all the residents were—or should be—sleeping.

Felice definitely had active surveillance on Lizzy. Even if he hadn't already been alerted, Xavier would have spotted the car right off. The car itself was as bland as a car could get, but he knew what vehicles belonged in the neighborhood, and this one didn't. The guy inside was taking care to keep a low profile; he wasn't smoking, but he *was* drinking coffee to stay awake, and Xavier didn't need night-vision goggles to spot the movement of his hand as he lifted the thermos cup to his mouth.

Before actually arriving at her house, Xavier had made a thorough reconnoiter of the surrounding area. Everything was clear. This was exactly what Forge had said it would be: low-level, just one guy.

Knowing how the game was played, he wasn't surprised they'd put eyes on her. But he hadn't picked up any prior intel on the move, which meant Felice McGowan was behind the surveillance, not Forge. And it meant she had used people outside the usual network.

That wasn't good news for any of them. She had

taken control from Forge on this; Forge might have balked at the idea and this was nothing more than Felice having her way, but Xavier didn't like the use of outside people. That signaled a breakdown of trust.

Trust was all they had holding this thing together. It was an armed, guarded, lots-of-safety-nets-in-place kind of trust, but it worked because they all knew each other and the situation was limited to their small group. Outside people . . . he didn't know their training, didn't know how they'd react in a fluid situation, didn't know how much they knew or what their orders were.

He'd rather deal with a skilled professional any day than an amateur. There was no telling what the fuck an amateur would do. They were as likely to open fire at a sudden noise as they were to totally screw the job by going to sleep. Hell, he didn't even know if this guy was armed, or with what. Though knowing Felice, he'd bet on armed.

He sometimes imagined their group as all of them standing in a circle, aiming at each other's heads. Forge was undoubtedly the most dangerous and capable of the group, outside himself, and then perhaps only because of his younger age and active training. But whenever he pictured this scenario, his weapon wasn't trained on Forge; it was on Felice, because she had the most to lose, and that made her the most likely to break the status quo. She would want to protect what she had, and she might decide the only way to do that was to eliminate the rest of them.

Like that idea hadn't occurred to each and every

one of them. He had his own safeguards in place, and Al Forge wouldn't be Al Forge if he didn't, also.

One day, which might not come around for years but could happen at any time, Felice was going to be a problem. He might or might not survive, but then again, the same odds applied to her.

In the meantime, he had to continue on the course he'd set for himself five years ago—longer, if he went back to when he'd first agreed to live a double life in preparation for the unthinkable, in case it ever came to pass.

Nothing he could do about that. All he could do was handle the present, which meant he had to get into Lizette's house—while it was under surveillance.

He smiled in the darkness. He liked a challenge.

Sometimes the gods smiled, because a light rain began falling. *Perfect.* For someone sitting inside a parked car, that had just cut visibility through the side windows down to nothing more than a blur. It wasn't just the rain, but the inevitable fogging that would occur. In the same situation, Xavier would have lowered the window and let the interior of the car get wet, because surveillance, not staying dry, was the objective, but the human instinct was to shut out the rain.

Xavier reached the rear of her house and took a quick peek around the corner, keeping his body flat against the wall and rolling his head just enough to get a line of sight on the car across the street.

If the gods sometimes smiled, other times they downright laughed. Abruptly a light was turned on inside the house just up from where the guy was parked. A couple of seconds later, the porch light was turned on, the door opened, and the robe-clad homeowner stepped out with a small dog bouncing around his feet. The little dog immediately dashed into the yard to take care of his business.

Human nature being what it was, the guy in the car had probably lain over in the seat so he wouldn't be seen; if he hadn't done that, he had at least slid way down in the seat, and all of his attention would currently be on the pet owner, hoping the guy either didn't notice his car or didn't recognize it as not belonging.

Xavier figured he couldn't have been handed a better opportunity. Silently he slipped around the corner of her house and approached the back door.

He could hear the neighbor saying something to the dog, his tone more querying than angry. Xavier imagined it was something along the lines of *Are you finished yet?* He didn't care what was said, because as long as the neighbor stayed on the porch, the guy in the car wasn't going to be watching anything else.

Xavier spared a quick glance to see that the dog was now happily prancing toward the owner, wagging its tail. He had just a few seconds left before that perfect distraction ended.

The keys, one for the doorknob and one for the deadbolt, were in his hand. He kept them separate, so they wouldn't clink against each other. Swiftly he unlocked both locks, each one clicking smoothly and almost silently; he put one key in his left pocket, one in his right, then gently turned the knob. He eased inside, closed the door, then stood very still and listened.

He was in the kitchen, with light coming in through

the window; there were lights from the oven, the coffeemaker, and the microwave as well, small but effective. He heard the hum of the refrigerator but nothing else, no creaking of the floors or fabric brushing against walls, nothing to indicate that she'd been awakened by his almost completely silent entry. Faintly, from outside, he heard the air-conditioning compressor kick on, and a moment later cool air began blowing from the vents.

That was good. Air conditioning covered a multitude of small sounds.

Beyond the kitchen, the house was dark. That was the way she liked it when she slept—dark, like being in a cave. There were no night-lights for her, no bathroom light left on to illuminate the hallway. The dark worked in his favor.

He made his way through the kitchen, noting that the clocks all displayed the same time, three thirty-two. Lizzy kept her clocks synchronized. He wondered if she realized why, if somewhere in the back of her mind she knew how crucial a minute could be. He himself had an instinctive sense of time, one that he'd learned to adjust according to what time zone he was in, and he could usually nail it to the minute without seeing a clock. For operations he always synchronized with team members, but that was more for their benefit than his. He'd always appreciated Lizzy's punctuality. She'd been dependable down to the second.

He didn't have to fumble around, figure out where he was or where she kept things. He was familiar with the layout of the exterior and the interior because he'd seen pictures. Lots of them. Even though

he'd never been here, this wasn't entirely unfamiliar
territory.

She was asleep just down the hall. He could almost
feel her there, her presence pulling at him, and he had
to make a conscious effort to focus on the task at
hand.

Lizette knew she was dreaming, because she recognized the dream. It was the all-white house again,
except for that one three-dimensional room that held
all the colors, as if the colors from the rest of the
house had been bled away and put in that one room.
But she wasn't in the colored room, she was in the
biggest white one, everything muted and quiet.

He was here, her Mr. X. She couldn't see him,
couldn't hear him, but she knew he was close by. She
could sense him as strongly as if he were in the same
room, watching her. She spun around, checking every
corner, every white wall, every window, but the room
was empty except for herself.

Wait a minute, she thought. What was going on?
Was this a dream, or reality? It felt real. She'd been
here before. But—oh, yeah, that had been a dream
too. Her heart began beating faster, because X had
been in that other dream, and he was waiting for her
in this one.

He'd be in that bedroom where all the color was,
the one room in this massive house that seemed more
real, more tangible, than all the others. Her body responded, knowing he was near, instantly craving
what she'd gotten in the last dream: not just sex, even
though it had been powerful and earth-shattering

and almost—*almost*—nothing-else-matters sex. Because something else did matter, something stronger that pulled her to him.

But where the hell *was* he?

She walked from one room to the next, searching for the one room with color, but it wasn't where it had been the last time. Damn it, why wouldn't the rooms stay in one place? She grew more and more frustrated as she got more and more turned around. She was completely lost now. Hallways twisted and turned, grew longer as she tried to reach the end. She was so frustrated she felt like kicking a wall. He was *here*—somewhere. She felt him on a cellular level, down deep where instincts ruled alone and logic went out the window. But if she didn't find him soon, it would be too late; he'd go away, find something else to do. He was always going away.

And then she smelled him. He had a faint, masculine odor that was his and his alone. His skin, his clothes, the soap he used . . . it all added up to X. Perhaps no one else would note the scent, it was so light, but she did. She'd inhaled his scent on more than one occasion, had closed her eyes and breathed deep and been soothed and excited and inflamed by the way he smelled.

She followed her nose and her instincts. She quit thinking and just walked forward, drawn onward. And finally there it was, the room she'd been searching for. She knew it was the right room before she even opened the door, but she watched her hand turn the knob and push the door open, watched all that vivid color bloom at the threshold. And there he was, waiting for her, always waiting. All this time, if only she'd known where to look.

"Lizzy." That was all he said, one word, her name, but it was enough.

Xavier knew the details of this house he'd never been in before tonight almost as well as he knew his own. Even though it was an older home, it had been renovated at some time, opening up the interior to a more modern floor plan. The living room and dining area were open to each other, one to the left of the front door and the other to the right; the kitchen was separated from the dining area by a half-wall.

Moving into the living room, he looked around; again, the room wasn't completely dark. Light seeped in past the edges of the heavy curtains over the windows, plus there were the electronic lights: a small blue one on the cordless phone charger, a bright amber light from the cable box, a red dot on the DVD player. The soft, multicolored glow allowed him to see all the furniture in the living room, and a sweeping glance told him what he was looking for wasn't there. Damn it, he hoped she hadn't carried everything into her bedroom, because that could get dicey. He stood in one spot and did a slow three-sixty, carefully examining every chair, the floor, every flat surface—

Aha. There they were, on the round table in the dining area—the shopping bags from this afternoon's jaunt into Virginia.

This very-early-morning visit—he wouldn't call it breaking and entering since he did, after all, have a key—wasn't the safest course of action, but he had to know. Where had she gone, and why? What would take her into Virginia when everything she might possibly need could be found within ten miles of her house? She had been put in this location for that very reason, to make her world small. Routine was their friend. Routine kept Lizzy alive. Her days were usually predictable down to the minute, allowing for traffic variables.

But not today—rather, yesterday afternoon, when she'd left work. She'd gone in the opposite direction. She'd driven too fast. She'd gone way the hell into Virginia, then turned around and come back, and on the return trip she'd gotten off at an exit that she'd burned past on the first half of her trip. She hadn't gone just one exit down, as if she'd missed that one; she'd gone several exits down. It was as if she'd been trying to shake a tail.

Except Lizette wouldn't have known how to even spot a tail, much less how to shake it. Lizzy, however, would.

Lizette was a neat freak. Lizette would have unpacked the bags and put everything away. These out-of-character things were little, but they told him a lot.

There wasn't enough light for him to see the bags as well as he needed to, and he didn't dare move them. The rustle of plastic might be enough to wake her, especially if she was recovering some memory and was more wary. Not only that, she might have memorized the exact position of these bags and their contents. He did things like that, automatically, so he'd know if anyone had been in his space.

He pulled a small penlight from his pocket. He'd placed black electrician's tape over the end so only a thin sliver of light shone through. He glanced at the window behind him, the window that faced the street. She had blinds in here, bracketed on each side by curtains. The blinds were closed, but even the faintest light would seep through the slats, noticeable even in the rain. Shit.

He had to take the chance. He moved so his body was between the window and the shopping bags, bent close, and turned the little light on directly over the bags. Just for a split second, long enough only to identify the store name on the bags; then he switched off the light and stood there with his heartbeat galloping in his chest. He, who was legendary for his cool under fire, was about to break a sweat as the meaning hit him square between the eyes.

Shit, shit, and double shit. A sporting goods store might seem innocent enough, but they were great places to stock up on certain equipment, whether you were into sports or not.

Two bags and a shoe box lay empty on the table. What the hell else had she bought?

One of the unopened bags had the receipt stapled to it.

He wouldn't have to open the bags if he could get a good look at that receipt. The bags held some bulky stuff, and he wanted to know exactly what it was. But to read the receipt, he'd have to turn on the light for at least ten, fifteen seconds. That was just begging to get caught.

His options were to pick up the bags and take them into the kitchen, away from the window, which would make *some* noise no matter how careful he was; or to tear the receipt off the bag and take it into the kitchen where he could read it, alerting Lizzy for certain that someone had been there. His last option was to take the chance of turning on the penlight and reading the receipt right there.

Option C. If he had to make the guy outside disappear, so be it.

He didn't *want* to kill the guy, though; the poor sap was just doing a job, and taking a decent stab at it by staying awake. Couldn't fault that.

The kitchen towel.

He remembered it, a red-and-white check, hanging on a ring beside the sink. It wasn't folded any particular way, it was simply hanging there. Going into the kitchen, Xavier studied the towel for a moment and concluded that the only thing she had done out of the ordinary was make certain the towel hung exactly the same length on both sides. And that wasn't even Lizette; he'd seen Lizzy do the same thing, way back when.

He pulled the towel from the ring and went back to the dining area. Draping the towel over the penlight so virtually none of the thin beam of light would be visible from outside, he thumbed the button and in the dim light read the list of her purchases:

A backpack. A knife. A rope. Three canisters of pepper spray. And she'd paid cash for them, so the purchases wouldn't show up on her credit card.

He turned off the penlight and closed his eyes, standing there for a moment as adrenaline flooded through him. No doubt about it now, not that he'd doubted his instincts anyway. But this was proof. She was back, or on the way back.

Lizzy was either getting ready to run or she was getting ready to fight. Would she recall everything, or just bits and pieces? How much did she remember now? Not much. If she'd remembered specifics, she wouldn't be asleep in her own bed right now; she'd be gone, her backpack filled with these purchases and who knows what else. Would she have filled out the paperwork to begin the process of buying a weapon? No, not in a place like that. If she was looking for a weapon, she'd go deeper into Virginia for an off-the-books weapon, either find a county flea market or make a black-market buy on a street corner. If she started making unusual trips on a regular basis, they were in trouble.

No, *she* was in trouble.

Piggybacking on the surveillance in place on her car, phone, and electronics wasn't enough, not now. He had to know where she was at all times; he couldn't take the chance that she'd shake her tail, ditch the car, leave behind this house and everything she'd known for the past three years. Even if she only partially recovered her memory, she was capable of doing just that; she'd be frightened, and not understand exactly what was going on.

If she ran, she'd take the backpack; why else would she buy it? It wasn't as if she were going to school or taking up hiking. Shit, he was going to have to make some noise if he took the backpack out of the plastic bag. He could tell which bag it was in, just as he could tell, now that he knew what she'd bought, that the receipt was stapled to the bag that held the pepper spray.

He needed to get to that backpack. He had other options, but he wanted to cover as many possibilities as he could.

Maybe he could work his hand inside the bag without making more than a rustle. Having full access to the backpack would be the best option, but circumstances weren't in his favor.

Reaching into a pocket, he removed a small pouch that contained three small, almost undetectable trackers. There were smaller ones; some were microdots, but they were more difficult to place, and he wanted to keep his time in here to a minimum. He removed one of the trackers. He'd put each of them into an individual resealable plastic bag, and marked each bag with a different number so he'd know which tracker he was putting on what. Removing one, he turned the plastic bag toward the dim light coming through the closed blinds, and could just make out the number 2. Okay, 2 was going on the backpack.

Working carefully in the darkness, because he didn't want to drop the little fucker, he eased his hand into the bag. The plastic rustled, but he moved in slow increments and the sound was faint, nothing more than a scratch. He felt straps. Not good enough. Easing his hand deeper, he brushed against a flap, which would probably cover a zippered pocket. Good enough, even though he couldn't see what he was doing. Carefully turning his hand, he attached the tracker to the underside of the flap.

Then he just as slowly pulled his hand out of the bag.

One down, two to go.

He took the towel back to the kitchen and looped it back over the ring, carefully adjusting it so both ends hung evenly.

Now things got tricky.

She didn't hesitate, simply walked forward, undressing as she approached him. There were no second thoughts, no thoughts at all, just instinct and need. Skin to skin; she needed it. Him inside her; she needed it. She wanted to feel her climax building and building until she screamed when she came, and she would. In this room she could scream if she wanted to. She could take what she wanted, live with abandon. Here she could live.

X folded his arms across his chest and stood there waiting, not undressing himself, just waiting for her. Always waiting. She pushed her underwear down her legs, stepped out of them without hesitation, without embarrassment or fear. She reached him, smiled up into his dark eyes, and began to undress him. When she removed his shirt, she took a moment to bury her face against the warmth of his bare chest and deeply inhale. He smelled so good, so real, and she could feel the heat of his skin against her cheek, the way the hair on his chest tickled her nose.

Even though she knew this was a dream, it was the best dream ever.

But as great as this was, she wanted more than just the smell of him—much more.

Tugging at his belt, she unbuckled it, then unzipped his jeans and slipped her hand inside, wrapping her fingers around him and feeling him harden, push against her fingers. He made a deep sound in his throat, more than a hum, not quite a growl.

She pushed his jeans down and off. In real life they'd have had to deal with his boots, but this was her dream, and she didn't want boots slowing her down. She was already wet, ready, empty without him. She wanted to push him down and straddle him, taking him hard and deep, but then she'd come and it would be over. She'd wake up, trembling and gasping for air. Not yet! She didn't want to wake up just yet. It was too soon. She wanted to feel him, smell him, savor every inch.

His hands wound in her hair, holding her close, making sure she didn't slip away. She loved his hands. They were big hands, powerful hands that could kill or pleasure, hurt or heal. Some people were afraid of those hands, but not her.

X lifted her off her feet and walked toward the bed. This was how she liked him best: naked, hard, impatient. When X was impatient, when she was rocking his world the way he rocked hers, he could make her feel . . . ravaged, and treasured, and loved.

Lizette's feet dangled inches from the floor. She soared. She wanted him so much, and he was right there, he was with her, she could wrap her arms around his neck and hold on even as she flew, really flew. And because this was a dream, maybe she could fly. She laughed a little, dangling there in his arms as he moved to the bed . . . and then she looked to the side and saw her face in the mirror. Her laughter died away as she stared at herself. That was her old face, the one that had been taken from her. She closed her

eyes, tight, and when she opened them again her face
was the new one, the one that she knew wasn't her.

Or was it?

Which one was the real her? Which one did X
want?

Which face did he love?

A bigger question: Did he love her at all? After
what she'd done?

Then he laid her on the bed and she couldn't see her
face in the mirror any longer, and that was just as
well. She didn't want to look; she wanted to feel. She
didn't want to wonder; she just wanted to hold X and
follow her body's lead.

For a moment they just lay there on the big bed,
chest to chest, legs intertwined, hearts pounding. They
were eye to eye, and for a moment Lizette felt her
breath catch. Good God, he was beautiful! Not pretty,
there was nothing pretty about him, but seen with her
heart he was . . . beautiful.

And whatever face she wore, he didn't care. Behind
this face she was still *her,* and that was all that mattered to him. Yes, he loved her. He still loved her.

He kissed her throat as if they had all the time in
the world, but Lizette was suddenly certain that they
didn't. They had no time at all, not together. She
would live in her world and he would live in his and
there would be no more *this.* Maybe there would be
the occasional dream, if she was lucky. No more
dreams of him at all, if she was not lucky.

"Now," she whispered.

He half laughed, half growled. "Not yet."

Lizette opened her mouth, started to say *please,*

but she didn't. Begging would only make him more determined to take his time.

They didn't *have* time.

Lizette shuddered, head to toe. She didn't want this dream to end, yet she couldn't wait to have him inside her. She could stay here all night, just holding him. Her body throbbed, and she knew she'd be doing good to wait another full minute.

More than anything, more even than the urge that pulled her forward faster and faster . . . she didn't want to let X go, not ever again.

Xavier went down the hall toward her bedroom, his movements fluid and ghostly, his footsteps as silent as if he were drifting above the floor. The last thing he wanted was for her to wake up. It was dark. Not being able to see him, she'd automatically think he was a rapist or murderer; any woman would. Hell, even if she did see him, she'd still think that. She hadn't recognized him in the pharmacy, after all. If she woke up and turned on the lamp, saw him in her home dressed as he was in dark clothing and armed, would her memory come rushing back or would she simply panic and start screaming? He'd bet on the panic and screaming.

Her bedroom door was open. She lived alone, after all; there was no need to close an interior door. He eased inside and stood for a moment, looking at the bed, at her.

The alarm clock, and the blue light on another cordless phone, gave off enough light for him to see. She was curled up in the bed, dark hair on an almost-flat pillow, covers pulled up to her neck—and one bare foot sticking out from under those covers. Some things never changed. No matter what they did to her face, her brain . . . she was still Lizzy, deep inside. He should have known, they all should have known, that one day she'd break free from the prison they'd put her in.

On the bedside table, inches from the bright clock, sat a tall can of something. He grinned. He'd bet his ass it was wasp spray, or something like that. No handgun, at least not yet, but she'd armed herself anyway. Near the base of the can lay her cell phone—and beside the phone was the battery. Until she put the battery in, the phone couldn't be tracked. Yes, she was waking up, breaking free.

Another thing about her had held true. Lizzy was a purse fanatic. She loved handbags, and would save money to buy one good leather bag, rather than several cheaper ones. Other women he'd trained, and trained with, would forego handbags in favor of pockets or fanny packs, but not Lizzy; she'd held on to her purses. She didn't just drop the chosen bag anywhere in the house, either; she'd always taken it into the bedroom and put it on a chair. She might move the chair around, but that was where the purse went.

Currently, the bedroom chair was maybe four feet from Lizzy's head, just on the other side of the bedside table. The bag was white, so he could easily pick it out, and it had a long strap. This was the tricky part. Maybe she didn't have a gun, but Lizzy had always been a good shot, and if she got him in the eyes with that wasp spray he'd be temporarily blinded.

God only knew what she'd do to him then, while he was at such a disadvantage.

He hooked the strap with a finger and noiselessly lifted the purse, got the cell phone from the bedside table, then backed out of the room as silently as he'd entered. The kitchen, where there was more light, was the best place for him to do this.

Once he was there, he put the purse on the counter and got to work. He was just about to place another tracker—this one was marked with a 1—in the inside zipper pocket when he paused. This was Lizzy, the handbag fanatic. She'd have more than one purse. She'd regularly changed handbags, to match her outfit or her mood or whatever she needed for the day. She could easily swap to a different purse tomorrow.

Not the purse, then. He noted the placement of her wallet, then carefully pulled it out and opened it. It was leather, oversized the way women's usually were, had a place for a checkbook but no checks. What it did hold was cash, a couple of hundred dollars' worth. There were also a couple of credit cards, her driver's license and insurance card, and a couple of receipts. He tried to read the date on one of the receipts, but there wasn't enough light, and he was running out of time.

It was a good bet that no matter what purse she carried, this wallet would be in it. He removed the bills and set them aside, planted the tiny tracker underneath a bit of torn lining and replaced the cash exactly as he'd found it, then slid the wallet back into the purse.

Next up: the cell phone. If she was smart enough to remove the battery, that meant she intended to keep it with her. This new phone, a replacement for the one she'd dropped and broken on Friday, was a simple flip phone. No smart phone for Lizzy, which was a good decision on her part. Normally he'd put the tracker inside the battery compartment, but if she was taking the battery out after she used it each time, that upped the chances she'd either see it or perhaps dislodge it.

For a few seconds, Xavier studied the phone. The light was better here in the kitchen, but it still wasn't great, so he went as much by feel as he did by sight. There were very few nooks and crannies, and none of them were right. Finally he tested the edge of the keyboard cover. It was rubbery, not a hard plastic. He pushed his fingernail under the edge, lifted it, planted the tracker beneath the cover, and then pressed it down. Not a great placement, but he was limited by not being able to use the battery compartment.

Purse and cell phone in his hands, he retraced his steps to the bedroom and placed both exactly where he'd found them, being careful not to let the phone click against the table as he released it.

He took a deep, silent breath and looked down at her.

If she woke up, he had no place to go. If she opened her eyes she'd see him, in the light of her alarm clock. He should leave, but now that he was this close to her he couldn't tear himself away, not yet. Seeing her in the drugstore had just made the hunger more intense. To have the luxury of actually seeing her, watching her sleep, he'd risk getting a blast of wasp spray in the eyes.

Lizzy. Thick dark hair, slightly curly, tousled now in sleep. The shape of her face was different now, but the curve of her lips was the same. That bare foot was the same.

The smell of her was the same.

His hands remembered the feel of her.

There had been times when he'd held her under him and fucked her until she screamed. And then she'd done the same thing to him, though she'd teased him and said that, being a manly man, his scream was more like a long grunt.

His fingers curled as he resisted the urge to reach out and touch her. His dick twitched, wanting more than just that. Shit, he had to get out of here before he did something beyond stupid.

Less than twenty minutes after letting himself into the house, Xavier let himself back out. It was still raining, which was a godsend. The surveillance car was still in the same place, but he couldn't see any movement inside it. Maybe the rain had lulled the guy to sleep, despite the coffee. Maybe he was concentrating on pissing into a bottle. Xavier had been on surveillance himself, so he knew how it went. He was glad he wasn't the one having to sit in that car.

He silently locked the kitchen door, both locks, then eased around the back of the house, going from shadow to shadow. When a couple of houses were between him and the surveillance car he picked up speed, wanting to get back to his truck and check the laptop, make sure the trackers were working. Then, assuming everything was working as it should, he'd go home and grab a power nap before Lizzy woke up and got started on her day.

He had to be prepared. Lizzy was waking up in more ways than one, and the shit was about to hit the fan. He knew which way he was going to jump. He'd made his choice years ago, and right or wrong, he'd stand by it.

Lizzy was alive, but she hadn't been living.

Fuck it all, neither had he.

In her dream, he parted her legs wider with his knee, and then he was there, plunging deep. She gasped, not in pain but in relief and pleasure and a sense of connection she'd never known before. She was part of him; he was part of her.

A mirror she hadn't noticed before—she was pretty sure it hadn't been there before—was suddenly over the bed. It was as big as the bed, reflecting the dream back at her. The face . . . which face did she wear? The old one or the new one? Did it matter?

She could close her eyes to escape the unsettling image, but instead she focused on X, on the broad shoulders and muscled back and hard, round ass. He had the best ass she'd ever seen. Their bodies were entwined on the bed, his tanned skin making hers look so pale, his hard body making hers look so soft, what she could see of herself. He was bigger, wider; he almost engulfed her. But as different as they were, they fit together.

She studied his strong legs; the way he moved . . . easier now, almost gently. Thrusting in and out in a slow rhythm that gradually, oh so gradually, increased in speed and power.

Lizette closed her eyes as she gave over and let herself come and come and come. She screamed, her

back bowing as she clutched X to her, felt him come
so deep inside her . . .

He whispered something, but she couldn't tell what
he said. She frowned at him, opened her mouth to
say, "What?" Whatever he'd said was important, he
wasn't someone who chatted just to hear his own
voice, but before she could form that one word, before he could answer—

She opened her eyes. Her body lurched, every muscle tensed . . . and then she relaxed, unwinding one
muscle at a time until she was melting into the mat-
tress. Every muscle in her body felt weak and heavy.

She needed to go to that Walgreens more often. If
X regularly shopped there, maybe she'd run into him
again. Maybe this time she wouldn't freak and run
like a scared rabbit. She could give him her number,
ask him out for coffee, and then . . .

Yeah, right. Lizette Henry, sex-starved stalker. As
if real life might possibly come anywhere close to a
dream. As if a man like that one didn't have a wife,
or a girlfriend. Or both.

It was raining. She closed her eyes and listened to
the raindrops on the window. The rain on the roof
and the windows created a soothing sound that might
lull her back to sleep, though the dark morning hours
were winding down, edging closer to dawn. She wondered if she'd dream about X again or if that part of
the night was done. She wondered if she'd forget the
details of the dream, come morning.

Right now the dream seemed so real, she was almost positive she could still smell him.

Chapter Fourteen

Felice McGowan never wasted her time worrying about status or perks, or any of the other ego traps that kept the majority of people in D.C. so preoccupied. In a perfect world, she would have a personal driver who always delivered her right to the door of where she was going, and no one would ever question her authority. Those were the two items on her private wish list, but the world wasn't perfect, so she forgot about it and dealt with reality.

Reality, in this case, was that she had to go out in the rain like everyone else, that most good plans usually went to hell somewhere along the line, and because of the nature of the game she had to go to Al Forge instead of telling him to come to her. His willingness to do so wasn't in doubt, but she worked at NSA now and she didn't want him there, didn't want the super-snoopers to see them together. Their relationship was completely off the books, and had to stay that way, for both their sakes.

In one way she had it easier than Al. She wasn't involved in the day-to-day, off-the-books surveillance of Subject C. Al not only oversaw that, he was also officially working under the large umbrella of Homeland Security. What he truly did was so wrapped in layers of need-to-know and for-your-eyes-only that probably even the President didn't have the complete dossier on him. He'd started out at Treasury, with the Secret Service, then switched to DOJ, and from there God only knew everything he'd done.

The NSA had the goods on everyone who was on the grid—meaning everyone except maybe the homeless and a few hermits—but she hadn't been able to access everything in Al's file. There were gaps that probably corresponded to some interesting international events, but she hadn't tried to match them up. When push came to shove, the country needed people like Al. Back in the day, she'd had a couple of gaps in her own dossier.

What Al used to do, Xavier now did. But Al had always kept his personal compass set on true north—meaning the best interests of the country—while Xavier was a wild card. When he'd started out she'd thought he was as true blue as Al, and God knows his skill level was off the charts, but along the way he'd gone a little rogue. Her confidence in him had been eroding for the past four years. But Al still trusted him, still believed in him, and that carried more weight than Al probably realized.

She didn't rationalize what they'd done. She couldn't. Every time she thought about it, she still got a sick feeling in the pit of her stomach. Her head recognized the necessity, but her heart bitterly regretted every action they'd taken, and mourned the outcome. All of them had lost pieces of their souls that day, pieces they'd never get back no matter how much they devoted themselves to their work.

And now there was this thing with Subject C. No

one had wanted to eliminate her, but everyone had recognized that she was the linchpin, the central weakness, that could not only take all of them down but also irreparably damage the country. Despite what Al perhaps thought, Felice wasn't eager to give the order; still, she understood that such an action might be necessary, while Al couldn't seem to admit that.

The thing was, for a while they'd been so close, the whole team, and people who went through such an intense event together developed a sense of family, of connectedness. Al's loyalty to his team was legendary. But Subject C hadn't been a part of the *team;* she'd been a tool the team had used.

They'd planned to eliminate the *threat* she posed to them, right from the beginning. As long as she wasn't a threat, Felice was content to let her live.

As long as she wasn't a threat.

There were disturbing details surfacing now, each of them small and easily explained away. However, taken as a whole, those details formed a completely different picture, one that Felice didn't think they could afford to ignore. It was a picture that said Subject C was becoming a threat.

The building that housed Subject C's surveillance was an ordinary two-story redbrick; the lettering on the door said *Capitol Temporary Services.* If anyone happened to wander in looking for a temp to fill in for a sick or vacationing office worker, there was a reception area, a receptionist, a "manager," and, if necessary, a temp could actually be found. But given that the erstwhile business didn't have a listed phone number, did no advertising, and walk-in business was nonexistent, that had never happened. Every now and then a not-too-bright guy would get the idea that "temporary services" was euphemistic for "call girl" and come in to negotiate a rate, but that was about it. Twice people had come in asking for directions.

Inside, the security was top notch. She nodded to the receptionist, who she knew was armed. Her thumbprint opened the first set of reinforced doors, and from there she progressed through additional layers until she reached the upper level. No building was completely unbreachable, of course. There was always a way to either get inside or destroy it. But this building wasn't in the center of power or action, and it was so bland as to be almost invisible.

At its most basic level, the building functioned as intelligence and support. Al Forge ran his black ops, and one very small portion, completely insulated from the rest, was dedicated to the surveillance of Subject C.

Al wasn't immediately available, so Felice left word she was there, and she went to the tank to wait. There was very little opportunity for silence in her world, and the tank was completely silent except for her own breathing, her own footsteps, her own little noises and no one else's. No one was watching her, no one was gauging her reactions, no one was waiting for a decision—well, at least not at this very moment. She selected a pod of French roast and made a cup of coffee, then sat down to enjoy her solitude. Al wouldn't keep her waiting long, so she had to make the best of it while she could.

She had some decisions to make, decisions that she didn't take lightly. Al's warning that Xavier knew where she lived and where her daughter lived wasn't something she could ignore. Al had meant it as a warning, and she had taken it as such.

She could shrug off any implied danger to herself, because she had accepted that possibility from the outset, but when her child was threatened . . . there was no shrugging that off. Ashley was her heart. She couldn't bear the thought that anything might happen to her daughter, that Ashley wouldn't get to live life to the fullest, to love and be loved, to have children, to grow old and see her family grow, to have a fulfilling career. She wanted all of that, and more, for her daughter. She wanted everything. Selfishly, she also wanted to see her own grandchildren someday.

She would not, ever in this lifetime, tolerate a threat to the precious life that was her daughter.

She couldn't spirit Ashley away, hide her from all danger. Ashley was a continent away, doing her postgrad work at Stanford. She was an excellent student, a self-driven overachiever who was willing to work her butt off to reach her goals. But she was also young, and even if Felice explained the danger to her, Ashley wouldn't understand the gravity of the situation, wouldn't cooperate with a massive interruption of her plans.

Therefore, something had to be done about Xavier.

Al entered the tank then. Whatever his thoughts were about her presence here, so soon after her last visit, they didn't show on his face. He'd make a killing at the Vegas poker tables if he ever decided to take up gambling. "What's up?" he asked casually as he, too, went to the coffeemaker and selected a pod.

Al wasn't a casual-type man. He could project the attitude if he wanted, but he was always thinking, always weighing, always trying to steer events his way. He knew why she was here.

Nevertheless, Felice went about systematically outlining the situation and her intentions—some of them, anyway. "Subject C is showing more signs of . . . instability," she replied. "Nothing dramatic, but out of her usual routine."

He waited until his coffee cup was full, then removed it and sipped before saying nonchalantly, "Such as?"

She felt a flash of annoyance that he'd asked, because they had trackers on Subject C's car; they knew exactly where she'd gone yesterday afternoon. She never took Al for a fool, and he returned the favor. If he was doing this dance, it was for a reason.

"You don't think driving miles into Virginia to a strip mall, bypassing several malls much closer that have the same stores, is a break in her routine?" All she put into her tone was mild curiosity.

He sighed. "Did she do anything nefarious at these stores?"

"She went to a sporting goods store."

"The horror," he said, keeping his tone so bland that the unexpressed sarcasm was sharper than it would have been if he'd snapped at her. Despite herself, Felice found herself smiling, because she liked a good comeback. "Her credit card shows she bought some running shoes, a jogging outfit, and some wasp spray."

She made a dismissive gesture. "I know that. I also know no charges at any other stores showed up, so she either paid cash for what she bought at them or she went specifically to that store and nowhere else.

Again, she passed other, closer, sporting goods stores. Why that one? Why so far into Virginia?"

"Maybe she hadn't planned to stop anywhere; maybe she just went for a drive, on an impulse."

"Please," she said, leaving the *Don't be an idiot* unspoken. "She's programmed *not* to be impulsive. If she's becoming impulsive, then the process isn't holding. And taking a spontaneous drive isn't the only thing different that she's doing."

"Such as?"

"She went running late yesterday evening when she got home. The impression my man got, the very words he used, was that it was as if she was starting training."

"That's just someone's impression, and I assume you used people who know nothing about her. She bought running shoes and a new outfit yesterday, then she went running. That isn't exactly unexpected. For all we know, people in her office started talking about dieting, getting in shape, and she decided to go along with it too."

Felice thought about that. "Feasible," she finally agreed, because it was. Kind of on the outer limits, but still within the bounds of feasibility. "*If* she had activated the new cell phone she bought, which she hasn't. She went to the trouble of buying a new cell phone the day after she broke hers, but she still hasn't even put the battery in it. Hell, why didn't she let them activate it in the store? That was on Saturday. This is Tuesday. All of the little things, taken together, form a picture I don't like."

He was silent, which meant the deal with the cell phone had bothered him, too. That wasn't normal behavior. Going for a drive, doing some impulse shopping, maybe going for an after-work jog—those things were unlike her, but not, in and of themselves, enough to make anyone push the panic button.

But he couldn't explain the cell phone. Who bought a cell phone and didn't put the battery in it? People like them, that's who, people who knew just putting the battery in activated the GPS, put out a signal that let them be traced. All over the world, people were voluntarily carrying automatic tracking devices that, knowing the nature of the world and governments, could one day be used to hunt them down and keep them under control.

"Given that all of this started when her supervisor possibly alerted her to the difference in time lapse," she continued, driving her point home, "we have to assume that did trigger some sort of mental . . . adjustment."

"Even if some of her former personal qualities are resurfacing, that doesn't mean her memory is," Al said. "She has no way of accessing any records, no way of knowing where to start. Even if she did look, all she'd find is a gap of two years. All the paperwork is tied up, and leads to dead ends. You know that. We covered every base."

"Unless her memory comes back, too."

"What are the odds of that? Aren't you more likely to get hit by a lightning bolt when you walk out the door?"

"Yes, of course, given that the odds of getting hit by lightning are surprisingly high. But you tell me: considering the subject matter, exactly what kind of odds can we afford to tolerate concerning Subject C?"

She had him there. The only logical answer was zero. None.

What she wanted was for Al to accept the reality of the situation and stop protecting Subject C. She had her own resources, but nothing like what Al could pull into action. If he would handle the people and let her handle the spin, they could come through this— maybe damaged, with doubt and suspicion following them for the rest of their lives, but those lives at least wouldn't be spent in prison, and on death row at that.

"I think you're borrowing trouble," he finally said. "Even if she *did* remember everything, what's she going to do? She, of all people, will want what we did kept quiet."

"Another question about odds: how likely is she to recover *all* her memory? Given the process, a partial recall is the more likely outcome."

"Given the process, it's a wonder she's a functioning human being at all," Al said sharply.

"She agreed to it."

"Only because the other option was a bullet in the head."

Felice had the beginnings of a headache, and she rubbed her forehead. Nothing about this situation was going to be easy. Al obviously wasn't going to step up to the plate, even though they were practically getting slapped in the face by the danger signs. She'd have to handle it.

Very well, then, she'd do it her way.

But for Al's benefit, she said, "Fine. We'll just keep an eye on her for a while longer. You'd better pray you're right, or we're all going down."

Chapter Fifteen

Discovering that she wasn't in such bad physical condition after all was a nice surprise, Lizette had thought as she got ready that morning. Her thighs were a little sore, but not bad. When she got home from work this afternoon and had a better dinner than just a protein bar, she'd go again—and a little farther this time, maybe faster. She probably shouldn't, she should probably let her muscles rest a day, but she was already eager to hit the pavement.

She was just getting in her car in the driveway when Maggie, clad in sweatpants and a tee shirt, came out on her front porch.

"Lizette, wait a minute!"

A little annoyed, a little harried—after all, a morning chat wasn't in her schedule—Lizette paused and looked at her neighbor over the top of her car. "I have to get to work—"

"I know, this'll be quick." Maggie hurried to the edge of the porch and beckoned Lizette over. For once she didn't have the little yapper with her, though as soon as Lizette noticed that fact she heard the dog begin barking inside the house, protesting being left alone.

Resigned, Lizette went over to the porch, stepping

gingerly through the dew-wet grass. She so didn't want to go to work with wet feet. "Is something wrong?"

"Could be." Maggie wasn't wearing any makeup, Lizette noticed, and she looked a bit younger without it. That was strange. "Listen—don't look, whatever you do don't turn your head, but there's been a strange car parked on the street since yesterday. One car left about seven this morning, and another took its place. It's like they're watching someone. I don't like it, makes me feel weird. I wonder if they're casing the houses in the neighborhood, looking for one to rob."

Strange that when someone told you not to look somewhere, it was hard not to. Lizette concentrated on not looking. Chills ran over her entire body. So it wasn't her imagination; someone *was* watching her. She didn't know whether to feel gratified or terrified. *Don't look, don't look*. She tried to think what to say. "Should we call the police, have them come check it out?"

"I don't know." Maggie looked nowhere except at Lizette. "It just strikes me as worrisome."

If it was a burglary gang casing the neighborhood, Lizette knew exactly what she should do—and suddenly she knew how to handle the other possible situation, too.

"I'll take care of it," she said firmly. "Thanks for keeping an eye on things."

Maggie looked a little startled. "What're you going to do?"

"Get his tag number."

And she did. She didn't have to back out of her driveway this morning because she'd backed in the afternoon before, in keeping with her new parking mode. As she started the car she carefully examined all the cars parked on the street and spotted the intruder almost immediately, even though the car itself was unremarkable, a beige domestic sedan. She knew what cars belonged on this street, and that wasn't one of them. And there was a man in it, a man who was kind of slumped to the side as if trying to hide from view. If she hadn't been alerted, and hadn't been looking for him, she might well have driven right by without noticing anything unusual.

He was parked so that if she took her normal route to work she would turn in the opposite direction from where he was parked; he'd be able to pull into the street right behind her. That meant she couldn't easily get his tag number.

There was also the concern that he might pull a pistol and shoot at her, but she didn't think so. Whoever was watching her had done nothing except watch; she didn't know why, she didn't know who it was, but so far no one had tried to harm her. And if Maggie *had* spotted some would-be burglars, they weren't likely to be armed, because the jail sentences were so much worse if they were caught with weapons.

Cautiously, she stopped at the end of her driveway, looked both ways for traffic—nothing in sight—and pulled into the street. She immediately stomped on the brake, slammed the transmission into reverse, and, tires squealing as they fought for traction, shot backward toward the suspicious car. She zoomed past in reverse and saw the guy's startled face looking out the window.

As soon as she was past him, she slammed on the

brakes again, quickly scribbled down his tag number, and pulled even with him and stopped, hitting the button that lowered the passenger-side window. Cautiously, he also lowered his window. "Hey," she yelled angrily, showing him the notepad where she'd written down his tag number. "If you're casing houses in *this* neighborhood to rob, buddy, you'd better think twice, because I've got your license plate number."

He couldn't have looked more stunned if she'd rammed his car instead of just getting his tag. "I— what? *No*. I'm not—honest, lady, this isn't—"

"Then you need to get your ass off this street," she barked. "And don't tell me you've been waiting for someone, not all this time. You think people haven't noticed you? *Git!*"

He got.

Her heart was beating faster, she noticed, as she watched the car turn at the first intersection and disappear, but it was kind of a pleasant sensation, as if she were riding some kind of high. She raised the passenger window, lowered the driver's window, and gave Maggie a thumbs-up and a grin as she drove past. Maggie returned the salute.

Two birds killed with one stone, Lizette thought with satisfaction. If the guy had been a burglar casing the joint, he was gone. If he'd been a private detective or something like that who'd been watching *her*, he was still gone, but the report he'd give was that neighbors had noticed him and she'd gotten his tag number and accused him of being a burglar. She was still flying somewhat under the radar.

* * *

As soon as he was out of sight, the man in the beige car thumbed a number into his cell phone. "I've been made," he said tersely. "A neighbor spotted me. I saw them talking. Then the subject got my tag number and accused me of casing houses, said she'd give the number to the cops if there were any robberies."

There was a pause as his handler weighed the ramifications. "Are you certain that she didn't make you beforehand?"

"I can't be certain, but I did see the neighbor looking out her window several times, and as soon as the subject came out to go to work, the neighbor came hot-footing it out of her house and called the subject over to talk to her."

"Okay. Regardless, you're burned. I'll call this in, let the client know."

Thirty seconds later, Felice said, "Discontinue observation."

She disconnected, then erased the call history from her phone. She'd do it her way from here on out.

Chapter Sixteen

Diana had another errand to run at lunch—new sneakers for her youngest, who had for some reason decided to flush one of his, requiring a visit from a plumber—and Lizette had her own errand, so they went their separate ways.

Lunchtime traffic was a bitch, as always. Getting to her bank took twice as long as it would have during a non-rush period. Lizette was kind of glad for the delay, because what she was about to do felt either important or stupid, and she wasn't certain which it was.

How much money should she take out in cash? She was able to save some of her paycheck and was consistent about it, but she had her mortgage and utilities to pay, and real estate in the D.C. area, even the more distant communities, wasn't cheap. She had some money in CDs, despite an interest rate that was so low she was almost paying the bank to take her money, because it was safe. Most of her savings were in a 401(k).

She had roughly five thousand dollars in her checking account, but her mortgage payment was automatically deducted from the account and if she emptied it out she wouldn't be able to make her payment. The thought horrified her. She'd never had a check bounce, never been behind on any of her payments.

But if she needed cash to survive, if she suddenly had to bolt—

Taking out two thousand seemed to be a nice compromise. She'd have enough to function, but that would leave enough money in the account to cover her mortgage, for the next payment at least. After that, she didn't know.

Maybe she was morphing into someone who was way more spontaneous and knew all kinds of spy-shit stuff, but she just couldn't make herself skip out on a bill.

Spy shit? The thought was electrifying. Holy crap! Was that it? Was that what she'd been involved in?

It kind of made sense, but it was scary. She couldn't see herself as a spy. But then, if she'd been through some kind of brainwashing that had turned her into someone else, she wouldn't see that, would she?

Her head was beginning to hurt, which she took as a sign to stop thinking about it and just take care of business. At least the headache felt more like a normal headache, and hadn't ambushed her. Maybe that was a sign she was adjusting, or—or something. She sighed. It seemed as if everything had multiple possible explanations, and how the hell was she supposed to guess the right answer when the most reasonable of the explanations were the ones that didn't feel right?

The bank was busy. She checked the time; if she was going to have lunch at all, she'd have to get something to go and eat it on the way back to the office.

By the time she'd finished the transaction and had

two thousand dollars in cash safely stowed in her wallet, she had half an hour left before she had to be back at her desk. There was a barbecue restaurant not far from the office; it wasn't her favorite, but at least it was fast, and saved time because she'd pass it on her way back.

She thought about calling ahead and placing her order, but that would mean putting the battery in her phone, and she felt uneasy enough that she simply couldn't bring herself to do it. Phones gave her the heebie-jeebies now, thinking that someone might be listening to every word she said.

By the time she pulled into the parking lot of the restaurant, she had twenty minutes left. The restaurant enjoyed a decent crowd, because even though the food was only acceptable, it was fast. Some customers were eating at the handful of tables in the joint— placing their orders at a bar, getting their food on a tray, then selecting their own table—while others were leaving with to-go boxes in hand. There were three employees behind the counter, and unlike the girl at the sporting goods place they seemed to enjoy their jobs, even joking with the regulars.

Lizette ordered a sandwich to go, which she could at least eat on the way back to work. The man behind the counter, a potbellied bearded guy who looked old enough to be her father, winked at her as he offered her change. Every woman who came through the door probably got that wink and a smile. She sized him up, classified him as harmless, and headed for the exit. An older woman coming in held the door for her. Lizette smiled, nodded her head, and continued on into the warmth of a summer afternoon that smelled of smoked meat.

She hadn't taken two steps before she noticed the black car slowly moving through the parking lot, two men, and they seemed to be checking the cars because each one was looking to the side, the driver toward the left, the passenger toward the right. She skidded to a stop, watching, the back of her neck prickling. Maybe it was her imagination, but when they reached her car the driver seemed to hit the brake for a moment, as if they were taking a harder look.

Assess the threat.

Oh shit, oh shit, not a headache, not now!

She forced herself to just look at the men, concentrate on them.

She did, and the pain faded to a bearable level— still there, but she could function. And, damn it, she'd assess the threat if she wanted to, she thought angrily.

Assessing took only an instant. The passenger now had his head down. Both men were wearing hoodies, the hoods up and forward as if they were hiding their faces. The hoodies were wrong for the hot weather, very wrong.

She wasn't the only customer who'd noticed the car, the way it was crawling through the parking lot, and the two occupants who weren't acting like people looking for a quick sandwich or plate lunch. A few people were on their way to their cars and one man stopped in his tracks, his body language shouting wariness as he watched the car crawling past, one aisle over. The D.C. area was notorious for drive-by shootings, almost always gang related, but collateral damage was still damage.

The driver looked around, and his gaze seemed to stop on her. Maybe he'd said something to the passenger, because the other man's head came up and he, too, seemed to look right at her.

Then he leaned out the window, and she saw the weapon in his hand.

She dropped her lunch and dove to the side, automatically reaching for the weapon she didn't have. The first shot went high, hitting the plate-glass window behind her; glass shattered, shards went flying. Screams punctured the air. The man who had stopped to watch the two men in the car threw himself to the ground.

Lizette rolled, then crouched behind a heavy newspaper machine. It wouldn't stop a bullet, but there were cars between the shooter and her, so maybe he couldn't see where she was. Her heart pounded, banging away in her chest, the roar of blood as it rushed through her veins so loud she could barely hear the screams that were erupting all around her.

Most people either flattened to the concrete or ran for whatever cover they could find, but one man stood frozen in front of the newspaper machine, a middle-aged man who looked around, wild-eyed, still holding the big bag with his to-go lunches in it. "Get down!" Lizette screamed at him.

Another shot. The man screamed, the to-go bag dropping as he wheeled around, clutching his shoulder. He stumbled, went down.

Lizette swiftly darted her head around the newspaper machine, a lightning-fast peek—and saw the shooter taking aim at her.

She threw herself to the side. The third shot killed the newspaper machine.

She'd seen his face—some of it, anyway. Caucasian male, mid-thirties, at least two hundred pounds. He wasn't firing without purpose; he'd looked directly at her. *Drive-by, my ass.*

She rolled, and another bullet hit the concrete behind her. She rolled in the opposite direction, and the newspaper machine took another one. She threw herself back in the other direction; the next shot went right over her head and hit the brick wall of the restaurant. Shards of brick cut her arms, stinging but not wounding.

Shit! She was pinned down, had no weapon, and all the shooter had to do was keep her pinned down until he had a clear shot.

The car was slowly moving forward, the shooter getting a better angle on her with every second. What kind of weapon did he have? He'd shot six times. Did he have a revolver, an automatic, how many in the clip?

The analysis was flying through her thoughts, somehow coolly divorced from the adrenaline searing her veins. This was not going to be good. She had nowhere to go.

The potbellied, bearded man who'd winked at her came out of the front door with a shotgun braced against his shoulder. He wasn't smiling anymore. He pulled the trigger, the boom deafening at such close quarters.

"You goddamn bastards!" he yelled, his face red,

swiftly pumping another shell into place and bring-
ing the shotgun back to his shoulder with one smooth
move.

The shooter yelled and ducked, and the driver hit
the gas. The car fishtailed in the parking lot, the rear
bumper catching a customer's car.

The shotgun boomed again, right over Lizette's
head. A steady stream of inventive cursing was turning the air blue. *You go, buddy! Blast their asses!*

Her ears were ringing from the gunfire. No, wait—
sirens, maybe. She couldn't really tell.

The black car peeled out of the parking lot into the
street, nearly taking out a couple of oncoming cars.
Tires screamed as hapless drivers swerved, caught up
in the unfolding drama and unable to do a damn
thing about it.

Not her problem.

Lizette jumped up and grabbed her purse, which
had come off her shoulder when she was rolling around
trying not to get shot, and bolted for her car. Everyone
would be expected to stick around to give statements
to the investigators, but she wasn't about to. She hoped
the shotgun guy didn't get in trouble because she'd
chosen his place to get a barbecue sandwich.

Not her problem.

She had to get out of here.

She was almost to her car, keys in hand, when she
froze in mid-step. The car—she'd have to leave it behind. She couldn't take the risk of staying with it.
They'd found her, not once, but . . . how many times?
The grocery store, that same car she kept seeing in
her rearview mirror before dismissing it to her imagination, those times she just felt as if she were being

watched. They knew what she drove, what her tag number was—hell, maybe even had a tracker on it. She needed another car.

She spotted a new customer pulling in, not knowing what was going on, other than that he'd just missed being in an accident when the traffic in front of him had almost creamed a car leaving the parking lot. She raced toward him as he opened his car door and stepped out, then hesitated, finally noticing the chaos in front of the restaurant.

"What's going on?" he called to her, his tone anxious. He didn't feel threatened by her; most men didn't feel threatened by a woman.

"There was a shooting," she said as she got closer. She made her voice breathless, panting. She assessed his car. A Chrysler, silver-gray like hers, probably a V-6.

"What? Was someone killed?" He stepped back, looking as if he might get back in his car.

"I don't think so." She slowed, looked back over her shoulder. There was a crowd around the wounded man. The shotgun-toting man—manager, owner, whatever he was—was staring down the street as if waiting for the black car to return.

"You're not leaving before the cops get here, are you?" he said, frowning at her. "Everyone should stay. I didn't see anything, but . . . hey, are you all right?"

There was no time to do this easy, no way to talk her way into that car.

"Sorry," she said sincerely, and punched him in the throat—not hard enough to kill, but hard enough to send him to his knees, keys dropping, hands going to

his throat as he gasped for breath. She grabbed the
keys from the pavement and rolled him to the side,
then slid into the driver's seat and started the engine,
all in one smooth motion.

She did take care not to run him over as she backed
up into the aisle, thinking in one part of her brain
that it didn't do her a damn bit of good to park poised
for a quick getaway if she ended up leaving her car
behind and stealing one that wasn't properly situated.

"Sorry," she said again, glancing in the rearview
mirror to watch the man struggle to his feet. He'd be
fine. She could have kicked him in the balls, but he
hadn't done anything wrong so she'd chosen the only
other option she'd been sure would work. How she
knew that . . . how she'd known to precisely pull the
punch so the man would go down without a fight but
not suffer permanent damage . . . not a clue.

She couldn't keep this car for very long. The police
were already on their way, would be here in minutes,
if not seconds, and now they had not only a supposed
drive-by shooting but a car theft to investigate. She
had to assume the police would enter the parking lot
from the main road, so she circled around the building and took a back exit, searching her mind for the
best route.

Best for what? Escape. Freedom. Survival.

And then she saw them, the shooters in the black
car, circling back as if they intended to have a second
chance at her before the cops got there.

And they saw her.

Lizette hit the gas and took the first side street she
reached. Coming straight at her, she could see flash-

ing blue lights. *Great.* She was driving her stolen car right toward the police.

She had the fleeting thought that maybe if she flagged down the cops—no, that might save her for a little while, but she'd end up in the pokey for at least a while, because she'd just punched a guy and stolen his car. She wouldn't be safe there; she'd be trapped.

At least the cops weren't actively looking for her yet.

Maybe. Cell phones and radios were faster than any car.

From that second on, Lizzy stopped thinking and acted on instinct. There was a moment of terror as she gunned the engine and bulled into traffic, much the way the black car had earlier. Tires squealed, horns blared at her. A white pickup truck came within a hair of T-boning her. A woman in the car right beside the truck took her hands off the steering wheel and covered her eyes, which wasn't the most helpful thing she could have done. Thank goodness she also hit the brakes.

Anxiously, Lizzy glanced in the rearview mirror. Damn it, it was set for the much taller owner. She reached up, adjusted it, then moved the seat closer to the steering wheel because she could barely reach the gas pedal. Was the black car following? At the moment she couldn't spot it, but that didn't mean it wasn't there, just that it could be blocked by vehicles between them. Would they risk it, with the cops so close? Maybe, maybe not. How bad did they want her dead? How pissed were they that she wasn't in a car they could conveniently track even if she did get lucky enough to shake them for a little while?

Lucky, hell. At least she could drive. She'd realized that the day she'd evaded the man from the grocery store parking lot, and again last night, when she'd found joy in speeding along the interstate. If she shook them now, they'd have no way of finding her.

Then what?

She was running for her life; one wrong turn, one miscalculation, and she was dead. At this speed she'd probably take someone with her, maybe several someones. She didn't want that, didn't want to hurt anyone, but she had to escape.

There it was, the black car, weaving in and out of traffic the same way she was, though more recklessly. One car they met ran off the road, dust flying.

This wasn't going to last. By now the cops had a description of the car she was driving, and they could call ahead. They had resources: spikes, a roadblock, helicopters. She hadn't just carjacked the guy, she was involved in a shooting, and they'd be looking hard for her as well as for the guys in the black car. Once they had overhead eyes on her she was sunk.

Traffic began to clear, making way for her and for the black car.

"So much for making it look random," she muttered. "Chase me through the outskirts of the city and run me off the road or shoot me after this . . . no way everyone won't know you executed me. No way." Execution? Yes, that's what this was meant to be. She didn't know who she was talking to, but whoever it was, she was definitely pissed at them.

She took the next ramp that would dump her on the interstate, two wheels all but leaving the pavement as she made the sharp turn. She was heading into Virginia again. Only a few minutes had passed since she'd peeled out of the parking lot in a stolen car, and she didn't have much time. *No helicopters, please, not yet.*

The black car followed her onto the interstate. Their engine was more powerful than hers—which was definitely a V-6, damn its puny little cylinders—and they had no trouble gaining on her. Her foot was pressed to the floor, and they were still gaining. She watched the rearview, gripping the wheel, judging the moment. *Closer, closer.* The car was coming up beside her, on her left. They were flying down the interstate at over a hundred miles an hour, side by side, the V-6 steady but not giving her a lot of extra power. The man in the passenger seat, hood pushed back down, aimed a black handgun out the open window at her.

She slammed on the brakes, yanked the steering wheel sharply to the side, and spun so she was facing the wrong way on four lanes of interstate. Oh, shit! Nice move. Where the hell had she learned to do that? The black car was stopping, too, but now flashing lights in the distance signaled that cops were on the way.

"Fuck!" she said violently, her vision blurring at all the traffic coming toward her, and she hit the gas. A hundred miles an hour on the interstate was scary. *Any* speed going the wrong way on the interstate was enough to give even the most hard-core adrenaline junkie a high.

She left the roadway much faster than she wanted to be going, but she had to get off the road or have a head-on with a semi. She sailed off the shoulder, the car taking to the air for a moment before landing on the gently sloping grassy hill and heading for a stand of trees. Shit! Tree, car—the tree always won. She'd really hate to get away from the bad guys and basically kill herself by driving into a fucking tree.

She'd said "fuck."

For one little frozen-in-time moment, that struck her as the most unlikely thing she'd done in the past terror-filled fifteen minutes.

She spun the steering wheel, eased off the gas, and slid the car to a hard, jarring stop that rattled her teeth. The passenger side crumpled against a tree.

Then she bailed. She grabbed her purse and ran, sprinting away from the interstate. The sirens were still at a distance, but it wasn't as if she could hide the car. Her tracks were plain in the grass, not to mention the traffic was horribly snarled directly behind her, and, oh yeah, here was a wrecked car.

Would they have a good description of her, what she looked like, what she was wearing? Most eyewitnesses gave god-awful accounts, completely missing hair color, miscalculating how tall someone was, how old, but the guy with the shotgun had struck her as a man with a good head on his shoulders and sharp eyes in that head. There was no way to know, and no time to worry about it. She needed to put distance between her and this whole situation.

As she raced across the ankle-high grass, she remembered that she hadn't taken the time to wipe her prints from the car. But—what difference did that make? Whoever was trying to kill her knew damn well who she was, and if her prints were on file somewhere . . . well, who was she kidding? Of course her prints were on file somewhere. The big question was whether or not they were in the AFIS files that cops accessed, or some other kind of file.

Given the locale and general topography, she couldn't expect to remain undetected for very long. The trees thinned, giving way to asphalt and a playground that had seen better days and a street lined with apartment buildings. There were a number of people out and about, in the park and nearby. They probably saw joggers all the time, but how often did they see a jogger wearing office attire and carrying a purse? In the distance, even over her own heavy breathing, she could hear the whap-whap of a helicopter, probably a news crew but possibly a police helicopter. Other people heard the same thing, shading their eyes against the hot sun as they looked up. A plane could drone overhead without anyone so much as glancing up, but helicopters always got people's attention.

Whoever was in the helicopter, reporter or cops, would be looking for someone who was running, so that someone couldn't be her. She stopped, clutched her purse tight, and looked up, shading her eyes with one hand as she mirrored what other people were doing. There were several women in the park, many of them with children. If she just didn't run, she'd look like everyone else.

Hide in plain sight.

Lizzy stood in place and looked up. She wondered if anyone on the street would mark her as a stranger, if they would notice she'd been running when she arrived, that she was breathing hard and that her cheeks were red. But there were a lot of apartments on this street, and there was no way anyone would notice someone who didn't belong, the way Madison—the much-too-savvy child who'd helped Lizzy deface her own car—had noticed in that little complex. God, that seemed so long ago, and it had just been . . . three days?

The helicopter was flying low, banking over the interstate where, Lizzy knew, the traffic was a snarled nightmare. From here, though, no one could see the highway or how backed up the traffic was.

One man asked, his question directed to no one in particular, "What's going on?"

No one seemed to know. The helicopter turned, heading back the way it had come. Lizette looked at the woman next to her, shrugged, and walked away as if she knew exactly where she was going.

Hah. The truth was, she had no idea beyond her next step.

Chapter Seventeen

Xavier grabbed some much-needed sleep in the safe room in "J. P. Halston's" condo, tilted back in his chair, his booted feet propped on the desk. He could have slept in his own bed, but being where people could find him—and by that he meant not his own people—struck him as a little risky right now.

An instant message had alerted him about the confrontation Lizzy had had with the surveillance dumb shit. God, that was such typical Lizzy, slick and ballsy.

But none of the others knew Lizzy the way he did. The way she was playing it, there were still reasonable explanations for everything. She was keeping them guessing, and his people were watching and would let him know if anything unusual happened. He already knew Felice had met with Al again very early that morning, and he also knew that, after Lizzy's confrontation with her surveillance, whoever Felice had hired to do the job had been pulled off.

That would be the smart thing to do, not push Lizzy, let her settle back into her routine. The biggest question was, did Felice know how *not* to push? She had too much confidence in her own cleverness, which meant she was constantly underestimating what other people could and would do to fuck up her plans and schemes. In her world, all she had to do was give orders, and she expected them to be followed. In the real world, people disobeyed orders all the time. If it wasn't in their own best interests, people could be amazingly uncooperative.

So she would be shitting bricks that Lizzy had blown the surveillance put on her. Al would be . . . God only knew. Predicting what Al would do at any given time wasn't easy, which was why he was so good at what he did.

Felice was completely predictable. Al was the opposite. So why did he trust Al the most?

Because Al had been through a lot of the same experiences that he himself had dealt with, that was why. Al knew what it was to take live fire, and to return it. Al knew what it was like to kill someone. What they did was real to him, not an abstraction. Five years ago, they had all become involved in a bad situation; four years ago, the bad situation had devolved into a nightmare. How they'd handled it was something that kept them all tied in an uneasy alliance.

They all had to live with what they'd done. All except Lizzy. She'd been the outsider, the one deemed untrustworthy. Considering she'd been at ground zero of the plan Xavier didn't see how she could be untrustworthy, but he had to admit she'd had a hard time dealing with it afterward, and that was what had tipped the scale against her. She'd been a mess, withdrawn, crying a lot. The solution had been a bullet in the head or undergoing the process. Lizzy had chosen the process. Yeah, some choice. Lose her life, or lose herself.

He himself hadn't had a choice, not at the time. Either way, he lost Lizzy, and he'd been damn pissed about it.

But he was nothing if not tactically aware, so even though he hadn't been able to stop that snowball from rolling downhill, from the beginning he'd been working on his trip wires. By the time Felice noticed he wasn't falling in line like a good little soldier and was ready to turn on him too, she'd found out that if he went down, so did she, along with everyone else who'd been in the group.

Originally there had been eight of them. Two of them were now dead. One had died a natural death; the second one had been helped along. Xavier knew, because he was the one who'd done the helping.

Himself. Lizzy. Al. Felice. Charlie Dankins. Adam Heyes. They were the perpetrators, and the survivors. Charlie and Adam had both retired, gotten on with their lives, secure in the knowledge that they'd done the right thing and content to let Felice and Al handle any situations that might crop up in the future.

Xavier could have done the same thing . . . except for Lizzy. He had kept watch over her since she'd been installed in her new life, all her fire and spontaneity destroyed—or so they'd thought. Thank God the others had been so convinced of the success of the process, and thank God they'd been so wrong.

He'd given up hope, accepted that the chemical brainwash had been permanent, that his Lizzy was gone forever and only that dull shadow of her remained. Al and Felice would have been equally as confident that nothing would change. Then she'd gotten sick, and the Winchell woman had dropped that verbal clue that things in the world weren't as the incurious, routine-bound Lizette thought they were.

No—*wait*. Damn, he should have seen it before. The vomiting. The severe headache. That hadn't been a virus; that had been her brain beginning its recovery, fighting through and around the memory-wipe process. *That* was why she hadn't reacted at all to Winchell's comment: she'd already been aware something was going on. And at the first feasible opportunity, she'd destroyed her cell phone.

She probably didn't remember everything; she might never get all of it back. But her basic personality was reasserting itself, which meant the process was breaking down. That was a good thing to know, concerning the future applications of the process—because it *would* be used again, maybe already had been.

Al would need to know that, at some future date, but definitely not now. If they knew the process was breaking down, Lizzy wouldn't live out the morning.

But for now, everything had settled down. Lizzy was at work, none of his network of watchers was reporting anything alarming, and he was able to get some sleep.

He was awakened at noon by an alert. He swung his feet down from the desk, sat up in his chair, and studied the computer screen. Lizzy was in her car, and moving. It was lunchtime, so that wasn't unusual. Everything else was normal, too. There was some old coffee left, so he zapped it in the microwave, threw a sandwich together, and downed both as he monitored her.

The trackers showed her stopping, and the screen

gave him the address. Another screen gave him the physical picture of her location. Shit, she was at the bank again. A big alarm sounded in his head. She'd stopped at the ATM yesterday on the way home from the sporting goods store. Why was she going back to the bank less than twenty-four hours later?

Cash. She was getting more cash. She knew better than to use a credit card, would know it was instantly traceable. Not by regular cops, no, but Felice's people, Al's people, his own . . . hell, yeah.

Was she planning on running?

He sent out an alert code, eyeing the movement of Lizzy's car on the map. Now she was heading back in the direction of the office. She stopped again; he pulled up the address of a barbecue restaurant. She was picking up lunch. Okay, everything still mostly normal, except for the bank. Al's analysts might or might not catch that, because a different analyst was on duty now and he wouldn't necessarily know that she'd stopped at the ATM the evening before. The surveillance records were destroyed daily. Al got updates, and he'd sure as hell catch that anomaly *if*— big if—the analyst now on duty reported that she'd gone to the bank.

He'd just swallowed the last of the bitter coffee when all hell broke loose.

His computer screen blew up with a red-flagged message, and simultaneously his secure land line began ringing.

"Fuck!" He snarled the word as he surged out of the chair. He knew *exactly* what was happening: that fucking Felice had bypassed Al and was acting on her own. If she succeeded, if anything happened to Lizzy, he'd blow that bitch's world apart.

He answered the blaring phone as he read the message: *Attempted hit going down.*

"Are you on site?"

"Almost there. Just got the message."

Another IM came through: *Owner outside with shotgun, returning fire.*

"Did you get that?" Xavier asked. He had his Glock out and was checking the clip, slapping it back in. He couldn't sit there reading IMs when Lizzy was under fire. The coldness he always felt was settling in his veins, his stomach. If they killed her, within the hour the world would know what they'd done, but Felice's ass was his. No matter what precautions she put in place, no matter where she went, he'd get her—and he'd make her pay.

"Yeah, I'm almost there. Shooters are peeling out."

"Do you see her?" That was the most important detail, the one on which his life, and the lives of several others, hinged.

"Not yet. I'm just pulling in. Shit! There she is! She's coming straight toward me!"

She was alive. The fist squeezing his heart eased its iron grip.

The world hadn't ended.

"I'm on the way," Xavier said tersely. "Keep me updated on the secure cell." He broke the connection and went out the door.

Felice wouldn't hit only Lizzy. She was far from stupid. The big question was, would her people try to take him here at the condo, or aim for a more secluded area, such as the stretch of road a couple of miles down, which was the fastest route to where Lizzy was?

They couldn't have known where Lizzy would stop to get lunch, but the restaurant was on the way back to her office, so they might have originally planned to hit her there, but then the opportunity at the restaurant presented itself and they went for it. Setting up on his own most direct route, to get him, would be a logical move.

Felice wasn't using Al's people; he'd have known if she was. Al himself would—maybe—have prevented it. The big question was: was she using other operatives, or had she gone outside and hired civilians?

Civilians. They would know only what she told them, they wouldn't have any contacts that might trip her up, and the cost would likely be cheaper, which would make it easier to hide the money in some unrelated item.

What she would do was have eyes on him, to alert the team when he left the condo.

He had options. He could take his truck, leaving from his private garage on the first floor of the condo—or he could take "J.P.'s" car, and leave from that unit. He also had a motorcycle stored at another secure location. But those vehicles were unknown, and perhaps that wasn't what he wanted. The best option might be to drive his known, expected vehicle, draw out the team that was on him, deal with it now. That would get them out of the way and send Felice scrambling to replace them.

Moreover, driving his truck might make them think his guard was down, that he wasn't expecting a move on him. Felice would know better, and so would Al:

his guard was never down. But the men she'd hired wouldn't know, and that was to his advantage.

He spotted the eyes as soon as the garage door lifted and he drove out: a white Chevrolet Malibu, parked five or six units up, opposite side of the street. One guy.

Dumb asses. How obvious could they get? Okay, rephrase that: maybe not dumb asses, but definitely civilians. He shouldn't underestimate them, but react as if they were seasoned veterans of black operations.

Less than a mile from the condo, he picked up a tail. Not the guy in the white Malibu, but a gray truck, a Dodge. Smart move; the truck would put the shooter on the same level with him if he attempted a shot while speeding down the road, the two trucks side by side. Risky way to do something, but a possibility they should consider, and on a perverse level he appreciated that they'd covered that base.

Two men, he noted as the gray truck drew a car length closer. He didn't spot a backup, not even the guy in the white Malibu. Just two? Fuck, he felt insulted.

But now he could deal with the team on his own terms, in his own way. He swerved in and out of traffic but drove smoothly, easily, not as if he were trying to shake a tail, but as if he were in a hurry to get somewhere. They fell back, but not too far.

As luck would have it, the empty stretch of road wasn't empty; a couple of cars and a semi came barreling past, spaced just far enough apart that the gray truck couldn't pull even with him. Shit, now he had to string them out. He could easily have taken them off the road with his heavier, reinforced vehicle and handled the problem there, but now they were entering a more populated neighborhood and the chances for either of them to act had just gone down.

In the meantime, what was Lizzy doing? His secure phone had buzzed a couple of times, but he kind of had his hands full at the moment.

He hit a stretch with a long string of traffic, preventing the shooter from moving in on him, and grabbed the phone. Yeah, yeah, don't text and drive. He did what he had to do.

The texts made him laugh out loud. *"She mugged me and stole my car."*

"Cool."

His guys were the best. The muggee would take a lot of teasing over the coming months. He thumbed a reply: *"Got 2 on my ass. Will handle. Can you tail her?"*

"No can do," came back the almost instant reply.

"K. I'll pick up her signal once I handle these 2 bozos."

He put the phone down, relief coursing through him. Lizzy was not only okay, she was functioning in a way none of them had expected, not even him. She'd mugged one of *his* guys? Okay, so not one of them would lift a finger to her, but still . . . yeah, it was cool.

And he still had the two on his ass to deal with.

His favorite park for running was one that would be perfect for him now, partly because he knew every inch of it. It was the right terrain for serious runners who liked some challenge in their workouts. The lunchtime traffic was thinning, but it still took him almost ten minutes to reach the park. The last of the lunchtime runners were just finishing up their routes, and there were several places to park. The jogging trails would be most crowded early in the morning and late in the afternoon, when the weather wasn't so brutally hot, so with a little luck he shouldn't have to deal with any witnesses.

The men following him might wonder what the hell he was doing here, but what they thought didn't matter as long as they followed him. They could reasonably look at his stop at the park as a godsend, allowing them to corner him in a secluded area. He repressed a snort. Yeah, right. Dream on, buddies.

If they wanted him in a place where there were no cameras, no witnesses, their wish was about to come true.

He parked his truck near the head of the dirt trail and bolted for it, disappearing into the heavy cover as the gray truck wheeled into the parking lot.

To his left, the stand of trees thickened; limbs hung over the trail. The location he had in mind was a thickly wooded portion of the trail, where it wound back and forth in sharp curves that created blind spots, with boulders and thick bushes providing additional cover.

He plunged off the path, behind the cover of some big tree trunks, drew his weapon, and waited. The position was a good one, allowing him to see the running path as well as the most likely route if they decided to play it safe and stick to the woods beside the trail.

Best tactic was for them to do both: one coming up the trail, the other in the woods.

Right on cue, he heard footsteps pounding on the path, then slowing, moving ahead more cautiously.

Through a small break in the trees, Xavier saw a man move past. Mid-thirties, just starting to lose some hair along the temples, the guy looked like thousands of other men in the area—casual clothes, nothing threatening about him at all.

Xavier knew where that guy was. He switched his attention to the wooded area, straining to hear a rustle, a snap, the clatter of a rock. Where was the other one?

The first man moved into view, his head swiveling. Xavier stood motionless, his drab clothing blending into the background. The human eye, particularly an untrained one, saw motion more than detail. He waited, studying his prey through a tiny opening in the brush and trees, noting the noise suppressor on the weapon in the guy's right hand.

Thank you, buddy, Xavier thought as the man passed him by, and he silently stepped onto the path behind him.

He took him down with a massive punch to the back of the neck. The guy grunted as he went down, the only sound he had time to make as Xavier wrenched the suppressed weapon from his hand, pressed it to the back of his head, and fired.

The man twitched once, and that was it.

Even a suppressed shot wasn't silent; the other man on the team might have heard, depending on how far away he was. Xavier assumed he'd be close; otherwise they were piss-poor tacticians. Likely he'd think the shot came from his partner's weapon—which actually it had—but he had no way of knowing whether or not Xavier's weapon was also sound-suppressed. Only a complete idiot would yell, "Did you get him?"

and these guys weren't idiots. Too inexperienced to be playing this game with him, but not idiots.

Xavier stepped back into the woods, quickly, cautiously, surveying the area in all directions, waiting—

A bullet smacked into the tree six inches from his head.

Xavier dropped down and rolled away, lifting his own weapon and searching the shaded, wooded area for movement, for a breath that wasn't as quiet and controlled as it should be.

Nothing.

Could be the man on the path had been designated as expendable from the beginning, and the shooter in the woods had used his partner to flush Xavier out.

Not bad, he thought. Wouldn't work, but not bad.

Shooter number two couldn't be far away. Xavier hunkered down, breathing slow and easy. He could outwait this guy, but he had things to do and he was getting impatient. Maybe the oldest tactic in the world would work. Moving silently, taking care he was completely hidden, he picked up a small rock and tossed it to the left. It didn't make a big noise, but he hadn't wanted it to. Instead it was the kind of soft sound a slip of the foot might make.

A shot fired; he saw the flash, and then he heard the shooter step forward, one almost-silent step in the dirt and fallen leaves. It was enough.

Xavier fired twice, and the second guy crashed to the ground. Not taking any chances, staying low, he moved toward the fallen man, eyes on his target.

The guy wasn't dead. Soon, but not yet. When he saw Xavier, he tried feebly to lift his weapon.

Xavier stomped his boot down on the guy's wrist,

then put a bullet between his eyes. It took only a moment to return to the path and drag the first shooter's body into the woods before the hue and cry was raised and Felice knew her team had failed. The time it might buy him could be critical. He scraped his boot along the disturbed dirt on the path, wiped his prints off the weapon, and stuck it back in guy number one's hand. That might entertain the detectives a little bit, especially if the weapon could be traced back to the dead man.

He went back to his truck. Just in case anyone had seen it and connected it to the two dead men in the woods—he didn't see how, but people did strange shit, like take pictures of vehicles with their cell phones—he'd need to stow the truck in a secure location other than his condo and use a different vehicle for a while.

As he left the parking lot, he used his cell phone to pull up the program that would tell him exactly where Lizzy was.

Chapter Eighteen

Instead of working her way out of the city, Lizzy worked her way in. D.C. was a big, crowded city teeming with people: tourists, politicians, everyday residents living their lives. She could blend in if she had to. There was abundant public transportation, especially in the heart of the city, but there was no way she could risk the Metro. There were too many cameras, and too few exits if she was cornered.

Thank goodness she had some cash. Her paranoia—which had not been paranoia at all, as it turned out—had served her well.

She strode down the sidewalk as if she knew where she was going. Her mind churned. What the hell good were all her supplies, when she'd left them at home? Damn it, she should have put everything in the backpack and thrown it in her car. Yeah, she'd had to dump her car, but . . . oh, hell, she was second-guessing herself. Would she have had the opportunity to swing by her car, grab the backpack, and take off again? As things had played out, no. She'd screwed up. She should have taken the backpack into the restaurant with her. A lot of people used backpacks in the city; she wouldn't have stood out.

But now those things were as lost to her as if they

were locked in a vault somewhere, and she'd wasted the money buying them. She didn't dare go home. If the bad guys didn't get her there, the police would. She was a car thief, and, oh, yeah, she'd also committed assault while stealing the guy's car, so she was pretty sure that had moved her into a whole different category of criminal. She wasn't just a thief, she was a dangerous thief. Yeah, home was pretty much out of the question.

Which begged the question: were *they* the bad guys, or was she? If she couldn't remember, how was she to know? She might have done something really horrible in the past. After all, she seemed to be pretty good at evasive driving, and she was drawn to hunting knives and guns and pepper spray. Why?

She waited for the question to trigger a headache, but nothing happened.

No, she had to be logical about this. They had obviously known exactly how to find her. If she was such a bad guy, why wouldn't they have done something before now?

Instead they'd waited, and watched. Nothing had happened until she'd started remembering. Despite her best efforts to act normal, she'd done things out of the ordinary, such as ditching the people following her, destroying her cell phone and not turning on the replacement, and oh yeah, let's not forget the surprise trip into Virginia. To anyone on the alert for such clues, she'd practically taken out a billboard.

Hindsight was so crystal clear, which did her a hell of a lot of good. She should have done *nothing* for several days, maybe even a week or so. Crap.

Moaning about it didn't do her a damn bit of good.

She needed to figure out what she should do now, under the circumstances as they were rather than what she wished they were.

Her first instinct was to run, to get as far away from the area as possible, but wouldn't they be expecting that? Good guys or bad guys, they would be expecting her to run.

She needed time to think, time to get her bearings and come up with a plan.

The woman she'd become, the boring, predictable woman whose face she didn't recognize as her own, would be in a panic now. But the woman she'd been before, the woman who was trying to come through, *that* woman wouldn't panic. She knew the value of control, calm . . . a plan.

She felt as if she were divided into two people: Lizette who never did anything, and . . . who? Who was she, really?

Lizzy.

The name sounded in her mind like an echo from far away, so faint she could barely hear it. Instantly pain shot through her head, but it faded almost before she could begin focusing on something else.

Did this mean . . . hell, she had no idea what this could mean. She remembered her parents sometimes calling her Lizzy, so that wasn't exactly a missing memory. In college she'd been Liz, but . . . somewhere along the way she'd morphed into Lizzy, so had she somewhere along the way morphed back into Lizette? Why couldn't she remember exactly when?

Because it had been something gradual, something that had just happened, rather than an event. "Lizzy" felt right, though. "Lizette" now felt like a shoe that pinched. Too bad the two were still at war; she knew she needed to do something, but *what*?

Follow your instincts. They've gotten you this far.

She was a target; she knew that. She didn't know who was after her, or why, but she knew she had to find a way to hide. There would be no going home, no calls to friends, no retrieving her car. She'd never go to work again, never walk or jog around that familiar block. Whoever was after her knew what she looked like, but at the moment they didn't know where she was. How long before that changed?

On instinct, she swerved into the next drugstore she passed. She smiled at the cashier near the front door, grabbed a basket, and started shopping. Hair dye? No. Her hair was brown, a common color. Hair that was obviously dyed would stand out, and they might be on the lookout for that, they might expect her to go blond or red. Instead she bought hairpins, so she could pin her hair up. That would disguise the length and style, and was preferable to a bad haircut accomplished with a pair of scissors in front of a hotel room mirror.

Scissors might come in handy, though. She selected a good, sturdy pair and put them in the basket. Scissors weren't as good as the knife she'd left behind, but were better than nothing. The drugstore didn't stock hunting knives or pepper spray, damn it.

She also got a hat with a wide brim, which would come in handy not only in hiding her face, but in protecting her from the heat of the summer sun. She bought an oversized tee shirt, cheap tennis shoes, and socks. The store didn't stock any pants, but thank goodness she'd worn pants to work that morning instead of a skirt. They would suffice until she could do more shopping. She also tossed a cheap, oversized purse into her basket, along with some travel-sized toiletries and a pair of too-big sunglasses.

They—whoever the hell they might be—were looking for a frightened middle-class businesswoman on the run. That meant she had to be someone else.

She could do that, she thought with an unusual surge of confidence. She could be someone else.

She'd done it before.

Because he knew where Lizzy was, thanks to the trackers in her wallet and cell phone, Xavier didn't rush to intercept her. She was okay, for now; she'd be scared and confused, but given the evidence that she was regaining her memory, likely not as much as an ordinary citizen would be. She'd given Felice's men the slip, and been smart enough to abandon her car, so now they had no way of tracking her. She hadn't been hurt, and she'd acted decisively. Giving her time to settle down some seemed like a good idea. He'd never hear the end of it if she managed to take him down, too—and she had, in the past; not often, but he knew better than to let his guard down around her.

He had to dump his truck and secure other transportation, and that took time. J.P.'s car was out, because Felice's people would pick him up again when he went back to the condo. He might get away with leaving from J.P.'s garage instead of his regular unit, but why take the chance when he could get to the motorcycle in the same length of time? On the motorcycle, he could go faster and get into tighter places, be completely anonymous, and the helmet would prevent any facial recognition program from nailing him.

If he knew Felice, the failure of her assassination teams—both of them—would make her double down in her efforts. Whether or not Al had been in on it was debatable; probably not, or outside teams wouldn't have been used, but with Al it was always best not to assume you knew what he'd do in any given situation. Briefly he thought about calling Al, but in the end decided the call would be a waste of time. Even if Al wasn't in on the attempts, by now he'd know about them, and what he did from here on out was his call. Whether he was teaming with Felice or not, what he'd say to Xavier would be the same thing in both instances, therefore nothing was to be gained. In any case, Xavier would rather let them worry about the complete lack of contact from him. Felice would be scurrying to beef up her protection, and her daughter's protection, which would pull some of her resources away from actually locating Lizzy. Good enough. Felice would pay, but not right now. Lizzy was his current priority. He'd get to Felice in his own time.

He checked Lizzy's location again; she'd been steadily working her way toward downtown, but she'd finally stopped. He tapped a key, zoomed in on her location. Drugstore.

A big drugstore was kind of like a department store these days. She could pick up any number of items that she'd need, such as a change of clothes, sunglasses, maybe not any kitchen knives but there would definitely be scissors, nail files, things like that. She might change her hair color. There were a lot of possibilities, and he'd taught her most of them, though she'd probably come up with a new wrinkle on her own. Being on the run was tiring; not the physical effort so much as the state of hyper-alertness, watching everyone around you, gauging every move, seeing everything as a potential threat. He himself could go for days, with a little chemical help, but Lizzy was out of practice. She was going to wear out soon, and find a place to go to ground. He watched the two blinking dots that marked her location.

She was on the move again. He'd get his motorcycle, do some reconnoitering on his own to get a solid sense of what Felice was doing; then he'd go to Lizzy.

She couldn't very well stop and change her appearance in the middle of the street, but she did put on the wide-brimmed hat and sunglasses. That would help to hide her face from any cameras she walked past. She was tired, but she had to keep moving. Her legs ached; she'd worked up a sweat, and the adrenaline burn had disappeared, leaving her feeling limp and wrung out. She wanted nothing more than to find a place to sleep.

Buck up, girl. This is no time to be weak. She had to keep her wits, not let her exhaustion lead her to take shortcuts that could leave her vulnerable.

But she did need somewhere to stay, so she focused on her situation. There were a lot of hotels near the tourist attractions, but none that would rent her a room without ID and a credit card. She needed a place that would rent her a room for cash. No hotel would go for that, unless . . .

Unless she found a place with an impressionable or bribable desk clerk. It would have to be a small place, not the best hotel in town—not even a moderately decent hotel. She needed to find a one-star or no-star hotel that was independently owned, desperate for business. She walked some more, until the area she found herself in was not exactly nice—but not exactly the pits, either. This little cluster of less-than-magnificent motels was maybe five miles from the Mall.

Though she was so tired she was almost stumbling, she still made herself walk around the motels, examining the layout of the rooms, the parking lots, the points of access and egress. None of the places was perfect, but an older, redbrick establishment met most of her requirements. Number one, there weren't many cars in the parking lot, so they might be amenable to trading cash for discretion. The rooms all opened up to the parking lot; she didn't want to be stuck in a room with nothing but a narrow hallway beyond her door. And the fact that the place was old meant there were actual windows in the bathrooms. The windows were high and small enough that she'd have trouble fitting through, if it came to that, but if things were desperate enough that she needed to go out the window, she'd do it if she had to strip off and slick shampoo all over herself to squeeze through.

Something else in the motel's favor: it was here. She was tired, she was hungry, and her arms ached from carrying the drugstore shopping bag. It hadn't seemed all that heavy at first, but the weight was wearing on her. And the longer she was out in the open looking like, well—herself—the more danger she was in.

She looked in the office window. The desk clerk was a young woman, thank goodness. A woman was more likely to empathize with a hard-luck story, and she wouldn't expect a blow job in return for a favor. The clerk looked bored and impressionable. Both factors would play in Lizzy's favor.

She opened the door and took off her hat, heaving a little sigh as she approached the desk.

"May I help you?" the clerk asked, her face brightening at the prospect of an actual customer.

"Yes, I'd like a room. Ground floor, if you have it." Given the small number of cars in the parking lot, a ground-floor room should be available.

The clerk—her name tag read Cindy—smiled and tapped her computer keys. "How many nights will you be with us?"

This was where it would get tricky. "Just one."

"Great! I'll just need your driver's license and a credit card."

Lizzy bit her bottom lip. Her picture might have been shown on TV by now. Maybe not. Would they bother with breaking news for a stolen car and a car chase? Would they show her driver's license picture? Had she even been identified yet? Fortunately there was no television in the tiny lobby, and even if there had been, Cindy didn't look as if she'd care much about the news. Soap operas, maybe, or reruns of game shows.

"Cash," she replied, digging for her wallet. "I don't have a credit card."

Cindy paused, wrinkled her nose. "The owner says

there has to be a credit card on record, in case of damages to the room."

Lizzy paused, as if considering the problem rather than dismissing it. "I can give you an extra deposit," she finally said. She didn't want to spend more money than necessary, so she said, "Twenty dollars? Thirty? When I check out in the morning you could inspect the room and give the deposit back, so I'm okay with doing that." Meaning she didn't intend to be doing anything that could possibly damage anything in the old building.

"Well . . . that might be all right. I'll just need your driver's license."

This was the really tricky part. Lizzy tensed and put an anxious expression on her face. "I—uh—I'd really like to not have my name on the record."

Cindy immediately shook her head and sighed. "We don't do that. Sorry."

Lizzy let her lower lip tremble. "I understand. I just . . . it's my husband. I can't let him find me. I have a way out of town, and once I'm away from D.C. I think I'll be safe, but . . . but that won't happen until tomorrow."

Cindy's blue eyes got big. "Husband?"

Lizzy nodded. She let her real fear and anxiety show through.

"You could call the cops . . ."

She gave a bitter laugh. "He's a city politician. He knows . . . too many people. I can't trust the police." And wasn't that the truth, she thought wryly.

Cindy looked at her computer, pursed her lips, and sighed again. Lizzy was already wondering where she could try next—she couldn't go much farther—when the woman said, "Maybe . . . 107 isn't rentable right now because the last person who stayed there punched a hole in the wall and pulled the towel rack right out of the wall, and the damages haven't been repaired yet. I could put you there, for one night. Just one," she repeated, shaking a finger for emphasis.

"Oh, God, that'd be great! Thank you!" Lizzy said fervently, opening her wallet and taking care to keep it turned so Cindy couldn't see the credit cards in their slots. Before she could pull out any cash, though, Cindy said, "Nah, keep it."

Lizzy raised her eyebrows slightly as she looked across the counter.

"My mom's second husband was a real asshole. I get it."

It was a symptom of her fatigue that her eyes burned with tears at the young woman's kindness. In spite of that, she pulled out a hundred-dollar bill and pushed it across the counter. She didn't trust loyalty she hadn't bought, didn't want to owe anyone anything. "Thanks, but take it." She wiped her eyes and managed a weak smile. "It's his money, anyway. I'd like to spread it around while I can."

Cindy shrugged and took the hundred. It would probably go into her own pocket, which was okay; her job likely paid minimum wage, and every buck counted. She slid a key card across to Lizzy, who slipped it into her pocket as she gave the clerk another thank-you smile and headed out the door.

She was nowhere near home free, but she had a place to spend the night, and that was more than she'd had five minutes ago.

* * *

Anger wasn't a new emotion for Felice, but control was essential in her job and it had been a very long time since she'd allowed herself to show much emotion at all. Normally that wasn't a problem; right now, though, her temper was so white hot and intense she could barely contain herself, and it kept bubbling dangerously close to the surface. She had to appear as if nothing had gone wrong; she had to smile at her secretary as she walked out of her office—it was always a tight smile, but a smile nonetheless—and nod to the guard at the gate as she drove out of the parking lot. She ignored everyone in between.

Son of a bitch! How could something so simple go so wrong? All she'd gotten was an innocuous text on her burner cell: *The project failed*. She didn't get the details, and that was what she needed to know asap. She couldn't think everything had gone wrong, so what portion of it had failed? Lizette would have been the easy part; the odds were the team put on Xavier had failed, and getting him had been the most important task. She'd strongly emphasized that, requested very good people. Now, if the worst-case scenario had come true, a very angry Xavier was on the loose and hunting.

It struck her how vulnerable she was right now, driving home alone, unprotected. She had defensive driving skills, but her handgun was at home. Her normal job didn't require firearms. Even if she had it with her now, if Xavier came after her, her only chance of survival would be sheer luck. Felice didn't trust luck. She trusted control, meticulous planning, and preparation.

She gripped the steering wheel so tightly her knuckles turned white. It took every ounce of self-control she possessed to stick to the speed limit. She needed to get home as fast as possible, but a delay if she got stopped for speeding would cost her more time than this relatively slow speed. She needed to make a call, and she didn't dare do so if there was even the most remote chance that anyone would overhear. Her home, office, and car were swept often for bugs, but she wasn't foolish enough to believe that she could speak freely anywhere in this town, especially now.

She'd been pleased with the planning and preparation. The plan had evidently fallen apart in execution, though. Damn it! She'd been assured that only top-notch people would be used. Evidently, instead of the A-Team, she'd gotten the B-Team—and "B" stood for "Bozos."

Despite her tension, she reached home without incident. Still, the tight feeling between her shoulder blades didn't ease until she had parked in the garage and lowered the door. Even then, she carefully examined every corner of the garage before she got out of the car. She knew what Xavier was capable of, and she didn't take anything for granted. When she unlocked the door and entered, the alarm system began its warning beep; she punched in the code, relocked the door, then went straight to the den and got her weapon from the desk drawer. She checked every room in the house before she dared let her guard down. Until this was over, she'd have to be very careful.

Then she retrieved the burner cell phone from her purse. She'd have to get a new one; they were intended for one-time use—hence the term "burner," though of course sloppy people disobeyed that protocol all the time. She'd never thought she would be one of those people, but she didn't have time to get a new phone and she needed to know exactly what had happened.

She took both the gun and the phone into her bathroom. She turned on the water in the whirlpool tub, then flipped the switch that activated the modern rock-and-water feature in the corner. Normally the sound of the rushing water was very soothing to her, but now she didn't notice it other than as a means to an end. When the tub was full enough, she turned on the whirlpool motor. She stood between the tub and the waterfall; anyone who was trying to listen in would have a hell of a time trying to make out words over the white noise.

She made the call. When her contact answered she said tersely, "What happened?"

There was a short pause. Maybe he was trying to come up with some reasonable excuse for his failure, but in the end he said simply, "Both projects failed."

Felice was stunned. "Both?" Good God, how could that happen? Xavier was a difficult proposition at any time, but the other should have been a cakewalk. This was worse than the worst-case scenario. "How is that possible, unless your people are completely incompetent?"

"The attempt was at a restaurant. The owner decided to play hero with a shotgun. My men got away, but they missed the target."

"You colossal fuckup." She was so angry she could barely speak. She seldom resorted to vulgarity, but she was the one who could pay a very large price for this man's failure. He could shrug and move on to other clients, while she was left to deal with a catastrophe.

"The shotgun wasn't expected. Things happen."

"I expect your men to do as they're instructed." Lizette should be dead. For God's sake, she was barely human! Okay, that was an exaggeration. But you couldn't wipe away a portion of someone's memories and a chunk of her basic makeup and expect her to continue to function at her previous level. Getting to her should have been child's play. "Tell me they picked her up again."

"Not yet. She stole a car in the parking lot and got away."

"So she isn't in her own car now?" Felice pinched the bridge of her nose. "That doesn't make sense. Her car was right there; why steal another one?"

"I can't say, unless she was so panicked she wasn't thinking."

"In which case she'd return for her car when she calmed down. Has that happened?"

"No, her car is still sitting at the restaurant."

Felice looked at the ceiling as she pulled in a deep breath. She'd been right all along, then. The little things out of the ordinary that Lizette had been doing were because, against all odds, she was recovering her memory. It wasn't supposed to be possible—but they all did things every day that a hundred years ago would have been considered impossible. Even Al wouldn't be able to explain away leaving a perfectly good car behind and stealing another one.

"There's more bad news," continued the deep voice at the other end of the call.

"I suspected as much." Her voice was tight.

"The team I sent after the other target were both found dead in a park a little more than an hour ago."

Even though she'd been expecting that, she still felt as if the ground dropped out from under her. She put a hand on the bathroom vanity for support. "I didn't hear anything about bodies being found this afternoon." And she would. The NSA heard everything.

"You wouldn't. We tracked their car when they didn't check in, found the bodies, and cleaned it up."

"And the target?"

"He didn't go home. We haven't picked him up yet, but we will."

Scenes from *The Terminator* flashed before her eyes. Xavier would be like the robot; he would keep on coming no matter what they did, killing everyone who got in his way. That was the downside to providing intense, advanced training to people like him; it was great when he was on your side, but if he ever turned on you—

She had a panic room; she'd installed one five years ago. But she couldn't live there forever, and what about her daughter? This could continue for some time, if Xavier was on the run. Besides, it wasn't in her nature to hide from trouble. She had to handle this; she had to come up with a plan to finish the mission. Felice grabbed onto her rioting emotions and tamped down the fear she couldn't afford to wallow in.

"My daughter, Ashley—I want her picked up and secured."

"If she objects?"

"She can object all she wants; I want her under lock and key until this is done." Ashley wouldn't like it, and she was definitely her mother's daughter, Felice thought; she would carry a grudge for a long time. But she'd take having her daughter angry at her over having to bury her only child any day of the week, without hesitation. Xavier was ruthless. If he couldn't get to her any other way, he would use her daughter against her. Anything was possible: kidnapping, torture, murder. If the situation were reversed, Felice had no doubt that she'd do whatever was necessary. And if she herself would do it, she had to assume Xavier would go to the same lengths.

She would protect her child at all costs.

The cost would be high. Ashley was independent, or trying to be, and she wouldn't like being hidden away, missing out on the two summer classes she'd been taking, removed from her friends and all their social activities.

Tough shit. Ashley's safety was more important than anything else in this world.

"I gave you two assignments, one easy and one admittedly not so easy. You assured me both would be handled, and instead your people have been completely incompetent. The situation is royally screwed up. How are you going to fix this?"

"I have someone in mind," her contact said. He didn't even sound urgent. Perhaps he was accustomed to jobs going wrong, which wasn't a good thing. On the other hand, he did have an impeccable reputation. "If you want to pay the money to get him, he's a real badass, a specialist in his field. He isn't required often, but in special circumstances he's . . . invaluable."

Felice didn't ask how much money he was talking about, because at this point it was immaterial. And if this badass guy was the best, why hadn't he been employed to do the job in the first place? Deeply annoyed, she snapped, "I don't care how you get it done, just do it." She wouldn't be safe, her daughter wouldn't be safe, until Xavier was dead. And none of them would be safe until Lizette was in the ground. She should have been put there years ago.

"Yes, ma'am. I'll get him on the hunt."

"Call me when my daughter is secured." She ended the call and stood there in deep thought for a moment, mentally running through scenarios and possibilities. One in particular stood out: if she had to get her hands dirty and take care of matters herself, she was starting with him—and she had no doubt that he was well aware of that fact.

Chapter Nineteen

Room 107 hadn't been occupied in a while. In addition to the hole in the wall and a catty-wampus towel rack, the room was musty-smelling and dusty, which told her the small hotel had a problem with cash flow. A hideous gold and orange bedspread covered the single bed, and—she noted, pulling a corner of the spread back—there were no sheets. Lucky for her, there was one forgotten towel in the bathroom.

"Great," she muttered. "I'm not completely shit out of luck."

Priorities. She was starving. Lizzy grabbed some ones from her wallet, along with the loose change from the drugstore, and headed for the vending machines three rooms down. Key to her room in one hand, money in the other, hat and sunglasses on, she strode to the lineup of machines. Junk food wasn't what she'd had in mind for supper, but since she'd never gotten to the barbecue sandwich her stomach was trying to crawl through her spine. She was so hungry she didn't care if all the offerings were stale.

There wasn't much to choose from: sodas, water, chips, cookies, crackers. She loaded up, went back to her room, and once the door was closed behind her she dropped her "dinner" on the single table in the room, removed the hat and sunglasses, and sat down in the only chair.

For one moment, one horrendous split second, she thought she was going to lose it, just break down and sob. She swallowed hard, looking up at the ceiling as she willed herself not to break down now.

She'd been running since she'd realized those men were shooting at her, so until this moment she hadn't really had time to think about how truly bad this all was. But she wouldn't cry. She refused to let them get the best of her. She focused on the next step, which was to get herself fed. Then she'd shower, get some sleep. She had to get some rest or she wouldn't be able to keep going. Those things she could handle. After that, she needed a plan . . . and she didn't have one.

She had to get out of town, but how? Public transportation would be under surveillance. Considering the number of cameras in the Metro, her hat and sunglasses wouldn't be a sufficient disguise. Bus? Maybe. That was a possibility. She could pay cash and hope she could change her appearance enough not to raise any alarm. But still, the idea gave her the heebie-jeebies. Her car—which wasn't a safe option anyway, obviously—was out of the picture. And she couldn't very well walk out of D.C.

Damn it, she thought irritably, she was going to have to steal another car. A bit more discreetly this time around, so the theft wouldn't be reported for several hours. Which meant she couldn't snatch the keys out of a driver's hand, unless she was willing to resort to kidnapping. Lizette Henry, carjacker.

Maybe.

It would be better, though, to hot-wire an older car.

New cars with their computers and antitheft systems weren't an option, but something older, maybe with a really kick-ass engine: a gas guzzler, an engine that roared. Why did that thought give her a bit of a thrill?

Exactly how did one hot-wire a car? Lizzy thought about it as she opened a pack of cheese crackers with a thin smear of peanut butter sandwiched in between. She took a big bite. They were stale. No surprise there. Damn it, she should have bought some food at the drugstore. They would have had protein bars, which would be better than this. But she'd been in a panic at the time, and she hadn't been thinking clearly—not clearly enough, anyway. It was the kind of stupid mistake that could get her killed. Yeah, she might starve to death.

Back to the immediate question: did she know how to hot-wire a car? She asked herself this again as she wolfed down the rest of the first stale cracker and moved on to the next one, washing it down with a long swallow of cold, sweet Coke.

Yes. Yes, she did! She could almost see her hands confidently crossing and twisting wires. The process was so clear in her mind, she might have done it just yesterday. No, not yesterday, but more than three years ago, in that two-year blind spot.

She waited for the blinding headache, the nausea, the internal warning that she could not go there. Nothing. She closed her eyes in relief. With everything else that was going on, she didn't think she could deal with those headaches now. If one of them hit at the wrong time, it could get her killed.

Two packs of crackers, two Cokes, and a bag of potato chips later, she was finally full. Tiredly she dragged herself into the bathroom. This long-neglected unit wasn't stocked with shampoo and soap, but she'd bought the basics, so she was set. Maybe while she was in the shower she could come up with more of a plan than "steal a car," which, as far as specifics went, left a lot to be desired. Where to find the car? When should she leave this room? Where should she go after she stole a car?

Under the spray of the shower, she tried not to think about anything but getting clean, washing the day off her body and out of her hair.

Seriously, the shittiest day ever.

At least as far as she could recall, which—ha-ha—wasn't all that far.

She got out of the shower and used her one towel to dry both her body and her hair, then pulled on her oversized tee shirt. She wiped the steam from the mirror and looked again at her new face. She did remember seeing it in the mirror every morning for the past three years, but now she also remembered that it wasn't her face. And she remembered without pain. Progress was definitely being made, but she wasn't certain she'd ever truly get used to that face, as if something deep inside her was mourning what she'd lost.

"What did they do to you?" she asked the face in the mirror, which, of course, had no answers and a whole helluva lot of questions.

She turned on the TV in front of the bed. The motel didn't get many channels, and it wasn't a very good TV, but all she wanted was a look at the news. Did they have her name, her photo? By morning would everyone in the city be looking for her?

Get real, a cynical little voice said. What made her think her little carjacking was of that much importance in a city with D.C.'s murder rate?

While she waited for the news to come on, Lizzy sat on the end of the bed and packed her belongings into the big, cheap bag she'd bought at the drugstore. Her smaller purse went in the very bottom, everything else in the middle, and the scissors placed so the handles were at the very top, easy to grab if she needed them. She wished again for her backpack, those power bars, the knife, her new running shoes.

She wouldn't make the same mistake with this bag that she'd made with the backpack; from now on she'd take everything she had with her wherever she went. It wasn't as if she'd be carting around a huge suitcase.

The story about the supposed drive-by at the barbecue restaurant was one of the first stories on the news, and Lizzy held her breath as she waited for the bit about the stolen car and the assault on the driver. It didn't come. The newscaster mentioned that a bystander had been wounded, but he'd been treated at the hospital and released, and then they moved on to other news.

Huh. Just as her cynical little voice had said: a stolen car wasn't exactly news in D.C., but the way it had happened, where and when . . . She felt a little dissed. Here she'd been so worried, wasting all that energy, and evidently she didn't rate even a blip on the dangerous-criminal radar.

She didn't change channels but kept listening, in case they added that part of the story later. But— nothing. There wasn't any mention of a chase and attempted murder—hers, by the way—on the interstate, either.

No, they don't want anyone else to find you. They want you to themselves.

Forget the police. That was so much scarier than being wanted by the police.

It was possible they'd shown her face on another news broadcast, or on another channel, but she didn't think so. The mysterious "They" were controlling everything, even the news that was released to the public. Again she wondered if she was the good guy or the bad guy. She didn't know, and at the moment she didn't much care. Her only care, her only priority, was to survive.

Looked at logically, though, she thought she had to be a good-guy type. She didn't feel any homicidal tendencies, nor did she want to knock over an armored car. If she was a bad guy, her badness seemed to be limited to car theft, which was way too minor to have people trying to hunt her down and kill her. There had to be more. She just didn't know what that "more" was.

It was too early in the day for her to go to bed—at least, it would be on a normal day. But this wasn't a normal day; she didn't even know what normal was, anymore. She was tired, and she needed to get rest where and when she could. After getting fully dressed, in case she had to run in a hurry, with her bag filled with everything she currently possessed sitting on the floor beside her bed, she closed her eyes.

And slept.

She'd assumed, when she first closed her eyes, that

if she dreamed at all her dream would be one of fear, a nightmare about the unknown, about them.

Instead she dreamed about X again: X in her room of color, and in that big bed. Even in her dream she was a little surprised that he'd shown up again. This time she was on top and he was the one wearing handcuffs. He liked it. Not as much as when he was in complete control, but still . . . he liked it. Interesting. X liked a touch of kink. He liked her. And oh, the sex was good. It was dream sex, but that was infinitely better than nothing. Which was what she'd enjoyed the past however many years. Nothing. Nothing and no one.

She whispered into X's ear, as she moved slowly, taking all of him in, riding him as if it were the last time, the only time. *I should've let them kill me . . . It would have been better than this, easier . . . No, no, they did kill me, and you let them . . .*

Lizzy woke with her hands clenched and her heart pounding. It was dark outside. She wasn't wearing a watch, the clock on the bedside table was blinking the wrong time, and she didn't dare put the battery in her cell phone just to check the time. She should probably dump the cell, but she couldn't make herself do that quite yet. What if there were an emergency and she needed it? As in making a call to 911, screaming for help because someone was trying to kill her? Yeah, she'd keep the phone for a little bit longer, at least until she had some sort of concrete plan.

She didn't dare turn on a light, since there was likely a new desk clerk on duty by now and if he or she looked this way and saw there was a light on in room 107 . . . well, she didn't want to take that chance. But with the heavy curtains tightly closed, she took a small risk and turned on the television. Just seeing what program was on helped her to narrow the time to within the hour. Flipping through the channels until she found a twenty-four-hour news station, she stopped. There, in the bottom left-hand corner, was the precise time.

She needed the precise time. Time was important. With a flick of her thumb, the television went dark again.

She'd slept five hours, which was amazing, all things considered. Another hour, maybe two, and she could venture out, find an old car, and hot-wire it. No way could she stay here until morning. The desk clerk's intentions had been good, but what if Cindy had second thoughts? What if she told a friend who told a friend who told the wrong friend?

She couldn't trust anyone.

If she stole a car that was parked overnight, it shouldn't be missed for several hours. She should find a house, then, or an apartment building. Maybe a motel like this one, where maybe someone had been careless enough to leave his keys in the ignition. It happened all the time. But she wouldn't do it at this motel, because it would bring too much attention to the place. Cindy would definitely talk if she thought a woman she'd helped had stolen a paying guest's vehicle.

By tomorrow morning she could be well into Virginia, maybe even North Carolina. She could dump the car before sunup, and at that distance away from the city a bus would be safe enough. Well, as safe as anything else.

A plan. Finally.

And until then? She didn't think she could sleep anymore. If she tried she'd be worried that she'd sleep too long, and that would keep her awake. Since the pain of remembering seemed to have disappeared, she sat and tried to remember . . . something, anything. Just some small things, such as where she'd lived, whether she'd worn her hair short or long, if she'd gotten a flu shot every year. She had for the past three years, but what about before that? That two-year gap remained stubbornly blank.

Less than an hour later, she heard the roar of a powerful motorcycle engine as it pulled into the parking lot. Someone coming in late would probably also sleep late, and the idea of stealing a motorcycle and flying out of town with the wind in her hair was oddly appealing. Did she even know how to ride one? Oh, hell yeah. She couldn't pull up any particular memories, but she was suddenly certain that she was no stranger to a motorcycle. She'd already decided not to steal a car from this parking lot, but she was curious. She had to look.

With the lights in the room off, no one should be able to tell that she'd parted the curtains just enough to peer into the parking lot. The motorcycle's parking lights went off just as she looked out, so she knew precisely where to focus.

The bike was on the other side of the L-shaped lot, parked beneath the one broken streetlamp in the area. For a moment the man who stepped away from the motorcycle was so lost in darkness she could barely make out his shape, but then he moved through a lit section, and her heart stopped.

Him. The man from Walgreens.

X.

Okay, this was taking coincidence way too far.

He stayed in shadows as much as was possible, given that the parking lot was so well lit. Was it her imagination, or was he walking straight for her? His gait was smooth, strong, confident, as if he knew right where she was—and he was coming to get her.

Shit! He was one of them!

Lizzy moved fast. She slung the strap of the big bag over one shoulder, smoothly pulled out the scissors, and darted into the bathroom. There was enough light coming through the small window for her to at least orient herself. She could go out the window, but there might be a better way. Swiftly she unlocked and opened it, hoisted herself up, and used the tip of the scissors to break one of the frosted glass panes. The sound of breaking glass wasn't horribly loud, but it was . . . enough. Maybe. Leaning out the window slightly, she made a soft sound, an exclamation, and then she made a fist and popped it against the window frame.

And she waited.

He didn't make her wait long. It was darker here, behind the hotel, but she knew where he'd appear and her gaze was there when he came ghosting around the back of the building thinking he'd find her there, either halfway out the bathroom window or sitting dazed on the ground after falling on her head. Sucker.

She eased down, tiptoed toward the door, and left the room as quietly as possible. She ran along the concrete sidewalk that ran the length of the motel. For a split second, she thought about stealing his bike. No, that wouldn't work. This guy, these people, obviously had some sophisticated way of tracking her down. He'd surely have a way to track his own vehicle, maybe through some satellite GPS system that could disable the bike when he called it in.

She didn't have much time before X realized she hadn't gone out the window and headed back this way, so she had to move. Her direction was chosen by patches of darkness, by paths where she could remain out of sight.

Lizzy found a shadow along the hotel wall, where she stopped, held her breath, and listened. X might search for her out back for a while, he might investigate the immediate area beyond the broken bathroom window and attempt to track her from there, but he wouldn't spend a lot of time doing that. In no more than a minute or so, probably sooner, he'd figure out what she'd done and come steaming back this way. And she was on foot, at least for now.

Just to make things fair, she thought he should be on foot, too.

Taking a chance that he was alone, that there wasn't someone close by, watching, Lizzy took off at a run toward X's motorcycle. Her first thought had been to run away, to head in the opposite direction, but this was too good a chance to pass up. She didn't have a plan, but she was quickly learning to trust her instincts, to listen to that inner voice that had kept her alive until now. When she reached the motorcycle, happy for the moment that he'd parked it in the darkest spot in the parking lot, she took a couple of seconds to look it over. She had to tamp down her appreciation for the fine machine in order to do what had to be done.

She dropped to her haunches, took the scissors, and cut the spark plug wires. How did she know those were the spark plug wires? Who knew? She didn't understand where the knowledge came from, but it really didn't matter. As soon as it was done, she felt a short-lived rush of relief. Then she stood up and walked away. It was tempting to run, but if anyone was watching, a brisk walk would raise less alarm.

She didn't dare go back toward her room, so she kept walking away, onto the narrow strip of pavement between this motel and the next and then toward the main road. She kept an ear cocked for sounds behind her but didn't hear anything. She let herself enjoy the luxury of a small smile. He was going to be so pissed when he couldn't start his bike.

Unfortunately, she couldn't take the time to truly enjoy her act of vandalism. Bits and pieces of knowledge were coming back to her, and while she'd seen cars quickly and easily hot-wired on TV, TV generally sucked at accuracy. She did remember hot-wiring a car, could see her hands doing the work, but her memory was telling her it wasn't quite that easy. She either had to get under the hood or else she needed a portable drill to remove the ignition. Either method would require tools; her bag felt damn heavy, but unfortunately there weren't any tools in it, unless you counted the handy-dandy scissors. They wouldn't get her a car, though, unless she used them to threaten a driver and take his keys.

She reached the main drag and turned left, breathing a sigh of relief that she'd made it this far without being tackled from behind. She hadn't heard any footsteps, but she was beginning to not assume anything was beyond X's capabilities. She risked looking behind her, and almost went limp with relief when she saw no one following her. Deep down, she'd really expected to see him coming toward her, his steps completely silent, a menacing figure of darkness.

Who the hell was he? She was suddenly, irrationally furious that she'd had those great erotic dreams about a man who was trying to kill her. It was as if her subconscious had pulled a really sick joke on her.

Forget about that. Who he was, and why he was after her, was far more important. This meant their initial meeting in Walgreens hadn't been accidental, and, if she had to take a wild leap here, not their initial meeting at all. He was someone from those missing two years. On some level she'd recognized him, and that was why she'd abruptly panicked and run. It was the running that had tipped him off that some of her memories were coming back and that she was now, somehow, a threat to him.

What didn't fit was the surveillance. Why watch her at all? If he intended to kill her, he'd had other opportunities before this morning.

Because he wasn't the boss. Someone else, somewhere, had analyzed the information on her and made the decision. X was part of the wet team.

Wet team. Her head throbbed, and she stumbled to a stop, her vision blurring . . . and then the pain faded.

Lizzy inhaled deeply, braced herself, and deliberately made herself think, "Wet team."

No pain. She started walking again.

It was as if each time her conscious thoughts ventured into an area that had previously been blocked, her brain was getting shocked, as if she'd touched an electrified fence. But once that fence was down, she could go to that section again without getting shocked.

Okay, hokey analogy, but it worked for her. When she had the time, she'd wonder how she even knew what a wet team was, but right now she had more pressing concerns.

About a block down the street she saw the neon lights from a bar. She started to cross to the other side to avoid the bright lights that would make her too easy to spot, if anyone was looking there, but then it struck her that there was no better place to find a car with the keys inside. Drunks did serve their purpose, now and then.

She hurried down the sidewalk, taking occasional glances behind her, but her luck was holding. She even smiled a little, thinking of X back at the motel parking lot, still trying to start his motorcycle. No, by now he should have found the severed spark plug wires, unless he was taking the time to thoroughly search the old motel. She could only hope her luck was that good. She'd allow herself to hope, but she wouldn't bet the farm on it. She'd continue with her own plan.

She stopped before she reached the bar and studied the parking lot, looking for men outside taking a smoking break, which would be a situation she wanted to avoid. She didn't see anyone, so she eased forward. Starting at the back of the parking lot, working her way to the front, gave her more cover for a longer period of time; she'd be exposed at the street for only as long as it took her to check that last line of cars, and maybe not even then if they were all newer models.

She checked only older cars that weren't as likely to have active alarm systems, looking in the windows to see if they were unlocked, or maybe even had the keys in the ignition or the cup holders. People did stuff like that all the time. She didn't have all night, and luck wasn't with her. Even the drunks took care to lock their car doors in this part of town.

Disappointed, Lizzy sought the shadows of a Dumpster and leaned against the side of it, ignoring the smell, ignoring the fact that the cheap-ass drugstore tennis shoes were already rubbing a blister on the heel of her right foot, feeling the presence of X as acutely as if he were breathing down her neck. She'd slowed him down, but she had come nowhere near stopping him. She had no idea how, but they clearly had some means of locating her. Now when he caught her he'd just be mad.

And he would catch her, if she didn't find wheels now.

The bar door opened and she sank back deeper into the shadows. She heard soft voices, getting louder as the people came toward her, but she stayed where she was. She was as well hidden here as she'd be anywhere else. A couple walked past her, arm in arm. Maybe—no. She dismissed the idea almost immediately. If she was going to jack a car, she didn't need to take on two people. They'd come out of the bar, sure, but neither of them was staggering or weaving, or talking too loud. If they'd been drunk she might have been able to overpower them both, but they weren't.

She watched as they got into a dark red crossover vehicle, talking the entire time, and never even glanced in her direction. They pulled out of the parking lot, and she was once more alone.

That truth hit her like a ton of bricks. She was literally and completely alone. There was no one she could call for help, not without giving her location away and putting anyone who might be willing to give her a hand in serious danger. There in the humid night, crouching by a Dumpster, she felt scared and small and helpless.

Instantly she rebelled. She'd admit to the scared—she was scared spitless—but she was damned if she was helpless. One way or the other, she'd either get away or go down fighting. And if she fought hard enough, even if she lost the battle, the disturbance might attract enough attention that they didn't get away with whatever it was they were doing.

Boy, that was some solace.

The bar door opened again, and a man half-stumbled his way through the lines of cars. He was singing some country song to himself, not loudly, but enough so that she could tell he'd never make a living at it. At least he was a happy drunk, and he was alone.

He sang the same two lines over and over as he shuffled unsteadily across the gritty parking lot. He jingled his keys in accompaniment.

Lizzy swiftly ran through her choices. She could wait until he reached his car so she knew which one was his, knock him down, take the keys, and drive off, but how long would she have before a report was filed? Not long, and more than anything she needed time. Another approach was called for, and this happy guy seemed to fit the bill.

She stepped out of the shadow of the Dumpster and put a smile on her face as she walked toward him. "Hi."

He took a single step back, surprised, and then he smiled, too. "Hi. Where did you come from?"

Her drunk was under thirty, thin, at least six feet tall, and dressed in jeans, tennis shoes, and a worn tee shirt that revealed just how skinny he really was. Even though he was a lot taller than she was, she could take him in a fair fight . . . not that she was known for fighting fair . . .

She quickly dismissed that last, odd thought. "I was just hanging out, and I noticed that you really shouldn't be driving in your very happy condition."

He shook the hand that held the keys in her direction. "I can drive just fine."

"I'm sure you can, but since it's not necessary, why don't you let me drive you home?"

His face lit up. He had a really sweet smile. "Hey! Are you with one of those volunteer groups that drives people home when they're tipsy?"

Tipsy? This guy was so drunk, he was about two seconds from landing on his ass.

"Yes I am," she replied, seizing the opportunity he'd just given her.

"Mothers of . . . no, wait . . . Desnit . . . nesigda . . . drivers."

"You're exactly right," she said firmly. "I'm with Mothers of Designated Drivers, and we really should go so I can get back here and help someone else, later tonight."

He gave her that sweet smile again. "Okay." Then he handed her the keys—with a remote, thank goodness—and waited.

"Good decision," she said, and hit the unlock button on the remote. Lights flashed on a car close to the end of the line.

"Hey, that was smart," he said as she took his arm and led him to his car. He leaned so heavily on her, stumbling, that she began weighing the odds they'd both end up sprawled on the pavement. If he went down, he'd take her with him.

But they made it. She propped him against the car, a white compact, foreign made but common enough to blend in on the interstate.

"What's your name, honey?" she asked as she opened the back door for him. He all but fell inside and lay down on the seat, twisting to fit into the small space.

"Sean," he said. He added his last name, but mangled it so much it actually sounded like "subwoofer." The odds were almost a hundred percent against that, but she didn't care about his last name so she didn't ask for clarification.

"Nice car, Sean." She tossed her bag onto the front passenger-seat floorboard and adjusted the seat and the mirrors. "You keep it so clean."

"It's my sister's car." He giggled; a weird sound coming from a semi-grown man. "I'm not supposed to drive it, but her car is a lot nicer than mine, and she's out of town so she'll never know." Then he made an exaggerated shushing sound.

"I won't tell, I promise. It'll be our little secret. Now, you take a nap while I drive you home."

"Okay," he said agreeably, and then he went silent.

Lizzy pulled out of the parking lot and turned in the opposite direction of the motel. What was X doing? Surely by now he had at least tried to start his motorcycle.

"Good luck with that," she muttered.

"What?" Sean asked from the backseat.

"Nothing, sweetie, you just take a little nap. We'll be there in no time."

He was so far gone he hadn't even thought to give her his address. Apparently a volunteer for Mothers of Designated Drivers was supposed to have psychic powers for divining addresses.

Within minutes, Sean was snoring. He'd probably sleep for hours, if she let him. She could just drive, with him sleeping off his drunk in the backseat. But if she did that, he'd be more sober when he woke up and therefore more difficult to deal with. Not only that, his location would be a direction pointer for the people searching for her.

X had found her easily enough before. She didn't want to do anything to help them.

How were they doing it? She was tempted to toss everything she hadn't bought at the drugstore that afternoon out the window. Anything she had that she'd owned before could have a tracker on it. The most likely culprit was the cell phone, even though it was in pieces. It was a constant, the one thing she always had with her. She didn't see how they could have gotten to it; she hadn't left it anywhere . . . unless someone had broken into her house while she was sleeping.

Oh God, that so freaked her out just thinking about

it. She should just throw the damn thing out the window.

But not yet. There had to be a better way, a way that would confound them and cost them valuable time. And just because the cell was the most likely item didn't mean she could just assume that was the means they were using.

Lizzy drove west on I-66, her mind spinning as the miles passed. Thinking about the cell phone made her think about the people she called. That was a very short list: Diana. It was a sad testament to the past three years of her life that she didn't have anyone to call but one friend. And she didn't dare call her, not with that damn phone.

Wait. Sean would have a phone, right? Everyone had a cell phone, these days.

She'd gone far enough. Lizzy took the next exit and pulled into the parking lot of a closed service station. Stopping at the side of the building, near the back, she got out and opened the rear door, and tugged and pulled until she got a groggy Sean out of the car and on his feet. For someone so skinny, he sure was heavy.

She put her arm around him as she urged him forward, using the opportunity to pick his wallet from his back pocket.

"This way, sweetie," she crooned, leading him toward the Dumpster just behind the building.

"This isn't my house," he said, sounding confused.

"No, we're just making a quick pit stop."

"Oh. That's okay."

"You know, Sean," she said as she lowered him to the ground as gently as possible, behind the Dumpster where he'd be out of sight from the street and the gas station, until morning at least, "you really should give up drinking. It doesn't agree with you at all."

"Yeah, yeah," he said, as if he'd heard that before. He sighed and leaned back, then he was asleep again, his head lolling against the side of the Dumpster.

She swiftly, lightly patted his front pockets and located his cell. She used two fingers to ease it out. Then she got back in his sister's car and drove away.

She drove farther west for a few minutes before she keyed the phone, making it light up. It was an expensive smart phone; too bad she couldn't keep it a while longer. No way could she call Diana at home in the middle of the night to say goodbye, or anything else, but she hated to just disappear.

She dialed Diana's work number, and when prompted, hit the key that would allow her to leave a message.

"Hi, Diana," Lizzy said, and for a moment the voice was . . . hers. It was the easy voice of the woman she'd been for the past three years, not the voice of the woman who would roll a drunk and disable a motorcycle. "Just wanted to let you know that I won't be in today." That was an understatement. "Or tomorrow." She hesitated to say more, not wanting to let them know Diana meant anything to her, but then realized if they'd been watching her all this time, if her phone had been bugged, they already knew. There was no hiding it at this point. "Thank you for being such a good friend. I'll miss you, but things are going on and . . . I quit. If I'm ever able to get in touch again, I will. Take care." She ended the call before she started crying.

Damn it, they'd not only stolen part of her former

life, now they'd cost her her home, her job, and her friend. If she could ever get her hands on the sons of bitches who were doing this to her—

She pulled into the right lane, rolled down the passenger window, and violently threw Sean's phone out of the car. It might survive the landing, but probably not. If they triangulated the call they'd be able to tell she'd been in this area, and, like the passed-out Sean, the clues would lead them west.

She was like Gretel, but without a Hansel leaving breadcrumbs to lead them home.

Chapter Twenty

The little shit had completely tricked him. Xavier was torn between fury and laughter. On the one hand, she'd really pissed him off by vandalizing his Harley, but on the other hand, pretending to go out the bathroom window had been a slick move. He was proud of her. Exasperated as all hell, but proud.

She'd been on foot and he figured he could easily catch her, but then what? She'd fight like a wildcat, in which case he could either knock her out and sling her over his shoulder—not a good thing on a public street—or he could *not* knock her out and throw a fighting, screaming Lizzy over his shoulder, also not a good thing. Cops would be all over him within five minutes. Okay, ten, considering the part of town they were in. Either way, he was now on foot and had no way of transporting her anywhere.

His best option was to just let her go; it wasn't as if he couldn't catch up to her later, as long as she didn't figure out there had to be a tracker on her somewhere, and ditch everything she had with her, including her clothes. The Lizzy he knew wouldn't hesitate to do exactly that. The fact that she was still partially Lizette threw in an unknown factor, making it harder to predict what she would or wouldn't do.

He had to deal with his motorcycle, too, get the spark plug wires replaced. The motorcycle was still the best way for him to travel anonymously.

He also needed to come up with a plan, move some people into place. If Felice thought he wouldn't hit back, she was bat-shit crazy. No way would he let this go unanswered.

It went without saying he'd be burning his bridges in this country. Taking out a high-ranking employee of the NSA would bring down all kinds of shit on his head, especially if Al had gone along with Felice in the assassination attempts. He'd thought about it some more and even though Al would have used different people and different methods, that didn't mean he hadn't agreed to let Felice handle it. Xavier couldn't assume Felice was acting on her own authority.

If she could use the NSA's resources to track both himself and Lizzy, they were probably as good as dead. The average citizen had no idea of the extent to which their own government spied on them. But if she did use the NSA, that was an official link between them that might bring up questions. She could resort to that later, but for now Xavier bet that she would still be using her outside sources. As she lost each battle, she'd escalate to the next step.

That wasn't Xavier's way. One step at a time was stupid. If it were him, he'd go straight for the big guns, annihilate the threat, and move on. Why waste time dicking around?

But getting to her wouldn't be easy. She'd take precautions now, after her first attempt had failed. He might have to take out Al at the same time, something that would be infinitely more difficult. And he had to deal with Lizzy.

Tactically, he should remove the threat first, then go after Lizzy. That was what Felice and Al would both expect him to do, to follow training and deal with the immediate threat. But even though he'd been protecting Lizzy all these years, none of them knew that he and Lizzy had been lovers during most of the training and operation phase. Al thought it bothered Xavier because a woman had been killed during the action, and afterward he had become more protective, angrily rejecting the need for the memory wipe that they'd performed anyway. When he and Lizzy had been together, they'd gone to great lengths to keep their relationship private; hookups and affairs did happen between operatives, but because of the extremely sensitive nature of the mission, they'd both thought their connection should be kept on the down-low.

That was then. This was now. When it came to Lizzy, to hell with tactics. She was on the run, she was scared, and Felice would still be searching for her. Xavier wanted to get to her first. Even if she didn't remember him, even if she was now running from him as much as she was from Felice, he could calm her down and get her to a safe place, convince her that he'd never hurt her. He wanted to know how much she remembered, how much of Lizzy had surfaced. The essence of Lizzy was back; that she had even partial recall was more than he'd ever hoped.

He placed a call, knowing his chops were going to get busted, big time. "I need a tow for the Harley." He gave his location, and waited for the fun to begin.

There was a pause. "You have an accident?"

He could just say it had quit on him, but he wasn't going to put the blame on such a fine machine. "She cut the spark plug wires."

He heard a muffled snort of laughter. "No shit? Fuck, I'm in love."

"Don't get any ideas, dickhead. She's mine. Just make the arrangements."

Sitting in Sean's sister's car in the parking lot of a Leesburg, Virginia, twenty-four-hour Walmart, Lizzy watched the people around her, looking for anything suspicious, and furiously thinking.

She had to figure out how X had found her.

She'd ditched her car; that had been the most likely means of tracking her. But he'd still found her within hours. So there *had* to be a tracker on something she was carrying. But what?

She pulled her purse from the bottom of the shopping bag, took out the cell phone and battery, and stared at them. The phone hadn't been turned on, hadn't even been activated. She'd been so careful, was there any way in hell X could have tracked her through this phone? But how else could he have found her so soon?

Maybe "They" had implanted a chip in her skull, or something. Maybe they weren't tracking her phone; maybe they were tracking *her*.

Except the idea didn't trigger even a glimmer of a headache, unlike the memories she'd come to accept as a real part of her unknown life. Still, she spent a few minutes raking her fingers through her hair, feeling her skull for a small raised section. *Nada*. Finally she shook her hair back and sat there feeling like the fool she would definitely have looked like to anyone who'd happened to see her.

That didn't rule out the possibility of an implant on her back, but there wasn't any way she could check herself for that. Or maybe laparoscopic surgery had implanted a chip on her liver, or something like that.

No, no Band-Aid scars on her belly.

She was running out of ideas, and was back to the phone. Except that didn't make sense. The phone hadn't been out of her possession since she'd bought it, and had never had the battery installed, much less actually been turned on and used.

She could have tossed the cell phone out the window miles back, just to be on the safe side, but she hadn't. Watching people come and go at Walmart gave her a better idea, anyway.

She took a long, considering look at her handbag, then sighed. She really liked that bag, and she carried it a lot. She liked it so much, in fact, that she probably hadn't changed bags in at least a month, which was a long time for her. That made the purse a suspect, too.

She sighed again, then seized the bag and turned it upside down, dumping the contents into the plastic drugstore bag. The purse was leather, butter soft, and just the right size for her essentials, but it wasn't impossible that it was bugged—unlikely, but not impossible. It had to go. If she had the time she'd search it, take it apart seam by seam, to be certain, but time was not her friend. Every delay held the potential for disaster. She had to keep moving.

She'd slowed X down by cutting his motorcycle's

spark plug wires, but she didn't kid herself that the delay was anything more than temporary. All she'd done was buy herself a little time—if she was lucky, if he was working alone. If he wasn't, which was far more likely, then he'd have backup, maybe just around the corner. He could be closing in on her right now.

No, if he'd had backup close by, X would have found her by now and she'd be . . . what? Dead? In custody?

Beneath him in bed, her legs wrapped around him . . .

God! She shoved the thought away. She had to be one sick puppy, having sex thoughts about the man who was trying to kill her. Damn those dreams; if she had another one, she might have to punch herself in the face, just because.

She removed the cash—less than sixty bucks— from Sean's wallet and stuffed it down into the shopping bag, wishing as she did that he was a wealthier man who'd carried more money on him. She considered his credit card, dismissed it as too risky, then dropped his wallet into her purse.

Even though the lit parking lot was an oasis of light in the darkness, she put on the hat and sunglasses. Let people think she was weird, or some politician's wife up to no good, though why anyone would meet a lover at Walmart she didn't know. People did weird things every day, especially at Walmart. There were cameras *everywhere,* and she wasn't ready to be spotted.

As she walked toward the well-lit store, she fingered the cell phone, searching for some clue as to how X had found her. She ran her fingertips along the phone, the case, even the battery. Her attention was split between the phone and her surroundings, because she couldn't let anything slip by her, but she wanted to know *how*. She wanted to know why, too, but at the moment the how was more important.

Then she felt it. There, under the 7 on her keypad, the smallest of bumps. She could barely feel it, would never have paid any attention if she hadn't been looking for something, anything, out of the ordinary.

"You *asshole*," she said beneath her breath as she walked into the Walmart. An employee standing by the shopping carts looked up sharply, and Lizzy smiled at him. "Not you."

The man acknowledged her with a nod, but he remained wary. Good. He'd remember her. When X showed up maybe he'd waste some time searching the aisles for her, because he'd be so sure she was here. He'd be wrong.

But when the hell had he gotten his hands on the phone? The only possible answer was that he, or someone else, had broken into her house while she was asleep and planted the tracker. God, that was a creepy thought, but what else could it be?

That also brought up another question: if someone had been in her house, and this someone wanted her dead, why hadn't she been killed in her sleep?

Because something had changed—and the only thing she knew of that had changed was herself. By taking the small steps she'd taken, she'd set off a situational alarm. The thought had occurred to her before, but the tracker on the cell phone was proof positive.

Finding the tracker was a relief. Now she knew how he'd been doing it, and she knew for certain what to do. She placed the purse in the cart seat and wheeled toward the grocery section, trying to move fast without looking as if she were in too much of a hurry. She grabbed a bag of orange-slice candy from an end of the aisle display and tossed it into the cart, just to make it look as if she were actually shopping. Paper plates went on top of the candy.

People who shopped at this hour of the morning apparently weren't in a hurry. Why would they be here at this hour? They worked weird shifts, or wanted to avoid the crowds, or maybe they were just night owls. They meandered down the aisles, stopping with their carts turned to the side, blocking anyone else who wanted to go down the same aisle. And man, what a motley crew they were: druggies, men on their way home from a bar, people who looked as if they never left their houses at all by the light of day. That one looked as if he might live in his car. She shouldn't judge; she might be next. But, damn—over there was a woman wearing pink camouflage tights two or three sizes too small, teamed with a lime-green tank top and no bra. Lizzy blinked and hurried past, lest she be blinded.

She passed a man with a black eye, a limp, and a cart filled with beef jerky and beer. Dang. With her hat and sunglasses, and her too-big drugstore tee shirt, Lizzy fit right in. She even qualified as one of the better-dressed shoppers.

Come to think of it, she'd love some beef jerky of her own, just to have something to eat that didn't come out of a vending machine, but she couldn't take the time to actually go through a checkout line. X would be behind her, and she didn't know how close he was. He might not be the only one, this time.

Her heart jumped at the idea. Fear could stop her in her tracks if she allowed it, so she shook off the feeling of panic. She had to push forward, one step at a time.

There were a few people in the grocery section of the huge store, but she found an aisle that was momentarily deserted. She popped the battery into her cell phone and switched it on, then swiftly pushed her cart to the next aisle, where a short, plump Hispanic woman intently studied the labels on two different cans of soup. Like Lizzy, the woman had placed her purse, a huge red tote-bag kind of thing, in the cart's seat that was intended for a toddler's butt or a loaf of bread—or an unguarded purse. And, hallelujah, that purse was wide open at the top. Lizzy didn't even slow down as she walked by and dropped the phone into the bowels of the big red bag. Considering the depth and girth of that purse, it might be weeks before the phone was discovered—if it didn't ring.

She moved on to the frozen foods, plucked Sean's wallet from her purse, and reached into the cold case for a pizza, leaving the wallet behind as she removed a large pepperoni and tossed it into her cart. Another crumb. Figure *that* one out, Mister X.

On the next aisle over she parked her shopping cart, with the empty purse, candy and all still in it, and made a beeline toward the exit. As she went past the checkout lanes she whipped off her hat and her glasses, fluffed her hair, and hoped that the employee who'd noticed her walking in wouldn't notice her walking out, in case X arrived while the woman who now had Lizzy's purse was still shopping.

She thought of all the things she'd like to buy here: boots, a different hat, protein bars, water, a knife or two or three. But not here, and definitely not now. There would be another Walmart, farther down the road. Or better yet, a string of smaller stores that were less likely to have working security cameras. Maybe she could find a flea market, though for that she might have to wait for the weekend. She'd definitely need a new car before then. Hell, she'd need to dump Sean's car by morning, because as soon as he woke up and could get to a phone the theft of his sister's car would be reported.

As soon as she dumped that car, she was going to turn south. Every clue would lead west, and she'd be going toward Florida instead. Would that work? Was it enough of a head-fake to spring her free?

There were still plans to make, decisions that had to be made, but for the first time on this long day Lizzy could truly imagine herself making it down the road.

One step at a time.

While his guy grumbled about being called out in the middle of the night for transport and repair, Xavier leaned against the wall of the windowless garage and once again studied the map on his cell. The mechanic— Rick—was one of his people, a whiz with engines of all kinds as well as a more-than-decent sniper.

Changing spark plug wires wasn't a difficult or time-consuming job. He could have done it himself if he'd had the parts, but it was a plus to have someone on his payroll who had a quiet place to do the work as well as the spare parts and the expertise.

Xavier had checked Lizzy's progress often since calling Rick. He'd followed her progress away from the hotel, then west on I-66. Two blinking dots, representing her cell phone and her wallet, had stayed together—until now.

For the first time since he'd planted them, the two dots separated. Xavier pushed away from the wall, frowning as he watched and considered the possibilities. He ran his thumb over the screen and zoomed in for detail. Walmart. The cell was still in the store, but the wallet was walking out.

Quickly he ran through the options. Had she planted the wallet on someone leaving the store while she stayed to shop, or had she planted the cell on someone still in the store and then made her escape? His money was on the wallet being with her. That tracker would be more difficult to locate, and a cell phone, small as it was, would be easier to drop in a pocket or purse while passing by.

Though all she'd have to do was set the wallet on a shelf and walk away, and someone would pick it up.

Worst case, she'd found both trackers, or else was simply getting rid of everything she'd had on her when she'd run and was starting fresh. If she did that, then he'd lost her. Violently he rejected that thought. No matter what, he'd find her. He had a starting point, that Walmart in Leesburg. She'd be picked up on the parking lot cameras, and he'd find a way to get access to the recording. He'd at least have an idea of what she was driving.

All he could do was watch the trackers. If one—or both—moved to a site nearby and stayed there, it was most likely not in Lizzy's possession. If one object stopped at a house or apartment nearby while the other kept going, he'd have her.

"How long?" he asked sharply.

"Almost there," Rick growled. He was still grumpy about his interrupted sleep.

Xavier dialed, put the phone to his ear. "Anything?" he said when Maggie answered.

"They're watching her house," Maggie said. Despite the hour, she sounded as alert as if it were high noon. "Slow drive-bys, the occasional car parked on the street for an hour or so before moving on. This afternoon a package was delivered. Well, almost. The so-called deliveryman rang the bell, looked in the window, then started nosing around. I went outside and offered to sign for the package for Lizette, but that spooked him and he left—with the package, which judging by the way he held it was nothing more than an empty box, just an excuse to get close, in case anyone was watching. No one has gone inside yet, but that'll happen soon."

"She's not going back there," Xavier said.

"Of course not. She isn't a fool." Maggie sounded insulted on Lizzy's behalf. "Further instructions?" she asked.

"If they make a move on the house, call the police. As a concerned neighbor," he added.

"I can handle them myself, if you'd just let me . . ."

"No." He didn't need dead bodies piling up on Lizzy's doorstep. "I'm just trying to keep them busy." And annoyed. They had to be wondering how an office worker could so efficiently elude them and have them running around like monkeys.

Maggie sighed, obviously disappointed. "My next assignment had better be a little more exciting than this one. The excitement factor has gone up the past few days, but watching an empty house is pretty damn boring."

Xavier watched Rick finish up the repair job. "But you like the dog," he said.

"Yeah, Roosevelt is a plus." Then she went back to all-business. "I'll let you know if matters escalate here, but my guess is when they see no results from their stakeout they'll move on." She paused. "Is she all right?"

"As far as I can tell." Xavier ended the call and leaned against the garage wall again, watching the blinking dots that grew farther and farther apart. If he was lucky, in no more than an hour or two he'd be able to identify which tracker had stayed with Lizzy. If she'd gotten rid of them both . . . he was royally screwed.

Chapter Twenty-one

The morning sun was streaking the sky with pink when Lizzy reached Front Royal. She found a McDonald's and parked Sean's sister's car in the rear, where several employees had parked, backing the compact car into a small space so the tag wasn't visible from the parking lot. Someone would be looking for it, sooner or later. She took a moment to wipe down everything she'd touched, then got out and locked the car. She even wiped down the keys with her shirt, then, still using her shirttail to hold them, laid the keys across the back of her hand and tossed them into the Dumpster, hitched her bag over her shoulder, and started walking.

She was tired. The five hours of sleep she'd managed at the beginning of the long night had helped, of course, but stress and adrenaline had sapped almost all of her energy. She couldn't keep up this pace for much longer. She needed to eat, and somehow she needed to grab a nap, even if only a short one. Fatigue would make her clumsy, both physically and mentally.

She thought about going into McDonald's—good coffee—but she was leaving the car there, so it seemed a good idea to find somewhere else to eat. Where she ate might not matter, but at this point no one knew who'd stolen the car and she didn't want to definitely connect herself to it. Would McDonald's have a security cam? She knew for certain some of them did. She didn't want to take the chance.

She started walking, and once again cursed the cheap shoes she was wearing. On the other hand, at least she had shoes.

She didn't have any idea where she was going, but she headed toward what seemed like a busy section of town. Her choice worked out. A few blocks down the road she saw a plain, boxy building with a neon "Open" sign, and when she got closer she could read the lettering on the window: "Sam's Cafe." Below that was the welcome information that the cafe served breakfast, lunch, and dinner. *Good for Sam,* she thought as she went inside.

She stood for a few seconds, getting her bearings. No hostess, so it was seat-yourself. Bathrooms straight ahead as she'd come in the door. She made a beeline for the ladies' room. She was starving for real food, but some needs were more urgent than others.

While in the bathroom she washed her face and hands, finger-combed her hair, then washed her hands again. She made a face at herself in the mirror. Thank goodness she'd been able to shower at the motel, but she was beginning to feel icky again, even though she hadn't done anything more strenuous than drag Sean out of the backseat. She needed to buy some new underwear, too. She didn't have any spare clothes with her, so she couldn't even stop and do laundry unless she wanted to stand around buck naked while her clothes washed and dried. Having even one complete change of clothes would make a world of difference.

First things first, though. Next up: food.

The restaurant was evidently popular with the locals, because it was busy, with most of the booths and tables filled. Unease prickled along the back of her neck as she studied the scant selection of empty tables. She wanted something closer to the kitchen and the rear exit. As she hovered there looking for a place, a man slid out of a booth toward the back, and she hurried forward to take his place while the waitress was still busing the table.

She was not only starving now, she was going to need a lot of energy in the coming hours, so she ordered a huge breakfast: ham and eggs, biscuits, coffee. Grits were offered, but she turned them down because even though she'd heard about them she wasn't really certain what a "grit" was, and the waitress asked if she wanted to substitute home fries. Potatoes? Oh, hell yeah.

While she ate, she thought. She didn't know this area, but she was in a good-sized town that should be able to provide everything she needed for the next step.

She wasn't sure how she knew, but she was fairly certain there was a bus station in Charlottesville, which would be somewhere around . . . seventy, eighty miles from here, by back roads. She needed to pick up a map and study it, make certain her memory, such as it was, wasn't deceiving her.

Split the difference and say, seventy-five miles. She could walk it, but while that wasn't impossible, neither was it practical. She didn't have that kind of time to just mosey down the road. She could try to hitch a ride, but could she trust anyone who would pick her up? Hell, no. She couldn't trust anyone, period. Look what trusting her had cost poor drunk Sean: his sister's car, which he would get back, but for which he would have hell to pay when his sister found out what had happened; his wallet, which he might get back, depending on who found it in the Walmart freezer; his phone, which was toast; and his sixty bucks.

She had money, she had a lot more than Sean's sixty bucks, but she had no idea how long what she had would have to last her, and every dollar would count before this was done. That was assuming this was ever really finished, that she would eventually be able to find a place to settle, establish a new identity, and have some semblance of a real life. Unless and until she fully regained her memory and knew exactly what was going on, she couldn't afford to stop for longer than a brief rest. She was going to spend some of that money, though, because she had an idea about how she was going to get to Charlottesville.

The stores she needed probably wouldn't open until nine or ten, and she didn't want to go to another Walmart even though she could get everything she needed there in one stop. There were too many cameras, and she didn't want to establish a pattern. Smaller stores would be better.

The waitress was friendly, but thank goodness was too busy to strike up a conversation. Lizzy ate, she planned, then she paid and left.

Today was going to be tough, but she'd have to push through it. She wouldn't have an opportunity to sleep for a while. When she got to Charlottesville and was on a bus heading south, then she'd sleep. How well she'd be able to sleep on a bus was up in the air, but any sleep was better than none.

In the meantime, she had to keep moving, keep going forward.

About a mile down the road she found a nice little shopping center. A few of the stores opened at nine, so she was in luck. In a Dollar General store she bought beef jerky, peanut butter crackers, a kitchen knife—it was better than nothing—a box of Band-Aids, and three bottles of water. More water would have been better, but space and weight were an issue. Right now, she had to carry everything she owned, and water was heavy. There would be places to buy water on the road.

Moving on to a Big Lots, she also found a backpack; the selection was limited, but at this point she didn't care. The main thing was that it was big enough to hold all her possessions. She got a dark green one, as well as a baseball cap and sunscreen, thick socks, a wristwatch, a few pairs of clean underwear, and a box of wet wipes. Next she went to a convenience store and used the bathroom to clean up some, change her underwear, put bandages over the blisters on her heels, and don a pair of the thick socks to better protect her feet.

Then she was ready for the final stop: a bicycle shop.

She tucked her hair up under the baseball cap and slid the sunglasses on. Disguise in place, she walked in the door of the shop and immediately looked around for security cameras. She spotted one immediately: a mounted half-round black camera with a blinking light. She tensed for a second, then noticed that the red light on the camera was blinking too fast.

The camera was a fake. She relaxed, shifted the backpack, and settled the straps around her shoulders. She'd already packed it with all her new possessions, as well as everything else she'd been carrying, and it was too damn heavy, but she'd deal. At this point a heavy backpack was the least of her problems.

The bike store didn't exactly do a booming business on a Wednesday morning. The only other person in the store was an older man behind the counter; he looked up and greeted her as she walked past. "Anything in particular I can show you?"

"I'm just looking around," she said. She thought he was probably the owner, given his age and the fact that he seemed to be going over a checkbook, but she couldn't be sure.

She found the sale section of the store. She couldn't afford the most expensive bicycle here, the good performance road bikes were well over a thousand bucks, but she didn't want a piece of crap, either. If just the cheap bicycles were on sale, she'd have to fork out more money than she wanted to, but she needed something good with enough gears to handle the terrain. Was there such a thing as last year's styles in bikes?

There were just a handful of bikes on sale; there was some variety, but only one model that looked as if it would fit the bill. It was black and kind of dull-looking, despite some blue detailing, which was okay with her; she didn't want anything flashy. She flipped over the sale tag and winced a little. Even on sale, the bike was still a bit more than she'd wanted to spend. Moving down the line, she checked the other bikes;

they were cheaper, but didn't have the gears she'd need.

When the old guy realized that she was interested and not just browsing, he came out from behind the counter and joined her. "Can I interest you in one of these?"

Lizzy removed her sunglasses. "I like the black one, but it's pretty expensive. Do you give a discount to customers who pay cash?"

In the early morning hours, the cell-phone signal had stopped at an apartment building less than a mile from the Leesburg Walmart; the wallet signal continued moving.

Xavier considered the matter as he cruised through the cool early-morning hours just before dawn, the big Harley rumbling beneath him. It wasn't impossible that Lizzy had dumped both wallet and cell, which would have made catching up with her much more difficult. Not impossible, but definitely more difficult, and dangerous for her. If her training was coming back she might have thought to discard everything she'd had from before, but he was betting the farm she still didn't have back her full operational cognizance. Instinct, yes, and native intelligence, but the rest of it . . . probably not yet. She'd obviously found the tracker on the cell phone, and after that most people would then think they were safe; they wouldn't consider there being a second tracker. He was *almost* confident that she'd kept the wallet with her, for now.

But for how much longer?

There were a couple of different dangers here. For

the time being, she was safe from Felice; they'd completely lost her when she dumped her car. The first danger was that she'd recover enough of her training that she was able to give *him* the slip. At her best, Lizzy was damn good, and predicting her actions was never easy. The second danger was that she'd recover more of her memory and remember him—but she didn't know how to contact him, so she might well double back to the D.C. area in an effort to find him. If she did, the street cameras and all the other NSA capabilities would identify and locate her, and she might as well have a laser target painted on her back.

As long as she was moving away from D.C., though, he was content to follow.

In Front Royal her speed—rather, the speed of the wallet she carried—changed. Odds were Lizzy had dumped whatever car she'd stolen to get away from D.C. and was now on foot, a move that assured him she still had the wallet in her possession.

As long as she kept the wallet on her, he'd be close behind.

He could have caught up with her during the night, not long after his bike had been repaired. But then what? If he roared up behind or alongside her on the interstate, she'd just panic. Maybe she'd gotten her hands on a gun and would try to shoot him; it wasn't as though he could shoot back. Maybe she'd simply panic and drive off the side of the road, wreck her car, hurt herself, or be killed.

His approach needed to be smoother than that. For now, he just wanted to know where she was. He wanted eyes on her. No, that wasn't quite right. He wanted *his* eyes on her.

She was easy to find, thanks to the tracker, but he had to make certain she didn't spot him. According to the tracker and the detailed map overlay, she was in a Dollar General store in a strip mall. He parked his bike at the end of the mall, almost completely obscured by a van, and a few minutes later watched as she walked out of the store, juggling her purchases. That answered that question: she still had the wallet.

He couldn't very well confront her here and now. There were too many witnesses, too many ways it could go wrong. Knowing she still had the wallet on her was all he needed, for now.

In the meantime, he was starving, and he needed caffeine in the worst way. He watched until she was safely inside another store, then started the Harley and headed back toward a restaurant he'd passed driving in. He'd let Lizzy continue to believe she'd shaken him, that she'd gotten away, and when she was in a more remote area he'd find a way to talk to her. She couldn't just keep running; eventually she'd make a mistake and Felice would be there.

He didn't rush through breakfast, but took his time and gave Lizzy a little space. After the waitress had cleared away his dirty plates, he sipped on a last cup of coffee while he watched the tracker on his cell phone as it moved away from Front Royal.

What the hell?

Something didn't make sense. The tracker didn't give him her exact speed, but close enough. She was moving along too fast to be on foot, but too slow to be in a car. Maybe if there was heavy traffic on that road, construction that had traffic at a crawl, but . . . not likely. The traffic on the road he watched moved steadily enough, and she wasn't too far away. If the road she was on had construction, the locals would know and avoid it, but he didn't see any increase in traffic on this road. Of course, he wasn't familiar with the local patterns, so when the waitress came back to ask if he wanted another refill, he said, "I'm good. Maybe you can tell me something. Is there any construction in the area? I'm heading south, and I need to make good time."

"Not that I know of, and if there was, there'd be someone in here bitching about it all day," she said.

"Okay, thanks." When she'd left, he checked the image on his phone again. He watched for a while, puzzling it over as he finished his coffee. After a few minutes her speed varied. She moved along pretty slowly for a few minutes, then there was an increase in speed before her speed leveled out again.

Something occurred to him. There was one rather far-fetched possibility that actually made him smile. He switched the mode to topographical and laughed. That slow speed had come on one side of a hill, the burst of speed on another.

She was on a bicycle.

He was impressed by her thinking. No ID was required to buy a bicycle, no registration to worry about, she had enough cash on her to afford one, and she wouldn't have to worry about driving a stolen car or hitchhiking and being picked up by a nutcase. And who would think to look for her on a bicycle? She'd surprised even him. That was part of the fluidity of her thinking, because absolutely no one would expect her to escape on a bicycle. With a helmet and sunglasses on, she'd also have a damn good disguise. No one would look twice at her.

The road she was on would eventually lead to Charlottesville. He checked a couple of things with his phone and discovered there was a bus terminal there. She could dump her bike and buy a ticket to anywhere. That terminal was far enough away from D.C. that it probably wasn't being watched, close enough that she might remember the location from her training. She'd had multiple escape routes memorized, and one of them might have included the Charlottesville terminal.

He definitely didn't have to worry about catching up with her, not as long as she stayed on the bicycle. He'd been worrying about when and where to confront her, her reaction to seeing him again, the difficulty of any witnesses being present. If he let her wear herself out, the coming confrontation would be much easier . . . for him, that was. It wasn't a small consideration. When he'd been training her, she'd occasionally cleaned his clock. Not on a regular basis, but often enough to make her cocky. Not many people could take him down, but she was just sneaky enough to surprise him a couple of times, and she didn't mind playing dirty. In his mind, he could still see the glee in her smile the first time she'd managed to put him on his back.

Another cup of coffee was called for, after all. Xavier lifted his empty coffee cup in a silent request for a refill. There was no reason he couldn't sit here for a while and let Lizzy get a bit farther down the road. He could even think of it as payback for what she'd done to his motorcycle.

She had her bike, and he had his. The coming chase would be no contest.

Oh good lord, yes, she had let herself get into terrible shape. Lizzy simultaneously pedaled and cursed every cookie she'd eaten in the past year, every extra pound. There weren't many of them, thank goodness, but oh, if only she'd started running a couple of months ago instead of just this week. If only she were in the same shape she'd been in back in the day.

She paused in her thoughts. What day was that, exactly? She didn't know, but she did know she once would have been able to handle this trip without feeling as if she were being tortured.

The straps of the cheap backpack, being thin on the padding, cut into her shoulders. Her legs ached. Her butt was numb. Sometimes she'd stand up to pedal and give her butt some relief, but that was harder on her legs.

She'd been on the bike about an hour. There was currently little traffic on the two-lane road, so she chanced a glance at her wristwatch. Assuming it was keeping correct time . . . make that forty-five minutes. Evidently being tortured made time pass more slowly. By her calculations she had another four hours and fifteen minutes of cycling time, and that didn't take into account the breaks she'd have to take along the way.

She ached everywhere, and she needed a bathroom already. Maybe she should have said no to that third cup of coffee at breakfast. If necessary, she could make a trip into the bushes on the side of the road, but that would be a last resort. Not only were there homes behind the trees that lined the road, there could be poison ivy, ticks, mosquitos.

She would laugh, if she weren't afraid the laughter would turn to tears. Someone was trying to kill her, and in the past twenty-four hours she'd resorted to car theft—twice—stolen drunk Sean's cash, lied to an impressionable young woman to get a motel room, and possibly led stone-cold killers to an innocent late-night shopper's door. She no longer knew who she was, and she didn't even have time to think about that, not until she was safe, but here she was, worried about modesty and the dangers of Virginia roadside wildlife.

She couldn't let herself dwell on that. She had to concentrate on moving, on surviving. When she was safe, then she'd think about stuff.

One step at a time.

Every hard uphill battle came with an eventual blessed downslope, but really, how could Virginia be mostly uphill? Why didn't the down portions ever seem as long as the up portions? That was just wrong. She treasured the moments when she could sit up and catch her breath, let the wind rush into her face, let her aching muscles relax. Traffic was light on the two-lane road, but on occasion she'd be forced to move to the far right edge, coasting along as a car sped past. Usually those cars would shift over and give her some breathing room, but now and then they didn't, blasting by so close that the force of the air would make her wobble. Some people were jerks.

She wasn't oblivious to the possibility that X might be driving one of those cars. All he'd have to do was run her down, plow his car into her, and then drive off, leaving her as nothing more than a wet spot on a back-country road.

Her instincts had tried to tell her about him, there in Walgreens when she'd panicked and run. Then her hormones had played a nasty trick on her with those sex dreams, and she'd let that tangle up her thinking. It really pissed her off now, that she'd wasted perfectly good dreams on the asshole who was trying to kill her.

Thinking about X distracted her for a while, but not long enough. Soon her aching legs had retaken priority in her thoughts, damn it.

When she rounded a gentle corner in the road and saw the gas station straight ahead, she could have cried, she was so happy. Bathroom, more water, something to eat, a few minutes of rest, however brief. She had to keep moving, and she was already so sore that she knew if she stopped for too long she'd never get started again.

Two meetings with Felice in the tank in less than a week was noteworthy. Al hoped that no one in the building was actually making note. He was surprised that she came as quickly as she did when he contacted her, but considering what she'd done . . .

This time he was waiting for her, standing with his arms crossed. As soon as the door closed behind her, he spoke.

"You stupid bitch."

She stopped in her tracks; her shoulders went back and her face tightened. He had her on the defensive.

"I did what needed to be done," she responded. "I did what *you* wouldn't do."

"No, you've royally fucked things up. It's bad enough that you made this decision on your own and then went outside, but to go to an outside team of incompetents calls into question *your* competence. It was a stupid move."

It wasn't smart to call Felice stupid twice in a couple of minutes, but at this point he didn't care if he pissed her off. If she was going to send a team after him, she'd have already done it. Even worse, if Xavier thought for a minute that Al had been in on the plan, he was coming, too. Al had always known what they'd done might come back to bite him in the ass, and here he was, waiting for a bullet or worse. Xavier was the "worse."

Felice recovered her composure and walked toward the coffee machine. "I have people on it."

"Your people," he said, "not mine." She continued to methodically make herself a cup of coffee. Al hadn't heard from Xavier since the failed hit on Lizzy, not a word. And that meant Felice hadn't just gone after Lizzy, she'd also made an attempt on Xavier. She'd obviously failed, or she already would have bragged about her success in taking out the infamous Xavier.

"I understand that this isn't what you wanted, but now that it's under way, you have to agree that we can't call it off. The ball is in play. We have to see it through."

"Agreed," Al said curtly.

Felice sipped her coffee, fighting to keep her gratification at his acquiescence from showing on her face;

that would be too much like gloating. "I ordered the elimination of both Subject C and Xavier. Given his interest in her, I saw no other choice."

"You should have come to me."

Her look was withering. "You never would've agreed. You'd have tried to talk me out of it, at the very least. I saw what needed to be done, and I took care of it."

"No, you tried to take care of it and you failed."

Again, that withering look. Felice didn't like to fail, and even more hated having her few failures pointed out. "I've brought in a specialist to finish the job."

"That's all well and good, but how do you expect your so-called specialist to *find* Xavier?" If Xavier was in the wind, they'd never locate him—unless and until he wanted to be found. And if he did, that would be very bad news for them.

"That's his problem." Felice took her coffee cup, cradled it, took one sip.

Al stared at her for a long moment, burying his rage deep. They knew that Xavier had trip wires that would make the details of what they'd done public, in order to protect himself and Lizzy. It would be devastating for the country if that were to happen. Even if they managed to plant doubts about him and the story, to clean up the mess, to paint Xavier as nothing more than a conspiracy theorist, the details he released would remain. The conspiracy theory would live, perhaps forever. And if enough people believed it . . .

"No, it's *your* problem. He will come after you." Al tried to remain outwardly calm. "Tonight, two years from now, at any time in between." He noted the way her shoulders tightened again. "I suggest that you put your specialist on your house. If you're lucky, Xavier will show up sooner rather than later. He'll find Subject C, secure her, and then he'll come after you. If he decides to wait, if he takes more time to plan and doesn't act while he's still pissed, you won't have a prayer. But if he reacts in anger and attacks now, it's possible your specialist can intercept him at the house and end this."

"And Subject C?"

"If I were you, I'd deal with Xavier first and then worry about what your fuckup cost us where Subject C is concerned."

"You could offer to help," she said. "You have the personnel."

Was she fucking kidding? Al clenched his jaw, but he kept his cool, as much as was possible given the situation. "That wouldn't be smart, at this point."

Her quick agreement to meet this morning finally made sense, though: she wanted him to help her clean up the mess she'd made. She didn't know him at all if she thought he'd risk any of his people to track down another one of his own because she'd screwed up.

"If he contacts you . . ."

"You'll be the first to know," Al said dryly.

Felice left her half-full cup of coffee sitting on the table and left the tank without looking back.

Al followed her, retrieved his weapon and cell phone, and headed for the room where Dereon Ashe was on duty, listening for activity at Subject C's house, watching the monitors on her car, listening to activity in her office. If that duty had been dull before, it was now beyond boring. There was nothing to listen to. If enough of Lizzy had come back, there was no way she'd risk returning to any place or person she'd known as Lizette. The question was, how much had come back? Just enough to make her run, or enough to make her dangerous?

Felice would take his advice and put her specialist on her own home. Maybe she'd even think of him as a double-duty off-the-books employee, a bodyguard for herself as well as someone who could take Xavier down when he came after her. Xavier would be looking for that move; when he moved in on Felice he'd be looking for someone like her specialist. If he didn't, then he wouldn't be the man Al himself had trained, years ago.

Felice thought she had everything well in hand, but Al would put his money on Xavier any day.

Chapter Twenty-two

Three hours. Three hours and fifteen minutes of misery and determination. This section of road was straight, thank heavens, but she could use a downhill coast right about now. Her muscles were on fire, from her neck to her ankles. Her butt was beyond numb.

She was passing through a small collection of businesses that likely constituted some kind of township, but if there had been a sign she'd missed it. She *had* seen a sign that said the speed limit was 3.0, which had distracted her until she'd realized the decimal point was a bullet hole.

For the past hour, her entire focus had been on moving forward while her body screamed for her to stop. Curse words she hadn't even realized she knew slipped from her lips as she pedaled. To anyone watching, with her backpack, helmet, drugstore clothes, and the now constant muttering, she probably looked like a crazy bag lady with a bicycle instead of a shopping cart, and she didn't freakin' care.

Maybe it was the constant pedaling, the rhythm, the steady sound of the tires on the road, or simply the fact that for the first time in a long while her mind wasn't entirely occupied with how to survive from one minute to the next, but as she struggled up one hill and coasted down the other side, a few memories suddenly eased into focus. She tensed, expecting the wallop of a headache that would knock her off the bike, but . . . nothing. No pain, no nausea. She relaxed and let the memories come.

The memories weren't anything earth-shattering, and really not all that specific, just kind of general-knowledge memories. She hadn't always worked in an office, hadn't always been a predictable, routine-bound, never-miss-a-day, nine-to-five employee. *Chicago. A security firm.* Not some little fly-by-night PI outfit, but a top-notch security firm with offices located in a tall building in downtown Chicago, with windows that overlooked the city. The firm had attracted a lot of high-profile clients. She'd worked as a bodyguard on more than one occasion; men especially liked her because she didn't look like a bodyguard, but she could shoot like one.

And drive. Her heart skipped a beat. So that was where she'd learned evasive driving, how to spot a tail and lose it. The job also explained why she'd so often reached for a handgun that wasn't there. Once there had been a time when she'd never been without her weapon.

There was still nothing that would explain why she'd lost her memory of that time or why anyone would want her dead, but her previous occupation explained a lot. It was a relief to know that these newfound skills she possessed had come from a legitimate job and not . . . well, *not*.

When she actively tried to remember, something blocked her, something got in the way. So as she pedaled along the side of the road she didn't make an effort to think about anything in particular; she just let her mind go free, and that's when the images played through her mind.

There were faces, the images of people she'd worked with; some were clearer than others. She didn't reach for names, didn't want to force anything, but at this point any memory of her previous life was welcome. She hurt, she was tired; at times she just wanted to stop and pull onto the side of the road and sit there until someone found her. The memories kept her going.

If she just pedaled and let her mind go, more would come to her. And they did: a target range where she'd honed her skills. There'd been an office, too, but she hadn't spent much time there. She remembered getting on a plane to go . . . somewhere. If the memories didn't come easily she didn't force them, so when the plane didn't go anywhere she relaxed and let it sit there while she thought of other things, other places and memories.

A football game at Soldier Field, watching the Bears; laughing over a beer with . . . someone. Maybe a co-worker, maybe just a friend. She remembered being grabbed from behind, caught by surprise by a well-muscled and very tall man while on a job and still coming out on top, thanks to her martial arts training. She'd taken classes in college and had discovered an affinity for it. How had she forgotten that?

Stupid question. How the hell had she forgotten *anything*?

So, she'd worked as a bodyguard. She'd even been something of a whiz kid, picking up new weapons and skills with ease, managing to appear deceptively harmless when she needed to, while never losing her focus. She'd been more than a bodyguard, though that had been her primary area of expertise. On occasion she'd tailed a subject or two, she'd infiltrated a company to learn more about the CFO, she'd . . .

A car horn, too close and too loud, jerked Lizzy back to the present. She'd drifted too far to the left and had alarmed or annoyed the driver who wanted to pass. She jerked the bike back to the right, lifted a hand in acknowledgment of the car, and pulled her brain back to the present. Wouldn't that be a trip, to shake X, come up with a plan, start to remember, and then get run over by a random car? That would just be *too* unfair.

The car passed, and Lizzy had the road to herself again. Maybe it was best to just accept what she'd remembered and not push for more—not yet, anyway. It wasn't in her nature to let something like that drop, but now wasn't the time. She didn't want to deal with the pain and nausea, and she knew she shouldn't let herself get too distracted. She wasn't safe yet.

None of what she remembered explained the memory loss or why someone was trying to kill her. There were a couple of possible explanations for the selective amnesia and even the facial reconstruction: a car accident; a bullet in her head—though surely there would be physical evidence of that, a scar no surgery could completely disguise. She could come up with explanations for the surgery and the memory loss, but there were very few that covered both. As to why someone would now be trying to kill her . . . she needed more information before she could make sense of that.

At least she had an explanation for why she sometimes knew what she knew, such as evasive driving and hot-wiring a car.

Duh! Collections! Now she remembered. Before she'd become a bodyguard, she'd repossessed a car or two, or ten. The cars she'd hot-wired hadn't been stolen; they'd been recovered by the company to whom they rightly belonged when the purchasers stopped making payments. Of course, some recoveries hadn't been any more complicated than having a tow truck pick them up off the street, but some others had been . . . interesting, to say the least.

She'd liked her work as a bodyguard much better. The pay had been significantly better and she'd never been sent on a job that required her to get grease under her fingernails. At least, not that she could recall.

As she coasted down a small hill, she took momentary pleasure in the feel of the wind in her face and ignored the sad truth that another uphill piece of road was looming ahead. Crap. She didn't know how much more her legs could take.

Oh, God, she was going to die.

Lizzy didn't think she'd ever before been this tired, not even during training. A couple of times, when her legs and back hurt so bad she didn't think she could go another inch, she got off the bike and pushed it. At least that used different muscles, and walking was a hell of a lot easier than pedaling. After all, she walked every day of her life. When this was over, she'd pay money not to ever have to park her ass on a bicycle again.

And speaking of asses, even *that* was sore.

She didn't remember ever being sore when she was a kid, when she rode her bicycle every day. How did kids *do* that? Why didn't their little asses get sore? It just wasn't fair. She was running for her life, here, not just playing around the neighborhood.

At one point when she was pushing the bike she thought she heard the roar of a motorcycle coming up behind her, hidden by a curve in the road, and her heart nearly stopped. Quickly she left the road, shoving the bike through the high weeds on the side of the road until she reached some kind of bush. She laid the bike on the ground behind the bush, then flattened herself in the weeds beside it. At that point she didn't care if she was in the middle of a patch of poison ivy, or even if there was a freaking snake crawling up her leg. Her heart was pounding so hard her ribs were reverberating.

She buried her face against the earth, the smell of grass and dirt filling her nose, leaves prickling against her skin, and listened to the deep, coughing, almost tiger-like roar that signaled a Harley, as it got closer and closer. X's motorcycle was a Harley. No other motorcycle in the world sounded like it, in her opinion.

Chills ran over her entire body. Dear God, how had he found her so fast? She'd dumped her car. She'd dumped her phone. She'd dumped her purse. She was on a *bicycle*.

At least she'd chosen a black helmet instead of the bright pink one that had caught her eye. Pink would stand out, even among these weeds. Black just blended in. The bright spokes on the bicycle tires . . . would they flash in the sun? If she had time she'd pull some weeds to cover the bicycle, but she didn't have time; the motorcycle was right *there* and she didn't dare look, didn't dare move—

It roared past without the rider even letting off the gas, and Lizzy went limp with relief. Then she quickly lifted her head to stare at the swiftly receding figure to see if she could tell for certain if it was X, if that was the same Harley.

No way to tell, not from the back, and not at the speed at which he was traveling, disappearing around a curve. The best she could tell was that the rider looked like a big man.

So . . . inconclusive. Could be X, could be just another guy on a motorcycle. There were a lot of Harleys in the world.

But, if it *was* him . . . oh, shit. He was now in front of her, and she might run into him at any turn of the road. All he had to do was pick a good spot and wait for her.

On the other hand, this spot right here was pretty secluded. Cautiously she sat up and looked around: rural, no houses in sight, which was probably a good thing or her bolt into the weeds might have been witnessed. She could just envision some curious kid tromping through the weeds toward her, alerting X to her presence.

And, thinking this through, if that *had* been X, he had to be tracking her somehow and would have seen that she'd stopped, and he'd have stopped too. Ergo, that either hadn't been X or he didn't have a tracker on her. And if he didn't have a tracker on her, what were the odds that he'd be on this two-lane road heading deep into Virginia, right behind her? Almost zero. Logically, then, that hadn't been X.

She sucked in a deep, shaky breath. She'd felt safe on this road, on her bicycle, her identity hidden under the helmet and sunglasses. Her instincts had been right . . . she hoped. But if she heard any more motorcycles coming up behind, she was still going to get off the road and hide.

Between the walking and this episode, she'd lost enough time. She had to get back in the saddle— literally—and get going. Standing, she settled the backpack in the proper position again, tightening the straps a little because throwing herself on the ground had shifted everything. She pulled the bike upright, pushed it through the tall weeds to the road, and mounted up.

The short "rest," as stressful as it had been, had done her tired muscles a lot of good. Of course, the adrenaline shot caused by sheer terror had a lot to do with that, but she'd take whatever push she could get that would move her on down the road.

If she made it to the bus station alive, she was never, ever throwing her leg across a bicycle again. They were instruments of torture.

Pedaling steadily, she tried to distract herself by thinking of the satisfactory ways in which she could get rid of the bike. Simply leaving it on a sidewalk had no real payback; she wanted to do something that brought revenge, and closure. She wanted to shoot it. No pistol, so that was out. She wanted to set fire to it. She wanted to take a hammer and beat it to tiny little pieces. Both of those were viable options, because she could buy gasoline and matches or she could buy a hammer. Which one would be better, and less likely to get her arrested as being a danger to herself and others? The hammer, probably. People tended to notice fires, even small ones.

Traffic was light. Several cars passed her, but minutes would go by without anyone in sight. Up ahead she saw a three-way intersection, with a service station set square ahead. The sign for the road she was following indicated she should take the left. Oh, yeah, she remembered seeing a kind of dog-leg turn on the map; the road should be turning back to the right within a mile of the intersection.

But that service station was the most welcome sight she'd seen in a while. Her thigh muscles were killing her. She wanted some aspirin, a bottle of cold water, a protein bar, and she wanted to pee. Pee first, in fact.

It was the good kind of service station, with the public toilets inside. She wheeled the bike off to the side, and took the precaution of tucking it behind the trash bin so it couldn't be seen from the road. Then she took off her sunglasses and limped into the station.

The clerk, a middle-aged woman with frizzy hair and a warm voice, was talking to a younger woman who held a toddler on one hip and a little boy of about three by his hand. "Don't go anywhere, stand right here," the mother warned the boy, because she had to release his hand in order to pay for their fruit juices and her bottle of sweet tea. He squirmed and jumped up and down, but didn't wander from her side.

There were two other customers, both men; one was looking at candy, the other was in the back drag-

ging a six-pack of beer from the refrigerated case.
Neither so much as glanced at her.

The cool air from the air conditioning was more
welcome than a prayer. Lizzy went into the women's
bathroom—a single, so she locked the door behind
her—and heaved a giant sigh of relief at the coolness,
at walking instead of pedaling, at the fact that she was
still alive and well away from the D.C. area. The small
bathroom could use some updating and smelled
heavily of bleach, but it was clean, so she included that
in her relief.

After doing what she had to, she washed her hands
and dried them, then pulled the helmet off and held it
between her knees as she massaged her head. The
helmet was ventilated, but she'd still been putting out
a lot of effort and her hair was sweaty. Her ponytail
had suffered during the day, too, and was hanging
messily to one side, with a lot of escaped strands.

She pulled the band off and shook her head, rolling
her neck from side to side, loosening her shoulders.
She wet one of the paper hand towels and washed her
face, reveling in the coolness, before restoring her hair
to a much neater ponytail and wedging the helmet
back on her head.

When she left the bathroom, the young woman
with the two kids had checked out and left, the beer-
drinker was paying for the six-pack, and that same
guy was still trying to make up his mind about what
candy he wanted.

That struck her as a little strange, because men
usually had an idea what they wanted and went
straight to it. Women were the browsers. She eyed
him suspiciously, but he seemed like an ordinary guy,

in jeans and a tee shirt, a ball cap on his head. He certainly wasn't X. She gathered up a bottle of cold water and the aspirin, which, holy hell, cost twice what it would in a drugstore, and looked for the protein bars. The selection was small—one brand, chocolate or peanut butter. She got one of each.

As she checked out, the candy man finally selected what looked like a couple of Hershey bars, then moseyed into the pretzel and potato chip section. Maybe he had difficulty making decisions. Maybe he had some time to kill.

Lizzy slipped her sunglasses on as she stepped out into the glare and circled toward the back. Standing behind the trash bin, she opened the bottle of aspirin and popped two into her mouth, then twisted open the water bottle and washed them down. Maybe the aspirin would help; it couldn't hurt. She also ate the chocolate protein bar while she was standing there, so the aspirin wouldn't upset her stomach.

Checking her watch, she saw that she'd killed twenty minutes. She needed to be on the road.

Muscles that had relaxed began protesting again within a quarter of a mile. Once more she began trying to think of the most diabolical thing she could do to the bike when she didn't need it anymore.

She took the turn to the right, pedaling deeper into the rural countryside. There were hay fields filled with giant round bales of hay, pastures with cows in them, some horses. She'd known that this route would take her through the rural area, away from most of the towns and communities, but she hadn't realized it would be quite this empty. If she'd been in a car, she wouldn't even have noticed. Being on a bicycle, however, she was suddenly, acutely aware of how alone she was, and how helpless if some yahoo tried to mess with her.

No, she *wasn't* helpless. That was Lizette-thinking. She was Lizzy, who had taken some intense martial arts training, who knew how to fight and fight dirty, how to protect a client from a carjacking, a kidnapping attempt, or a simple mugging. Yeah, she'd been armed then and she wasn't now, at least not with a handgun—a situation she intended to remedy pretty damn soon. But she did have a knife, and the willingness to use it.

She caught the deep, rumbly roar of a motorcycle, coming up behind her.

Briefly, for a split second, she considered just staying on the road. After all, she'd decided there was no way X could be tracking her now. She'd shaken him off her trail. This was just another motorcycle rider; the hills of Virginia were popular with cyclists.

No. She couldn't take the chance.

Frantically she looked around; she wasn't in a great place. There were hay fields on both sides of the road, fields that had recently been mowed and baled. Off to the right about a hundred yards was a big shed under which the owner of the hay probably intended to store the bales, but that was a long hundred yards and the motorcycle was closing in fast.

Crap! All she could do was try to make it to the shed. No—one of the big round bales was closer, and she could hide behind it.

She didn't have time to get off the bicycle and push. Instead she turned it into the hay field, bumping across the rough field so hard it jarred her teeth, bent forward, pedaling as hard as she could. She had to fight to keep the bicycle upright, the ground was so rough.

She reached the first bale and jumped off the bike, crouching down, her heart pounding from exertion and fear even though she knew it was nothing, knew the motorcycle was going to blow right past her—

The loud rumble throttled down. It was slowing.

Her back against the bale, she rolled her head around for a fast peek. She saw the Harley. She saw the big man riding it, effortlessly holding the big Harley up across the rough field that had almost unseated her, black tee shirt clinging to his muscled torso, face hidden by a black helmet with a complete face shield.

X.

Chapter Twenty-three

Lizzy's mouth went dry and her vision dimmed. She had absolutely nowhere to go, nowhere to hide. She was on a bicycle. He was on a motorcycle, maybe fifty yards away and coming straight at her.

Quickly she unzipped her backpack and pulled out the kitchen knife. In the afternoon sun it looked dull and inadequate, but it was all she had. Unless there was something in the shed, maybe a pickax, a scythe, an awl—anything that would help give her an edge— the knife would have to do.

Though what good would any of that do against a bullet? It didn't matter. She couldn't just give up, not after all this. She had to keep trying.

She was running before she consciously made the decision *to* run, her body taking over, refusing to give up. She didn't bother with the bicycle; on the rough field, she was probably as fast or faster on foot than she'd be on the bike, as long as she didn't break an ankle. She ran, tired muscles forgotten, aches and pains disappeared. All she knew was desperate effort, a burning need to get to the shed before he did. And she prayed, prayed there would be something there she could use to defend herself, prayed, hell, that the farmer who cut these hay fields would drive in on his tractor to start moving hay into the shed. Anything.

She was running west, the afternoon sun hot on her face, blurring her vision. She didn't look back, didn't look to see how much he'd gained on her, just flung herself headlong across the stubby grass stalks. Twenty yards to the shed . . . ten . . . then she was there, the deep shade of the structure enclosing her. She skidded to a halt, temporarily blinded, bright spots swimming in front of her eyes.

Fiercely she squeezed her eyes shut, trying to regain her vision. Damn it! She should have thought about that—she should have squinted to reduce the amount of sunlight in her eyes. Now she was helpless for a few precious moments, and the deep rumble of the motorcycle was getting closer, louder.

No time! She gripped the kitchen knife, but she knew in her bones it wasn't enough. She had to find another weapon *now*.

She opened her eyes a sliver; her vision had adjusted enough that she could see to make her way deeper into the shed, working to the right, searching the periphery for anything she could use. Snakes . . . wouldn't there be a hoe or something around to kill snakes?

Yeah, that would work. A hoe against a handgun.

A hoe would be better than nothing, and that was pretty much what she had right now. A knife was for close-quarters combat. She needed something that would allow her to keep some distance between her and her adversary.

The rumbling engine cut off.

And there it was, by God, as if her desperate thoughts had conjured it out of midair: a hoe. The blade was rusted, the handle wasn't in the best of shape, but it was a weapon. She grabbed it up in one hand, knife clutched in the other, and turned to face Death as he approached.

He'd stopped the motorcycle twenty, maybe twenty-five yards away, and was sitting astride the Harley with his booted feet planted on the ground, calmly watching her as she scrabbled through the shed and finally came up with the hoe.

His black face shield caught the sun, reflected it back at her.

She was so frightened she felt dizzy, and spots swam before her eyes. She could hear her breath, her lungs pumping too fast, and dimly she realized she was hyperventilating. She had to stop, she had to get control of herself, or she'd have no chance at all. Deliberately she sucked in a deep breath and held it, forcing herself to calm down.

The dizzy sensation faded and her vision cleared. She squared off and braced herself.

Leisurely he dismounted from the bike, kicked the stand down, and stood the Harley on the hard-packed field. Given how uneven the ground was, Lizzy had the fleeting thought that he must have found the one piece of flat earth in the entire field. His movement still calm and deliberate, he pulled his chin strap loose, used both gloved hands to pull the helmet up and off and place it on the seat. Then he started toward her.

If he had a weapon, it wasn't evident. His hands were empty.

That didn't mean he didn't have a handgun tucked into his waistband in the small of his back.

No, that wasn't how he carried his weapons. He used a shoulder rig.

Her heart was already racing, and suddenly her blood was thundering in her ears. She heard a tiny sound vibrate in her throat, something wordless and uncontrollable. Her vision shrank down to a tunnel, centered on his face, the almost brutally carved structure of his cheekbones, the eyes as dark as night, focused like a hawk's on his prey.

There was kind of a saunter to how he moved, hips loose and easy, wide shoulders moving back and forth, his balance perfect no matter which way he needed to jump.

She looked at his face.

Time spun away from her, everything solid falling away. Dizzy, she put out the hand that gripped the knife and touched a support post, but she couldn't grab it without dropping the knife and she wasn't about to do that. Her chest heaving, she stared unblinking at him as past and present blended together in a swirl of color, of night and day, then and now.

His face.

She had watched him before, coming toward her just like that, as sure of himself as if he controlled everything in his world.

The quick flash of feet and fists, the thudding sound of flesh hitting flesh, the grunts as blows landed. His training partner scored a hit to the testicles and he went down, cussing through tight-clenched teeth, while she and her own training partner howled with laughter because he almost never lost a bout.

He didn't lose this one, either. He bowed his spine and flipped upright before his training partner could take advantage, and two quick pop-pops, one with his right elbow and the other with his left knee, sent his partner down. The man lay sprawled on his back on the mat, breathing hard and groaning. He tapped one hand on the mat in surrender.

X grabbed a towel and came to where she and her partner watched, his prowling stride as fluid and easy as before, his dark eyes narrowed on her face. Sweat dripped down his face, darkened his olive-drab tee shirt. "Why do women always laugh when a man gets kicked in the balls?" he growled as he swiped the towel over his face.

"Because they're so precioussssss," *Lizzy said in her best Gollum accent, still laughing because he was a little pissed. She so seldom got anything on him, she enjoyed it to the fullest whenever she did.*

"Damn right they are," he returned.

He was closer, his gaze still locked on her.

X . . . No, not X . . . but close. X . . .

Xavier.

His name was *Xavier.*

The name exploded through her brain, and suddenly it was there, memories cascading through the wall that had been breached. The days. The nights. She gripped the hoe handle with all her strength, using it to support her weight as she fought to stay upright.

Xavier!

He crawled over her, his naked body rubbing all over her, his powerful legs pushing between hers and spreading them wide, so that he settled into the cradle of her hips and loins. She loved that moment when he paused to guide the thick tip of his penis to her, loved the flex of his hips that nudged him inside her that first little bit. He was thick and hard and there was always that instant when her body was startled by the size of him, then she'd feel herself soften and relax and take more of him. He'd wait for that moment, hold himself back until he felt her accept him, and then he'd push deep, and she could never hold back a gasp at the hot slide of his flesh into hers.

Xavier. Oh my God, it was *Xavier.*

He stopped just inside the shadow of the shed, his head cocked a little to the side as he intently watched her. He didn't dismiss the knife or the hoe, not in her hands, though she had no doubt at all that he could take her. She hadn't trained in . . . however long it had been since they'd trained together. She was weak, out of practice, hadn't had enough sleep, plus she was exhausted from riding that damn bicycle for hours in the summer heat, while he'd been cruising on his Hog.

Fury blasted through her. Damn his eyes! He *did* have a tracker on her, somewhere. He could have caught her at any time, but instead he'd hung back, played games with her, let her damn near kill herself before he made his move. That probably *had* been him on the motorcycle earlier, leapfrogging ahead of her, enjoying the game. She was so furious, she'd have kicked him in his precious balls if she'd been able to. The day wasn't over yet, though.

"Lizzy," he said, his deep voice calm and dark, a little cautious, as if he didn't want to spook her. She realized he didn't know what, if anything, she'd remembered. "I won't hurt you. Do you remember me?"

Yes. There were still big gaps in her memory, but she remembered *him*.

She had loved him. Whether or not he'd loved her had been up in the air, still was, because she didn't know what had happened. But one thing definitely hadn't changed: she still did love him, she realized, otherwise her heart wouldn't be feeling as if it were about to burst. He was here. The long time apart felt as if she hadn't been living at all, as if her world had been gray and empty. Pain and joy and all kinds of anger unfurled in her, and she briefly closed her eyes. This was too much; she couldn't get a grip on any of her emotions, couldn't organize any of her tumultuous thoughts into any kind of order.

"Yes," she finally managed, all but whispering the word. She drove the knife point into the post, left it sticking there. She looked back at him, her lips trembling. "*Preciousssss.*"

No sooner had the word left her lips than he lunged, was on her, the impact of his body knocking the hoe to the ground. It would have knocked her to the ground as well except for the grip he had on her, both arms around her, and he lifted her off her feet and kissed her. His mouth was hot and firm and hungry; she didn't think she'd ever been kissed like that before, as if he were starving for the taste of her. He slanted his head and his tongue took possession of her mouth, and the impact on her senses was like being body-slammed.

Yes. Yes, she had been kissed like this before—by him. The rightness of it, the sense of belonging, sliced through her as sharply as any blade.

Her arms wound around his neck and she kissed

him back the way she used to, the way she'd done in the dreams that had been trying to tell her something, had all but been pointing at him and screaming *Him! Him!* She kissed him as violently as he kissed her, not caring if her teeth cut his lip, not caring about anything other than his taste, the feel of him, the hot smell of his skin, the fact that he was *here*.

He held her with one arm and with the other pulled the helmet from her head, dropped it to the ground. The helmet dispensed with, he began taking off her clothes.

He was so fast it was almost like being under assault. Her senses spun violently as she tried to orient herself. He wasn't going to—was he?—yes, he most definitely was. She instantaneously went from disbelief to acceptance, to need. It had always been like this with him, their attraction so fierce she felt as if her skin could barely contain her.

Within a minute she was naked from the waist down, and she didn't care that they were in a shed, and that the shed was open to the road that ran along the hay field. In the shadows, at that distance, probably no one could see anything anyway. And even if they could— she didn't care.

She cared about him. She'd found him again, or he'd found her. It didn't matter. They were together.

There was nothing to sit on, nothing to lie on except the ground, but he was strong enough that they didn't need either. He unbuckled his belt, unsnapped his jeans, and shoved them down just enough. Holding her braced against the support pole, holding her up with both hands gripping her ass, he surged against her. She locked her legs around him, lifted herself, opened herself, and he pushed in hard.

Time spun away again. The world spun away. Memory and reality collided; it was the way it had been before, the heat and stretching and almost-pain. There was no foreplay, no trying to arouse her, but he'd always had her number and could make her come even when she was trying her damnedest not to, just to spite him. She came easy for him, in both senses of the word. He kissed her, and she was turned on. He touched her, and she was ready for him.

She had been without him too long.

She felt the tension inside her building fast, rushing toward her like floodwaters. He thrust deep and fast, moving her up and down on him. She moaned, the sound raw. It was coming, that complete upheaval that was too intense to be mere pleasure, drawing all her muscles tight until she felt as if her entire body was trying to clamp around him.

Then she came, bucking in his arms, her fingers clenching on his back, her face buried against his throat as she tried to stifle the guttural sounds she was making. He drove her harder against the post, his hips pistoning; then his rhythm changed to something slower, rolling, deeper. He grunted—she remembered that grunt—a brief, hard sound before one long groan tore from deep in his chest, then she felt the tension seeping from his muscles as he slowly relaxed, resting his heavy weight against her.

She closed her eyes, drove her fingers through his thick dark hair, gripping the back of his skull. "Xavier." How had she lived without him?

He'd know what was going on. He could fill in all

the awful blanks in her memory. The important thing was that she'd remembered *him*. She loved him more than she could hold in, and now that they were together again she didn't plan on letting him go until she'd wrung him dry.

And then she was going to kill his ass for what he'd put her through today.

Chapter Twenty-four

"Awkward" wasn't the word for it.

Here she was half-naked—literally—with a man she'd just had sex with, but she wasn't certain exactly what was going on. Shouldn't she have gotten some of that settled before getting down and dirty with him?

She grabbed up her pants, holding them in front of her as if that would do any good. "Um . . . I have some wet wipes in my backpack." She waved her hand in the direction of the hay bale where she'd left everything in her panicked run to the shed.

He didn't seem to feel any of her discomfort. He slid a hard, muscled arm around her waist and pulled her to him for a minute; she automatically stiffened, but more in unease than rejection. Gradually she relaxed, her cheek resting on his shoulder and her hands pressed flat against his back, feeling the rippling muscles there, the heat that poured off him. Even if she didn't remember much detail about their time together, everything about him was so familiar, so right, from his smell to his taste to how their bodies fit together. He kissed the top of her head. "I'll get them. Don't slide that knife into me while my back is turned, okay?"

She *had* thought of pulling the knife from where she'd stuck it in the post, because she was uncertain and didn't know whether or not she needed a weapon. When in doubt, she thought, get the weapon and worry later about looking silly. Did that mean he knew her well, or was that simply what his life was like, that he had to look at everything from the viewpoint of potential for attack?

She was still scrambling for balance when he returned, but she'd left the knife where it was.

"I don't know what's real—" she began.

"We are," he interrupted, giving her one of those darkly intense looks. "We're real. Just go with that for now."

"There's a lot I don't remember. I didn't remember you until you were coming toward me. X. I thought of you as Mr. X."

He considered that. "Close enough. You were going in the right direction."

"Your name *is* Xavier?" she asked, just to be certain.

"Yeah, it is."

She stopped asking questions while she turned her back to clean herself; silly, perhaps, to feel embarrassed after what they'd just done together, but there'd been no time to become accustomed to him again. One second she'd thought he was about to kill her, and the next second her brain was firing erotic images at her. There was no bridge, no link between the past and the present.

She looked at the wet wipe in her hand, and something else smacked her between the eyes: they'd just had sex without using a condom, and she wasn't on birth control. Was this new? Had she been on birth control before? Simply not worrying about it had felt so normal, as if condoms had never been part of their love life, but she didn't know for certain. Everything was probably okay this time—her menses were due to start in just a couple of days—but from here on out they'd need to take precautions until she could get back on the pill and it became effective.

That was assuming they were still together, and both of them were still alive, that there was a "here on out."

Deep down, she didn't doubt the "together" part. And now that Xavier was with her, for the first time since she'd taken ill she wasn't frightened and lost. Okay, not *as* frightened, and still lost, but Xavier wasn't. She didn't know what was going on, but he would.

He'd found her. He knew she was in trouble, and he'd found her.

She pulled on her pants, thinking furiously. She could reach only one obvious conclusion, and she'd been smacked between the eyes so often in the past few minutes that she was beginning to feel like a punching bag. Turning, she snapped, "You *jerk*!"

He lifted his eyebrows. There was a sleepy, self-satisfied look in his dark eyes. "Yeah? How so?"

"*How so?*" she mimicked furiously. "Don't tell me you couldn't have caught up with me at any time. You let me half kill myself on that damn bicycle, instead of stopping me *hours* ago. That was you who passed me when I was hiding in the weeds, wasn't it?"

"Yeah, but it wasn't a good place."

She felt like smacking him. There wasn't an ounce

of apology in his tone, but then, there wouldn't be. He'd analyzed the situation, decided on his tactics, and that was that; did he ever second-guess himself? She didn't know, but she'd bet not.

"I needed a place with no witnesses, in case you didn't remember me."

"I didn't," she said, her stomach clenching a little as some of the backwash of terror hit her.

"Yeah, wouldn't that have worked out well, with me trying to wrestle you onto the motorcycle while you fought like a wildcat, screaming your head off," he said dryly. He hooked his left hand around the back of her neck, drawing her in for a long kiss.

That reassured her as nothing else would have done, but she still wasn't ready to let go of her ire. As soon as her mouth was free she said, "There were plenty of places— "

"I wanted you tired, to minimize any struggle. Are you tired?"

"Exhausted," she shot back. "You know what? That's a case of sound tactics and poor judgment. Because I'm not only tired, I'm sore in every muscle, and I'm *pissed*."

His mouth quirked as he considered the ramifications. "Tired is good, pissed isn't unusual. I'll try to do something about the soreness."

"Such as?"

"How does a hotel room with a whirlpool tub sound?"

The bicycle she'd bought just that morning—and spent a wad of dough on—had served her well, but she'd never before in her life been so glad to see the last of anything. She pushed it to the side of the road and left it there, figuring someone would pick it up within half an hour at the most. Then, backpack strapped in place and helmet on, she waited until Xavier had straddled the Harley before she stepped on the bar and swung her leg over the seat, settling into place behind him. This wasn't one of the big touring bikes, with the raised passenger seat and back rest; this was a machine built for muscle and speed, which meant he had to scoot forward as far as he could and she still barely had enough room to sit down. Another half inch, and she'd be on the back fender. She wrapped her arms tightly around his waist and laid her head against his back, because she would have to hold on for dear life.

He started the engine, and a heavy throbbing sprang to life between her legs.

"Good Lord," she muttered. "If a woman had one of these babies, she wouldn't need a man."

He laughed and squeezed her hands where they laced together on his stomach, then put the transmission in gear and eased onto the asphalt.

Because her position was so precarious, she deeply appreciated the way he handled the machine, as smoothly as if he were carrying fine china. The motorcycle seat was more comfortable than the bicycle had been, or she never would have made it. What would have taken her hours more—because she probably would have ended up walking the rest of the way—was reduced to about half an hour.

The hotel he chose was one of the big, historic five-star inns. He didn't have reservations, of course, but what he did have was a platinum card, with a name on it that bore no relation to "Xavier" in any way, not as an initial, a first name, a last name—nothing. Somehow she wasn't surprised that he had fake ID; they were obviously involved in something that made having false identities a very good idea.

In nothing flat the Harley was in a secure parking area and they were in a luxurious suite with a balcony, a fireplace, a king-size bed, and marvelous antique pieces. The bathroom was easily twice the size of her bathroom at home—or what used to be her home. The odds were she wouldn't be going back there, and even though she knew the life she'd been living was a false one, she still felt a pang at the idea of not seeing her home again. She didn't want to think about that, so she examined the tub. It wasn't a whirlpool, but she figured a long soak in hot water, plus a couple of aspirin, would be almost as good.

"I'm getting in that tub," she announced, bending down to turn on the water.

"Be my guest," he said from behind her, patting her butt.

"Jerk," she muttered.

He chuckled as he moved away. "I'm going to check my messages. Maybe you'll be in a better mood after you've soaked for a while."

There was a lot they needed to talk about, but neither of them seemed in any hurry to get into the heavy stuff, such as why people were trying to kill her, and what his involvement was—heck, what *her* involvement was. He seemed content to wait, and she was so tired, that suited her too.

Lizzy ran the water as hot as she could stand it,

then stripped down and stepped in. Gingerly she lowered her aching body into the tub, groaning as the heat seeped into her abused muscles. Closing her eyes, she lay all the way back, sinking down until her hair floated around her and her knees were sticking out of the water. She hurt from her toes to her neck. It was possible that the only part of her body that didn't hurt was her right earlobe, because she'd caught the helmet strap on her left ear and pulled at the stud earring she wore.

She wanted to just relax and soak, to let her mind float the way her hair was doing, but it wasn't possible. No matter what, her thoughts kept worrying at her situation like a cat with a ball of yarn. She wasn't safe; she might never be safe again. But at this moment she felt safer, *better,* than she had since she'd looked in the mirror and seen a stranger's face staring back at her. Her heart beat at a steady rhythm; she wasn't poised to leap from the tub and flee. Maybe tomorrow she'd be on the run again, but for tonight she could enjoy a simple hot bath, real food, and sleeping in a decent bed.

When she sat back up—because her knees really needed the heat more than her ears did—she opened her eyes and looked around the bathroom, all white marble and polished chrome. There was this big bathtub and a shower, double sinks, and a separate room for the toilet, as well as more thick, fluffy towels than two people could use in a single day. She'd say this for Xavier: when he found a place to hide out for a night, he had much better luck than she did.

Luck, hell! He was prepared for anything and everything. Having a fake ID and credit cards under a false name was much more effective than lying her way into an unrentable hotel room where she had to sit with the lights out, no sheets, and one crappy towel.

Xavier. X. The man of her dreams, literally. She was still highly pissed at him for letting her pedal that damn bike for so long before stopping her, furious with him for terrifying her, and yet—he was here.

Without him, she'd been bereft, and hadn't known it. Only now that he was back in her life could she look at the interval between then and now and see how drab and joyless it had been. Xavier was the color in the colorless world they'd stuck her in. In spite of everything, she was relieved that she could now remember . . . some of what had happened. She remembered *him* most clearly.

She still didn't know how things stood. Were they the good guys, or the bad guys? Xavier certainly could break either way. Maybe both; maybe neither. She thought about that, and realized it didn't matter that he wasn't a certified White Knight. Her life wasn't a black-and-white movie from the fifties where good and bad were easily defined and identified. White hats for the heroes, black ones for the villains. The real world was much more complicated than that. *Her* world was complicated.

No, *complicated* didn't begin to cover it. Her world was a cluster-fuck.

The door opened and Xavier came in—without knocking, of course, but even though she was a little uneasy at being naked in front of him, she didn't grab a towel, or otherwise show the modesty that felt out of place between them. He'd seen her like this before.

She might not remember exactly when, but she knew it had happened.

"I ordered food. It'll be here in forty-five minutes."

She looked up at him. The man towered over her, fully dressed, armed—she didn't know where he'd had the weapon hidden, unless it was in the small leather kit he'd carried in, but she was glad he had the big handgun. Even though logic said they were safe, he'd found her, so it followed that someone else could.

"What did you order for me?" She was grumpy enough that she wanted him to have ordered something she didn't like, so she could snap at him.

"Crab cakes. And cheesecake for dessert."

She loved crab cakes, and cheesecake was one of her favorites, too. He'd remembered. Did she know his favorite foods? Out of the murkiness swam an obvious answer: steak. He wasn't a picky eater at all, but he loved steak, rare.

Because she was still grumpy, she said, "I get first pick. I might decide I want the steak. I earned it today, calories be damned."

His lips twitched. "Yes, ma'am. So you remember about the steak?"

"Not specifically, but generally . . . yes."

He lowered himself down to sit on the floor beside the tub, taking her by surprise. He no longer towered over her, in a position of obvious authority. They were on the same level, almost face-to-face. She was naked and he wasn't, which she might have been naive enough to think put her at a serious disadvantage if it weren't for the way his gaze grew heavy-lidded as he looked at her breasts, and the dark hair between her legs.

He'd be naked too, before much more time had passed; sex between them had always been immediate and demanding. She knew this even without specific memories. They might not get their dinner finished before he was on her. Playing coy wasn't in the cards, not where he was concerned, not when she didn't know what tomorrow would bring. It sounded corny, maybe, like one of those fifties movies she'd thought about a few minutes ago, but life was precious. Sometimes it was too short.

And she was so tired of being alone.

"Tell me what happened," she said quietly.

He reached into the tub and trailed his fingers through the water. "What do you remember?"

"Not enough. It's as if there's a big dark hole in my head, and I can remember things around the edges of the hole—until I saw you this afternoon. You come from the two missing years, don't you?"

Instead of answering, he said, "When did you realize two years were missing?"

"Last Friday." She clenched her jaw. "I looked in the mirror and saw this face, and knew it wasn't mine. Everything else came from that."

"It made you sick."

"Sick, and with the headache from hell." Giving him a sharp look, she said, "So I was right: the house is bugged."

"Everything was bugged. The house, your phones, the car."

That was so repulsive, thinking of strangers listening to everything she said and did, that she closed her eyes and shuddered. He touched her cheek with his wet fingertips. "This should probably wait until you remember more on your own."

At that she opened her eyes. "What if I don't? And why don't I remember? Was I brainwashed?"

"In a manner of speaking. Not in the classic sense."

"Why? We were on a . . . a team together, weren't we? I can remember training with someone, a woman, but you were there too—"

"Yes, there was a team, of sorts." His dark gaze bored into hers. "Leave it for now, Lizzy."

She gave him an impatient glance. "Get real. Like you'd leave it alone, if this had happened to you? People are trying to kill me, and I don't know who they are or why."

That wasn't news to him. She saw it in his eyes, and suddenly she realized. "Wait—if they're trying to kill me, and you've been trying to catch up with me so you can protect me—are they trying to kill you too?"

"Yeah, but I'm better than they are."

He'd always been so damn cocksure of himself, and the worst part of it was, he had reason to be. She didn't have any specific memories, other than the one she'd had in the shed, but she *knew*.

She circled the conversation back around, searching for something he would tell her. Talking him around was going to take time. "How could I be brainwashed to lose two full years of my life? Well, and parts before that, too, because even though I know I worked in Chicago, at a big security firm, my memory is kind of like Swiss cheese."

"It was a chemical process," he said, his tone a little remote. "You were the third person it was tried on."

She'd been a guinea pig. That was almost as repulsive as knowing she'd been spied on like a lab animal—almost, but not quite. For spooky, dirty feelings, having every minute of her life listened to and examined was at the top of the list. "What happened to the other two?"

"One died from a heart attack. The other . . . the process wasn't as extensive, covered just a couple of months. He did okay."

"Is he still alive?"

He shrugged. "I didn't say that."

"Did this process kill him?"

"I didn't say that, either."

She reached out and pinched him, scowling. "I'm getting tired of hearing what you didn't say. Look at it this way: if I don't know exactly what's going on, then I don't know what to do, and I may make a mistake that will get both of us killed. I have to know what I'm—what *we're*—facing. Tactically, keeping me in the dark isn't a good move."

She saw the flare in his gaze, knew that she'd hit on the one argument that was likely to get his attention. Xavier was a born tactician, constantly weighing the odds, studying cause and effect, action and reaction. For every move, he had a countermove.

"I don't want to do anything that might . . . harm you," he finally said, shaking his head, and she knew she'd lost this particular argument, for now anyway. "This is uncharted territory. You're getting your memory back on your own, and that's probably what's healthiest for your brain."

"Can't you ask someone?"

He snorted. "The people I could ask are the ones who are trying to kill us."

"Well, that's a bitch," she said acerbically, earning a grin from him.

"No disagreement there."

Something else occurred to her, and she poked him. "You found me. You had me bugged, too, didn't you? I got rid of the cell phone, so what else did you have a tracker on?"

"I put three trackers on you, when I saw the situation deteriorating. One was on the backpack you left at your house."

"Okay. That and the phone made two. What else?"

"Your wallet. I figured that was the most likely item you'd keep with you, if you could. I was afraid enough of your old training would kick in that you'd dump everything you had with you and start fresh."

"My wallet." That meant he'd been in her house, gone through her things. "When? When did you put them there?"

"Monday night, after your shopping spree."

"You broke into my house? While I was asleep?" Outrage made her voice rise. He didn't look the least bit guilty. If anything, he even looked amused.

"It wouldn't make sense to break in while you were awake, now would it?"

"You went through my purse!"

"Guilty. Nice one, too."

"And I had to dump it in a Walmart store, damn it!"

"I'll get you another one."

"You're damn right you will." She blew out a cool-down breath, slicked her hands over her wet hair. As huffy as she felt, the hard truth was that if he hadn't put the trackers on her, he probably wouldn't have been able to locate her again and she'd be all alone in this mess. Not knowing what was going on, not having all her memory back, she'd have made some sort of mistake and been caught. He'd saved her life. Grudgingly she said, "Thank you."

He looked even more amused. "I know it kills you to say that. You're welcome."

"It doesn't *kill* me. I just don't like doing anything that makes you more cocky than you already are."

"Remember that, huh?"

"Enough . . . Preciousssss." With that out of her system, because he never liked being reminded of the few times he'd let people get under his guard, she crossed her arms on the edge of the tub and propped her chin on them. "Something really bothers me, though, more even than the creepy spying."

"What's that?"

"My face. Why did they change my face?" She heard the disturbed note in her voice and looked down, not wanting him to see the desolation she felt. It was silly, mourning for a face. This one wasn't ugly; she was still attractive. Some people might like this face better than her old one. But this wasn't *her;* she wanted to look in the mirror and see herself, feel that sense of being grounded.

He was silent a moment, as if weighing how much he should tell her. Finally he said, "To keep you safe."

"Safe? *Safe?* The very people who are trying to kill us are the ones who gave me this face, so how is it keeping me safe?"

Again that silence, that pause. "Because the people

who are trying to kill us aren't the biggest problem out there."

She squeezed her eyes shut, feeling tears burn. Oh, shit, that certainly wasn't anything she wanted to hear. What in God's name had she been involved in?

He was evidently finished answering questions, because he fluidly got to his feet. "The food will be here any minute. You should probably get dried off. You can always have another soak if this one didn't do the trick." He got to the door, then stopped. "By the way—"

She looked up, stubbornly blinking back the tears. No way was she going to cry.

"I like your face," he said softly. "It doesn't matter. I liked your face before, and I like it now. You're still you."

Chapter Twenty-five

He'd never told her he loved her.

They lay naked in bed together, the curtains pulled against the night, against the whole world. The room wasn't dark; one bedside lamp remained on, because she wanted to see him as much as he wanted to see her. Their lovemaking had been slower this time, longer, but just as exciting because a part of her couldn't get over the fact that this was Xavier, and she had been so long without him. She was still caught between everything feeling so new and different and at the same time so familiar. Her head was on his shoulder, his arm was around her, one hand absently stroking over her side, her arm, then brushing the backs of his fingers over her nipples. How many times had they lain together like this? She had no idea, but perhaps that was what made the memory surface.

Her heart squeezed in pain. Maybe he didn't love her. Even with the huge gaps in her memory, she knew that she loved him; that particular emotion came through loud and clear, despite everything.

He cared for her; it was evident in every kiss, in the way he touched her, watched her, in the controlled ferocity of his lovemaking. But caring wasn't loving, and how much of it stemmed from a sense of protectiveness, of guilt? Whatever had happened in the past, they'd been in it together, but she was the one who'd paid a big price.

"Don't feel responsible for me," she murmured, knowing that whatever it was they had, she didn't want him to feel bound to her for that reason.

He tensed beside her, the muscled arm under her head turning to iron. A few beats of time passed. "You said that before." His voice was sharp as he pulled his arm free and jackknifed to a sitting position.

"Before?" She frowned at him as she propped herself up on an elbow, tugged the sheet over her breasts—not out of modesty, but because she was a little chilly, with the air conditioning blowing across her. "I did? When?"

"Before you let them wipe your memory," he said curtly. "I was against it. There were . . . problems, but nothing I couldn't have handled. You sent me off on a wild-goose chase, and by the time I got back, it was too late." The black look he gave her said that he was still more than a little pissed about it, too.

"Wait a minute." She wiggled to a sitting position beside him, staring at him in astonishment. "I *chose* this? I agreed to it?" That couldn't be right; she couldn't imagine willingly letting someone wipe out a huge part of her personal identity. Never mind that it had been very skillfully done; she'd been living a perfectly normal life, with her earlier memories intact, until that morning less than a week ago. My God— less than a week, and her life had been completely turned upside down.

"Nothing I could do after that except take steps to keep you safe."

Damn it, this conversation was going in two different directions, and she wanted to follow both of them. "What steps? Keep me safe? And why did I choose to have my brain tampered with? What the *hell* was going on?"

He threw back the cover and got out of bed, stalking naked to the sitting area and coming back with a bottle of water. He twisted the cap off and drank deeply, then silently offered the bottle to her. She took it, sipped, then gave it back. "Tell me what happened. I don't want to be kept in the dark any longer, no matter what happened."

"You want to take the risk that not letting your memory recover at its own pace could cause some real damage?"

"I don't see how it could. Brain damage is a physical thing."

"How about emotional damage?" he demanded angrily. "I don't know what could happen. Telling you stuff might prevent you from ever really remembering."

This felt oddly familiar. She got the feeling that he seldom got angry, but that she'd always been able to push his buttons. She liked that; she didn't enjoy making him angry, but she did like that she could get to him when no one else could.

"Let me ask you something. Exactly what are you planning to do about this situation?"

His expression was instantly veiled, all anger wiped away. It was as if his face had been turned into stone. If he knew her as well as she thought he did, he probably already knew where this was going—and he didn't like it at all.

"Are you going back?" she prodded. "To D.C., or

wherever you have to go to take care of this little problem of people trying to kill you?"

"Yes." Just that one word, his lips barely moving, his gaze narrow and hard. "This isn't something we can run from. It has to be handled."

"What were you planning to do with me? Stick me somewhere, come back to pick me up when it's all over?"

"Exactly." He said it without a hint of apology in his tone.

"What if something happened to you? I'd never know, would I? You wouldn't come back, and I'd be a sitting duck, because sooner rather than later I'd need a job, a place to live, and then they'd have me."

"You'd be taken care of. I have people who'll make sure of that."

"How would I know them? C'mon, you know that isn't going to work. The odds are, more of my memory is going to come back and if you think I'd let it slide that someone had killed you, then you're full of shit."

"I don't need you to protect me," he snapped, then glared at her because he was doing what he'd just told her he didn't want her to do. "Fuck!" he said explosively.

"If I know what's going on, I'll make smarter decisions."

"Damn it all to hell and back, you never could just let something go, could you?"

"Beats me. I don't remember." She gave a little shrug, knowing how much it would annoy him.

"We're in this situation because you couldn't handle it before."

Okay, now *she* was annoyed. "Say what?" Exactly

what couldn't she handle? Yeah, she'd been terrified a couple of times since her memory had started coming back, but all in all, hadn't she done okay? She'd escaped an attempt to kill her. She'd shaken the people who'd been spying on her, and if Xavier hadn't been such a smart-ass and planted *three* trackers on her, she'd have shaken him, too. And as scared as she'd been, it was nothing compared to the downright terror she'd felt when he was riding the Harley across the field at her. She still owed him for that one.

His lips set in a grim line, he got back into bed and stuffed the pillows behind his back. "You let your emotions get the best of you. The decision was that you couldn't be trusted, so the options were the memory wipe, or a bullet."

"Wow, some choice." She didn't like what she was hearing. She didn't like that she'd evidently been weak. She'd handled some tough situations in her job, made some hard calls, and she'd lived with the results. What could have so upset her that she'd been judged unstable enough to be a threat to . . . whoever they were? "So when I started getting my memory back . . ."

"You were a threat to everyone."

"Including you?"

"Including me."

She was horrified that anything she'd ever done had been a danger to him. She had never thought of herself as a weak person, not even these past three years when she'd been such a dulled-down version of herself. What had been so bad that she'd broken under the strain?

"Tell me," she said brusquely.

"All right." He made the decision as incisively as a

surgeon would wield a scalpel, though the scowl on his face made it obvious he didn't like it. "You do need to know. But if you freak out on me, I'll drug you and keep you locked up somewhere. Got it?"

He would, too. She didn't doubt him for a second. "Got it."

He picked up his phone from the bedside table, slapped the battery in, and turned it on. He began tapping the screen; from where she sat on the bed she could see a web page loading. "Remember what I said," he warned, and turned the phone toward her so she could see the screen.

Lizzy frowned, startled, as she instantly recognized the image. It was a picture of herself, the way she used to be before she'd been given this new face. "That's me. Why are you showing me a picture of myself?"

"Because that isn't you. That was First Lady Natalie Thorndike."

"Get out," she said, disbelieving. She took the phone and stared at the image, trying to make the connection. Something tickled in her brain, a sense of repulsion, as if she wasn't supposed to go there. Pain stabbed at her temples and she caught her breath, laid the phone down.

"What's wrong?" he asked sharply, picking up the phone again.

"Headache," she managed, trying to breathe deeply and focus on something else. She thought about him, about the years he'd spent protecting her, and before that when he'd trained her for—

Well, that didn't work. She put both hands to her head and squeezed her eyes shut. "Sorry. It happens every time a new memory tries to come through. It isn't as bad as it was the first few times." Forget the Oscar Mayer wiener song; she had something much better to think about now, which was Xavier naked. Different kind of wiener. She almost laughed at the thought, and the pain ebbed. Opening her eyes, she smiled at him. He was watching her closely, not trying to help, gauging how well she handled the situation.

Deliberately she held out her hand for the phone, and was gratified when he gave it to her. She made herself look again—and felt another one of those clicks of memory. She examined the photo, and now she could see that this was an older version of her former self. The First Lady had looked extremely good for her age, whether from very good facial work or from genetics. Regardless, except for the hint of age on the First Lady, and the hairstyle, she and Lizzy had been identical.

Had been.

Was the First Lady dead? Lizzy didn't remember anything about her dying, but when she thought about Mrs. Thorndike, it was in the past tense.

"Is she dead?" she asked uneasily.

"Yes."

"When did she die?"

"Four years ago."

Four years, which put her death in the middle of Lizzy's two missing years.

Don't go there don't go there don't go there.

Despite the warning echoing through her brain, she swallowed and said, "What happened to her?"

"I shot her."

Lizzy went numb with shock. She stared at him, unable to say a word. He took the phone from her nerveless fingers, turned it off, and removed the battery. She focused on that because it was easier than thinking about what he'd just said. Even though she thought his phone was probably as secure as any phone that could be devised, he still took the precaution of removing the battery. His expression was as remote and cold as the Arctic landscape, and that scared her.

"Does the name Tyrone Ebert mean anything to you?" he asked, breaking the thick silence.

After a minute's thought, she slowly shook her head.

He reached out and tugged her close to him, settled her with her head once more on his shoulder. "That was the name I went by when I was transferred to the Secret Service."

This was too huge for her to comprehend, yet she sensed this was just the tip of the iceberg. Because it was so big, she seized on a detail, frowning up at him.

"Your name isn't Xavier?"

"It is. Tyrone Ebert was a carefully built alias. It stood up to a deep background check."

An alias like that wasn't easy to build, and only an agency like the CIA, FBI, or NSA could pull it off, build a background so solid that they couldn't detect their own work. There were compartments within compartments in any intelligence agency, some unknown to even the people who worked there.

"You were in the Secret Service," she said, feeling her way through the maze.

"For a while. I was assigned to Mrs. Thorndike's detail."

"But . . . why?" Why was he given an alias? Why

was he inserted into the Secret Service? She didn't have to detail all the "whys," because he knew each and every one of them.

"We called it a code-black situation."

"Which is . . . ?"

"When the President is committing treason."

The President . . . President Thorndike. Try as she might, Lizzy couldn't put a face to the name. She tried to think who had succeeded him. After him had come . . . President Berry, who had fulfilled the remainder of President Thorndike's term when—

She breathed deeply through the pain in her head, forced it away. She could get through this.

"Treason."

"We were investigating him."

"Who is 'we'?"

"I'll tell you who we aren't. We aren't the FBI. This was too deep, and the FBI is hampered by all kinds of laws and shit."

She started to protest that it was the FBI's *job* to investigate domestic threats to the country's security, but then bit it back. He was right; the FBI was hampered by laws and shit. That was why there were people like him, who would do the dirty work and then, when it was all tied up beyond doubt, "arrange" for the FBI and others to get the evidence practically dumped in their laps, so their hands were clean and they broke no laws in getting said evidence, which would have made it inadmissible in court. Some things were too important to let someone skate on a technicality.

"But where did I come in? The last I remember, I was working for a security firm in Chicago. I do remember some of the training with you, and . . . other stuff . . . but not any investigation or even how I met you."

"Other stuff, such as the fact that we were all over each other almost from the day we met?"

"We were? That fast?"

"Damn close."

Well, hadn't she known it, deep down? She'd even had the thought that she'd always been easy for him. She didn't even mind, because the attraction hadn't been one-sided; they got to each other then, and they got to each other now. She could push him further than anyone else would dare—and have fun doing it.

She cleared her throat. "Back to the story."

"The story is, when we started investigating Thorndike, we contacted someone who worked at the same place you did, for some technical assistance. He brought you to our attention. Except for your hair, you were a dead ringer for the First Lady. Do you remember anyone ever mentioning it to you?"

Lizzy shook her head. "No. But until Thorndike was elected, no one knew anything about her. If anyone said anything about it afterward . . . I just don't remember."

"We brought you in on the investigation, trained you. The idea was that, with the help of a couple of senior Secret Service agents, we'd be able to get you in and out of the President's private quarters without anyone thinking about it."

"Surely to God he wasn't stupid enough to keep incriminating stuff lying around the White House! Think of the staff, the aides—there's no privacy."

"Lying around, no. But everything leaves a trail, if you know how to look. And we weren't actually thinking about inserting you into the White House; it was on campaign stops, holidays, things like that, where the First Lady would act as a go-between for her husband and the Chinese."

The Chinese . . . something teased at her memory, but it was so vague, so deeply buried, that nothing solidified.

"Long story short, we were in San Francisco, and we slipped you into their hotel suite to search for intel on the payoffs. Thorndike made himself a huge fortune, selling the country out to the Chinese. Money has to be kept somewhere, and we were almost certain the First Lady was handling the transactions. With her family background, she knew almost all there was to know about the ins and outs of international banking."

"And she had this information *with* her?"

"During the meet and greets, a go-between would slip her a thumb drive during a handshake. On the thumb drive would be information about the latest deposit. They spread it around, to make a pattern harder to spot. She'd download the information to an off-site location, delete the information from her laptop, and destroy the thumb drive."

"So I had to get the thumb drive she'd been given in San Francisco, copy the info, and get out."

"And if anyone saw you, including the President, no one would think anything about it. You were dressed exactly as she was that day; your hair had been lightened and cut and done just like hers."

Lizzy took a deep breath, closing her eyes and taking comfort from the closeness of his big body, the heat of his skin under her hand. "But something went wrong."

"Fuckups always happen. Even when you plan for

them, you're hit by a different fuckup than the one you'd planned for."

She swallowed. "Was I the fuckup?"

"No. We'd arranged for the First Lady to leave the suite—took some doing—so the other agents didn't see her, but the heads of both details were working with us and we got it done. Then we slipped you in. The President was in his bedroom; he wasn't even aware the First Lady had left. You went into her bedroom, started running the water in the bathroom as if you were in there, located the thumb drive in the purse she'd carried that day, and began copying it."

She turned in his arms enough that she could look up at him. "So what happened?"

"We were sold out by another agent on her detail. He was working with us—we thought. Instead he was on the take with the Chinese, too. He panicked, told the First Lady what you were doing, and she went back up to the suite before you could get finished. He also gave her his weapon."

Lizzy fell silent, desperately searching her brain for the pieces of the puzzle, but all she could find was blankness. She had a sick feeling in the pit of her stomach, a dawning horror that made her want to stick her fingers in her ears so she wouldn't hear any more, yet what he was telling her was why all of this was happening now, why she was missing two years from her life. Even if she never truly remembered, she needed to know *why*.

"The President and First Lady together confronted you in her quarters," he said. His tone went calm and remote. "She had the pistol, but she didn't know who she was dealing with. From what you told us later, you jumped her, fought for the pistol, pulled the trigger, and Thorndike was hit."

She knew there was a lot he wasn't telling her; there were gaps and simplifications, details glossed over, yet there was no glossing over the biggest detail of all: she'd killed the President of the United States.

She didn't move, stayed locked in his arms. She felt numb and sick at the same time. Later she'd analyze everything he'd told her, poke and prod at the details, but for now all she could do was try to handle the essential fact that she'd not only killed someone—even if it might have been self-defense—but that someone had been the most important person in the world. It went against everything she felt as an American, that no matter what, agree or disagree, the life of the President should be protected. The possibility that she might have been defending herself was cold and scant comfort, because she couldn't remember, so she couldn't say for certain what had happened. She might have panicked. She might have lied about tussling with the First Lady for possession of the pistol. She didn't know and Xavier didn't know; he was recounting what she'd told him—them—after the President was dead.

"What did I do? How did you get me out?"

"You banged the First Lady's head against the wall, dazed her, put the gun in her hand, and hid in the closet. Both the details broke into the suite. The First Lady saw us, probably figured they were caught—guessing, here, because no one knows for sure—and she started shooting. She shot two Secret Service agents, killed one, a good agent named Laurel Rose. I shot the First Lady."

"How did you get me out of the closet, out of the suite?"

"For twelve minutes, we controlled everything: access to the suite, the weapons, the scene, everything. The senior agent of the First Lady's detail was down. I took over. We'd planned on you being in disguise when you left the hotel, so thank God we had that ready. Change of clothes, a wig, glasses. We got you changed, and out of there through a connecting room, and set everything up to make it look as though the First Lady shot the President because she had proof he was sleeping with her sister—which he was, by the way."

They'd gotten her changed, got her out. She didn't miss the way he'd phrased that. She sounded as if she'd been more of a liability than a thinking, functioning part of the team.

"You hadn't finished copying the thumb drive. You brought the original out with you, too. The evidence nailed him. He was selling not just technology details, but military secrets as well. After we had the situation handled, we talked it over and agreed to leave things as they were. A cheating husband was better than a traitor."

Oh, God, this hurt so much. She ached inside, as if she were being torn apart. Not only had she done something awful, but she'd dragged him and everyone else on their team into this with her. "You took an oath—"

"I took an oath to uphold the Constitution, to protect the country from its enemies, both domestic and foreign. In this case, the enemy was domestic."

Their own President.

"I was a loose end." She understood now why her memory had been wiped, why her face had been changed. Not only was it best that she no longer resembled the deceased First Lady, but changing her appearance would keep people from commenting on it, perhaps triggering a memory.

"We're all loose ends. All of us. But you kind of unraveled afterward, had a hard time dealing with it—"

"Ya think?" she shot at him, then shook her head at the anger in her tone. "Sorry. I made things impossible for the rest of you, didn't I?"

"I knew you'd come through it. You'd had a shock, we all had, but you're tough, and I knew you'd deal with the facts when you'd had enough time. But the others thought you were a liability, one that would get us all lined up in front of a firing squad."

"So . . . the brain wipe."

"Yes."

"What about the agent who was working for the Chinese, the one who gave Mrs. Thorndike his weapon? That's a huge loose end."

"He's the other one whose brain was wiped."

"Is he still alive?"

Xavier got that cold, remote expression on his face again. "What do you think?"

Chapter Twenty-six

Felice wandered restlessly through her house, staying away from the windows even though all the curtains were drawn. She could feel the darkness pressing against the glass, hiding the living ghosts who slipped unseen through the shadows. She didn't want to make a target of herself by letting her silhouette show, however briefly, against the curtains.

According to her contact, the specialist he'd called in was out there somewhere, watching, but no matter how good he was he was still just one man, and he couldn't watch all four sides of the house at once. Her contact had given her a name—Evan Clark—by which the specialist would identify himself if necessary, but she couldn't think of any reason why she should ever meet him face-to-face. That wasn't his real name, of course, but under no circumstances did she want that information.

What had been set in motion five years ago was rolling downhill to its inevitable conclusion, as unstoppable as an avalanche. She didn't feel good about it; this was the one contingency that they hadn't prepared for, hadn't anticipated—that the team members would, by necessity, have to eliminate each other in order to hold the secret safe. It was too big, otherwise. In the end, only one person could know.

Xavier and Lizzy had to die. Dankins, Heyes, Al Forge—they all had to die. If there was to be only one survivor, she intended to be that one. She had Ashley to think about. Dankins and Heyes had families, too, but she wasn't worried about their families, she was worried about her own. Wasn't that the way the human race was wired?

Once they'd all been so close, linked by the importance of the mission; she'd never respected a group of people more. Not one of them had taken the job lightly, but even so, going in, none of them had realized how steep the price they'd paid would be. How had it come to this?

Survival of the fittest. That was what they'd failed to take into account, the primal instinct to protect oneself and family.

In hindsight, this was something she should have done years ago, immediately after the mission had been completed, when no one was expecting it. The body count would have attracted too much attention, though, and now here they were. She had to eliminate all of them—do it herself, or have it done.

Xavier should have been first. He was by far the most dangerous, had been even before the bungled attempt on his life. Al was almost as bad, but he'd grudgingly agreed that taking out Xavier was the only thing they could do now, so she'd bought some time there. The main thing with Al was to act before he got his guard up.

The specialist would have to handle Xavier. There was nothing she could do herself; she'd have to be insane to even consider the idea of trying to handle Xavier. He *would* be coming for her, Al was completely right about that, and the best place to get her was her own home. When she was at work, she was untouchable. Xavier would expect her to take evasive actions going to and from work. He might think she would go to ground somewhere, but she couldn't live her entire life hiding from him and he'd know that. He'd also expect her to think she had everything handled, that her ego would blind her to her vulnerabilities.

She had an ego, but not where work was concerned. When it came to the job, her motto was simple: do it. No matter what, do the job. That was where they all underestimated her, but then she'd deliberately built that image. Winning was easier when the opposition didn't know what you were capable of doing.

If she knew Xavier, he wouldn't wait long. He'd hit fast and hard. She'd truly expected him before now; what had delayed him? Was he trying to find Lizzy? When Lizzy had left her car behind in the restaurant parking lot, they'd lost any way of tracking her. That didn't mean *Xavier* had lost her, though. The sneaky bastard probably had his own trackers planted on her. She had no way of knowing for certain, but she trusted when her gut told her something, and it was saying she was on the right track.

In that case, Xavier had gone after Lizzy, and was probably making certain she was in a safe place. That would make locating her more difficult, but she'd surface sooner or later. And every hour Xavier delayed was an extra hour in which she layered in another story, another false trail, another document that proved he was unstable and descending into insanity. Let all of his trip wires be sprung; he'd be just another nut-job conspiracy theorist. The evidence in the deaths of President and First Lady Thorndike was ironclad, right down to the DNA. Despite the unexpected circumstances, the plan had held.

This one would, too. The most worrisome factor for her was the time limit. This couldn't stretch on for too long.

Ashley was furious at being taken from college, of course. She so enjoyed stretching her wings, and now abruptly her feathers had been clipped. She was very much Felice's daughter, fiercely determined in everything she did. Felice could make the fiction she'd concocted—that the NSA had picked up on chatter that could indicate a domestic terrorist attack on Ashley's college—hold for a couple of days, but after that Ashley wouldn't buy it.

She didn't mind battling with Ashley, but she didn't want to alienate her forever. Being too heavy-handed would definitely push her daughter away. She would, if necessary, do anything to protect Ashley, but she'd do everything she could to make certain it didn't come to that.

On cue, her cell phone rang. It was Ashley's ring tone, the one she herself had picked out so Felice would know it was her and answer the call. She only hoped the men guarding Ashley had placed the call, instead of letting her call whomever she wanted. Sighing, she took the call.

"Hello, Ashley. No, nothing has been settled, one way or the other." She put weariness in her tone.

"Mom, this is ridiculous."

"Protecting you isn't ridiculous."

"Then why didn't you have the entire college evacuated?"

"Because if there is a legitimate threat, doing so would alert the perpetrators and we wouldn't catch them."

"So you'd just let people die?"

"Of course not. Investigators are working around the clock to make certain that doesn't happen, and I might add they're risking their own lives in doing so."

"Only if there's a real threat, and you don't know that for certain."

"No, I don't." Arguing with Ashley was like trying to nail gelatin to a wall. Her girl was slippery.

"So you intend to have me kidnapped and guarded every time you *think* there *might* be a threat?"

"Have I done this before?" Felice demanded.

A pause, then she heard a sulky, "No."

"Then give me a little credit. I evaluated the intelligence, and even though I personally think nothing will come of it, it's still credible enough that I don't want to risk your life. You'll understand when you're a mother."

Ashley made an exasperated sound. She would have continued arguing, but Felice said briskly, "I assume Mr. Johnson is there with you. Please hand the phone to him." Johnson was the name they'd chosen for Ashley's guard. Again, Felice had no idea what his real name was, nor did it matter.

"This is Johnson." The man's voice was calm. She was glad; whether or not he was a nice person didn't matter, so long as he *acted* nice in front of Ashley.

"Be careful with her cell phone. Don't let her have it again until this situation is resolved."

"Yes, ma'am. She won't like it, but you're the boss."

In the background, Felice heard Ashley demanding, "What did she say?"

"You may tell her exactly what I said. Keep her buttoned down tight."

Felice ended the call, smiling at Ashley's spirit even though it had been for nothing. She'd pay a price for this, but keeping her daughter safe was worth it.

Tomorrow . . . tomorrow she'd take care of Al.

Chapter Twenty-seven

Lizzy slept. She didn't know how, because despite Xavier's warning, the shock was so massive she'd been reeling from it. It didn't help that she had no memory of what she'd done; she believed him implicitly. *Not* remembering her actions was somehow worse, because she had no context through which to filter the things he'd told her. She didn't know what she'd thought, what she'd felt, what the other agents had done, where they'd taken her afterward or what she'd said and done. All she had were the bare facts, and on the face of it they were ugly.

Xavier could have told her more, and would if she asked, but all she'd wanted was time to absorb what he'd already said. "I'm okay," she said steadily. "Just let me deal with it, okay?"

He'd given her a sharp look, one she'd returned without flinching, so he'd given a brief nod, turned out the light, and slid down in the bed with her. She'd turned on her side so her back was to him, not to shut him out, but because that was what felt right. He'd put his heavy arm around her and pulled her back so she was nestled in the cradle of his muscular body. She rested her hand on top of his. The position, the feel of him, the familiarity, had combined with the sheer physical exhaustion of the day and instead of lying awake fretting about things she couldn't change, she'd gone to sleep within minutes.

She woke before dawn with his big hand sliding over her breasts, stroking and teasing her nipples into tight peaks. The things he'd told her the night before loomed over her, a heavy weight that could crush her. She shouldn't enjoy this, she thought dimly. She didn't deserve to laugh, to feel joy, yet pleasure was already blooming deep in her belly, so that she rose through layers of sleep into need, her breath sighing out, her body moving restlessly. That, too, felt very familiar, not just the sensation, but the timing. How many times had he awakened her in the early morning?

Maybe he understood something of what she was feeling, and that was why he'd chosen to wake her like this. She lived, and he wanted her *to* live, to find the fire and fullness of life that she'd once had. This, what was between them, was both trite and powerful. Civilizations had been risked, had fallen, because of love.

She could no more deny him than she could stop the beat of her heart.

His hand left her breasts and smoothed down her side and hip, over the curve of her belly. His touch firm, he dragged his fingertips through her cleft, found the soft, damp opening between her legs, and bit her in the curve between her neck and shoulder as at the same time he slid two big fingers deep into her. The heel of his rough palm pressed down hard on her clitoris, sending little lightning shocks all through her.

Her body bucked and shimmied under the triple

onslaught. A breathless little cry slipped from her lips and she turned her face against the pillow, fighting to contain the sensation, and the sounds she was making. What he was doing felt so damn good, and if she gave in it would be over far too soon.

He licked where he'd bitten, then bit her again. He shifted his position so he was lying half over her, controlling her with his weight. His other hand stroked over the coolness of her bottom, down, between her legs, touching where his fingers entered her and stroking, stroking, taking her higher.

There was so much sensation she was drowning in it, yet when he removed his fingers and slid his erection into her, she was jolted yet again. There was friction, heat, stretching, fullness. He flattened his hand low on her belly and braced her for his slow, powerful thrusts. She felt every inch of him dragging out, squeezing back in. And despite how much she wanted to make it last, all too soon she was lost to the delicious, maddening increase of tension, winding tighter and tighter inside her, until she couldn't take any more and went flying.

Even then, when the mindless spasms of pleasure eased, there was more. There was the feel of him moving hard, pushing deeper and deeper, until she heard that grunt he gave, followed by the rhythmic surges of orgasm. She loved it, loved that their lovemaking was as intense for him as it was for her.

Sweaty, lungs heaving, they settled together. He brushed her hair away from her face and rumbled, "You awake?"

Despite everything, she found she could laugh, the sound soft in the darkness. "No, I was faking it."

"I have to go back."

There it was, the decision that had been hanging over them for the entirety of the time they'd been together, which wasn't that long at all, only about twelve hours—twelve precious hours when she'd felt as if a missing part of herself had been restored. But they couldn't run for the rest of their lives, and Xavier wasn't a man who turned his back on a problem, anyway. Odd that her clearest memories, her strongest instincts, revolved around him; or perhaps it wasn't odd at all, given what they'd shared, how intense their time together had been.

"Yes," she said. "We have to go back."

"*We?*" There was iron in his tone. She'd known that particular argument wasn't over with, so this was as good a time as any to revive it.

"Yes, we. If you leave me behind, I'll follow. If you lock me in a house and board up the windows, I'll set the place on fire. Trust me. And don't tell me 'your people' will take care of me, because I'm not buying it. We're in this together."

"You'll hinder me. You're out of shape and out of practice—"

"Hey."

"Training shape," he clarified, running an appreciative hand over her breasts and hips. "Your instincts are good, but how long has it been since you fired a weapon?"

"My guess? Four years." Since she'd fired the shot that killed the President, in fact.

"It's a skill set that requires constant practice to maintain. You'd be lucky to hit the broad side of a barn."

That was an exaggeration, but in his world being able to hit a target wasn't good enough; the shot placement had to be precise.

"Not only that," he continued, "but you don't remember what either Felice or Al look like. Either of them could take you, and you wouldn't have a clue until it was too late."

Felice? Al? The names were new to her, yet they resonated. They were part of her lost years . . . "They're behind the people who tried to kill us?"

"Felice, definitely. Al, possibly. It has Felice's handiwork written all over it."

"How?"

"She used outside people. Al would have used some of his own people, and we'd both probably be dead."

"Al . . . what are his people like?"

"Me."

"Oh."

From out of nowhere swam an image of a lean, whipcord-tough man with short-cut, graying hair. "Is Al in his fifties, gray hair?"

Behind her, Xavier tensed. "That's Al. Have you seen him?"

"I *remember* him."

"If you remember anything *about* him, you know he isn't anyone to fuck with."

"But you don't think he's involved in this?"

"Oh, he's involved. The big question is whether he's helping Felice, trying to stop her, or just sitting on the sidelines waiting to step in and mop up."

"What does your gut tell you?"

"I'm not discounting anything."

She turned in the circle of his arms and looped her

arm around his neck, pressing her face to the warm skin of his shoulder. "Do you have pictures of them?"

"At my condo. I can't go back there yet. Possibly some of my people could come up with some surveillance shots."

"Just how many people do you have?"

"Enough to have backup whenever I need it."

As far as detail went, that was fairly useless.

He pinched her ass. "You've met some of them, in a way."

"I have?" Immediately she thought of nosy Maggie Rogers, and the full-blown suspicions she'd felt the day she first started getting her memory back.

"At the barbecue restaurant. The guy you punched and stole his car? Him."

"Oh, no." She was immediately assailed by guilt. "He was on our side, and I punched him!"

"He'll never hear the end of it, either. The others are teasing him nonstop, for getting mugged by the protectee. But it made him feel a little better when you cut my spark plug wires."

She didn't feel at all guilty about that. He'd terrified her enough that she thought he deserved a few cut wires, and she said as much, which earned her another pinch on the ass, followed by a rub.

She kissed his chest, loving his closeness, made all the more precious by the long, cold years without him. He could marshal some excellent, commonsense arguments against taking her with him; none of them made any difference to her whatsoever. She wasn't going to let him leave her behind. The sooner he faced that reality, the sooner they could return to D.C. and take care of business.

"The first thing we have to do is find a motorcycle shop and have a passenger seat installed on the Harley—either that, or we rent a car. It's too far back to D.C. for me to ride behind you the way I did yesterday."

"You aren't going."

"Yes," she said firmly. "I love you, and I am."

Maybe it was saying she loved him that did it. Maybe he'd gone into shock. But he'd fallen silent, and there were no more arguments. She doubted both of those possibilities, because this was Xavier; whatever had changed his mind, her emotions wouldn't figure into the equation.

She'd hoped they would rent a car, but he opted for the Harley. Not only did he not want to leave it behind, but the helmets provided them with perfect identity concealment. He located a shop that could install a small passenger seat with a backrest on the bike; then he bought her a helmet that almost matched his, so they'd look like one of those motorcycle couples who thought it was cute to dress alike. Even better, the helmets had radio capability, so they could talk.

He disappeared for a little while, leaving her to twiddle her thumbs in the bike shop. She wondered if he'd ditched her, after all, but he returned within the hour, wearing a shirt he hadn't had on when he left, a button-up chambray shirt that he'd left open over his tee shirt.

Lizzy lifted her brows at him in question, but he ignored her.

She sat down and flipped through a year-old magazine on bow hunting. She was anxious to be on the road, to start the endgame, but she felt as if she'd been through this countless times before, the endless waiting for the action to begin.

By noon, they were ready to head back to D.C. He got on the bike, she parked her butt on the much-more-comfortable passenger seat, and they headed northeast. Before they hit the interstate, though—a much faster route than the hilly, curvy route she'd taken the day before—he wheeled off the road behind an abandoned old service station, and from the small of his back produced a black automatic pistol.

"Here. You'll need this."

Cautiously, Lizzy took the weapon, and as soon as her palm closed on the butt of the pistol she was flooded with tactile memory, not just of the weight and shape of a handgun, but the buck of the weapon when she fired, the sound, the smell of cordite and gunpowder. It was a Sig Sauer compact, a nice weapon she'd used before, though the model wasn't her favorite.

"Thanks," she said, ejecting the clip and checking it, the movements coming back to her automatically, without conscious thought. She slapped the clip back into place. She didn't have a shirt or jacket to hide the weapon if she tucked it into her waistband, so she put it on top in her backpack.

"Ready?" he asked, the sound coming through the helmet's built-in earpieces.

"Yes." She might not be prepared, but she was ready. There was a difference, and she hoped he didn't make the distinction.

"One more thing."

She waited. The black face mask of his helmet turned toward her. "I don't think I've ever said this before," he said in a musing tone. "But I love you too, and that's why you're here. I'm not letting you get away from me again."

They stopped to gas up the Harley, and while Xavier stayed outside to pump the gas, Lizzy went inside to prepay and also to use the bathroom. The pump was activated, and he began filling the tank. The task was fairly mindless, so he began thinking about the situation they were heading into, whether or not they'd be facing both Al and Felice or just Felice. He'd worked with Al a long time, respected him, but if he was involved, Xavier would take him out without hesitation. He needed to start formulating a plan, so he wouldn't be caught unprepared no matter what happened.

No one had called his cell phone, but then they wouldn't, even though it was secure, bouncing off satellites, through encryption programs, and with every other safeguard he'd been able to access. If any of his people needed to get a message to him, they'd leave it on the number in the secure room of J.P.'s condo. Good old J.P.; she'd come in handy over the years. When he'd checked his messages the day before, there had been nothing, which was reassuring in a way but also worrisome. The situation in D.C. hadn't been static while he'd been chasing Lizzy down. *Something* was happening, but evidently nothing with his people, so none of their identities had been discovered yet.

He got out his phone and dialed the number, then input the code that let him access his messages. A robotic voice informed him that he had one new message.

His head lifted slightly, like a wolf's scenting the wind, when he heard Al's voice.

"There's a specialist waiting for you at our mutual friend's house. She expects you to come calling."

Xavier deleted the message, then cut off the pump.

The immediate message was simple: Felice had hired an assassin to watch her house and ambush him, because she knew he'd be coming for her. That part was easy. He really wouldn't have expected anything else, but knowing for certain gave him an edge.

The part that got tricky was whether or not Al had called him to make him think Al was on his side and not Felice's. Giving up the specialist was nothing; Al would do that without a qualm if it would buy him an extra second, a moment of hesitation or distraction, in which he could take care of Xavier himself.

The coming night was going to be interesting.

Chapter Twenty-eight

If she'd been heading back into D.C. on her own, Lizzy would have been terrified, but because Xavier was with her everything was different. *She* was different from the woman she'd been last week—hell, from the one she'd been the day before. She knew things about herself now, things that horrified her, but she was already beginning to feel as if there was a distance widening between what she knew and who she was. It had been a mere six and a half days, almost to the minute, since she'd awakened and seen a stranger in the mirror, and in those six and a half days she'd become someone who, instead of continuing to run away, was now racing back into danger.

Most specifically, *Xavier* was racing toward danger—danger, and, if he was right, a possible end to running, for both of them.

He'd told her about checking his messages while they were stopped for gas, but he hadn't told her anything else. Whatever message he'd received had disturbed him. No, not *disturbed*—that was the wrong word. Preoccupied. He'd gotten a familiar and grim look in his eyes, and the set of his mouth had become even more determined. He was going to war, and he was planning his moves. She knew he wanted to end this for both of them; she understood that running was not an option, unless they were prepared to run forever.

The blessed helmets they wore were the perfect disguise. Lizzy felt completely free as they roared down the interstate and into D.C. Even with all the cops, all the cameras, all the people looking for her, she and Xavier were virtually invisible. She liked that feeling. She wished it could last forever.

Twilight was fading into true night when he wheeled the Harley into the parking lot of a garage. The concrete was cracked, with weeds growing through the cracks. They weren't in the nicest part of town, but then . . . it was a garage, the kind where mechanics worked on mechanical stuff.

Older trucks and cars filled the small parking lot. Xavier balanced the Harley on its kickstand near the door to a small office. They both stretched, arching their backs to relieve muscles cramped from the long ride, but left their helmets on as they went inside. No one was in the waiting room to greet them, but she'd noticed several cameras in the parking lot and another mounted in the corner.

Xavier took his helmet off and placed it on the front counter. Urgently, Lizzy pointed at the camera. "It's okay," he said. "Closed circuit—for our use only."

Our use? That said a lot. She eased her own helmet off, shook her hair free, and set her helmet beside his.

"This is where you're going to stay," he said.

"*What?*" It wasn't quite a screech, but . . . close. Damn it, she'd *known* he was going to pull something like this. That didn't mean she'd give up without another argument, though.

"There's something I need to do, and I can do it only if I know you're safe."

She'd been right about that "going to war" look. "No matter what it is, you'll need backup."

"Not this time." He took her arm and led her through a side door, into a windowless garage that smelled of oil and gas.

Three men were there. One had greasy hands and stained overalls with the name "Rick" embroidered on the pocket; another was middle-aged, with a Marine-like haircut, who stood behind a waist-high table at the back of the room and was in the midst of taking a rifle apart and cleaning it. The third man was the poor guy she'd carjacked two days ago. She nodded in his direction. "Uh, sorry."

The other two laughed, though not long and not very hard. The victim just put a hand to his throat and kind of growled, "At least I got my car back."

On one wall a television had been mounted. It showed four camera views of the exterior and the office; their arrival had not been unexpected.

Lizzy looked up at Xavier. "Maybe this isn't such a good idea." She not only didn't know these men, but one of them had good reason to hold a grudge against her. Her lack-of-trust issue at the moment was perfectly reasonable, from her standpoint.

"It's the *only* idea." He led her past the three men—who continued to work as if they hadn't been interrupted—to another office in the back of the garage. Glass windows overlooked the work area, so it wasn't private, but there was a coffee machine, a couple of swivel chairs, a desk and computer.

"When are you leaving?" she asked, leaning against the desk and crossing her arms over her midsection.

"Not for a couple of hours."

She looked through the office window; she could see all three men from here. "And you trust these guys?"

"Completely. I wouldn't even consider leaving you here if I didn't. They've been helping me look out for you for the past three years. They're good at what they do."

Lizzy lifted her chin slightly, straightened her spine, and faced her biggest fear. "What if you don't come back?" She couldn't lose Xavier, find him, and then lose him again. It would be incredibly unfair, incredibly painful. After all this, she wasn't certain she'd even want to go on.

Of course, odds were without him she didn't stand much of a chance anyway.

"We'll get something to eat, you can get acquainted with them, and by the time I leave you'll be more comfortable—"

"Wait a minute. Stop trying to distract me, okay? You said you didn't need backup, but you were just talking about me, right? You're taking one of them with you, at least. Aren't you?" Surely he wasn't going to face the people who were trying to kill her—them—*alone*.

"No. I need to do this on my own."

Exasperated, infuriated, Lizzy threw her hands in the air as she paced around the small office. "What good does it do to have people who can help if you *won't use them*? Why go up against those people alone when it's not necessary?"

Xavier nodded toward the work area. "They know a lot, but they don't know everything and they can't. If anything goes wrong tonight, they don't need to be anywhere in the area when the shit goes down. They can't even know where I'm going tonight, who I'm targeting." He gave her a brief, hard smile. "You know how everything has to be compartmentalized. Need to know. I have to do this alone."

Given the magnitude of their secret, the small circle that knew the truth of the President's death and the cover-up that had followed, that made some sense. But still—

"You have to come back."

"I will." He cupped her chin, tilting her face up. "I have you to come back to, and that makes a helluva lot of difference."

"I'd feel better if I were helping."

"I know." Graciously, he left the *tough shit* unsaid.

"Instead I'm going to sit here, wondering and worrying, with a bunch of men I don't know and—sorry—don't trust, and . . ."

"I thought about that," Xavier said, then he leaned down and kissed her, a quick kiss, a brush of his lips on hers. "She should have been here by now."

"She?" Lizzy drew back and gave him a suspicious glare. "She, who?"

Then a new sound caught her attention: a yap. A very familiar yap. No, it couldn't be— She turned and gaped at the woman who was walking across the stained concrete floor, a dog held securely under her arm as she paused to talk to the other men. She stared up at Xavier. *"Maggie?"*

Xavier had been gone little more than half an hour, and already Lizzy was shaking. This went beyond worry. She was more terrified than she'd been for as long as she could remember, and that was saying something. It had been bad when it was her life on the line, but at least when she was on the run she could *do* something. All she could do tonight was sit and wait, knowing that at any time Xavier could be dying, that she might never see him, talk to him, hold him again. One thing she remembered about herself: she *hated* waiting.

Maggie, stroking a sleeping Roosevelt's fur, smiled at her. "I understand," she said softly. "Waiting is a lot harder than being in on the action."

"That's what you've been doing for the past three years, isn't it? Watching and waiting for something to go wrong." Maybe her voice was too sharp, but Lizzy was still pissed that her neighbor had been spying on her all this time—even though Maggie had been working for Xavier, even though her intentions had been good. She wasn't pissed at Maggie; she was pissed at herself, because she'd been so blind for the past three years that she hadn't figured out that something about her nosy neighbor wasn't quite right. No, worse—she *had* been a little suspicious, and had let it slide. Careless stuff like that could get people killed.

"I suppose I have been," Maggie said, not at all perturbed, "but that's not what I meant. When you're in our business, waiting for someone you love to return from a job is absolute torture." She smiled. "Being in the thick of things, the minutes fly past. Yeah, it's dangerous. Yeah, we're all adrenaline junkies to some degree. Any one of us would rather face bullets than . . . this. But sometimes *this* is required, and above all else, we do what is required."

Maggie knew what she was talking about; Lizzy accepted that. Maybe she knew too well. Who had Maggie waited for? Was she really a widow, or was that just part of her cover? Had she waited for someone who didn't return? Lizzy didn't want to know, not tonight.

"He's different with you," Maggie said. Maybe she saw the new fear in Lizzy and was kind enough to change the subject. "More . . . human." She smiled, and continued to stroke Roosevelt's fur. "Still Xavier, still the most capable man I know," she clarified, "but still, it does give me hope for the rest of us." Reaching out with her free hand, Maggie grasped one of Lizzy's and gave it a comforting squeeze.

After a while she said, "I'm different too, with him."

Maggie nodded, gave a slightly sad smile that told Lizzy the other woman's thoughts had wandered into a dark place. "That you are."

Felice looked up from her computer screen when her phone rang. She cast an apprehensive glance at the window closest to her, even though she knew the office was the safest place she could be, as she answered. Just knowing Xavier was out there made her nervous about windows.

"Felice. We need to meet."

Al. She'd been letting time tick down, trying to judge what would be the best time to call—not too late, because she didn't want to make it sound like an emergency and cause him to have his guard up, but not so early that there would likely still be some people about. Having him initiate the meeting was good; he'd be less suspicious.

"All right," she said calmly. "Where? Not the tank again; I've been there too often these past few days."

"Remember that abandoned warehouse in Maryland where we did some of the training? Will that do?"

"Yes, of course." The old warehouse would do better than nicely. It was perfect for what she had in mind. "When?" She'd let him set all the parameters; he'd feel safer. But he'd always underestimated her anyway; he'd never expect her to do her own wet work. She had, in fact, always kept her hands clean in that respect, but that didn't mean she was inept with a weapon, or that she was incapable of doing what was necessary. She practiced regularly. And she'd always known, deep inside, that she was capable of killing.

"Can you make it in an hour?"

"I think so. I might be a little late." She actually would have no problem making the hour time frame, but letting him think she'd be late might catch him the tiniest bit unprepared. Every advantage counted.

Maybe he'd decided to take a more active role in eliminating Xavier. If so, good for him; he might even have already done so, in which case he'd have saved her a lot of time and trouble. None of that would change her endgame at all.

On the other hand, it was more likely that Xavier had already struck back, in some fashion. It was worrisome that Al was being this cautious, that she could even consider he might be so spooked by Xavier that he felt this clandestine meeting was necessary. Then again, who knew Xavier better than Al?

Staying late at the office meant it was almost dark when she pulled out of the parking lot. The summer days were long, but it would be fully dark by the time she reached her destination.

She hadn't been to the old warehouse in years, not since they'd ceased training four years ago; she didn't think any of them had. It was best to walk away and not return. None of them had needed to continue training, anyway, except for Xavier. Where he worked out and practiced these days, no one knew.

The warehouse would still be in use by someone, though. It was an asset that wouldn't be sold, though it might be repurposed. It hadn't changed much, she thought as she approached at well below the speed limit. A wire fence topped with barbed wire surrounded the property, but the gate stood open. A number of streetlights kept the parking lot well lit. Maybe too well, but she would have to work with what she had. The building was longer than it was wide, made of rusting steel, and with windows so caked with dirt it was impossible to see what was on the other side. Al's car was already there, parked near the door. She parked beside him and got out.

Now that she was here, a whisper of unease ran along her nerves. How long had he been here? Minutes? Hours? She laid her hand on the hood of his car and felt the heat that told her he hadn't been here long; she could hear the clicks and ticks of a cooling motor. Good; if he'd been here so long that the engine had already cooled down, she'd think he was setting some kind of trap. Instead, he'd just gotten here.

She slipped her car keys into the right pocket of her crisp gray trousers and tucked her weapon into her waistband, at her spine. It wasn't her favorite place to carry a handgun, but if she walked in carrying or wearing it in the open, Al would know something was up. She'd never habitually carried a weapon, though she could make the argument that at this point she wasn't going anywhere unarmed.

A light was on, shining through the partially opened heavy metal door. A little bit of light from the parking lot might shine through, too, but not much thanks to the heavy coating of grime on the glass. She pushed the door open and paused, noting that the light came from one room on the right, at the far end of the hall, exactly where Al had said he would be.

Unease chilled her spine again. She changed her mind, drew her weapon. She wanted it in her hand. She could conceal it behind her leg. At the least, she wanted to hear what Al had to say. He might have some valuable information for her. Did he know where Xavier and Lizzy were? Did he have a workable plan for getting to them? But no matter what he said, he wasn't leaving that room alive.

She moved down the hallway, past closed doors and open ones, her eyes searching the shadows in what had once been offices and employee break rooms and goodness knows what else. Nothing moved, other than herself. Her steps were easy, silent. When she was close to the room where a light burned, she called, in as normal a voice as possible, "Al?"

"Come on in," he said, his voice as normal as hers. He even sounded a little distracted, not at all as strained as he'd sounded on the phone.

She shifted her weapon so it was concealed behind her thigh, walked forward.

The room where he waited was small and square, with a rusted door, an old desk, and two plastic chairs. She stepped inside and immediately spotted the camera, mounted on the metal desk, the light on that confirmed it was recording. Her gun hand remained low and hidden. Damn it, he'd taken the precaution of putting a camera on her.

He followed her gaze to the camera, his face betraying no emotion. "Just video, no audio," he explained. "The feed is being transmitted to an off-site computer. I thought it might keep us honest."

"Honest? That's a . . ."

His hand flowed up, quick and smooth. He was wearing a glove, and in that gloved hand was a weapon. Startled, Felice looked at him and tried to raise her own hand, but he was too fast. He fired, once, twice.

She was dead before she hit the floor.

Al kicked Felice's weapon away from her hand, even though it was obvious she was dead. One bullet to the chest, one in the head. She'd damn well better be dead. It would be humiliating to have so completely lost his touch that he'd missed such easy shots. He looked into the camera, then walked to the table to turn off the recorder.

He should be surprised that she'd arrived for their meeting with a weapon in her hand, but he wasn't. The fact that he'd fired before she'd even had a chance to raise her gun would ensure that if this video were ever uncovered, he wouldn't be able to claim self-defense. Not exactly the cold-blooded murder he'd planned, but the video would be more than incriminating enough. After all, he hadn't drawn his weapon because she had one in her hand; he'd drawn on her and fired without provocation. The gloves indicated premeditation.

There was no way to know if Xavier had gotten his message or not, if he was headed toward Felice's home and her specialist tonight, or tomorrow, or six months from now. Knowing Xavier, he'd bet on sooner rather than later, but there were too many variables to make a truly educated guess. No matter, really. Felice had to be out of the picture, and cleaning up the mess they'd made was his job.

Xavier should expect that Felice would have put someone on the house to wait for him, but when emotions were high, anything was possible. Giving him the warning was the least he could do.

Al patted down Felice's pockets and found nothing but her car keys. He took the keys and dropped them into his own pocket. She'd probably left her purse in the car, though what he needed might be in the glove box or sitting on the console. In any case, it wasn't here. He collected the camera and wiped down the room for any evidence that he and Felice had been here. The team coming in would do the same, and he trusted them to do the job well. But at the same time, he couldn't always rely on others to do what he had to do himself.

Like Felice, he thought as he stepped over her body.

He'd taken no pleasure in killing her; it was just a chore, like filing taxes or taking out the trash. It simply had to be done. She'd gotten them into a huge mess with her impatience, her unwillingness to listen, so he'd done what he could to mitigate the damage.

In the vast, open parking lot—open and well lit so that there was no place for anyone to hide—he opened the trunk of his car and placed the camera to the right, next to the laptop that sat there, green light indicating that it was on, Wi-Fi keeping the connection with the camera active. Al opened the laptop, and leaning over and slightly into the trunk he transferred the video that clearly showed him shooting Felice to a thumb drive, dropped the thumb drive into his pocket, and then deleted everything from the computer.

The laptop would be in pieces before midnight. He couldn't take the chance that the video might be retrieved somehow, someday. There could be only the one copy, if this was going to keep him alive.

That done, he slammed the trunk shut and walked to Felice's car. She'd been cautious enough to lock it, even though judging by the gun she'd been carrying, in her hand and ready to fire, she hadn't planned on being here for very long. Al unlocked the doors with her remote, opened the driver-side door, and leaned in. There was no phone on the console, but Felice's purse was sitting on the passenger-side floorboard. With a gloved hand, he snagged it by the strap and pulled it out of the car.

A state-of-the-art cell phone fit snugly in an inside pocket made for the device. That was her personal phone, and it wasn't what he was looking for. Carefully, he pushed aside a wallet and a small clear bag that contained lipstick and mascara, and near the bottom of the lined bag he saw the shape he was seeking.

Her burner cell was in a zippered inside pocket, buried deep. He removed the phone, then pressed the "contacts" button.

There was only one contact listed.

He thumbed the button to call the sole number programmed into the cell. When a man answered, Al said bluntly, "She's dead. Whatever you've been paid is all you're going to get, so call off your dogs."

"Understood." The man's voice revealed no emotion. This was just business, after all. He might regret losing a good customer, but other than that there was no reason for him to care that Felice was dead. "How should I proceed with the daughter?"

That was an unexpected question. Was Ashley being held hostage? No, of course not. Felice would have pulled her daughter off the street the moment she realized Xavier was a threat. "She's under your protection?"

"Against her wishes, yes."

"Let her go," Al instructed.

"What should I tell the girl about her mother?" Again the voice was cool, detached. Al suspected that voice would have remained the same if he'd instructed Felice's contact to dispose of the girl.

"Nothing. Just release her." Soon enough Ashley would learn—everyone would learn—that Felice had been the victim of a violent carjacking. It would be easier to make her disappear, maybe even more satisfy-ing to just wipe her off the face of the earth, but if she just vanished, that would leave too many unanswered questions. Her death would be thoroughly investi-gated; the team who'd been tasked with disposing of her body would have to do a stellar job. He didn't doubt that they would, and Ashley would have clo-sure.

Al returned the purse, sans burner cell, to the floor-board and tossed the keys into the driver's seat. The cleaners would be here within half an hour to finish the job he'd started.

He didn't intend to be here when they arrived.

Felice's contact immediately called "Evan Clark," hoping the man would answer. Not being able to reach him would be one thing; if the man did the job and there was no one to pay him, that was something else entirely, and definitely not good.

Clark didn't answer. Depending on the situation he might have his phone silenced, or hell, he might be out taking a piss. A message would have to suffice, and it wasn't one he wanted to leave in a voice mail. He sent a text message from a phone that would be in someone else's Dumpster within the hour.

Abort, Felice's contact typed. *The client is dead.*

Chapter Twenty-nine

Knowing someone was watching, and spotting that someone, were two different things. Crawling into position took over an hour, so slow and precise were his movements. Xavier knew where *he* would set up, if he were the one watching the house for someone like him to arrive, but there were several good options.

Felice commanded a very good salary. Like most people with money, she wanted space around her, which meant she lived in a neighborhood where the lots were measured in acres and the houses weren't all that close together. It wasn't the ritziest part of town, otherwise she wouldn't have been able to afford the acreage, but it was nice. Unfortunately, the big yard meant a lot of trees, a lot of landscaping, and a lot of places for concealment.

Any idiot would figure Xavier wasn't going to walk up to the front door and knock. Therefore, surveillance should be looking for a clandestine entrance.

Even knowing that, he couldn't spot the guy. The fucker was good. He'd chosen his spot well, and he wasn't moving. Either that, or he'd fallen asleep.

Xavier had taken up position well back from the house, far enough back that the hired gun was almost definitely between him and the house. There was a light on in one downstairs room. Was she watching TV? Catching up on paperwork? He wondered if she had enough confidence in her hired gun that she could sleep.

The answer to that was, Felice had enough confidence in her own decisions that she would sleep, secure in the knowledge that she'd handled things.

The one light in the house, though, was a big, blinding glare in his night-vision goggles. He turned his head incrementally, taking five minutes to move an inch, because sure as hell the specialist would have night vision too, and movement could get him spotted as easily as it could the guy he was looking for.

Patience was the key. The shooter had been in place longer than he had, which meant he would get thirsty sooner, have to piss sooner. That was assuming anyone was here at all, that Al wasn't playing mind games with him and had lured him here to set up a trap of his own. Xavier had always gone into any situation knowing it could be his last. Being aware had kept him alive so far—

There.

The man was practically dead ahead, not ten yards in front of Xavier. The only thing that had given him away was a not-quite-slow-enough movement of his head as he surveyed the property. He'd set up at least a third farther back from the property than Xavier had expected. Shit, at least he had to admire the man's tactics. This wasn't an amateur.

No, this was a dead professional. He just hadn't stopped breathing yet.

Xavier painted the back of the man's head with a pinpoint laser, aimed his silenced weapon, and fired.

Now he'd stopped breathing.

Swiftly, Xavier covered the ten yards, kicked the man's weapon away, then knelt and checked. Definitely dead. Medium size, medium build, medium . . . just medium, the kind of guy who could go anywhere without being noticed.

He patted down the shooter's pockets, looking for identification. Nothing, not that he'd really expected any; still, it was always best to look and make certain. He did find a cell phone, turned off. He didn't turn it on. Some cell phones made a hell of a racket when they were activated, playing tunes and beeping and chiming. He wiped it down and slipped it back into the man's pocket.

Even then, he didn't immediately go toward the house. A silenced shot was a long way from silent. While it wouldn't have been heard inside Felice's house, or in any of her neighbors' houses, Xavier had no guarantee that the specialist was alone. He waited another hour, watching, before he slipped down to the house.

Her security system was fairly standard. He bypassed it without a problem. The deadbolts on the doors were a bigger problem, but like most people, she had a back door with a window. He thought it was one of the stupidest things people could do. Why not just invite a burglar in? Using a diamond cutter, he sliced a round hole in the glass big enough for him to get his hand through, then opened the deadbolt as well as the simple lock on the doorknob.

He noiselessly entered.

He was out in less than ten minutes. The house was empty. Felice wasn't here.

She'd set her guard dog to watch an empty house, knowing Xavier would eventually come here looking for her.

Damn it, where the fuck was she?

Something was going on. Xavier didn't need his spidey sense to tell him that. Al had warned him about the shooter, and hadn't set up an ambush of his own even though he had to have known Xavier would be there sooner rather than later.

If Felice had gone to ground somewhere, would Al know? Had they had a falling out, a parting of the ways? If they had, Al had better be watching his own back—but then, so should Felice.

He was well away from the neighborhood when he made a decision. He wasn't on the Harley—it was too loud—so he wasn't worried about being heard inside the car he'd taken from the garage where he'd left Lizzy. Taking out his phone, he dialed a familiar number.

"Our friend definitely had company," he said when Al answered. "But she wasn't at home."

"And her company?"

"He's asleep behind the house."

"I'll have him taken care of."

"Do you have any information on our friend's whereabouts?"

"We need to meet."

Xavier had expected that. "Where?" He might be making a damn big mistake, but something was definitely going on, and he needed to know what it was. Al was his best bet for that.

* * *

It was the next day. Xavier and Lizzy had both arrived at the designated meeting place two hours early, and circled it several times in opposite directions. She hadn't actively recovered any more memories, but she was moving the way she had before, balanced and alert, instead of with the flat, unaware gait she'd used for the past three years.

Whether or not she ever fully regained her memory, she was herself again, full of piss and vinegar, and he loved her. No matter what, he wouldn't let them be separated again.

As proof of his love, he was even letting her ride the Harley without him. She knew how, and as soon as she'd thrown a leg over the Hog the muscle memory had taken over. Watching her, her movements at first tentative and then rapidly gaining in confidence, had been a real kick

She'd looked at him, her smile as bright as summer. "Hey! I can do this!"

"I know. Just be careful and don't let the weight get away from you."

"I know."

He kissed her, and she pulled the helmet on. She was his backup. Something hinky was going on, and they hadn't been able to find out what. Felice's house was empty, her car gone, and she wasn't at work. Al had gone to ground, too. Wherever he was, he wasn't showing his face. But there didn't seem to be any kill teams looking for him and Lizzy; if there were, they were invisible, because his people hadn't spotted a thing, and they'd been looking hard.

Now he had this meeting with Al.

Together he and Lizzy had surveilled the meeting place, checked the adjacent businesses, and now he was ready to take his place inside. Lizzy had his back.

He settled in, facing the door, thirty minutes before the agreed-upon time.

Al's first choice for this meeting had been an off-the-map, rarely used park; Xavier preferred their meeting place to be a bit more public, and Al had agreed. He respected Al Forge, and he trusted Al as much as he trusted anyone else in the business—but at this point in the game that wasn't saying much.

While he was on guard where Al was concerned, and would continue to be, he was much more worried about Felice. Where the fuck was she? None of his people had been able to get a fix on her, which couldn't be good. She was fully capable of turning on everyone, Al included. Maybe that was what this meeting was all about.

With a laptop in front of him, as well as two huge cups of coffee—one for him, one for the man he was waiting for—no one thought twice about him taking up the booth for so long. He was obviously waiting for someone, and he wasn't the only person in the coffee shop who took his time, sipping on overpriced—and bitter—coffee and taking advantage of the free Internet.

Al arrived right on time, not a minute early, not a minute late. He looked calm but sober, and he'd taken care to dress casually. Xavier couldn't say with any certainty that Al wasn't armed, but there was no shoulder holster, no loose jacket to disguise a gun at his spine. And in a crowded place like this one, surely someone was observant enough to spot a weapon, though likely the person would just think Al was a cop.

Ankle holster, maybe—no, almost certainly, because Al was as likely to leave the house unarmed as Xavier was. But he couldn't get to that ankle holster quickly—not quickly enough, in any case.

It was an indicator of the seriousness of the situation that Xavier even had these thoughts where Al was concerned.

Al slid into the bench seat on the other side of the table. "Is she here?"

"Close," Xavier said, and sipped his coffee.

"Should I be worried?"

Xavier's expression didn't change as he said, "Yes, you should."

Without responding, Al removed a thumb drive from his pocket and slid it across the table. "Do me a favor and turn the laptop so no one else can see the screen," he said in a quiet tone. He looked tired, older, and more than a little pissed about the way things had gone down.

Weren't they all.

Xavier popped the thumb drive into the slot on the side of the laptop and clicked on the icon that immediately popped up. The silent video began to play. The focus was brutally close, and the players were recorded clearly and cleanly. He could see the surprise in Felice's eyes when Al swiftly lifted his arm and aimed his weapon at her; then, moments later, he saw the determination that had been on Al's face as he reached toward the camera and turned it off.

"Jesus, Al." Xavier ejected the thumb drive—after

swiftly saving the file—and shut down his laptop. He slid the damning device back across the table, but Al shook his head. He didn't take it, just pushed it back toward Xavier.

"It's yours. That's the only copy, so for fuck's sake keep it someplace secure."

"Someone like Felice can hardly disappear without questions being raised."

"This afternoon her body will be discovered in a remote area of Virginia, the apparent victim of a violent carjacking."

Talk about surprises. He narrowly studied the man who'd trained him. "Why?" But he knew, as he asked the question, what the answer would be.

"I've got you two by the short hairs, and now you've got me in the same position."

Xavier leaned back. "Mutual assured destruction."

"Yeah." Al gestured to the coffee cup in front of him. "Is this safe?"

"I suppose."

Al wrapped his fingers around the cup. "You suppose?"

"It's gotta be cold by now and it tastes like shit, but I didn't put anything in it, if that's what you're asking."

Al lifted the cup and took a long swallow, then returned the cup to the table. "You're right. It is cold and it does taste like shit." He took another long drink. "But I need the caffeine, and frankly, I've had worse."

They didn't talk for a moment, as a young employee walked by—too close—and cleaned the booth directly behind Al. When the kid returned to the counter Al asked, his voice low, "Is she listening?"

"Yes."

"Am I going to make it to my car alive?"

"Yes."

"Good to know. If I was in her shoes, I'm not sure I'd be able to say the same. We did what had to be done, all of us . . ." Al shook his head and took another long drink of the cold, crappy coffee. "But that's not why I'm here. The information I've shared with you puts us on even terms, as I see it. I hope you see things the same way."

"I'm surprised," Xavier said softly. Not surprised that Al had killed Felice, but that he'd trust the evidence in anyone else's hands. She might have just disappeared. That would have left him and Lizzy looking over their shoulders for the rest of their lives, but Al would have been a lot safer if no one knew.

Perhaps. None of them was truly safe, and they never would be.

"Mind if an old man gives you some advice?" Al asked, his voice gruff but a lot more relaxed than it had been when he'd first sat down.

"Can't promise I'll take it, but sure. Shoot."

"Get a new job."

Not what he'd expected to hear. "A *job*?"

"I'm sure you have some sort of marketable skills."

He'd hear about that line later, when Al was gone and he met up with Lizzy. She was listening in; she was watching his back. She was probably laughing her ass off, right about now. No—she'd laugh later. Right now, she was looking down a barrel at the back of Al's head.

"Disappear," Al said quietly. "Change your name, change *her* name, move to Bora Bora, or Paris, or fucking Omaha, for all I care. Open a bakery or a tackle store, or hell, I don't know. A driving school, maybe." That made him smile. "Well, maybe not a driving school. Stay in one place for a while, make a few babies. Live, like a normal person."

"This advice from a man who's been married . . . how many times?"

Al shrugged his shoulders. "I could've made it work with the second ex-wife if I'd lived in Omaha and run a bookstore or a doughnut shop." His eyes darkened, deepened. "Get out. That's my last bit of advice to you. Just walk away. Live your life."

And with that he took his own advice. Al Forge stood and walked away without looking back.

Epilogue

Almost a year later, with the hot Texas summer sun scorching her skin, Lizzy braced herself on the shooting range of their security-training firm and sighted down the barrel of the big Glock in her hand. She wore ear protectors, which she hated because they added another level of heat to the already almost unbearable temperatures, and steadily pulled the trigger until the clip was empty. Then she reloaded and did it again.

Suddenly her heart began beating with a slow, heavy rhythm.

The hot, seared landscape blurred, and images began forming in her mind.

For the past year she'd been recovering bits and snippets, here and there, but never the central event itself. Most of what she'd remembered had centered around Xavier, the giddy delirium of their relationship and the uncertainty that had plagued her because he was—well, he was *Xavier*, skilled and lethal to an incredible degree, dark and sexy and sometimes scary, but always exciting. She'd have died rather than admit it, but on a professional level she'd felt completely out of her league with him, while in their personal relationship she'd demanded they meet as equals. In the end, though, when she was dealing with the shock and grief at what she'd done, it was his personal commitment that she'd doubted.

He was right. She'd been a mess. If the situation had been less dire, if they'd been able to give her a month to come to grips with everything, maybe the whole situation could have been avoided.

Xavier didn't think so. He thought that, no matter what, Felice would eventually have turned on them all. Maybe he was right. They'd never know, because beyond a doubt it was Lizzy beginning to recover her memory that had pushed Felice over the edge.

She did remember some things about Felice, and part of her mourned for the woman she'd known while they were training.

Now, perhaps because of the familiar weight of the pistol, the way it bucked in her hand, even the smell of burnt gunpowder, the protective curtain came down.

She remembered the high-heeled shoes she'd worn, the blue-gray suit with the darker blue silk blouse, an exact match of Natalie Thorndike's clothes that day.

She remembered Charlie Dankins giving her the signal, ushering her into the President's suite.

She'd gone straight to the First Lady's bedroom, to the elegant handbag that had been tossed on the bed. She had a small hand-held computer that could read the thumb drive, then copy the data to another thumb drive. She had just inserted the second thumb drive in the USB port when the bedroom door opened.

For a second they'd simply stared at each other, the

President, the First Lady, and herself. Then the First Lady had lifted her hand, and Lizzy had seen the gun.

She lunged toward the First Lady, coming in low, catching her gun hand, and shoving it upward.

The First Lady shoved her, surprising strength behind the move. The President leaped at her, trying to wrap her up and take her down, but Lizzy had rolled into the First Lady's feet and sent her staggering in an effort to keep her balance.

The First Lady rounded on her again with the weapon. Lizzy surged again, got her hand on the pistol, trying to jerk it away. Her finger slipped inside the trigger guard. The First Lady slung her hard against a table, and the impact made her hand jerk. Both of them had their fingers on the trigger when they staggered hard against a table, and the impact made her pull the trigger. Three shots. They all hit the President.

She saw the First Lady freeze, staring in horror at her husband.

Moving swiftly, Lizzy pounced. She grabbed the First Lady by the hair and slammed her head into the wall. The woman staggered, her eyes half-rolling back in her head.

"Here," Lizzy said, and gave her the pistol. Then she turned her so she was facing the President, and Lizzy herself grabbed up the dead-giveaway little hand-held computer, as well as the thumb drive lying beside it, and bolted for the closet. It was the only place she could think to go.

It was stupid. It was inevitable that she'd be found

there, but she had no other place to go. Already the door was being kicked down. There was a connecting room, but it would be locked.

There, in the dark closet, she listened to the uproar outside. She heard more shots. She stood frozen, her stomach knotted in panic, trying to fight through the horror of what had just happened. They were caught. There was no way out. All of them would be executed. And she'd killed the President.

She had very little clear memory of being gotten out of the suite. She knew it was through the connecting room, that the door had been unlocked. She remembered Xavier, everyone, moving fast, someone all but dressing her . . . dear God, that had been Felice.

After that . . . grief. Pain. Tears. The feeling that she didn't deserve to get away with what she'd done. Nothing they'd said had made much of an impact on her, not the proof of the President's guilt; all she felt was the rawness of her emotions that she didn't think would ever heal.

Except now . . . standing in the hot Texas sun . . . she suddenly realized that she *had* healed. The memory wipe had given her three peaceful years in which she had recovered. That hadn't been the purpose, but nevertheless that was the result.

And now she'd remembered the act itself.

She heard Xavier coming up behind her. She turned a little to watch him, because she couldn't *not* watch him. Black boots, jeans, olive-drab tee shirt. A thigh holster was strapped to his right leg.

He eyed the target. The shots were all grouped in

the tattered center. "You killed the fuck out of that one," he said.

She flinched a little, tried to hide the movement, but nothing concerning her escaped him. He frowned, gripped her shoulders, and turned her to face him. His dark gaze bored into her blue one, and his grip tightened.

"You remember." It was a statement.

"Yeah." She got the one word out, but it was a struggle; her throat felt thick, clogged with the tears she refused to cry. The time for crying was long past. She'd done what had to be done, and the knowledge was a burden she'd always carry. She would always grieve at what had been necessary.

Xavier wrapped his arms around her and pulled her against him, lending her the support of his big body. The added heat was one more level of hell, and yet having him there was all she needed.

"I'm okay," she said a few minutes later, because if it wasn't quite true now, one day it would be.

"You sure?"

"Sure enough," she said, and slipped her arm around her husband's waist. A small fuzzy dog began racing through the red dust toward them, yapping like crazy. She leaned down and scooped him up, held him the way Maggie had with her arm under his belly. "Roosevelt," she said, "stop that infernal yapping." Even though she knew the answer she asked again, "Exactly when is Maggie coming back?"

"Another two weeks, maybe." Xavier looked around at the facility they'd designed and constructed. Security people already came from all over the nation for advanced training. It was challenging enough that he didn't miss black-ops work much at all. Besides, he had Lizzy. That made up for losing the excitement of getting shot at.

Together they walked back to their offices, and the life they'd built together.

Read on for a special bonus excerpt from

RUNNING WILD

by Linda Howard and Linda Jones

Libby Thompson crossed her plump arms and tried to look stern, which wasn't easy considering the undeniable sadness she felt. "Don't give me that look, A.Z. Decker. Those puppy-dog eyes haven't worked on me since you were nine years old." Not that he'd had puppy-dog eyes even back then, and he certainly didn't now, but she'd learned a long time ago that the trick to handling him was to never let it show how blasted intimidating he was when he looked pissed and flinty-eyed, the way he did now.

Zeke glanced down and to the side, where Libby's bags sat. They were a hodgepodge of hand-me-downs, three different makers, three different colors: red, brown, and black. The bags were all stuffed so full they bulged and threatened to split their zippers wide open. Everything she owned was in those bags.

"I gave you two weeks notice," she said in her best no-nonsense tone, because if she gave an inch he'd have her talked into staying in no time flat. She couldn't let her guard down, not even for a minute. The trick was to remember that he looked at problems as things he could solve if he just didn't give up, which was great if he was working on your behalf, and not so great if you were on the other side.

"I tried to find a replacement," Zeke said accusingly, as if his failure was her fault.

"Really?" She snorted. "You put an ad in the *Battle Ridge Weekly*." That was when she'd realized he hadn't taken her seriously when she'd told him she was leaving, because if he had he'd have placed multiple ads in the newspapers in larger towns. As much as she loved him, that had really ticked her off. If he thought he could bulldoze her the way he did everyone else, then he was about to get his perception of the world rearranged.

"Two more weeks," he bargained.

She blew out a breath of frustration. In her fifty-seven years, she'd faced down a lot and not let life get her down even when she was widowed at a young age and left with a baby she needed to support. But from the time she'd first come to work here at the Decker ranch, she'd needed every bit of ability she possessed to stay ahead of Zeke. As a toddler he'd been a chubby, charming hellion; as a gap-toothed little boy he'd been a skinny, charming hellion; and since his teenage years he'd been a heartbreaker, with a whole lot of hard-ass thrown into the mix. He couldn't imagine not getting his way, and this time she simply couldn't let that happen.

She'd been working at this ranch house for thirty-odd years, at first part-time and later, after his mother remarried and moved to Arizona, full-time. She had her own room here, just off the kitchen. She knew this house as if it were her own, knew him as if she'd given birth to him. For thirty years she'd cooked, she'd cleaned, and she'd blessed him out when he needed it. She'd mothered him, mothered the ranch hands, and spoiled him rotten. And she was on her way out the door.

She sighed, and her gaze softened a little. "Zeke, I hate to leave you in the lurch, you know I do, but I promised Jenny I'd be there this coming weekend. She's at her wits' end, with Tim out of town on business more often than not and those three kids running her ragged, and another one on the way. She's my daughter, and she needs me."

"I need you," he growled, then his jaw hardened as he finally faced the reality, once and for all, that she was leaving. "Okay. *Damn it!* Okay. I'll get by."

"I know you will." Libby stepped toward him, patted him on one cheek while she went up on her toes and kissed him on the other. She backed away and was all business once again. "I think Spencer knows his way around the kitchen; he'll do until you find a replacement. I left a couple of cookbooks on the kitchen table. The recipe for my beef stew is in the one with the green cover. I know you love my beef stew."

"Thanks."

He didn't sound very grateful; he still sounded pissed as hell. Well, he could just stay pissed, because she'd made up her mind. Ignoring his sour mood, she continued, "I filled the freezer with stew, a pan of lasagna, and cornbread. There's a big pot of chicken and dumplings in the refrigerator for tonight. Once that's all gone, you can either find another housekeeper or you can get your ass busy finding another wife. That's what you really need, A.Z., a *wife*."

That was a safe gambit, because if there was one subject Zeke avoided, it was marriage. He'd tried it once and it hadn't worked, so from his point of view why should he put himself through the torture of trying again? He wasn't a monk, by any means, and if he put himself out to find another wife he'd find himself standing in front of a preacher in no time. He definitely wasn't hard on the eyes, with those broad shoulders, green eyes, and thick, light brown hair. The right woman would rise to the challenge of meeting him halfway—*if* he were looking for a wife, which he wasn't. All he wanted was a cook and a housekeeper, and that was a horse of a different color.

Not many women would be happy on a ranch in the middle-of-nowhere Wyoming. The nearest town, Battle Ridge, was damn near a ghost town these days. Well, not really; there were still stores, but ten years ago more than two thousand people had lived there, and now there were only about half that many.

And the bus came through twice a week. Libby was about to get on it.

"Well come on, damn it," he said, reaching for the bulging red bag. "It's time to get you to town. You're right, we'll find a way to get by until I hire someone to replace you. No one's going to starve, and I can damn well do my own laundry." He snatched up the brown bag, too, leaving the black one, the smallest one, for Libby.

She couldn't help it. Her voice softened some when she said, "You know, you could call your mother . . ."

"No," Zeke said sharply. Well, she'd known that was a nonstarter. He'd love a visit from his mother, but if she came her husband—Larry—would tag along. Zeke didn't begrudge his mother happiness, but he and Larry had never seen eye to eye. A few days here and there were about all he could stomach; no way would he ask them to move in for a stay that could turn into weeks.

"One of your sisters, then."

"No." This particular *no* wasn't as harsh as the first one had been. "They've both got families, kids, jobs. Neither of them could take that much time away to stay here."

Libby opened the front door for Zeke, since his hands were full, and he stepped onto the porch. Half a dozen hands were waiting by the truck, waiting to say good-bye to the woman who had become a second mother to many of them. For a couple of them, she was the first real caring mother they'd ever known. There wasn't a smile to be seen.

"Like I said, we'll get by." He shot a narrow-eyed look at Spencer, who shifted his feet and looked both guilty and confused, because he didn't know what he'd done to earn the boss's scowl. "Though we'll be lucky if Spencer doesn't give us all food poisoning."

"Things will work out. They always do," Libby said optimistically. She patted her hair, making sure all was in place, then rose on tiptoe to kiss his cheek again. "I'll be back for a visit every now and then," she said, going down the steps to say good-bye to all of the ranch hands.

Zeke wasn't as optimistic as Libby. As he drove her into town he tried not to growl his answers to her conversational tries, tried to be happy for her, but— *hell!*

He'd miss her. He couldn't remember a time when she hadn't been here. She was a spark plug of a woman, short and wide, with the kind of spirit that drew other people to her. When other women were settling into their senior years, Libby was dyeing her hair a different color every other week—it was flaming red right now—bossing everyone around, making plans to take her grandchildren on a hot-air balloon ride, and generally steamrolling through life. At the same time, she had the kindest heart he'd ever seen.

Damn it. He couldn't replace Libby. Someone else might do her job, but no one could replace her.

You'd think with the economy as tough as it was, hiring someone would be easy, but the area was trapped in a kind of catch 22, because people were leaving instead of digging in their heels and fighting to keep their lives intact. Battle Ridge was full of empty houses, most of them with FOR RENT or FOR SALE signs on them, and not a sign of any renters, much less actual buyers. Businesses were closing, families were pulling up stakes and heading south, where the brutal winters didn't hammer at you and you might still be unemployed but at least you wouldn't be freezing.

He'd try. So far he hadn't really put his mind to it, because he'd thought Libby would back out of her plans and stay here. It galled him to think he might not succeed, but he was enough of a realist to know that right now the deck was stacked against him.

Getting a woman to come out to the middle of nowhere for a lot of hard work and nominal pay—he wasn't a miser, but no one was going to get rich working at the Decker Ranch—wasn't as easy as she seemed to think it would be. Things didn't always work out. When God closed a door He didn't necessarily open a convenient window. No, Zeke figured he was pretty much fucked.

Battle Ridge, Wyoming, didn't look like much. Carlin Reed pulled her faded red Subaru into a parking space in front of an empty store and looked around. Probably there wouldn't be any jobs here, but she'd ask around anyway. She'd found work in some of the damnedest places, doing things that she'd never before have considered. Work was work, money was money, and she'd learned not to be picky. She wasn't above doing yard work, washing dishes, or just about anything else as long as it didn't involve prostituting herself. Her first attempt at mowing a lawn on a riding mower had been something worthy of a clip on YouTube, but she'd learned.

From what she could see, Battle Ridge had fallen on hard times. Her atlas gave the population as 2,387, but the atlas was six years old and, from what she had seen driving in, she doubted Battle Ridge supported that many residents now. She'd passed empty houses, some with FOR SALE signs that had been up so long they'd become dingy and weather-beaten, and empty stores with FOR SALE OR LEASE notices in the windows. Here in the west it would still be considered a fair-sized town, especially in a state the size of Wyoming with a grand total population of half a million people. Nevertheless, she had to deal with the reality that half the buildings she could see around her were standing empty, which meant she'd likely be moving on.

Not right this minute, though. Right now, she was hungry.

Traffic was light, but that was expected. Hungry or not, Carlin sat in the dusty four-wheel-drive SUV and through her dark sunglasses carefully studied everything around her, every vehicle, every person. Caution had become second nature to her. She hated losing the unconscious freedom and spontaneity she'd once known, but looking back she could only marvel at how unaware she'd been, how *vulnerable*.

The level of her vulnerability might change depending on circumstances, but she was damned if she'd add in the factor of not being aware. She'd already noted the license plates of the cars and trucks parked on each side of the street, and they were all Wyoming plates. There was little chance her movements could have been anticipated, because she hadn't known herself she'd be stopping here, but she still checked.

Two buildings down on the right was a café, the Pie Hole, and three pickups were parked in front of it even though two o'clock in the afternoon wasn't exactly a prime mealtime. The name of the café amused her, and she wondered about the person who had come up with it, whether it was a quirky sense of humor or a don't-give-a-damn attitude behind the choice. Her amusement was momentary, though, and she returned to studying her surroundings.

Directly behind her was a hardware store, and another small cluster of vehicles was parked in front of it. To the left was a general store, a Laundromat, and a feed store. A block back, she'd passed a small bank, and beside it had been a post office. Down the street she could see a gas station sign. There would probably be a school, and maybe people from fifty miles around drove their kids there. Was the town big enough to support a doctor or a dentist? To her, it seemed like a good deal: a thousand or more patients and no competition. A person could do worse.

After she'd watched for a few minutes, she settled back and watched some more, waiting for that inner sense to tell her when she'd been patient long enough. She'd learned to listen to her own instincts.

The normalcy of the activity around her seeped into her bones. There was nothing frightening here, nothing unusual going on. She got her baseball cap from the passenger seat, pulled it on, and grabbed her road atlas and hooded TEC jacket before getting out of the Subaru. Though it was summer, there was a coolness to the air that justified taking the jacket along, though she didn't actually put it on. The TEC was very light weight, just a couple layers of nylon, but it had so many pockets that it had actually taken her days to locate all of them. If she had to run, everything she needed was in those pockets: her ID, her money, a throwaway cell phone—with the battery removed and stored in yet another pocket—a pocketknife, a small LED flashlight, even a couple of ibuprofen and some protein bars. Just in case. Seemed as if these days she surrounded herself with just-in-case items and scenarios; she was aware *and* prepared.

She hit the lock button on the remote, and slipped the key and remote into her right-front jean pocket, then headed toward the little café; her leggy stride covered the distance at a fast clip, just one more detail about her that had changed during the past year. Once she'd never gotten in a hurry; now her instinct was to *move*, to get from A to B, get her business accomplished, then move on. While it was true that a rolling stone gathered no moss, she wasn't worried about getting mossy; more to the point, a moving target was harder to hit.

Still, when she reached the café door, her own reflection startled her, made her briefly check. Baseball cap, long blond hair in a ponytail, sunglasses—when had she acquired the whole Linda Hamilton–Terminator vibe? When had she become someone else?

The answer to that was easy: the moment she'd realized Brad was trying to kill her.

She opened the door of the Pie Hole; a bell over the door sang as she walked inside. Stepping to the side, she took a moment to do a fast assessment, looking for another exit—just in case—and evaluating the three men currently riding the stools at the bar counter, their legs spread and boot heels hooked on the railings just as if they were on horseback—again, just in case. There was no clearly marked rear door she could see from her vantage point, though there was one door with a plain KEEP OUT sign. Could be a storage closet or an exit. She could also assume there was a back door off the kitchen, though, and maybe a window in the bathroom. Not that she thought she'd need either, during this short stop.

The three men evaluated her right back, and she found herself tensing. She didn't like attracting notice. The more she stayed under the radar, the less likely it was that Brad would be able to track her. It was reassuring that there was nothing remotely familiar about any of the men, and their clothing proclaimed them local. She'd gotten good at judging what was local—wherever "local" happened to be—

and what wasn't. These men fit right in, from their creased hats down to the worn heels of their boots.

Still, she shouldn't have come in here. Too late she realized that *any* stranger would stand out in a place this small, where the locals might not all personally know one another, but they'd certainly recognize who belonged and who didn't. She didn't.

She thought about leaving, but that would attract even more attention. Besides, she was hungry. The best thing to do was the normal thing: sit down and order. She'd eat, pay the bill, then move on down the road.

The café itself was a smallish, pleasant-looking place, gray linoleum floor, white walls, an honest-to-God jukebox against the back wall, red booths along the street-front windows, and a smattering of small round tables in the center of the place. The counter, complete with a couple of clear pie cases and an old-fashioned cash register, ran the length of the right side of the room. A pretty brunette in a pink waitress uniform stood behind the counter, talking to the three men with the ease of long acquaintance; like the men, she'd glanced up at Carlin's entrance, and even through her sunglasses Carlin caught the brilliant glint of strikingly pale eyes, making her alter her grade of the waitress's looks from pretty to something more. Maybe that was why the three cowboys were camping on those stools, rather than the lure of food. Good. If they were flirting with the waitress, they were less likely to pay a lot of attention to anyone else.

The last booth was positioned against a solid wall; Carlin chose that one and instinctively slid in so she was facing the doorway . . . just in case. The plastic menu was inserted between the napkin holder and the salt and pepper shakers; she removed her cap and sunglasses and grabbed the menu, more from curiosity than anything else, because all she wanted was coffee and pie. She'd get something to eat, and use the break to study her map of Wyoming, figure out exactly where this little country road went, and pick a place to stop for a while.

She'd been so sure Brad wouldn't bother to follow her. She'd been wrong. This time when she stopped she'd take extra precautions. No one would get her Social Security number. There would be no bank account, no W-2, damn it; somehow she had to fall off the radar, something that was increasingly hard to do with everything computerized. He'd bragged about his computer skills, and she'd hoped that was all it was—bragging—but evidently not. She didn't know how he'd found her in Dallas, but he had, and she'd barely made it out alive. Jina hadn't.

If she let herself think about what had happened her stomach would knot in panic, and she'd feel as if she was strangling on her own breath, so she'd pushed the memory away and focused on simply moving, doing what was necessary to stay alive. He'd try again, but she was damned if she'd make it easy for him. Somehow she'd figure out what to do, a way to outsmart him, set a trap—something. She couldn't live like this forever.

But for now, she couldn't stay in any one place too long. Unfortunately, she didn't have enough cash to just keep driving around the country on a permanent road trip, so she'd *work* her way around the country. Ideally, she'd find some place to stay through the winter, which was why she'd ventured this far north.

People on the run tended to head toward warmer climes, bigger cities. She'd done the opposite.

She'd told Brad once that she hated the cold and joked about one day retiring to Florida. Maybe, if he remembered that detail, he wouldn't think to look for her in Wyoming.

She studied the menu. The offerings were simple: eggs, burgers, and a mysterious "daily special"—along with, of course, the "pie of the day." Today was Thursday. Maybe Thursday's pie was apple.

"What can I get you?" The brunette in pink arrived at the booth. She didn't carry an order pad, but with such a limited menu, there probably wasn't much need for one.

Carlin glanced up. "Kat" was embroidered on the breast pocket of the pink uniform, and the waitress's eyes were even more striking close up, a kind of electric gray that tended toward blue, as clear as a mountain lake.

"What's the pie of the day?"

"We have cherry and lemon meringue."

"I was kind of hoping for apple," Carlin said, "but cherry will be fine. And coffee, black."

"Coming right up."

After Kat walked away, Carlin placed her atlas on the table and opened it to Wyoming. Her finger traced the road that had led her to Battle Ridge. She followed it on beyond, to other names of other towns and other roads and miles and miles of nothing, on into Montana. In the periphery of her vision she saw Kat approaching with her order, and she moved the atlas to the side to make room.

A silverware set wrapped in a napkin and a small

plate bearing a huge slice of cherry pie were slid in front of her, followed by a saucer and an empty cup. Lifting the coffee pot from her tray, Kat expertly filled the cup. "Are you lost?" she asked, nodding toward the atlas.

"Not really."

"Where are you headed?"

That was the sixty-four-thousand-dollar question. "I haven't decided yet."

"That sounds like freedom," observed the waitress, and walked away without saying anything else.

Picking up her fork, Carlin took her first bite. The not-apple pie was amazingly good. For a minute, maybe two, she forgot all her troubles and simply indulged her taste buds. The crust was flaky and buttery, and the filling was perfectly sweetened. The coffee was good, too. She took a deep breath and realized that it was the first time in weeks that she could honestly say she was relaxed. It wouldn't last, but for now she'd take it.

While she was eating, a man came in for a slice of pie to go. Seemed as if she wasn't the only one who thought the pie was outstanding. Idly she listened as he and Kat chatted, about neighbors, about the weather. Maybe the waitress was as much of a pull as the pie, at least as far as the male populace was concerned.

Carlin looked out the window. Battle Ridge wasn't much to look at, that was a fact, but it had everything a small town needed, at least as far as she was concerned: a place to eat, a Laundromat, a general store. The people who passed by the Pie Hole all glanced in and waved, even though they didn't stop.

Pulling the jacket to her, she unzipped one of the

pockets to get money for her meal, instinctively counting the bills there. Oh, there was plenty for paying her bill, but not enough, not nearly enough, to get her by. Living on the road was eating through her savings faster than she'd expected.

She gathered her things and walked toward the cash register with money in hand. The man who'd come in for lemon meringue left, his gaze lingering on Carlin for a moment too long. There it was again; the look was curious, not malicious—she knew the difference—but one more person had noticed her.

Kat took her money, rang up the sale, and passed back the change. Carlin laid down a dollar tip. It wasn't much, but percentage wise it was generous, and no matter how poor she was she wasn't going to stiff a nice person who'd earned a tip.

Carlin knew she should take her atlas and go, but she didn't. There might be a job opportunity in town, but if she just drove away without asking, she'd never know. She slid her butt half onto a stool and asked, "How long have you worked here?"

A slow smile curled Kat's mouth. "Seems like forever. It's my place. I'm cook, waitress, manager, and chief bottle-washer all rolled into one."

Out of all that, one thing registered uppermost. "You made the pie? It was great."

"I did. Thanks." The grin widened. "Apple tomorrow, if you're still around."

"Depends on whether or not anyone around here is looking for help." Carlin figured there were two places in a town where pretty much everything would be common knowledge: the beauty salon and the café. She'd planned to eat, fill the Subaru's gas tank, and head on down the road, but now all of her plans were fluid, and she'd take advantage of whatever break came her way.

For a long moment, Kat was silent, her gaze still clear but not giving anything away as she did her own assessment. "Maybe. Can you cook?"

"I can learn." She could cook enough to get by, for herself, but she for certain wasn't on Kat's level.

"You got anything against doing dishes and mopping floors?"

"Nope." She wasn't proud; she'd scrub floors on her knees, if that was what it took to earn some money.

"Ever done any waitressing?"

"A little. It's been a while."

"Some things never change." Kat pursed her lips. "I can only afford to hire you part-time, and the pay isn't exactly great."

One thing she hadn't expected when she asked about available jobs was to find one here in this little café. She wasn't about to turn it down, but now came the tough part. "That's okay. The thing is . . ." She paused, looking at the three other customers to make certain they couldn't hear, then glancing out the window to take a quick study of the street before taking a deep breath and turning back to Kat. "I need to be paid in cash. No record, no taxes, no paperwork."

Kat's easy smile died, and something flashed in those clear eyes. "Are you in trouble? More specifically, are *you* trouble?"

Carlin tilted her head, considering that, then shrugged. "I guess you could look at it both ways, but I'd say *in* trouble."

"What kind of trouble? Legal or man? It has to be one or the other."

"Isn't that the truth," Carlin muttered, then said, "Man. Stalker, to be specific."

Small town didn't mean stupid. Kat's eyes narrowed. "Why didn't you go to the cops?"

"Because he is one," she said flatly.

"Well, that complicates matters, doesn't it?" Her eyes narrowed again. "There are bound to be good cops, too, wherever you're from. I really hate the thought that one bad apple can force you to take to the road. Maybe you should try again."

"Twice was enough to suit me."

"Oh." Kat stared at her, hard, her gaze as sharp as a knife's edge. Carlin had no idea what she saw, but whatever it was, her next words were brisk and decisive. "You're hired. Just part-time, like I said. Some cooking, the easy stuff, but mostly cleaning, waiting tables. I do all the baking. Business is okay, but I'm hardly raking in the dough. I'll make it worth your while, though. Still interested?"

"Yes." She said it without an instant's hesitation.

"Do you have somewhere to stay?"

Because Carlin had just now—as in the very second Kat had made her offer—decided to stick around, the answer to that was a big *no*. She shook her head. "Do you know where there's a room I can rent? Nothing too expensive, just a room with a bed." She hadn't seen a motel driving in, but surely there was someone in town who would rent her a room.

Kat tilted her head toward the single restroom door at the back of the café; beside it was that closed door that was decorated with a KEEP OUT sign. "I have a place upstairs. You can stay there. No charge for employees," she added. "It's really more of an attic, but in the winter I stay up there when the weather's so bad I don't want to drive back and forth from the house. Might as well have someone living up there," she said, as if the offer wasn't a big deal. It was, at least to Carlin. She wasn't so proud that she'd argue about paying rent. Every dollar she saved gave her more of a chance of not getting killed.

Besides, it wouldn't be for long. She'd make a few dollars, catch her breath, maybe come up with a more permanent plan. "Thank you." She managed a smile. Having the near future settled took away some of her anxiety. "I can start right now; just tell me what to do."

"Good deal." Kat offered a hand across the counter. "Since we're going to be working together, I should introduce myself. I'm Kat Bailey."

Carlin hesitated a moment, thinking hard, then took the offered hand. She wasn't ready to give her real name to anyone, not until she knew exactly how Brad had found her the last time. Not that she didn't trust Kat; she'd simply learned that she really couldn't be too careful. Her gaze scanned the counter. A few feet away was a full bottle of ketchup, and inspiration struck. "Hunt," she said swiftly. "Carlin Hunt."

Kat snorted as she ended the handshake. "Well, at least you didn't look at the floor and tell me your last name was linoleum."

Caught. She wasn't a very good liar, and that had to end. Like it or not, she had to get better at spinning tales. Catching her breath, Carlin waited for the offer of a job and a place to stay to be rescinded.

But Kat merely gave her a brisk nod, and that was that. "Get your stuff; you can at least get unpacked before you start work." Evidently, a fake surname wasn't something that upset Kat Bailey's apple cart.

As Carlin went out to the Subaru to fetch her backpack, she blew out a huge breath of relief. She had a place to stay and a way to make a few dollars, a way that didn't require a lawnmower or a weed eater. And tomorrow there would even be apple pie.

It was the first time in a long while that she'd been able to think of a "tomorrow" that wasn't full of anxiety and uncertainty.